TAKE MY *Heart...* FOR DINNER

BOOK ONE

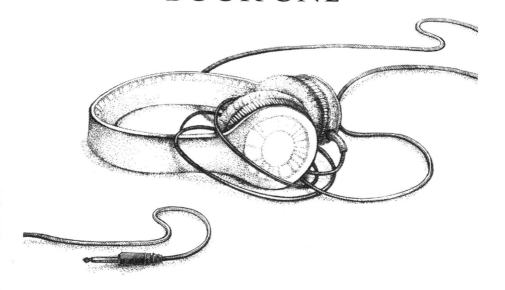

MAXWELL AND VALERY KOFMAN

Enchanted Worlds

authorHOUSE®

San Francisco 2016

AuthorHouse™
1663 Liberty Drive
Bloomington, IN 47403
www.authorhouse.com
Phone: 1 (800) 839-8640

Illustration and Cover Elena Kotova

Published by AuthorHouse 03/07/2017

ISBN: 978-1-5049-8221-4 (sc)
ISBN: 978-1-5049-8219-1 (hc)
ISBN: 978-1-5049-8220-7 (e)

Library of Congress Control Number: 2016903351

Print information available on the last page.

This book is printed on acid-free paper.

Table of Contents

About the Book 5

About the Authors 6

Foreword 7

Prologue 12

PART ONE..17

Chapter 1. Last School Bell..18

Chapter 2. It's Not Easy Being Tourists 25

Chapter 3. Terra Incognita 41

Chapter 4. In The Harbor 61

Chapter 5. Alive 72

Chapter 6. Downstream 89

Chapter 7. At the Roots of Cannibalism...........................99

PART TWO...127

Chapter 1. The Awakening..128

Chapter 2. Deeds of Bygone Days 152

Chapter 3. In The Meantime 167

Chapter 4. Computer Genius...186

Chapter 5. Picnic In The Forest......................................203

Chapter 6. Dynasty of Broken Hearts.............................232

PART THREE...257

Chapter 1. Highlanders 258

Chapter 2. A Day Of Collapsed Hopes 292

Chapter 3. Escape..301

Chapter 4. Deliverance...336

Chapter 5. How To Do Business In New Guinea.............364

Chapter 6. Celebration..386

Chapter 7. To Everyone According To His Deeds...........410

Epilogue 425

Glossary 429

About the Book

Take My Heart ... for Dinner is the first novel of the trilogy, Enchanted Worlds. A chain of unexpected events pulls Ben, a high school student from a prosperous family in New York, out of his usual comfortable surroundings and throws him into a terrifying yet fascinating world filled with uncertainty and suspense. The novel is not just the story of the adventures of a young man who gets sucked into an enthralling whirlpool of events; it is also an attempt to lift the veil of mystery that lies over a hitherto uncharted society, and digs deep into the heart of Terra Incognita.

This coming-of-age book is intended for a wide range of readers as it explores history, social and cultural customs, and the traditions of an ethnic minority, unraveling fascinating aspects of a society unknown to civilization.

About the Authors

Maxwell Kofman, the younger author of this book, is a high school student in California. A seventh-grade school essay, for which he got a perfect grade, planted the seed-idea for this book in his mind.

As the story and characters grew in his head and begged to be let out, he used his free time between school and various hobbies and wrote this novel. Over the last three years, the plot for the trilogy was also born. Currently, Maxwell is on the threshold of his college education, and is looking for a school that fits his interests. New ideas for the next book in the trilogy have also taken firm root.

Valery Kofman is an engineer who has experienced life in several continents, and his never-say-die attitude has infected his son, encouraging him to follow his dreams. Inspired by his son's book concepts, Valery joined the venture, helping Maxwell overcome his writer's block to bring the characters from his imagination to life in book form.

Foreword

So, dear reader, you opened our book and have read thus far already. Well, we are pleased that it has attracted your attention. At this point, you still have the opportunity to close it, and find another more enthralling and informative book for yourself. We urge you to take advantage of this chance right now, before it is too late. We are confident that after just a few pages you will not be able to put this book aside until you finish its very last page. In the meantime, please allow us to introduce ourselves.

My name is Max. I am fourteen years old and in the ninth grade at a high school in California. And this is my father, Valery . . .

. . . And I am no longer fourteen, unfortunately; or perhaps, fortunately.

And this is our book, our joint project, an attempt to describe a series of events from the perspective of two generations integrated into one novel. We hope that we have succeeded in doing that, but of course, you will be the judge, dear reader.

What is this story about? You may well wonder.

It is about the unknown, or the unexplored to be more precise.

Is there anything in the world that is still unexplored? This may be the next question that comes to mind. There are no unidentified stars left in the sky for many millions of light years around. We split an atom's nucleus like a walnut, and do not even get us started on electrons, as they have been serving civilization for over a century. Images of Moon craters are as common now as pictures of the Eiffel Tower in Paris, and we control the Mars Rover like a child playing with a remote-controlled toy car. What else is out there that is still unexplored?

Believe it or not, there is plenty unknown to us on Earth, just waiting to be discovered. The thing is, we always look skyward and deep inside, but we often lose sight of what is on the surface, right next to us. As we travel through the universe, explore the outrageous depths of the sea, observe neutrinos knocking electrons from their orbits like bowling pins, here, within arm's length (measuring on the cosmic scale), there is a land that has not yet been affected by nanotechnology. Leave alone nano, even regular technology does not exist there, as we cannot apply the word technology to the process of making a stone axe.

Oddly enough, there are plenty of such places on Earth. However, we are going to talk about only one of them. It is a place where two worlds coexist in full harmony—today's modern world, mad and always rushing, driven by rapid scientific advances; and the primitive world of yesterday, calm and relaxed. This world, inhabited by hundreds of aboriginal tribes living in impenetrable forests, on inaccessible mountaintops and on impassable marshy swamps, lies just a hundred miles away from modern buildings, equipped with the newest technological developments.

How is this possible in a small country with a national budget that barely exceeds the cost of spacecraft launched into orbit every year? What impenetrable forests are you talking about? We were able to reach the deepest seabed, overcoming the substantial pressure of a multi-kilometer water column, but can we not penetrate through dense forests? How can we call mountain peaks unreachable when thousands of people have climbed the world's tallest, Mount Everest? How can we call bog swamps impassable if we have drilled oil wells a dozen kilometers into Earth's crust?

However, it is true. These forests, mountains, and marshes are truly unreachable, and many tribes continue to live in primitive and isolated communities, despite all the world's scientific and technological achievements.

Why are we spending so much money trying to find another civilization a few million light years away? Maybe we should explore our own world more fully before venturing off into others. We could use just a small portion of the budget allotted for space discovery to meliorate marshes, bring water and electricity to such remote places, and send kids to school. Maybe one of these tribal children would become the Edison and Marie Curie of our time, and defeat cancer or AIDS, or invent alternative fuels for future engines. In twenty years, your investments could easily be paid off a hundredfold.

But we keep on studying black holes and galaxies, penetrating even deeper into the Earth's crust, while right next to us, to this day, there are a groups of people who continue to live the same way as their ancestors did for thousands of years, feeding off small rodents and practicing cannibalism, among other traditions and rituals.

Of course, civilization will gradually penetrate into these remote places as well, though with a delay of a few hundred years. Tourists who want to spend their vacation in exotic places are slowly finding their way there. It is possible nowadays to see people from these ethnic minorities with the newest camera or computer. More and more people in these tribes now refuse to wear traditional outfits and have switched to comfortable clothing and footwear. They have integrated modern tools, household items, and everything else that civilization offers us, into their lifestyle.

However, the major drawback of this integration with modern culture is the inevitable and irreplaceable loss of colorful tribal rituals, traditions, and languages. Today, there are many dialects on the verge of extinction. Even though linguists are trying to preserve them, there are very few people in these tribes who can still speak their native tongue. But rituals . . . well, some of them have long been classified by humanity and local authorities as a criminal offense, and their rejection is more a merit to society than an ethnographic loss.

However, this book is not about anthropology. All the above is just a backdrop for the stage on which the events unfold, a bit funny, sometimes sad and cruel, but overall as diverse and unpredictable as our life. The plot of this book is fictional and any similarities that you may notice are nothing but coincidences. History has had even more paradoxical happenstances, and to say that such events have never happened would be a little hasty, especially since many of the facts in the book were taken from the history of that region.

Some episodes may seem brutal, and my father and I had a long, heated argument whether to leave them in their original form or remove completely from the story, as this book is intended for adolescent readers. Nevertheless, we decided to leave everything as it is, with only a little edited text to minimize the description of the violent and bloody scenes. It is impossible to describe the events occurring in the book using dull, conservative language, as it is impossible, for example, to express a toothache with a mathematical formula. Therefore, dear reader, if you consider yourself a sensitive person or if you are easily offended, just skip the scenes that may well seem far too bloody and ruthless.

However, this book is not about the violent traditions of ethnic minorities either. It is just a story about the adventures of a young man who . . . well, maybe you should read it yourself.

Prologue

Rain in the jungles can be described as exceptional. It is a natural phenomenon that everyone should experience at least once in their life. It starts abruptly, without any indication or warning from the meteorologist on the local news. A clear blue sky suddenly fills with heavy clouds, saturating the air with moisture, and within minutes water simply pours down on the ground. Everything happens so quickly that a man who came out of his hut on a bright, sunny day to go pee under a fern might come back home soaked to the skin.

During such rain, all living things in the forest disappear. Animals flee into their burrows, while birds fly into tree hollows or rush under the cover of wide banana palm leaves. Even insects hide in the smallest of gaps in the tree bark, so that they are not washed away by the strong flow of water.

The rain usually stops as suddenly as it begins—after a few minutes or an hour, or maybe a few months. But thereafter the soil is soaked with never-drying puddles that house swarms of mosquitoes.

During one of those rainy days, when all living things in the forest hid under the protection of their homes, a girl ran swiftly through the trees. She was probably no more than ten years old, with black hair, slanted eyes, and high cheekbones—the typical appearance of a dweller of Southeast Asia. She raced through the forest, ignoring the heavy rain, jumping over fallen tree trunks, the dirt on the moist ground splashing under her bare feet. She squeezed through dense bushes and their long twigs lashed at her face. Her path led downhill and in some places the slope was so steep that she slipped on the wet clayey soil and fell face-down in the dirty slush. But she was up again in seconds, continuing to run toward her destination. Only on one occasion did she slow down, when the road became too steep.

The weather had let her down; it was obviously not perfect for this sort of outdoor trip. The day had been so beautiful, the sun had shone brightly in an azure sky, without a single cloud on the horizon. She had not planned to go anywhere and was helping the other women cook supper for the villagers. All of a sudden, a man entered the buambramra[1]. He picked up a piece of baked yam, tossed it into his mouth, and mumbled with his mouth still full.

"You know, I was in the village yesterday and met Beida, our postwoman, and she asked me to tell you that she received a package—"

He had barely finished the sentence when the girl leaped up and ran out the front door and into the woods.

She knew this road to the village very well. She had grown up in these woods and knew every tree, every bush around here, and had walked along this path for several miles, using only her instincts as a compass to lead the way.

As she was running through the forest, it had started to rain, not just any rain but a real tropical storm. But she continued running despite the downpour, hastily scrambling over the many fallen trees and bushes along her muddy path, leaving behind remnants of the grass-fiber skirt that she wore over unpretentious canvas clothing. Her hair, which was usually intricately arranged and framed in a circle of small colored feathers that came from the indigenous bird-of-paradise, was now a disheveled mess, covered with clay and hanging on her shoulders in a dirty, tangled mess. The two beautiful feathers on the sides completing the crown had fallen off somewhere along the way.

Very little of the colors on her face remained either. The bright yellow with orange paint and a bit of white around her mouth, common in her tribe for all men, women, and children as a tribute to local fashion, was now completely washed away. Instead, her face was covered in brown mud streaks from the fall and swipes made with her dirty hands. The only thing from her original outfit that remained intact was a long necklace, sagyu[2], thickly wrapped around her neck. It was composed of the fangs of wild boar and dogs hung on a string. Actually, a more accurate description would be small teeth. Nice big fangs were trophies, a status of respect that hunters wore to showcase their hunting achievements, while smaller teeth were given to children to make jewelry with. The girl had accumulated so many of them that she could wrap her necklace around her neck a few times. She still had enough teeth leftover to make a hand bracelet, samba-sagyu. But for that, she had to mix it with seashells and pretty little rocks found on the beach. Nevertheless, it was a beautiful piece of jewelry.

Despite the atrocious weather and the long distance she had to traverse, she made it to the village much faster than usual and quickly opened the front door of the post office. The girl tried to speak, but she couldn't say a word around the pounding in her chest. She just stood in the middle of the room, trying to catch her breath like a fish out of the river. Muddy water dripped from her hair and clothes onto the clean wooden floor. An old woman came from the backroom, and looked reproachfully at the puddle of water and muddy footprints that the girl's bare feet had made.

"I will clean it all up, Aunt Beida," the girl said, sounding pathetic. "I was told that you have for me . . . that you've received . . ."

The old woman nodded and, without saying a word, went to the back room. A minute later, she brought out a package and handed it to her.

The girl was about to grab the box, but when she looked at her wet, muddy hands she pulled them back, afraid to dirty the package, neatly wrapped in thick paper and sealed with scotch tape. The old postwoman handed her a towel, and the girl quickly wiped her hands and face and finally took the package. She then sat on a chair and stared at it. The small box was covered with colored stamps from the post offices of a dozen different countries, and the large sticker in the middle was labeled with an address that read: To: Papua New Guinea, Madang, Province Madang, Tribe: Wagaba. For Emma. She did not pay attention to the sender's name, knowing who this package was from. Besides, there was plenty of time later to read the text on every label and postage stamp thoroughly. The girl, Emma, was impatient to unwrap the package. She tried at first to carefully remove the paper, but the sticky scotch tape held it very well. She then tried to tear it with her nails, and even tried biting it. But her teeth, which were sharp and strong enough to chew hard vegetables, could not tear the tape of the packaging. The old woman handed her a pair of scissors, putting an end to her suffering. Emma looked at her gratefully, then cut the stubborn tape and finally unwrapped the package. Inside the box, she found a piece of paper from a school notebook with only a few words: Elementary, my dear Watson, and under the paper, as expected, there was a book, The Adventures of Sherlock Holmes.

Memories of events that happened not so long ago came back to her. Emma smiled and hugged the book to her chest, despite her wet and muddy clothes. But the next moment she was sitting on the dirty floor weeping loudly, bitterly expressing her grief, as children cry about their favorite broken toys, or as adults mourn the unfortunate demise of their loved ones.

Part One

"... Today is only yesterday's tomorrow..."
Uriah Heep, Circle of Hands

Chapter 1. Last School Bell

The school bell rang suddenly. A few minutes earlier, Ben had been staring intently at the wall clock above the white board, watching its second hand move sluggishly from one digit to the next, like viscous honey flowing out from an open jar. The teacher had been lecturing in a monotonous voice, but Ben had not been listening and had struggled to keep his eyes open. Attempting to stay awake, he plunged into a haze of pleasant thoughts about his coming summer holiday, which was to officially begin the next day. It promised to be exciting and a bit unusual; this year they planned to go to Australia. Ben had never been to the southern part of the globe, and he found it rather odd when his father told him that currently, in June, it was winter in Australia. Winter in the middle of summer was something quite outside Ben's experience.

The trip was mainly to visit some distant relatives on his father's side—either his aunt and her husband, or perhaps his uncle with his wife. Ben could never figure out which was which, and didn't care to find out. He had never seen them before, and frankly, he didn't really want to, as he had lived for fourteen years without knowing them, and could happily live the rest of his life the same way. But his father thought otherwise. He hadn't seen these relatives since they had moved to Australia many years ago, and he longed to visit them.

A change of scenery was much needed, as they were all tired of vacations to the tropical Caribbean islands. This was a chance to diversify their experiences, visit another country, and learn about different cultures. Ben suspected that the Southern and Northern Hemispheres looked alike, and the tropical islands on both sides were equally boring; but at least it was a change.

Unlike Ben, the Australian relatives were excited and enthusiastic about the upcoming visit of their nephew with his family and were eagerly preparing for their arrival. They planned the entire trip for them, booked excursions around the country, and even bought them an expensive cruise with a newly opened line from Australia to Papua New Guinea and the Solomon Islands. These places were still unknown to most people and had only recently become a blooming destination for tourism.

Ben was looking forward to this long and exciting trip. The only thing that bothered him was the unnecessary delay in his private project. However, it could be even beneficial, giving him an opportunity to examine the program code from a fresh perspective upon arrival. Ben and his best friend, Marcus, had worked on this project for almost a year now, but there was still a lot to do. This complex and multi-level project was their pride and joy, their brainchild, and had no analogy in the modern computer world. The project would be very significant if all turned out as they hoped. The only part that gave them a little discomfort was the label "not quite legal" as they termed it. However, upon further discussion, they had agreed that there was nothing illegal about it.

"It's not illegal, just a little . . . unusual," Marcus tried to convince his friends.

He was actually right. Imagine this situation. A burglar breaks into someone's house, and, instead of stealing, he leaves lovely flowers and a box of fine cigars for the sleeping owners. Would the burglar's actions still be considered a crime? Trespassing is a punishable offense under relevant articles of the Criminal Code, but in this scenario, the thief's actions would only bring joy to the hosts when they woke up in the morning and found these gifts awaiting them. It is unlikely that they would go to the police to complain about the unexpected gifts, although they might be a little surprised and curious. But this is just an abstract example; they weren't going to leave flowers and cigars for hosts, nor did they plan to break into a house. They planned, however, to breach other people's computers.

No, they did not consider themselves hackers. A hacker is someone who breaks into a computer for the sake of personal gain. But their team did not need money. They were all from wealthy families, attending an elite private school, and had plenty of pocket money, thanks to their parents. Their school was expensive and inaccessible to people below a certain income level. And, if necessary, they could easily make money for themselves. There were always people out there who needed to get their computers fixed, viruses cleared, a program written, or a website created, and they would be happy to pay decent money for such services. Ben and Marcus had strong knowledge of this kind of work, and this was the type of knowledge they were trying to gather, summarize, and organize into a single database for their project. Each member of the team had certain specialized knowledge that when summarized could be used by all participants. But that was only a small part, the first step required to implement their grand idea, which had no equivalent in the modern computer world.

No, they were not creating computer viruses either. In fact, the boys hated people who did that. In their opinion, hackers who spread viruses were mediocre computer "geniuses," losers, sick-minded people who found pleasure in someone else's suffering.

Viruses were not something that worried them. Their computers were well protected, and even if they did get infected, it wasn't a big problem either. Computer viruses were nothing more than annoying mosquitoes, an insignificant bug that diverts people's attention from important matters. However, for beginners trying to learn some basics, it could be quite destructive. Seriously, what kind of pleasure or satisfaction was there in spreading "Melissa"[3] or planting a "Trojan"[4] onto a beginner's computer? Okay, you've managed to cripple their operating system's registry, or erased some important documents. So what? Where is the excitement? No, letting loose viruses was not what Ben and Marcus had in mind when it came to fun and enjoyment. They had a better idea that exceeded anyone's wildest imagination, an idea that would raise adrenaline levels in the bloodstream just by thinking about it.

It had all started with Marcus's invention. He was the leader in their friendship when it came to computers. One night he came to Ben's house and shouted excitedly, "I got it, Ben! I finally got it!"

At first Ben did not understand what had caused his friend's excitement, as Marcus could barely explain himself through his agitated enthusiasm.

"How can you not understand?" Marcus exclaimed, gesticulating frantically with his hands. "It is simple, my dear Watson. Just read this." He then tossed a flash card to Ben.

Ben grabbed his laptop and plugged it in. After a brief review of the files, he stared at his friend. "Well, you certainly have ambitions, Marcus. You don't consider yourself a Napoleon by any chance, do you?"

"No, I don't. They didn't have computers during that time, if you must know."

"Yeah, I kind of knew that already. I think I've read it somewhere." Ben laughed. "But you certainly set your ambitions quite high."

"It has nothing to do with my ambitions, Ben, just simple knowledge of computer technology and pure math, that's all. I think that—"

It was at this moment of his reverie that the long-awaited bell rang, breaking a chain of pleasant memories. The second hand had finally completed its last lap around the clock face, connecting the electric circuits of the bell. The end of this lesson marked the completion of yet another school year and the yard exploded with the noise of moving chairs, classroom doors slamming, and the laughter and joyful chatter of delighted pupils sharing their plans for the summer with each other. The teacher was trying to complete the last few sentences of the lecture, but nobody was listening anymore. In fact, nobody had been listening to him for the past hour as they all had been too busy doing a silent countdown to the first day of the summer vacation.

Students were saying their goodbyes; the girls hugged, while the boys gave each other intricate handshakes. Children exchanged addresses and phone numbers as some of them were going to a different high school next year. Ben congratulated himself for surviving his final year of middle school and pondered what high school would be like as he started to head toward the parking lot to wait for his father. Marcus spotted Ben in the crowd and came up to him.

"So, Ben, are you still going on vacation tomorrow?"

"Yes, we are leaving early in the morning and will be gone for a month."

"Can you at least take your laptop with you?"

"I thought we already discussed that. I can't work productively while I'm on vacation. There would be no rest for me, and no work would get done either."

"I know. It's just . . . pity, we won't be able to initiate the project by the new school year as planned. Oh well, I guess we will start later. No big deal."

Two more boys who were also involved in the project came up to them.

"Hey, Ben, you didn't tell us where you are going on your vacation," said the shorter of the two boys, who was nicknamed Bob. His original moniker had been "Baby" as he looked like a ten-year-old kid even though he was fourteen, but when he sat at the computer and demonstrated certain skills that very few adults had, his name quickly changed from Baby to simply Bob.

"We're going to Australia to visit my dad's relatives. From there we'll take a cruise to Papua New Guinea."

"Wow, that's pretty awesome. You'll get to see all the cool parrots and monkeys. I also want to go there one day!" exclaimed the second computer genius, Richter, nicknamed after the pianist for his virtuoso typing ability.

"He might find some parrots there, but there are no monkeys in their jungles," Marcus said. He knew a little bit of everything in the world; that was why they called him Mr. Webster, in honor of the famous lexicographer.

"What do you mean?" Ben asked in surprise. "There have to be monkeys. It's a tropical rain forest. There are monkeys in every jungle."

"Yes, in every jungle, but not in New Guinea. They have marsupials instead."

"Do you mean kangaroos?"

"Yes, a kangaroo is a marsupial too, but there are many kinds of them; this one is not like the ones in Australia. It looks different. Sorry, I forgot its name. It is a rare animal that lives on trees."

"By the way," Bob interrupted, "I also heard that they have cannibals there."

"Cannibals? The ones that eat people?"

"Yep! That one."

"Come on," Ben said, doubtfully. "There are no cannibals these days. This is the twenty-first century, remember? Cannibals don't exist anymore."

"Well, let's ask our expert," said Richter. Everybody turned toward Marcus. "Mr. Webster, have you heard about cannibals in New Guinea?"

"Actually, I did read an article in the newspaper about it, but I don't know how true it is. Besides, I think no one truly knows. It's not like cannibals, even if they did exist today, would ever advertise their food preferences. It is all just speculation."

"C'mon, aren't you tired of this anthropology yet?" said Bob. "Let's talk about the Project for a change."

"Sh-sh-sh!" they all hissed at him.

"Shut up, Bob, someone might hear! Let's talk about this outside," Marcus growled. They hastily said goodbye to their friends and went towards the parking lot, where no one could hear them. They all had taken an oath of secrecy, stronger than any CIA agent's pledge. This was primarily because their project was classified as "not quite legal." If someone found out about it, the consequences could be unpredictable and unpleasant for everyone involved.

As soon as they were away from prying ears, Bob resumed the topic.

"So, what are we going to do about the Project?"

"Nothing!" Marcus replied firmly. "We all agreed on the path forward, didn't we? Everyone does what they are supposed to do, and Ben will finish his part when he comes back."

"Yes, I know. It's just a pity about the delay. I wanted to finish it as soon as possible."

"We all want to finish it rather quickly, but we cannot rush things. If we aren't ready to start at the beginning of the school year, we will begin later," Marcus concluded.

They all wished each other a fun summer break, shook hands, and left to greet their parents at the parking lot.

Ben jumped into his father's open top Porsche, leaned back and closed his eyes. The fresh breeze felt enjoyable on his face and it flowed through his hair, as the car quickly started to speed away from the schoolyard. He was in a great mood; school was over, and the summer break had just begun. Two months without homework, lots of rest, and an exciting, worry-free vacation would start tomorrow.

Fortunately, he couldn't look into his future and see what life had in store for him. That's how God intended it to be. We will also not jump ahead of ourselves but will let events unfold as they come.

Chapter 2. It's Not Easy Being Tourists

Every vacation, regardless of its length and destination, invariably ends too quickly. You wait for it for so long, count the days and even hours before it starts, but once the long-awaited day comes, time suddenly flies at the speed of a departing train. Until now, it was patiently waiting at the platform, but following the whistle and the clanging sound of the wagons hitching, it starts to pull away picking up speed, and minutes later, it's just a small speck barely visible on the horizon.

This vacation was no exception. Although it had just begun, the days seemed to rush past at frightening speed. The grueling flight from the Northern Hemisphere to the Southern one, followed by tears of joy at the reunion with relatives (it was actually Ben's great-aunt, his father, Rupert's, aunt, and not an uncle) was already left behind. Two weeks in Australia zipped by, jam-packed with visits to museums, beaches, trips around the country and, of course, family dinners in the evenings to the accompaniment of laughter, shared memories, and stories about everybody's current lives.

And now the tears of joy were transformed into those of sadness at their forthcoming departure. Rupert's elderly aunt, delighted with the visit of her nephew, bought them a surprise gift—tickets to a newly opened cruise to Papua New Guinea. However, the gift had lost its element of surprise. Unable to keep it to herself, she had impatiently revealed it to Margaret, Ben's mother, over the phone before their arrival. It was an expensive gift for an old lady, considering her meager pension, but she flatly refused when Rupert offered to reimburse her for the tickets. She replied reasonably that if she split the price of the cruise through all the years that she had been away from them, not been able to buy presents for birthdays and holidays, the amount would be insignificant. Also, considering that she had no other relatives left, she insisted that they accept this gift from her. Rupert couldn't find a convincing counter argument and had no choice but to give in to the old lady.

The next day after long goodbyes, Rupert and the rest of the family flew to Cairns in northern Australia, where they began their journey aboard the luxury cruise liner. New Guinea had not always been a popular destination and was closed for regular tourist seasons, but now the country, surrounded by an aura of mystery and adventure, had an influx of visitors from all over the world.

Every day, the ship anchored at one of the tropical islands of the Malay Archipelago, where tourists would explore local attractions, enjoy the beautiful scenery, and return to the ship tired but happy, moving on to another destination the following day. Again, the days flew by one after another, and the vacation entered its final phase. Soon they would reach the end point of their cruise, the town of Rabaul, and then fly back to New York. But in the meantime there were still three days of the holiday left, and tomorrow they planned yet another stop. The ship will anchor in a picturesque bay near the town of Madang, one of the largest cities in Papua New Guinea. Tourists could debark by tenders to the small coastal village and attend fascinating excursions on the shore and in the interiors, including a trip to town. Those who were not interested in sightseeing could spend a relaxing day on the white sandy beach.

The cruise liner sailed smoothly in the Bismarck Sea, breaking the mirrored surface of the azure water, forming ripples of small white waves. The slanting rays of the setting sun, half-hidden behind the horizon, refracted a blood-red glare on the glass tableware and on the starched white tablecloth. Ben was sitting in the restaurant,

enjoying the magnificent view. He was exhausted. The past few action-packed days on the shore had been very exciting, but had also completely drained all his energy. Every night they returned to the ship tired, as if they had spent a hard day at work, and later just sat quietly on the deck, sipping cold refreshments.

Of course, the natural beauty of the islands was exceptional with its stunning beaches, clear water, white velvet sands, diverse wildlife, and the fascinating ethnic culture. Each island offered tourists endless opportunities for excursions and sport activities, and Ben participated in many of them, together with his parents. They went surfing and snorkeling, hiking inside dense forests, and biked along the shoreline. The next day they were on another island and everything started again: the sea, the beaches, the activities, and the remarkable tours. That day Ben and Rupert had gone scuba diving in shallow waters, not deeper than twenty feet; for beginners, even such a small depth was quite an experience. The diving instructor had quickly given them a brief introduction, explained the basic rules of scuba diving, and shown them how to maintain neutral buoyancy. But as soon as Ben and Rupert geared up and went into the water, they realized that diving was much harder than it looked. The most difficult part was getting into and out of the water, carrying the substantial load of air tanks, lead ballast, and other diving gear. But the pleasure of experiencing the silent and amazingly vibrant underwater world exceeded their expectations; it was well worth all their efforts. After lunch, they had gone biking along the scenic waterfront of the island before coming back to the ship, exhausted. They had quickly showered and now relaxed at the table, waiting for dinner to be served.

Waiters scurried between the tables arranging the cutlery, taking orders, and pouring drinks. Rupert was indifferently flipping through the pages in the brochure that he had bought at the local souvenir shop and blissfully sipping amber Scotch from a pot-bellied glass. Surprisingly, he had found a pretty good selection of alcohol on the ship and now was sampling one of the numerous varieties on board. Most likely his ancestral genes—he was of British descent—dominated his blood since he preferred Scottish whisky, specifically from the Balvenie brewery, to all other brands.

Margaret kept herself busy studying the entertainment schedule for the next day. As soon as they had boarded the ship, she had rushed to the excursion desk, taken a list of the tours available, and was penciling in possible trips in the next port of calling, Madang. The waiter came to their table, refilled Rupert's glass with another shot of alcohol, and took their dinner order. Margaret put down the pencil and leaned back in her chair.

"What are you reading?" she asked Rupert after the waiter left.

"I bought this brochure at the souvenir shop; a short tourist guide to Papua New Guinea. I thought it would be nice to know a little bit about this country: geographical location, history, economy, and so on. I don't think we are going to visit this region again anytime soon."

"I hope we don't come back here in the near future," Margaret replied.

"Why not? Don't you like it here?"

"Of course I do. It's very . . . pretty," she said, carefully choosing neutral words. "Amazing beaches, tropical forest, wildlife; but surely we didn't have to travel across the globe for it! The Caribbean islands or Hawaii are quite similar, with the same beaches and nature, but more civilized, with changing rooms, showers, and toilets. But anyway, it doesn't matter now, since we are already here. So, tell me, what's in your pamphlet?"

"It's just an overview of the country." Rupert flipped a few pages of the brochure. "For example, historical and geographical information—this island is the second largest in the world after Greenland. It is divided into two countries: the western part is the Indonesian province, Irian Jaya, and only the eastern side is Papua New Guinea. The country received independence in the mid-seventies, but before that, it was administratively owned by Australia . . . Hmm, what else is in here?" Rupert flipped through a dozen pages. "The geographical location—water-locked by the Arafura Sea from the west, and the Coral Sea from the east, Indian Ocean on the south—"

"Okay, that is enough geography for me," Margaret interrupted.

"Oh, here's a fascinating fact," Rupert continued, after skipping a few more chapters and sipping Scotch from his glass. "The island is rich in deposits of oil, gas, gold, copper, and other minerals. However, over forty percent of the population still lives below the poverty line."

"So what?" Margaret shrugged. "Do you know how many countries in the world live in poverty? Many of them have even worse statistics."

"Of course, I know that, but not all of these countries are rich in natural resources that could be exported. Also, they don't have any coastal land that could bring income from tourism and fishing. But here they have all the conditions favorable for a strong economy, yet the country continues to be in poverty."

Rupert skimmed through a few more pages.

"Here's another amusing fact: in today's New Guinea, there is more uncharted land than in the North Pole, especially in the western Indonesian part of the island. This country is also called 'Terra Incognita,' which in Latin means 'Unknown Territory.'"

"How is that possible?" exclaimed Margaret. "Unexplored land in the twenty-first century? Especially with neighboring countries like Australia, China, and Japan?"

"There are many places on the island that are unreachable—dense jungle, high mountains, and the southern region is very swampy. But you are right, it is not clear how there could be any unexplored spots on the map today."

Rupert flipped through to the end of the brochure and put it aside.

"Actually, that's all the booklet says about this country. But I found some captivating information on the Internet before our trip that you cannot find in any booklet for tourists."

"About what?"

"For example, some local tribes here practiced cannibalism until just recently."

"What do you mean 'recently'?" Margaret asked suspiciously.

"Well, that's a good question. Officially, the fight against cannibalism began after New Guinea's declaration of independence in the seventies and lasted more than ten years. But according to unofficial sources, this struggle continues to this day. It's impossible to completely eradicate the traditions and rituals of one's ancestors in just two decades. Also, many tribes live in remote, mountainous areas, and the authorities neither have access nor control over these territories. So no one knows what's going on up there."

"Why didn't you tell me this before? Maybe we should have gone to another place instead, or even stayed in Australia?"

"That's *exactly* why I didn't tell you earlier. I didn't want to scare you!"

"Dad, are you serious? Do they have cannibals here?"

Until then, Ben had not participated in the conversation; he had been sitting quietly, looking out the window, but Rupert's last remarks caught his attention.

"No, Son, I didn't say that. I just said that no one actually knows what's going on in places that are unreachable. It is quite possible that somewhere out there, this horrible tradition exists even today."

Margaret wanted to make a comment, but Rupert interrupted her.

"I know what you're about to say. Believe me, in the places where we're going, cannibalism doesn't occur anymore. It is a civilized country like any other. We've already been here for a week, and we haven't met a single cannibal yet."

"How can you be so sure?" Margaret was not ready to let the subject go. "Do you think their food preferences will be written on their forehead? And what about the face and body paint and those awful necklaces made of some kind of teeth? Isn't that a symbol of cannibalism?"

Rupert laughed.

"Well, dear, that's obvious. Their face coloring and fangs on a string are nothing more than a way to impress the tourists and make a few bucks if someone wants to take a picture with them. It has absolutely nothing to do with any of their rituals and traditions. Haven't you noticed that the locals in the places we visited wore normal clothes? Men wore jeans and shorts, and women also dressed in usual clothes. They are actually civilized people, even though they are originally tribal. For example, did you know that men in many of the local tribes don't wear clothes? They only have this thing called *koteka,* a long tube that covers their genitals. It is made of wild dried calabash."

"That's an unusual outfit." Margaret chuckled. "And most importantly, very convenient and inexpensive. They just go to the garden, get themselves a calabash of the desired . . . uh . . . size and length, and wear them. There is no need to shop for new clothes."

"Calabashes don't grow in the garden; it is a wild gourd. Besides, the length of the *koteka*, by the way, is determined by the social status of the man in his tribe and has nothing to do with the size of his genitals. Papuan tribal women also don't wear any clothes, except a bag over their head that falls behind and forms a pocket. They carry vegetables, firewood, and even newborn babies in it. Have you seen something like that in those ports where we've been to?"

"No, I have not," Margaret said honestly.

"Of course not. You will never see it in places that are visited by tourists. All the natives in these ports wear normal, civilized clothing. Sure, it is not Dolce & Gabbana, but not bags over their heads, either.

Although I did see some women wear straw skirts in a few previous ports, but I am sure that is probably more of a holiday decoration put on the top of their usual skirts and dresses, just to entertain tourists."

The waiter approached their table and began to serve dinner, and they had to temporarily stop their conversation.

"Maybe somewhere deep inland, people still dress like their ancestors," Rupert continued after the waiter left, "or rather, don't wear clothes at all. It is possible that they also practice some of their brutal traditions from the past, but we have no business to be there."

"Still, I don't understand why we couldn't go somewhere else? Why should we put ourselves in danger, even if the chance of meeting these awful cannibals is very slim?"

"I'm telling you, there is absolutely no threat whatsoever." Rupert now regretted that he had started this conversation and hastened to change the subject. "Actually, Papua New Guinea is a more civilized country than their western neighbor, the Indonesian part of the island. I would not dare to go on vacation there. By the way, tourists don't visit these places very often, even now. For example, there is a cannibal tribe called 'Yali,' discovered only in the mid-sixties, and I wouldn't be surprised if they remained cannibals even today."

Margaret had cut a small piece of steak on her plate while Rupert was talking and was now looking at it skeptically.

"Hey . . . you! What's your name . . ." She summoned the waiter serving their table. "I requested my steak rare, but you brought it well done, a piece of burnt meat. Please take my dinner back and explain to your chef the difference between a soft, juicy steak and the overcooked one that you served me."

"I'm sorry, madam. I will exchange your order immediately." The waiter began to collect the dish from the table. "But I thought that the steak was—"

"You don't need to think, just go and ask him to make me the one that I ordered."

"Yes, of course, madam. I will bring you another steak right away."

"And while you are at it, please refill my glass with the same wonderful Scotch you brought me earlier," Rupert said, taking advantage of this situation.

"So what about Yali? You were telling us about them and cannibalism," Ben reminded his father once the waiter had left. Unlike his parents, he had an excellent appetite after such a tiring day. Strangely, this story interested him because of the conversation on the last day of school, where the all-knowing Marcus had mentioned cannibals when Ben had told his friends he was going to New Guinea. At that time, Ben hadn't paid much attention, as his thoughts had already been on the vacation, but now his curiosity was piqued.

"Yeah, Yali," Rupert continued. "They are considered the most dreadful cannibals, and despite their height, or lack thereof, they induce terror in their neighbors! The majority of them are short, as the average mature man barely exceeds five feet. They kill and eat their enemies and grind the inedible body parts and bones to dust and disperse it with the wind. But even the Yali can't be compared to the other cannibal tribe, the Asmat. In fact, when we talk about cannibals, we imply the Asmat tribe. Compared to them, the Yali are nice and sweet people."

"Yes, they sound very nice and friendly," Margaret said sarcastically, but Rupert ignored her comment.

"Yes, they are. If you are nice to them, they will treat you accordingly."

"Like you, Mom, friendly toward your steak." Ben grinned.

"The Yali fight simply to protect themselves and their tribe, and unlike the Asmat, they hardly ever attack their neighbors without a reason. The Asmat, on the other hand, strike with purely gastronomic motives, capturing and killing men and women from other tribes, and then dining on dead bodies. Their favorite meal is the brain of the defeated enemy mixed with sago worms. They collect these maggots from rotten trees and put them into the open skull of the deceased or even of hostages who are alive, then—"

"Wait, Dad," Ben broke in to say. "Something doesn't sound right. Brain with worms? That is just wrong!"

"There is nothing wrong with that. There are some worms that are quite edible. Actually, they are not worms, they are the larvae of the Woodcutter Beetle and many tribes eat them. By the way, in some countries even—"

"No, I am not talking about that. I mean how can they eat meat with meat? Brains, worms—both belong to the same food group, which is proteins and fat. They should eat human brains with vegetables, fried potatoes, and salad. In the open skull with the brain they could add some . . . what was that, sago? So add some sago leaves, shred a few cucumbers, onion or garlic, a little bit of seasoning and spices, salt, pepper, and some olive oil. Then mix it well. If the owner of the brain was killed just recently, the blood is still fresh and there is no need for olive—"

"That's enough!" Margaret slammed her hand on the table so hard that the glasses rattled. She looked at the piece of rare steak on her fork and threw it back on the plate in disgust. "Can we talk about something more pleasant during dinner? Let me finish my meal, and then you may continue sharing these delightful details with each other. Without me!"

"Yes, of course," Rupert reassured her. "Let's change the subject. This is very dark humor of yours, Son."

"Humor is only as dark as the subject," Ben replied, grinning.

Rupert quickly changed the subject.

"Did you know that the Asmat are excellent woodcarvers? They make absolutely stunning wooden statues, figures, and masks, using primitive tools. Their crafts are sold at art auctions in Europe and exhibited in museums there. This region is known for various rare trees, which are very expensive, and their wood-carved sculptures are considered museum exhibits. Also, it's not just the Asmat; woodcraft is part of the culture of the Mamberamo, the Vano, and other tribes. For Mamberamo, woodcarving is actually part of their religion, as they believe that their tribe came from the tree, therefore the wooden statues represent their origin. For them, it is a kind of icon that they worship."

Through the entire dinner Rupert talked about various tribes and their customs. He told them about people living in trees—the Korowai, the Kombai, and the Asaro; clay people who wore masks, which they believed would scare away evil spirits, and also confuse the enemy during war. The stories were captivating and informative. Even Margaret listened with great interest, while eating her steak. It was evident that Rupert had thoroughly prepared for the trip, reading all he could find about this country and the numerous tribes within it.

The next day, after an early breakfast, the whole family sat comfortably on the top deck in the lounge chairs by the pool. The sun was just above the horizon, and the air was refreshing. Soon it would be impossible to sit on the sundeck because of the strong tropical heat. Margaret was looking overboard, down at the lower level, where crowds of tourists were impatiently jostling their way into the tenders, rushing to get ashore. The excursion that they had booked earlier was scheduled for the afternoon, and there was plenty of time, so they decided to wait for the main crowd to dissipate. Rupert lit his first cigar and browsed through the local newspaper, sipping the pricey Scotch. He looked into his glass and thought for a moment that it was probably wrong to start the day with the use of strong alcoholic beverages. But a vacation is the only time that one can get away from daily routine and do things one would never do in everyday life. Anyway, who said that it is wrong? If something gives you pleasure and is not detrimental to others, then it is not wrong at all. The health risks of consuming alcohol were the same throughout the day, so why should one wait until evening? But of course, this was only a rhetorical question and did not require an immediate answer.

Rupert went deep into the local newspaper, and Ben detached himself from his surroundings, putting on his favorite Beats headphones, which he did not take off even during meals. He reclined in a lounge chair, surrendering to his thoughts, or rather, enjoying their absence. The past six days of the cruise had been exhausting, and all he wanted right now was to spend just one day on the ship in peace, sipping refreshments, reading a book, and occasionally cooling off in the clean seawater swimming pool on the deck. But instead, they had planned another excursion into the jungle. As always, the indefatigable Margaret insisted on this trip. Last evening during dinner she had read through the brochure and selected the most desirable tours for consideration. Out of all the excursions offered, Margaret decisively steered away from everything that was related to the beach and water sports. All the previous islands had looked identical: the same beaches, the same crystal-clear water, velvety white sand, and fish (well, perhaps the fish were different, who knows!). Therefore, it was decided to dedicate the remaining two days of the cruise to informative excursions and sightseeing, after which, if time permitted, they could go to the beach as well.

A consolidated list of three excursions was offered to the family for discussion in the music lounge, where they moved to after dinner.

They settled comfortably in the deep salon chairs. Music was playing softly. Rupert sipped his Scotch and studied Margaret's options for entertainment at the shore.

First on the list was a six-hour bus tour of the town of Madang, visiting the cultural center, the local museums, and acquainting visitors with the customs and traditions of the place. After that, the tour offered a visit to the lighthouse—a memorial in honor of the sailors who died during the World War II New Guinea campaign, and the island's liberation from Japanese occupation. At the end of the tour was a walk around town and, of course, to the famous market Mercado de Madang, where tourists could buy souvenirs made by native craftsmen.

Next on the list was a three-hour excursion into the jungle to observe the tropical flora and fauna of the island. The third one was an evening tour to a waterfall with a breathtaking view of the sunset, where the rays of the setting sun reflected in the particles of the falling water.

After a short debate, the tour to Madang town was crossed from the list, as nobody was interested in exploring it, even though it was the fifth largest city in the country. Preference was given to the waterfalls, and that was almost finalized. But then, suddenly, Rupert remembered that at the next port of Watam, near the Sepik River, there was a similar trip planned. It was finally decided to take the tour to the jungle.

That's how one small remark impacts the future and determines our life. If he hadn't said anything, it would have been different, but once the words were spoken, a course was set. The scale that swayed toward visiting the waterfalls tilted back in favor of the jungle, and whatever was going to happen—happened.

Actually, the decision wasn't made in the most democratic way. Margaret insisted on an excursion, and Rupert, as always, agreed with her, slightly adjusting the route. Ben cut himself off from the conversation with his headphones. He did not want to go anywhere at all, but didn't say anything, knowing he didn't stand a chance at winning against his mother.

We are probably going to miss lunch, Ben thought regretfully, *but if we return to the ship right after the tour, then there is a chance of getting something at the snack bar before dinner.*

The sun rose higher, producing intense heat. Waiters on the upper deck were serving cold beverages, and the music started to play loudly, entertaining the passengers who did not want to leave the comfortable ship for the questionable tropical beauty. The pool was finally open, and children immediately rushed into the rejuvenating water.

Ben looked around. The amount of people on the deck had increased significantly. It appeared that at the end of the cruise, more and more tourists preferred the comfort of the ship to the beauty of the tropical islands. Yet many tourists still hurried ashore for another portion of excitement. Finally, the crowd on the lower deck thinned out, and Margaret touched Ben's shoulder.

"It's time to go."

Rupert downed his Scotch and got up. They went toward the exit, and a few minutes later stepped into the tender for a ride to the shore. Ben looked back at the receding ship. For no apparent reason, he was troubled, but immediately let go of his brooding thoughts.

If you can't get out of the tour, then at least try to enjoy it, he said to himself cheerfully, and boldly stepped ashore as soon as the boat was moored to the pier.

Chapter 3. Terra Incognita

The festivities on the quay reached their peak as usual during the arrival of the tourist ships. The loud motley crowd nudged, swallowed, and whirled Ben in different directions as soon as he stepped on shore. Souvenir vendors rushed to intercept tourists at the pier, begging them to come to their shops and take a gander at their goods. Owners of small boats approached tourists, offering them fishing trips, or sightseeing on the small, secluded islands scattered throughout the bay. Many natives were standing in exotic attire, faces painted in bright colors, their intricately styled hair decorated with colored feathers. They were wrapped from head to toe in bizarre necklaces. For only one euro, tourists could take a memorable photo with one of the colorful specimens of the local ethnic minorities. People could also take a picture with a beautiful parrot, or a huge, scary-looking, yet absolutely harmless spider, or even with snakes. Children were selling exotic fruits, peeled and neatly sliced. Music playing on the ship anchored in the harbor reached the shore, complementing the sense of celebration. Tour buses were coming and leaving one after another, whisking tourists away on interesting and adventurous excursions. Some tourists were back from their tours, while others waited eagerly for their bus to arrive.

The new tourists from the ship mixed with those who had already explored the local wonders and were getting ready to head back to the boat. Many were still sitting on the white sandy beach enjoying the lovely weather and the ethnic food along with cold beverages in the small restaurant nearby in the shade, rather than rushing to the comfort of the ship. They were serving seafood: fresh fish, the catch of the day wrapped in the leaves of an unknown plant, along with rice and vegetables.

However, the main entertainment here was the marketplace, which occupied almost the entire port area. Endless stands were packed with a variety of colorful, unpretentious handicrafts from local artisans. The counters sagged under the weight of souvenirs made from wood, clay, seashells, and colorful pebbles. Traditional masks were mixed with bamboo flutes, souvenir spears, bows, arrows, and stone axes. Tourists flooded the island, sweeping away handmade jewelry, primitive tools, whimsical figurines, masks, and amulets.

In the few years since the first cruise ship went into operation, the souvenir trade had become a profitable business for the residents of the coastal towns. The entire population of the region adjacent to the harbor swarmed to buy all kinds of crafts from the masters of the surrounding tribes, and resold the lot with a large markup. Many of these souvenirs were made from indigenous rare wood, and were intricately hand-crafted. But the tribal masters quickly realized that they were selling their goods to the villagers for a pittance and repeatedly raised their prices. Many of the natives who had access to the port began to sell their souvenirs directly to the tourists at full price, eliminating the middle men.

However, there was enough profit for everybody. With each cruise ship hundreds of tourists bought out all the souvenirs and crafts, leaving dollars, euros, pounds, rubles, yen, shillings, as well as local kina and toea[5] in its place. As the demand for goods exceeded the rate at which local craftsmen could make them, Chinese manufacturers, sensing the vacuum in the market, overwhelmed the country with replicas of the original products. The replicas, unlike the originals, were made out of plastic painted as wood instead of the actual precious wood, but that didn't stop tourists from buying the souvenirs, and money kept flowing out of the tourists' pockets, improving the economy of the local towns and villages.

Ben strolled along the market alley, bored. He didn't want to buy anything, as they had already amassed enough presents at the previous ports. Now he looked at these souvenirs indifferently, just to kill time before the beginning of their tour. Every now and then he took a souvenir from the counter, and Margaret immediately handed him an antibacterial wipe as soon as he put it back. Ben was annoyed with his mother's bacteria phobia, but he dutifully accepted each wipe and cleaned his hands to avoid any confrontation with her.

Margaret was terrified of bacteria, and every time she came on vacation, she was prepared for any possible illnesses. She had supplies of medicine for fever, cold, inflammation, vomiting, cuts, burns, and upset stomach. The quantity of medical supplies in her bag was sufficient for the entire family, even if they had to take these pills daily. But luckily, so far, there was no need for that. She also kept wet and dry antibacterial wipes, antiseptics, plaster patches of all sizes, and even a small roll of toilet paper, just in case. Before traveling to the Third World countries, she also made everyone take a full recommended course of vaccinations against typhoid, cholera, hepatitis, diphtheria, tetanus, encephalitis, and other exotic diseases.

Ben felt someone pull on his sleeve.

"Mister, do you want to buy an amulet?"

A girl, probably no more than ten years old with her face painted in accordance with local traditions, and a necklace made of teeth from unknown animals mixed with seashells, offered him a selection of small wooden (or plastic—tough to tell at first glance) figurines on a section of lace. The string was so stiff that wearing it would surely bruise his neck.

"Please, mister, get one for yourself. It's not expensive, just one euro."

Ben would have gladly given her the money without even buying her craft, but his wallet, which had become much lighter after all the previous ports, was on the ship.

"Thank you, but I don't have any—"

"Oh, you don't have any euros? Well, then, one dollar and fifty cents, please."

"No, I don't have any dollars either, sorry." Ben smiled.

"Ah, Australian dollars?" The girl nodded understandingly. "Then it will be two dollars."

"I have only rubles!" Ben joked, not even knowing what a ruble looked like.

"Seventy rubles." The girl calculated without any hesitation, unaware of the teasing in his words.

Such unexpected knowledge of the exchange rates of different currencies deserved respect and had to be rewarded.

"Dad, give me a few bucks," Ben said to his father. "I'll pay you back on the ship."

Rupert gave him a few bills, of which Ben took two single dollar bills and gave them to the girl. She wanted to give him the change, but Ben stopped her.

"Don't worry, keep the change."

"Thank you, mister," she said, carefully folding and putting the money somewhere in the hidden corners of her clothes, and then handed him the figurines he had purchased.

Ben was about to reply, but the girl rushed after another potential customer.

Wow. No one has ever called me 'Mister' before. I'm just a few years older than her, thought Ben, while going to the next souvenir kiosk. *Or maybe not older, perhaps just taller.*

But a moment later thoughts of the girl were left behind as he saw a small shop nearby. Ben rushed to the store hoping to buy some food. At his age he always had a good appetite and never refused a snack between meals. Besides, they were going to skip lunch and get back to the ship right before dinnertime. Inside the store, Ben headed straight to the food section, ignoring the shelves with everything else. He got himself a few packs of chips and some sweets and went to the cashier. But Margaret was on high alert and promptly snatched his bags away.

"We are not going to buy any food." Margaret was a zealous opponent of any kind of junk food, especially in places like this.

"But, Mom, I'm hungry."

"It's okay, you can wait until dinner. You know that we shouldn't buy food in here. I got you some fruits." She handed Ben two apples and a banana. "If you are hungry just eat fruit, it's much safer and healthier."

The cruise administration prohibited people from taking food from the ship, but Margaret had managed to sneak out a few fruits and a few bottles of drinking water in her bag. Ben immediately ate the banana, knowing that it would rot faster, and put the apples in his backpack for later. His need for food was further tortured when the delicious smell of grilled seafood mixed with unknown spices and herbs suddenly wafted out from the small outdoor restaurant nearby, where people were having lunch and drinking cold beverages in the shade of wide umbrellas. Ben sighed sadly. His mom would never agree to have lunch in a place like that. Just the thought of it was giving her a strong allergic reaction.

Margaret, as if she was reading Ben's thoughts, quickly made a wide detour from the restaurant, and went to the end of the market alley, toward the local beach—a narrow strip of sand behind several huge boulders scattered along the shore. It didn't have any beach attributes like lounge chairs, parasols, changing cabins, or showers; nevertheless, there were plenty of people. The water was crystal clear, and people were plunging into the sea to escape the midday heat. Ben would have loved to go for a swim, but it was time to return to the parking lot for the arrival of their tour bus. They decided to come back to the beach before boarding the ship to wash off the dust and sweat.

The tour bus, with the colorful but faded advertising of the Madang Travel Agency, was already parked, and the driver cheerfully greeted the passengers. The bus was old and rusted in many places from exposure to constant rain and the humidity; it had a canvas top, and no air conditioner.

I'm glad we didn't go to Madang, Ben thought. He wasn't enthusiastic about spending even a few hours in the bus without an air conditioner, but the long trip to the town was even less appealing to him.

Actually, this excursion promised to be truly interesting. It isn't every day that a city dweller gets a chance to escape into the wilderness of equatorial rainforests. A man living in the concrete jungle of the big city must periodically escape to uninhabited nature, reunite with his roots, and visit the place where he came from and to where he will return at the end of his lifespan, completing the cycle. City parks with picnic tables and volleyball nets strung between trees don't count as nature. It has to be real, primitive, and mysterious as created by God, or whatever natural force one might believe in. The forest that they were about to visit was the best example of such a place.

The young cheerful driver with a warm open smile invited them to board the bus. There were not many people who had booked that particular afternoon excursion, and the bus was only half full. Most

46

of the jungle enthusiasts chose the morning tour instead, so they could spend the entire afternoon at the beach. Margaret and Rupert took the front seat, while Ben walked to the back of the bus, wanting to sit alone taking the entire row for himself.

The driver counted all the passengers, waited until everybody got their cameras ready, and began the tour. He spoke decent English, with a heavy Australian accent.

"Good afternoon, Ladies and Gentlemen. My name is Hubert, and I will be your guide and the driver. Please sit back, relax, and enjoy the ride."

Hubert stepped on the gas, and the bus slowly entered the thicket, rattling and humming with its eight cylinders, sixteen valves, and various metal joints. The road was gradually going uphill, and the surrounding landscape was changing accordingly. During the short three-hour journey through the dense forest, Hubert was going to make several stops and walk through the jungle to explore rare and interesting species of local flora and fauna, such as the rainbow eucalyptus tree grove, and the iron tree, among others. With some luck, the excursionists could also see unique birds and animals. At the end of the tour they planned a long walk to the natural habitat of the beautiful birds-of-paradise.

It turned out that Hubert was an excellent tour guide.

He talked nonstop about the flora and fauna with the usual "look to the left, look to the right," instructions every guide gives, and passengers obediently turned their heads in the indicated direction, clicking the shutter buttons of their cameras. Hubert drove through areas with coffee shrubs and rare iron trees, named for their brown rusty color, commonly used by local tribes for medicinal purposes. They saw many sago palms, the favorite tree of every tribe, as more than half of their daily food came from it.

Hubert also told them about the rich and diverse fauna of the island and even showed them the Doria tree-kangaroo, a species that looks like a small bear because of its thick brown fur. All of a sudden, Hubert stopped the bus, opened the door, and told the passengers to get out quietly, and then pointed to a hefty two-colored bird, sitting pretty low on the branch of a tree, indifferently looking at the crowd of excursionists.

"This bird, named crested or bicolor pitohui, commonly lives in this region, and should never be confused with the parrot," Hubert explained to the excursionists. "This bird does not get scared easily, and may even let you get pretty close. But never try to pet it, as it is very poisonous. There is a strong toxin in its plumage that can paralyze your respiratory system, limbs, and even heart muscles. The likelihood of death for those who want to pet this cute bird is small, but the consequences could be serious."

Unfortunately, they did not see any other unique animals, but Hubert told them about many species indigenous to the jungle, even though they weren't around.

During the first half of the tour, Ben listened to Hubert's narrative intently. He even walked with the group through the woods during short stops. But soon, on the way to their last stop, his mind stopped absorbing information. It became a jumble of names of animal species, mingled with that of plants, birds, snakes, butterflies, and even insects. His eyelids became heavy, closing involuntarily.

In addition, he felt cold and sick from the shaky bus ride on the winding dirt road. He had come to the shore wearing only a thin T-shirt and had not even thought of bringing a warm jacket on such a hot day. But now, at a higher elevation, the air became dry and chilled. The sun's rays could not penetrate the lush tree canopy, and a fresh breeze was blowing into the open bus. In the back row, Ben found a roll of canvas used for long-term bus parking. He unwound half of the roll and crawled under the tarp, put his head on the backpack, stretched out, and was lulled to sleep by the drone of the driver's voice.

Ben woke up from a sudden silence. As when you fall asleep on the couch in front of a loudly playing TV, you wake up as soon as someone turns it off. Apparently people were wakened not from the loud noise, but from the sudden change of sound levels. He was surrounded by complete silence, broken only by discordant bird songs somewhere high up in the trees.

Ben opened his eyes and listened to the sounds of the forest for a moment, wondering why it was so quiet and why the bus was not moving. He quickly realized that everyone had gone out to watch the birds-of-paradise and left him to sleep in the bus. At first he was upset that his parents had left him alone, but then he sighed in relief. The last few walks in the woods to observe the local vegetation had been more than enough, even though the trees here were quite rare, not found anywhere else in the world. The only tree that had impressed Ben was the rainbow eucalyptus. It changed its color depending on its size, its age, and even the season. Also, the tree bark becomes darker in color as it matures, and when exfoliating, exposes the internal lighter fiber colors. As a result, the tree trunk looks like an artist's palette. The grove of these trees had been unrealistically colorful, like a miscellaneous set decoration for the movie *Alice in Wonderland.*

The rest of the exhibits though were excruciating to Ben. He was a city boy and had very little interest in nature, wildlife, and vegetation. He was much happier in the comfort of his home with a computer on the desk, a box of pizza, and a bottle of soda. Nature, forests, and local beauty were for aborigines or Papuans, or whatever their politically correct name is. This is their land, their world, where they feel the most comfortable and cozy. After all, if the Papuans came to New York, they would not feel comfortable in the midst of skyscrapers, shopping centers, and endless freeways. As they say: to each his own.

Ben did not want to get out from underneath the canvas cover. He felt warm and comfortable under the pile of rigid material. But he was hungry again, probably from the fresh air and the walk through the woods. Ben remembered the apples his mom had given him before the tour started. He got one out of the backpack under his head and was ready to take a bite when he noticed a strange unknown creature the size of a large cat staring at him from the nearest window opening. Ben looked at the animal curiously, trying to identify it, careful not to make any sudden moves and scare him away. The animal looked at Ben, probably with the same thoughts.

It was obviously some kind of marsupial. Ben recalled some information from a zoology lesson, but with that, he exceeded his knowledge on the subject. Then he remembered his conversation with his friends on the last day of school. Marcus had been talking about some marsupials, but not kangaroos. Ben wrinkled his brow, trying to remember whether Marcus had mentioned its name.

I wonder what kind of animal that is, Ben thought. *If only Marcus was here, he would be able to identify it for sure.*

He decided to take a picture of this furry creature and send it to him for identification as soon as they got back to the ship. Trying not to make any sudden movements, he disconnected his iPhone from the headphones around his neck and prepared to take a shot. However, it was nearly impossible to take the picture from under the tarpaulin. Ben slowly put the apple on the seat in front of him and carefully got out from under the tarp on the floor. He held the phone, ready to photograph the mysterious animal, but it suddenly disappeared, taking the fruit with it. Ben looked out the window. The unidentified creature was sitting nearby in the tall grass, happily eating his apple. Ben got off the bus and cautiously sneaked up to a distance suitable for photographing, but as soon as he got close, the stubborn creature ran further into the woods with the half-eaten apple in its paws.

Why didn't I bring my camera with the long-focus lens? Ben cursed himself while chasing the beast. *I didn't want to carry a bulky, heavy camera, and now I have to chase this thing around the woods.*

But Ben was also stubborn and wasn't going to give up. Besides, it was a pity wasting the apple, since dinner was so far away. He got closer again. The high, dense grass almost hid the animal. Another step and once again, the animal ran farther. After playing catch-up with Ben, the unidentified creature ran quite far into the woods and climbed up a tree, grasping the trunk with three paws, the fourth clutching the remnants of the apple. The branch it settled on was located in an area free from any leaves and was a perfect spot for a picture. Ben was already too far into the thicket. He knew that it was easy to get lost in the forest, but right now, the bus with the colorful advertising was nearby and clearly visible through the trees, and he courageously stepped into the woods without further hesitation.

He snapped a few shots from different angles and looked through the photos. Some of them were blurred, and in the others the creature was blocked by branches. He had to get to the other side of the thick bushes and take a picture from there. Ben stepped over to the other side while staring intensely at the screen, trying to find a better angle, and suddenly realized that his leg could not find any ground underneath. Ben looked down and saw that he was at the edge of a deep cliff overhanging an abyss that had unexpectedly appeared behind the bushes. Of course, it didn't really appear suddenly; the cliff had been there for thousands, or maybe even millions, of years. But it was sudden for Ben, as it hadn't been visible from the other side of the bushes. He looked into the deep abyss, dazed, his mind refusing to accept reality. The edge started crumbling, and rocks began falling down into the abyss. Ben was losing his balance, standing on the edge of the cliff. He immediately threw away his now-useless iPhone, desperately trying to regain balance and find support, grasping thin twigs, clutching onto leaves and vines.

Stupid, how stupid! How foolish of me! Ben looked for something else to grab onto, terrified. At the last moment he saw the animal sitting on a branch, probably enjoying Ben's misery; he could have sworn that the creature was grinning mischievously, showing its sharp, small teeth, and the next moment he fell into the abyss.

The noisy crowd of tourists were loaded back into the bus, loudly sharing their experiences with each other. Their long walk through the woods had been refreshing, and everyone was in a cheerful mood, charmed by the local glamour. Margaret and Rupert took their places. Rupert looked back at the pile of tarps in the back row.

It's a shame Ben slept through this walk, he thought.

Hubert once again raised the microphone.

"Well, Ladies and Gentlemen, did you like the tour?"

"Yes, we did," all of the passengers shouted sincerely.

"With that, we conclude our journey in the wilderness. If you have any questions, feel free to ask me—otherwise relax and enjoy the scenes on the way back to the port."

Hubert turned off the microphone and started the bus.

The walk through the jungle to the habitats of the bird-of-paradise had exceeded everyone's expectations. New Guinea is considered the world's capital of this beautiful bird, being home to almost forty out of forty-five known species, and such a tour was a real godsend, even for the most demanding bird-watchers and photographers.

These kinds of tours are always associated with the risk that the birds may not be there when tourists arrive. No one can guarantee that the promised birds and animals will be found, as wildlife always lives on its own schedule, and is not always synchronized with the timing of any excursion. Often, disappointed sightseers had to leave without seeing these pretty feathered inhabitants of Terra Incognita. But today the birds were generous to the tourists and stayed perched on the branches of trees, ignoring the cameras pointing at them.

Margaret had counted about a dozen different species of birds, although she wasn't sure that these birds belonged to different classes. Males and females of the same species may significantly vary in the color of their plumage, shape, and sizes. At first, she demanded detailed explanations from Hubert for each bird that she saw, but after a while, the English and Latin names, and descriptions of birds confused her, and later she could hardly distinguish between a cockatoo, golden-red pheasant, or even hornbill. The only exception was the emperor bird, as their beautiful plumage could not possibly be muddled with any other species. The image of that gorgeous bird is even emblazoned on the national emblem of the country, and on local banknotes and coins.

The confusion was at the end of the tour, when the joyful excursionists were heading back to the bus, discussing the birds. Margaret also decided to demonstrate her knowledge and said that she liked the crowned pigeon less than the royal starling. But Hubert replied with a grin that they hadn't seen crowned pigeons at all, since those birds prefer swampy soil, and therefore lived on a lower level of the hills. He explained that what Margaret had seen was a Goliath bird and that these two birds were often confused with each other because of the similar plumage. The only reason he had mentioned the pigeon was for comparison with the Goliath bird. The rest of the way to the bus Margaret was silent to avoid further confusion, relying on Rupert's memory and pictures.

The bus was speeding along the narrow road through the jungle toward the port. Perhaps the word "speeding" doesn't quite describe the ride, or the word "road." It was just a dirt path winding through the forest, avoiding the stumps of tumbled trees, potholes, and other natural and man-made impediments. But for this road, the speed they were traveling at was tremendous. The passengers were swaying from side to side on sharp turns and road bumps, and those who wanted to take a nap on the way back had to give up any attempts at it. Hubert was in a rush to get back because he had another group for the late afternoon excursion to the waterfalls. This tour had taken a little longer than expected, as the tourists were observing rare birds and didn't want to leave, and now he was making up for lost time.

Margaret and Rupert, who had planned to take a nap on the way back, had to hold on to the handrails instead, to avoid falling from their seats at each turn. Margaret kicked off her shoes and flexed her legs. Her new shoes had been too tight and uncomfortable for the long walk through the jungle.

I shouldn't have worn these shoes for this trip. Perhaps I should have brought a less expensive pair, but something more comfortable.

Rupert also tried to stretch his legs but had no room in the narrow seat space, so he rested his legs in the aisle.

"Now I understand why Ben chose the back seat. He has much more room back there."

"By the way, how is he doing there? Have you checked on him?" Margaret asked, suddenly remembering her son.

"He crawled underneath that dirty tarp and fell asleep. I think he's getting tired from this vacation. He has already seen all of these jungles, birds, animals, and other exotic delights. I am glad that he did not come with us on this last hike."

"To be honest, I am jealous of him. He was resting all this time in the shade, while we were walking for half an hour through these awful woods."

"I'm hungry," Rupert complained. "It is almost dinnertime, and we didn't even have lunch."

"Yes, you're right! I wouldn't mind eating even that overcooked steak that they served me yesterday in the restaurant."

"It wasn't that bad, in my opinion. I agree they didn't give you the rare steak you ordered, but I do think you were over-reacting a little, Margaret. Besides, the waiter brought you what the chef had prepared. It's not his fault at all, and you should have been more polite."

"He is supposed to check the order," Margaret replied coldly, "rather than serving it blindly. Don't make me out as a spoiled lady. If I wanted a well-done steak, I would have ordered it exactly like that."

Rupert realized that, as usual, he couldn't win an argument with his wife and simply changed the subject.

"We should have eaten at the port before the tour. I saw a small restaurant there, and whatever they were cooking, the smell was pretty tempting! It was probably something from their local cuisine, some kind of seafood."

"How can we possibly eat at that filthy place!? Do you want to spend the rest of the vacation in the toilet? I'd rather wait until dinner. We are going to be on the ship in less than an hour."

Immediately, their imagination conjured a picture of a cozy restaurant on the top deck of the ship, dinner tables with white starched tablecloths, a variety of menu choices, and a bar with a wide selection of drinks.

Their conversation about food, though it increased their appetites even more, helped them kill the time on the way back to the port. The passengers poured out of the bus and rushed to the ship in anticipation of a hot shower, and unlimited snacks in the buffet before dinner. Margaret waited until all the other passengers got down from the bus, and headed to the last row.

"Ben, get up. Let's go. Time to leave. Benjamin?"

She pulled at the edge of the tarp. It slid to the floor, revealing Ben's backpack and an empty seat.

Ben was falling into the abyss. Experts say that during the last seconds of a person's life, his entire lifespan flashes through his mind like a movie on fast-forward: from the day of birth, up to the last tragic instant. How do these experts know all this? Who delivers this information to us if the next moment, the life of this person is abruptly ended in the most dramatic way?

Nothing like that was going on in Ben's mind as he was falling down from the cliff. Perhaps his mind simply didn't realize the full extent of the tragedy because everything happened so quickly. One moment he was running through the woods with the camera in his hands, and the next instant he was falling down into the deep abyss. But a moment later his mind didn't even have time for sentimental memories from his childhood. On the way down, Ben hit a huge tree.

Many years ago, a seed had blown into the crack of the hill, where it successfully sprouted. By some incredible miracle, this place had all the conditions necessary for the successful growth of the tree: plenty of sunlight, presence of underground water seeping through the hairline flaws in the rock, and the dirt, the smallest particles of which had been blowing into the cracks in the craggy formation for centuries. The little plant grew, matured, developed thick branches and powerful roots that penetrated deep into the rocky massif, and after many years, turned into a strong tree with a wide trunk, lots of thick and thin branches, and a lush crown.

Everything in life has a meaningful purpose, which, for this tree, was to save Ben's life. Salvation, however, was still far away—it was just a slight delay on the way to eternity, a gift given to Ben by Mother Nature.

Ben fell into the tree like a bomb into a tall building, destroying ceilings one after another, all the way to the basement. He squinted around, breaking branches and twigs that scratched his face. Problems need to be resolved in the order they arise, and at that moment, Ben's largest fear was that his eyes might get gashed. The new school year would start in a month, and the last thing Ben wanted was to show up in front of the new students without an eye. He fell lower and lower, until he reached the branches at the bottom that painfully hit his stomach, forcing him to flip over it like one would at the pull bar in gym. He managed to grasp onto the horizontal bough with both hands and hung there. But the branch was slightly thicker than the pull bar, and his speed was too high, so his right hand slipped and he was hanging above the deep precipice, holding on with only his left hand. By now it was time to shift the focus of his fear from losing an eye to falling into the abyss, which could have more serious consequences.

Fear and anxiety had caused his palm to sweat and lose its grip on the branch. Good thing it had rough bark on it, not like the smoothbore tree that Hubert had showed them during the excursion less than an hour ago.

What was the name of that smoothbore tree? Ben desperately tried to remember its name. *It was some kind of eucalyptus, satin or gummy. Yes, of course, satin eucalyptus. Gummy was the class of these trees, but the name was . . .*

For some reason it became unbearably important for him to remember that name, as if his salvation depended on it. Strangely, in the moment of extreme danger, his mind was grasping at something unimportant, refusing to focus on the essentials, protecting him from unnecessary stress. However, there was no time for secondary thoughts. The timer of his lifespan was counting its last seconds. He put together all his willpower and set aside unneeded thoughts and began focusing on the main problem.

Ben twitched convulsively, trying to reach the branch with his right hand, but that made matters even worse, and he was slipping more with every attempt.

Is that it? Is this really the end? Ben thought in horror. *Is this how I am going to die? But I don't want to die! I'm still a child. It's not fair! I still have so much to live for, a lot more I wanted to do with my life. What about school, my parents, Marcus, and little Liah? Our project still has to be completed—my friends need me.*

The unbearable sadness of his mediocre life made him regret all that time he had spent on computer games, movies, and even the time for sleep. But it also made him angry with himself and the stupid situation he'd gotten himself into because of his carelessness.

No, I'm not ready to die yet. I must do something, right now, immediately. I have to fight to the end!

The branch was slightly thicker than he could comfortably grasp onto, and Ben knew that he would not be able to keep a hold of it for much longer. He was running out of time.

"Let's not panic," Ben said to himself. "The time of tears and regrets is over. I should spend the last seconds of my life wisely."

Ben tried not to look down into the deep abyss, as he knew that the sight of the precipice would bring nothing but panic and fear and paralyze his ability to think clearly. But he felt the emptiness beneath him, sensed it with every cell of his skin, and even heard the silence of it. So, instead, he looked upwards. There were many thick, strong branches. If only he could reach out to one of them, just to get one branch above, and then get to the next one, and the next, all the way to the top of the tree, climb to the edge of the cliff from which he fell, and run to the port, to the ship, to his parents. He would take a quick shower, change out of his ripped clothes, and go to the restaurant for dinner.

Thinking of food reminded him that he hadn't eaten yet since morning, and that made him even angrier. It was awful enough to die at such a young age, but to die hungry was even worse. He looked around once again, trying to find anything that could help him get out of this situation. And he found it! It was his headphones. His great big, over-the-ear Beats headphones, the ones that allowed him to completely disconnect himself from the outside world, the headphones that he almost never took off! Now, at this difficult moment, they were here, sharing his suffering. They were stuck between two branches, at arm's length, and only the red flexible wire dangled in front of him, almost within reach, just a little to the side. Then his mind drew an elegant, relatively simple yet easy to execute plan. All he had to do was reach for the wire with his right hand, transfer the weight of his body onto the wire for a split second, and get a better grip with his left hand. Of course, the wire would not last for long, but all he needed was just one moment, that's all. With his left hand securely grasping the branch, his right arm could grab the left wrist, and help pull him up on the branch. Then he could get onto it, throwing one leg over, and easily reach the one above, then the next and the next.

So the number one priority was to reach that wire. He tried to grab it with his free hand and missed it by mere inches. It was necessary to swing both legs to the left and, on the return, move it to the right. This would give him enough momentum to get to the headphone wire. The time was up, and he had to execute his plans right now, as this was his only chance, there was no leeway for mistakes.

One: legs together, like a gymnast on the rings, sharp, bouncy swing to the left.

Two: the return movement of both legs to the right. The force of inertia moved his body, and his right hand grabbed the wire.

Three: his body weight transferred onto the wire, and the left hand relaxed for a moment, to get a better grip of the branch.

Four: at the count of four, a small, unexpected error occurred due to an unfortunate fact that Ben hadn't taken into consideration. His Beats headphones had played a trick on him: the wire was not soldered to the board, as Ben had thought, but was inserted into the connector. It popped out as soon as Ben transferred his weight to the wire. He was still looking with disbelief at the wire in his hand as his body was being swept down into the abyss. *I should have bought a Bose headphone with the fixed wire*, was his last thought before a horrifying shout of despair burst from his chest, scaring flocks of birds throughout the neighborhood.

Chapter 4. In The Harbor

The entire population of the village was buzzing like a disturbed beehive. Tourists who had just returned from an excursion, as well as the ones who were scheduled for the next tour, gathered in a circle, in the middle of which a furious Margaret was dragging Hubert by his uniform back to the bus, shouting so loud that her voice could have probably been heard on the ship, still anchored in the bay.

"We left my son in the jungle! Don't you understand? We have forgotten him back there, in the woods!" She took a deep breath and continued, "Alone, with wild animals, predators that will tear him apart! We must go back immediately!"

"But, madam, I have to take another group to the waterfalls. They've already paid for the tickets." Hubert was trying to detach himself from her in a polite way, but she was holding him so tight that he couldn't pull her off without hurting her. "You'd have to contact my dispatcher. Maybe he has free transportation and could make all necessary arrangements to pick up your son."

That was a lousy argument, as the dispatcher had already gone home to Madang, as he always did in the afternoon, after all excursion arrangements were made. Hubert knew that, but it was the only thing he could think of to say. Suddenly he saw a police officer, who had sought out the source of the commotion.

"Or perhaps you can ask the police? I am sure they can help you find another solution."

The police officer, the only representative of the local authorities in the port, was already trying desperately to come up with a reasonable solution. Unfortunately, nothing suitable was coming to his mind either. The situation was extraordinary and had not been addressed in any training or in written instructions and paragraphs.

However, Margaret did not want to contact the dispatcher, nor refer to any paragraphs in the police handbook, and kept pulling Hubert toward the bus.

When he realized that the local officials would not help, Hubert continued, "Besides, we have no predators in our jungles, except for . . . maybe snakes." As soon as he said it, Hubert immediately regretted it, because the word "snakes" made Margaret burst into tears and grab his shirt even harder, pulling him to the bus.

The situation was truly bizarre. All the other buses had left for an excursion to Madang, and would be back in the port right before the departure of the ship. There was no one else left to drive the boy's parents back to the jungle. But he also knew that he had to follow his work instructions, otherwise he would lose his job, and there were many people who would be glad to take his place.

Hubert felt sorry for this couple. On the other hand, it was not that big of a deal. The boy could walk back, or wait in the woods for another hour or two. Nothing would happen to him. Besides, there was still plenty of time before the ship's departure. Suddenly, one tourist who had purchased a ticket to the waterfalls tours spoke up.

"What if we go to the jungle instead? I don't mind seeing the nature in the woods. In fact, I couldn't decide between these two tours. So, if the others agree, we can change the route."

The crowd roared, expressing different opinions to the change in itinerary. Some agreed to go to the woods, others strongly opposed, while the rest were unsure yet. But within a few minutes, the majority of the tourists were convinced to visit the jungles instead of the waterfalls, especially after Rupert promised to reimburse everybody the cost of their tickets.

Inspired by their decision, Margaret desperately exclaimed, "Believe me, you will never regret it. Jungles are gorgeous and exciting. There's lovely nature, animals, and these birds . . . what was their name . . . oh, the birds-of-paradise. They are the cutest things you will ever see! We just came from there and enjoyed it so much."

Someone's reluctant voice at the back of the crowd said, "But I want to go to the waterfalls to take pictures."

Although it was mumbled, everyone heard him and turned their heads. A man with a bulky camera and a lot of photographic accessories hanging on his shoulders stood before the crowd and already regretted his words, yet he was persistent.

"You know, these waterfalls are unique. They are facing the west, and the mountains in front of them split apart almost to the horizon, opening the pathway for the rays of the setting sun refracted in little droplets of falling water. During the sunset the waterfalls are painted in many shades of red. It looks like the whole cascade is on fire. You cannot even imagine what a godsend it is for a photographer. I was so looking forward to this excursion."

"But did you see these colorful parrots and butterflies in the jungle?" Margaret began to lose her patience. "Believe me, they are much more gorgeous than the waterfalls."

"Birds are not my specialty. I'm a landscape photographer."

"Well, there are also plenty of landscapes; there are flowers, trees—"

"But I don't need that. I told you."

The situation, as always, saved Rupert, who had remained quiet until then.

"You know, we are making a stop tomorrow in the port of the Sepik River, with the waterfalls just like this one. But there are no jungles, because that area is swampy. Out here we are on higher grounds, with fresh air, dense forest, completely different vegetation, and gorgeous animals."

"Oh, really? Are you sure there will be waterfalls in tomorrow's stop?" the photographer started to give in.

"Well, of course," Rupert lied smoothly, "plenty of waterfalls. Once there is a river, then there are waterfalls, right?"

"Have you been there before? Have you seen it?"

"I have, many times."

"Are they also facing west, so one can see them in the rays of the setting sun?"

"They all face the west." Rupert shouted the last words back over his shoulder while heading to the bus with the other tourists and the disappointed photographer reluctantly followed him. Margaret was already inside, and the excursionists were taking their seats. Rupert jumped onto the bus, followed by the upset photographer. Hubert closed the door and drove back toward the jungles.

Margaret and Rupert stood in the aisle and looked out of the window openings on either side, hoping to see Ben, in case he had tried to walk back to the port. Hubert kept quiet during the entire trip and didn't make his usual jokes and remarks. He felt this would be inappropriate, given the circumstances. Everybody else kept silent too—all they wanted was to be done with this "excursion" as soon as possible. The most important thing right now was to find the boy and get back to the ship.

Soon they arrived at the place of their last stop. Margaret quickly squeezed out between the still-opening doors and jumped to the ground, followed closely by Rupert. The rest of the passengers also got off the bus and split in different directions to search for the boy.

"Be-e-e-n!" one shouted to the left.

"Benjamin!" echoed on the right.

But the jungle was silent, and there was no sign of Ben's presence. Only after a long, extensive search of that area did someone find evidence that Ben had been there.

"Come here! I found something." One tourist was holding an iPhone that he had noticed nearby. "I think it belongs to your son."

"Yes, it looks like his phone." Tears gushed from her eyes. "Where did you find it?"

"Over here, by these bushes. There is a steep cliff behind them," he continued. "I nearly fell down there myself, as it was hidden. But Ben might not have noticed it . . . and . . ."

Hubert took the iPhone and opened the photo app, scrolling through the last set of pictures, then showed them to Margaret.

"I think I know what happened. It seems that the boy saw an animal and wanted to take pictures of it. But the animal ran away from him and climbed on this tree where we are standing right now. You see this big branch on the picture? There is one just like that!" Hubert pointed at the bough on the tree. "Well, your son is very lucky. He saw one of the rarest animals of our region. Apparently, this is a tree-kangaroo, and I am telling you, not many people get to see this creature in real life. Unfortunately, this cutie is on the verge of extinction. The Latin name of this marsupial is *Dendrolagus*, which translates to —"

"To hell with the animal," Margaret growled. "I want to know where my son is, and not the Latin name of this monkey."

"But you are mistaken, madam, it is not a monkey!" exclaimed Hubert. "I told you, this is one of the rarest kangaroos. Apparently, it ran away from Ben and climbed on this tree. Please notice that the animal was partially blocked by the branch, while Ben was following him around to get a better shot. He must not have seen the edge of the cliff and . . ."

Everybody was standing quietly. What can one say at such a dramatic moment? Any words of comfort would sound false. Rupert tried to look down the cliff, but the thick bushes blocked his view.

"Somebody, please help me. Just hold my legs, so I can see if he is down there."

A few pairs of strong hands secured Rupert, holding him by the belt and legs, as he leaned over the precipice.

"I see a large tree growing down there, right in the middle of the cliff," commented Rupert. "But I can't see much past that; it is blocking my view."

They all called out Ben's name several times again.

"Is it possible he got stuck on that tree, or came down to the bottom of this cliff?" Margaret asked when rescuers pulled Rupert back.

"No, I don't think so. If he was there, he would have responded when two dozen voices called him. But in any case, we have to go down there. Hubert, how do we get there? Can you drive us? I will pay you for your time," Rupert said.

"You don't have to pay me. But we cannot go there by car since there is no road, just the impenetrable jungle. However, there is a narrow footpath we can walk through. Our residents use it sometimes when they go between villages or to the nearby tribes. This is my last tour for today, and I have nothing else planned after we come back to the port. I know this path a little bit, and if you want to go there, I could guide you. I don't think you can find the way yourself."

Hubert avoided looking into Margaret's eyes, afraid that she would read his gloomy thoughts. It was obvious that the boy had fallen off the cliff. Apparently, Rupert had come to the same conclusion when he looked into the abyss. He suddenly wilted, frowned, but said nothing to his wife, as he didn't want to sadden her until they confirmed his worst fears, of Ben's death, at the bottom of that abyss.

"Let's go," Margaret ordered, already marching back to the bus. All tourists went after her with a sense of relief that this "excursion" would be over soon.

"Wait, I just finished setting up my camera," the photographer shouted after them. He had set the tripod, chosen the perfect angle, aperture, and shutter speed, and was about to take pictures, and now, once again, he had to leave. This was unfair. But no one listened to his arguments as everyone was already getting onto the bus, and the unlucky photographer realized that if he delayed, they would leave without him. They didn't listen to him in the harbor, and they would not bother to listen here, in the woods. He hastily disassembled his tripod and ran to the already-moving bus.

Upon arrival at the port, Margaret insisted on going to the jungles immediately, but Hubert curbed her rush.

"Before we go, you better talk to your cruise agent, as there is a good chance that we may not come back in time to board the ship. Ask him to delay departure, if possible. Also, you need to take your luggage, in case the ship leaves without you."

It was a reasonable suggestion, and Margaret went with Rupert to talk to the on-shore cruise representative, who was supposed to deal with unusual situations like this. Their office was located in a two-story building, shared by all other port authorities. The cruise agent already knew of the situation and had contacted the customer service of the cruise company to report the incident, and by the time Margaret and Rupert walked into the office, the agent already had all the instructions.

"No, ma'am, we cannot delay departure. We have to maintain the schedule, and the ship will go right on time," he informed them as soon as they entered his office.

"What?! Are you going to leave us here?" Margaret exclaimed.

"Of course not! When you find your son, we will make all the arrangements for your transportation and book your flights home, for an additional fee, of course. But I suggest you also talk directly to the captain. Maybe he can offer you a better option."

They went to the ship and tried to persuade the captain to delay the departure for a few hours. If that was not possible and they had to stay on the island for a few extra days, their luggage and passports would have to be picked up from the ship anyway. Contrary to Margaret's doubts that the captain would refuse to talk to them, they were immediately brought to his stateroom. He thought it would be more humane to talk to the heartbroken parents in person than to give orders through his assistants. The captain already knew of the situation and sympathized with their problem, but he couldn't help them in any way. After hearing Margaret's request to delay the ship's departure until the next day, he just shook his head.

"No, no, and, again—no!" the captain responded adamantly. "You can't even imagine the consequences of such a delay. It will violate the navigational coordination with other ships. The ocean is not as big as it looks. There are strictly designated routes and schedules for the passage of shoals, and it has to be thoroughly coordinated. You have no idea what you're asking me. The port will charge us a huge penalty, and we are talking about hundreds of thousands of dollars. Also, what about the other passengers? We have over a thousand people on board. They all have plans, scheduled excursions, and tours at the next stop. We have agreements with several excursion agencies in the coming ports. No, it's impossible. Perhaps I can allow a short delay, for . . . let's say, two hours. I can make up that much on the way, but no more than that. But don't worry, soon we will arrive at the destination port and get new tourists on board, who will travel the same route as you did, only in the reverse direction. So, in three days, we will be in this port again. I will pick you up and provide our reserve stateroom for free, so you can go back to Australia, to the port where your cruise started. From there, you will make your own travel arrangements to get back home. Will this work for you?"

"Yes, thank you, Captain."

"Great! We were scheduled to depart at six o'clock tonight, local time. I will wait for you another two hours, until eight. Now, it is only three o'clock in the afternoon, so that will give you five hours to search for your son, and I hope you find him and return to the ship on time. But at eight o'clock, unfortunately, I will have to leave, regardless."

"Then we should get moving."

"Just one more thing." The captain paused. "Let's be realistic. As you already noticed, the jungles here are absolutely wild and impassable, and it is hard to find someone there. Besides, it will get dark soon, and that could also prolong your search, or even make it impossible, so you would have to wait until morning. Then you would need help from the police, as it will be difficult for you to continue the search in the jungle without help. I respect this country a lot and have full confidence in the local authorities. I am sure they will do everything possible to rescue the boy, and we will certainly inform them about the incident. But, I am afraid . . ." The captain stopped for a second, trying to choose a polite way to express his thoughts. "It will take a long time to overcome various bureaucratic delays. So, if you don't come back by the time of departure, I will also contact the Australian authorities and inquire about the rescue team. They may even bring military helicopters to search from the air. But it may also take a day or two for them to get here. So, finding your son today would be best, of course."

Margaret and Rupert returned to the shore after the captain once again expressed his sympathy. They brought their luggage from the ship, knowing intuitively that today's expedition to the jungle would not be successful.

"This is a jungle, not Broadway," Hubert tried to warn them. "It is going to be a long and difficult walk. Jungles are unforgiving to negligence, and we need to be well prepared for this expedition. Otherwise, instead of helping your son, we will have to seek help ourselves. We are talking about several hours of walking each way, through the dense chaos of the woods. It's nothing like a walk in the park."

Hubert looked skeptically at Margaret's shoes.

"Madam, you will not get very far like that. You should find a more comfortable pair for this trip."

70

Margaret was already close to being hysterical, and every second of delay was excruciating for her.

"But I don't have any suitable shoes, as I didn't plan to walk in the jungle."

Fortunately, the situation was saved by a tender-hearted woman, a German tourist from the ship who was standing nearby in the crowd of sympathizers. She offered to exchange her old, weary, but comfortable sneakers for Margaret's shoes. They both had the same size, and Margaret, without hesitation, gratefully handed the German lady her brand-new, expensive, summer collection designer shoes, which she had bought just before the trip.

"Can we go now, please?" Margaret exclaimed, barely holding back tears.

"Not yet, dear," said Rupert. "Let's stock water first; who knows how long we will be going through the jungle."

"And we also need flashlights," Hubert reminded them. "It will be dark soon, and we wouldn't be able to walk in the woods in complete darkness."

They collected a few bottles of water from the group of tourists who had gathered around them. Someone gave to them fruits and biscuits. Margaret gratefully accepted everything and put it in her bag. Four villagers offered to escort them to the woods, deeply sympathizing with their problem. Actually, all the people felt sorry for them: the villagers, tourists from the ship, officials, and many residents offered their help, but Hubert explained that large numbers of people would slow them down. He didn't want to take these four, either, but he thought that a few pairs of hands may come in handy in the jungle. Hubert knew the place well. The riverbank at the bottom of the cliff was strewn with large and small boulders. If the boy had fallen off the cliff, the chance of survival was slim. Most likely, he would have landed on one of the rocks, and they would need someone to carry the boy, or his remains, back to the village. They couldn't just leave his body lying on the rock. It would be inhumane, and not something a good, religious person would do. But even if the boy had somehow miraculously survived the fall, he would probably be badly injured, or at least have a few broken bones, so they would still need extra hands to help carry him out of the woods.

Also, Hubert had some serious doubts about this lady. Obviously she was a city woman and did not understand the difficulties of walking for many hours through the jungle. She would not be able to make it even half the distance required, and would also need help. Anyway, a few pairs of strong hands were always helpful in the woods. Out of all who wished to take part in the expedition, Hubert selected those who had powerful flashlights, solving the light problem at the same time.

Finally, all preparations were completed. Rupert left their luggage on the bus, and the small group, led by Hubert, disappeared into the jungle.

Chapter 5. Alive

Of all the human senses, the first that came back to Ben was his hearing. Lying on the muddy bank of an unknown river, Ben heard the sound of birds chirping mixed with that of the gurgling waters of the river and the growl of wild animals. The sounds were coming from everywhere. It surrounded him and penetrated deep into his brain, like an alarm clock that interrupts the sweet early morning sleep.

He lay there listening. At first he thought he had fallen asleep on the couch at home while watching an episode of *National Geographic* on his DOLBY surround-sound home theater. He wanted to shout to his mom to turn the volume down, and even tried to pull up the fallen blanket because he was cold. But he couldn't move at all!

And then he finally woke up. His consciousness was coming back to him, slowly, reluctantly pulling him back into reality. He waited another minute, but it was time to get up and face reality, which currently looked very complicated. Ben opened his eyes and immediately realized two important things. The first and probably the most important one: he was still alive! The second: he had no idea what had happened, where he was, and how he ended up here. His consciousness still didn't want to come out of the darkness, and refused to line up his thoughts in a chronological order to restore the chain of events. But slowly, his memory came back bit by bit, like elements of a picture on a blank sheet of photographic paper. First, vague outlines of the silhouette appear, then the most contrasting elements and small details show up, and soon the whole image is printed, down to the smallest detail.

His memory kindly drew him the entire picture, each step that had led to his transformation from being a careless tourist chasing this insidious animal whose name he still didn't know, to the condition of this helpless body lying on the bank of the river. He clearly remembered falling off the precipice, flying from the cliff like a hawk diving on its prey.

You didn't look like a hawk. Ben interrupted his own thoughts. *Hawks, when swooping on prey, stretch their whole body in a straight line, wings tight to their sides, claws together, beak slightly open, eyes keenly following the target. You were not a hawk for sure, but rather a stupid newborn chick that fell out of the parental nest. You were falling like a rock dropped from a cliff, waving your hands, screaming like a pig. Aesthetically, you were falling very badly,* the second Ben concluded.

Such a phenomenon or anomaly is well known in child psychiatry and is called Imaginary Friend Syndrome. Ben didn't know much, or rather, anything at all about child psychiatry, however, and didn't think his imaginary friend was an "anomaly." He was just another self somewhere deep inside of his mind. Second Ben was his best friend, and at the same time, his worst enemy. With him, Ben argued and fought, shared his thoughts, happy moments, sadness, and tragic moments, like the one right now. Depending on his mood, inner Second Ben was optimistic or pessimistic. But right now he was obviously in a sarcastic mood! Ben had neither the strength nor desire to argue with his inner self and left his sarcastic comment unanswered. Instead, he decided to focus on his physical condition. First of all, he was cold, and his whole body was shivering. Yet his arms and legs were numb.

I think my spine is broken! This horrific thought came to Ben's mind. *That's why I can't feel my body.* Ben had gotten his in-depth knowledge of medicine from an action movie he had watched recently. In that movie, a wounded soldier who was lying on the ground bleeding, holding his slippery, bloody guts coming out of his belly, begged his fellow soldiers, between the moans that is, to just shoot him.

"Shoot me, please, shoot me," he had begged. "I'm going to die soon anyway. My spine is broken, and I can't feel my body. Please tell my mom that I fought and died heroically . . ."

But his fellow fighters had looked away, not able to help, assuring him that everything would be all right.

It was possible that the symptoms during such an injury were completely different from his own, but there was no other knowledge available to him at the moment, and Ben decided to leave it at that for now, at least until he got more information. Instead, he wanted to assess damages and conduct an inventory of his body: arms, legs, head, and other smaller but nevertheless important body parts. The check on his hands failed immediately, as the right hand was gone. Completely gone! He saw a bloody mess near his shoulder where the arm used to be. It was completely torn off, leaving a nasty, bloody wound, mixed with mud and fragments of his shirt sleeve. He even saw small shards of bones of the forearm. The bleeding seemed to have stopped, as a dry crust covered the wound. Ben didn't feel the pain, but that was understandable—shock. During serious injuries, the human brain disables some nerves, to prevent the person from suffering strong, sharp pain, and the body goes into shock. Or maybe it wasn't shock, but rather the consequence of the spine fracture that prevented any sensation he may have felt. The experience of severe cold also fit well into the overall picture, like a small piece fitting into a jigsaw puzzle: he had probably lost a lot of blood when his arm got torn off. It was unclear why or how he was still alive. With this kind of wound, all the blood should have run from his body, like wine from a shattered bottle.

The loss of a hand, especially the right one, seriously disappointed Ben. His previous concern about losing an eye now seemed silly, and not a big tragedy compared to this bigger loss. Consequences of losing an entire arm were much more serious. He already foresaw the laughter of his peers when he would clumsily navigate his wheelchair in the schoolyard with only his left hand and a broken back.

My parents will have to buy me an automatic wheelchair, with a joystick control, so I can navigate with one hand. Thank God I still have at least that much.

Ben tried to move the fingers on his left hand, and he was soon freely moving his whole arm. It was progress, the first good news since his fall.

I'm still going to search for my right arm when my parents come to get me. It could be somewhere nearby, and it may be possible to somehow sew it back, he told himself. *Although, some animals probably already ate it by now, thanking their animal god for such an unexpected gift!* His heart sank at this.

It was time to evaluate the status of his legs. He tried to move one leg, but immediately had to postpone the inventory check: a sharp pain pierced through his body, one that hurtled him back into unconsciousness.

The rescue expedition penetrated deeper into the jungle, moving at a resilient pace. Oddly enough, the weakest link in the group turned out to be Hubert. At first, he walked briskly through the woods leading the small rescue team. On the way, he tried to draw their attention to unique plants and small animals, a habit from his tour guide role. He even showed them a decent-sized brown snake that flashed in the bushes nearby, and he told the group that this snake was one of the top five most dangerous snakes in the world. But the information about the local flora and fauna only irritated everyone. Of course, he realized the absurdity of his speeches, but he was hoping to divert them from further gloomy thoughts. He also tried not to think about what they were going to see very soon. In his imagination, he already saw the boy sprawled on the riverbank like a rag doll. The best-case scenario would be broken arms, legs, and spine. But if he had fallen on the boulders along the river, then they would have to scrape his remnants off the rocks and collect them separately.

We should have brought a few large plastic bags for his remains. The idea came to his mind as an afterthought, but he immediately dismissed it. *No, I am not going to do that. I am a tour guide, not a coroner. In the worst case, we will return to the port and call Madang for emergency relief teams to collect the cadaver.*

His pace slowed down involuntarily, holding back the advancement of the whole group, as if he was trying to prolong their arrival before facing the horrible reality. However, there was also another reason for his slowness, his sedentary lifestyle, and years spent behind the wheel of his tour bus. The once strong and athletic Hubert had gone out of shape. His slim, strong body had gained extra weight, and now every step in the woods was more and more difficult for him due to his decreased stamina.

Margaret on the other hand was in good shape, thanks to her daily exercise at the gym, and now she almost ran through the jungle along the treacherous path, driven by fear for her son. She easily passed the breathless Hubert, along with everybody else, and was now leading the rescue team, occasionally ridding her face of sticky webs with hurried brushes of her hand. Without any effort she jumped over fallen tree trunks, waded through the thick bushes and vines, and went step by step overcoming natural forest obstacles with the persistence of a programmed robot. Rupert also kept pace with her. Sometimes he even walked ahead and parted the branches of the intertwined plants and bushes for her, making a safe passageway. The rest of the rescuers also quickened their pace. Hubert, one of the last in the group, was sweating, indulging in his sad thoughts, and slowed down more with every passing yard. Occasionally he shouted to Margaret, correcting her direction.

The helpers who had volunteered to accompany them to the jungle were in the middle of the group. At the beginning they walked together, animatedly talking in their obscure dialect, but then, once the group stepped into the almost impassable thicket, they had to disband and walk single file along the narrow, barely noticeable path.

This trip hadn't turned out well for them. This was not what they were hoping for. They expected a leisurely stroll through the woods, with short but frequent stops to give the foreign guests a little breather. They wanted to impress them with their knowledge of the jungles and the ability to navigate through the tangled woodland. They wanted to tell interesting stories from their life, sitting around the bonfire, something like: "A fascinating thing happened recently . . ." and were also interested in having the chance to listen to the stories of foreign life from the dear guests. They wanted to make a good impression on them, and occasionally even make some money by offering a little help. But instead they walked, or almost ran, non-stop, through the woods for nearly two hours in complete silence. No, this was not what they expected when they had so eagerly offered their help, and already regretted it, but now had no choice but to endure the journey. After a few hours, one of them offered to make a short stop, but Margaret ignored him and continued walking. Now she had no need for anyone: neither guide nor helpers.

Soon the forest became noticeably lighter as the trees thinned out and after a while they were completely replaced by bushes. The air became relatively cool and filled with freshness, as the rescue team came out to the river. Hubert perked up, like a hunting dog.

"Stop! We are here!" he told the group.

Margaret stopped, trying to catch her breath.

Hubert pointed upward. High above them, in the middle of the cliff, a large tree grew right from the granite massif.

"Yes, this is the place," Rupert confirmed. "That is the tree I saw from the top."

Volunteers scattered along the riverbank in search of the boy. But there were not that many places to look. The whole terrain was open in all directions, with only occasional shrubs, leaving a short strip of land near the river covered with pebbles and large boulders. Apparently, these rocks had split off from the granite massif and fallen into the deep river. The water completed the job by smoothing them out and polishing their surface. Over time, the river had become filled with exposed rocks, and now they were all strewn along the bank.

Margaret came to the foot of the hill, looked up, and then drew an invisible straight line denoting the trajectory of the possible fall. The calculated point of Ben's contact with the ground was empty.

"He is not here!" Margaret exclaimed in despair, immediately bursting into tears.

He's not here! Hubert thought, with great relief.

Ben's second awakening differed completely from the first. Something was mercilessly shaking his shoulder. Through half-shut eyes, he saw a horrible, duel-horned beast with an ugly face and moving lips. A halo of light was shining around its head.

Strange, thought Ben, *usually only angels have halos, but this thing looks like Satan himself. I don't get it, am I dead and in heaven now? Or am I in hell?*

Immediately, his internal friend-enemy woke.

Who would let you into heaven? Second Ben mocked with his usual sarcasm. *Did you forget how you and Marcus gave that poor little boy a whirly?*

This incident had taken place at the beginning of the school year. Traditionally, the older students perform a rite of "initiation" for the freshmen of the middle school by dunking them in the toilet bowl. Ben and Marcus had waited for their victim, pulled him to the restroom, picked the boy up by his arms and legs, and dipped his head in the bowl—with clean water, of course. They were not monsters to dip him into excrements!

Was he not allowed into heaven because of this one small episode?

"What nonsense is getting in your head?" he protested against his own thoughts.

Ben finally came to his senses and fully opened his eyes. The monster didn't disappear, and suddenly, a thin voice spoke to him.

"Mister, get up. Mister, please, get up."

Ben always thought that the devil, or whoever lived in the underground world, would have a low, hoarse voice due to the constant heat and humid air around the boiling pot, but this devil had a thin, clear voice! Maybe it was an angel? He raised his head, and the glowing halo suddenly disappeared.

That's just the sun, Ben realized. *The setting sun illuminates its hair, creating the illusion of a shining halo around the head.*

One mystery was successfully solved. This was not an angel. The next moment both the horns disappeared. Actually they didn't disappear, but turned out to be regular feathers inserted into intricately coiffed hair on its head. The feathers were big and colorful, and in the light of the setting sun, appeared like horns.

"Who are you?" Ben asked, finally coming to his senses.

"I Emma. I hear you fall, so I ran," replied the monster in the same high-pitched voice, mispronouncing certain words with a heavy accent.

This is a girl, Ben thought. It was just a little girl, small, no more than ten or eleven years old, and not scary at all, just covered in face paint.

"I hear you fall," she repeated. "I no see, only hear, high fall, I not have time to save you in river. What's your name, mister?"

"Don't call me 'Mister,' please. I am Ben. Benjamin. How did I get up here?"

"River bring you to land. I look long time, no see first. I think you drowned."

"Wait, slow down, please. I can't keep up with you. Let's start from the beginning."

"You sit first. Lying not good, need to go. Dark very-very soon."

"I cannot sit; don't you see? I'm paralyzed and badly injured, as my spine is broken and my right hand is torn off. Also, both my legs are probably broken."

Girl Emma leaned over Ben and examined his wounds. Then, suddenly, she turned him to the side, freeing his hand from under his back. Immediately, millions of tiny needles pierced through his arm as the blood rushed into the veins and arteries. He gasped when he realized he had been lying on it all this time, causing the numbness, and because of his position, all he had been able to see was a bloody forearm. The blood had come from a deep cut on his shoulder, creating the impression of a bloody mess from a torn-off hand, and small pieces of river shells looking like shards of shattered bones from the forearm completed the illusion.

The theory of a fractured spine also crumbled to dust now. He felt every cell in his body. Yay! He had both arms and could move! Ben was not disabled! He also found an explanation for the cold and shivering. It was due to the long period of lying motionless near the water in soaked clothes after falling into the mountain river.

Besides, the air was chilling; the slanting rays of the setting sun did not provide much heat.

Emma soaked a piece of cloth in the river and carefully cleaned the wound on his shoulder. The cut was deep, with ragged edges, and it began to bleed again as soon as she removed the hard crust of dirt and gore. But it was so minor that Ben didn't even notice it. He was so overjoyed that both hands were in place and his spine was not broken that he wasn't even ashamed if he made a fool of himself in front of a little girl.

Meanwhile, Emma lifted his left pant leg and gently touched the knee. It was swollen so much that the kneecap was not visible. The right leg was better, but it was hurt at the ankle.

Emma shook her head doubtfully.

"Walk you cannot," she concluded after a quick examination. "Hurt right foot, left knee very bad swollen. I carry you cannot. You very far walk cannot."

But Ben was not as skeptical of his condition—in fact, he was relieved. He was alive! He had survived the fall from the high cliff and yet was still in one piece! The probability of survival from a fall of that height was even lower than winning the lottery. He was a very lucky person! All these small wounds and scratches would heal eventually; it was only matter of time. He was ready to dance with happiness, but as soon as he moved his leg (not to dance, of course), a sharp pain shot through his body again. This time he didn't lose consciousness, but involuntarily groaned, and his forehead immediately broke out in cold sweat.

How am I going to get back to the port? he thought wistfully.

But Emma, as if she could read his thoughts, said, "Return to the port you cannot. It is too far away. We go to our village."

"Where is your village?" asked Ben.

"It is close. We go there and they help your legs."

"I am not going anywhere! My parents must be looking for me already, and they will be here soon . . . probably."

"No," Emma said confidently. "From the port, here too far. No reach before dark. They look for you tomorrow. Morning we come back to port if you walk. Also, we have sheriff nearby. He has phone, and you call port or ship."

"Okay, you convinced me. But how am I going to make it to your village? I can't even stand on my feet."

"Yes, hard, I know." Emma nodded. "But I think everything. We swim river, then climb up hill, then it is very close in the jungle. I help you walk."

Ben looked skeptically at the girl. She seemed fragile, petite, almost a child. How could she possibly help him? But he said nothing, as there was no one else to offer help.

"Dark soon, hard to walk in dark. We must rush. Wait, I back quickly."

She got up and ran along the riverbank, picking up some wood on the way, and in a few minutes returned with an armful of thin and thick branches and twigs. There was a lot of driftwood of all sizes, and even tree trunks uprooted by the violent weather lay scattered along the riverbank. Emma grabbed a few twigs, broke a few sticks from a nearby bush, and then laid out the thick branches she had picked in the shape of a rectangle, making a frame. Then she deftly wove the thin branches overlapping them with each other and intertwining the frame. Using fresh twigs from the bushes as rope, she laced the whole structure and fixed the ends.

"Wow, good job," Ben said, looking at the light yet durable raft.

"I could done better, but we must hurry."

"But how do we both fit on this raft? It is not big enough for both of us."

"No, it is only for you. You go, I swim near. I good swim, don't worry."

"Do you think I would get on that raft and let you swim in the river?" Ben was outraged. "We either go on the raft together, or I am not going."

"Just wait little longer and we both no go! At night, river dangerous! You can crawl to water?"

"Yes, I can crawl," he muttered, "but I don't like this idea."

"You shouldn't fall off the cliff," Emma said acrimoniously, "then you would like it all. No argue. Crawl!"

He had no choice but to obey her order and crawled toward the river, doing his best to ignore the sharp bursts of pain caused by the movement. When he reached the water, Emma was already there waiting for him with the raft, holding it so it wouldn't get washed away. Ben crawled onto the raft. The water near the bank was shallow, and his weight pressed the raft down to the bottom. Ben tried to pull himself farther to the water with the stronger currents, clutching and pushing using the slippery pitfalls and snags, but he couldn't move the raft. His fingers slipped from the moss-covered boulders, breaking off his nails. Without his legs, Ben was as weak as a toddler. Emma also pushed the raft to deeper water. Never before had he felt so weak and helpless, and tears streamed down his cheeks mixing with the river water. It was a good thing he was lying face down and Emma could not see his tears.

Ben wanted to rewind his life to just a few hours back, to make this nightmare disappear. He would safely get on board the cruise ship onto a lounge chair on the deck, with loud music and scurrying waiters bringing him soft drinks and snacks at his first demand,

and, most importantly, he would be with his mom and dad. He even thought he could hear his mother's voice calling him, but the next moment, the river picked up the light raft and carried it downstream, toward other unfortunate events.

Hubert came to Margaret.

"Look, madam, it is too early to give up hope. I think I've found something!"

"What did you find? Tell me." Margaret instantly stopped crying. Hope reappeared in her eyes.

"You see, I was born and raised in this area. I lived in a tribe not far from here long before I became a bus driver. As a child, I would often go with the other tribesmen to hunt, and learned many useful skills from them, and also—"

"Make it shorter!" Margaret interrupted him impatiently. "Get to the point."

"Yes, of course," Hubert agreed quickly. "So, let's look at the whole situation. Presumably, your son came out of the bus to chase the tree-kangaroo, if I have correctly identified that animal, and fell off the cliff. As we know, there was a tree in the way of his fall, but it didn't stop him. Otherwise, he would have responded when we called him from above."

"I said shorter!" Margaret demanded. All the other members of this expedition also came to Hubert and listened with interest.

"Okay, but first, let's look at that tree that your son clung onto. Even though it didn't stop the fall, it significantly slowed him down, and changed the trajectory of his fall more to the left."

"Why to the left?" asked pedantic Rupert.

"Look at the direction of the branches." Hubert pointed at the tree. "It grows tilted because of the wind that blows through the canyon in the same direction for centuries. So the trunk and all the branches are slightly tilted to the right. Your son hit the bough, and that deviated his fall to the left. Now look at the trajectory from the bottom branch down. There is a wide ledge sticking out from the rocky massif. When Ben passed that tree, he should have hit that ledge and then gone down. Now, do you see these bushes below? If you remember, it's the same one I showed you earlier today during our excursion. They have very strong, rigid branches; this is how they adapt to the climate and rocky soil. In fact, their name in Latin is—"

Margaret opened her mouth to say something rude and offensive, but Hubert looked at her angry face and quickly returned to the topic.

"Well, it doesn't matter right now," he added quickly. "Sorry, I got carried away again. This is a result of my profession. So, as I was saying, your son fell on these bushes and continued his way down. And now, in the path of his fall, was that small tree. Can you see it? The tree is young, yet strong, and it didn't break under the weight of Ben's body. But once again, it significantly slowed him down. Do you see how some branches are broken off, and the top is kind of flattened?"

The farsighted Rupert looked up, squinting.

"Yes, I think you're right," he said. "I agree, that's exactly what may have happened."

"So, now trace the path a little lower on the left at these thick bushes underneath," Hubert continued. "The speed of his fall was already low, but obviously, they took the weight of his body, and threw him farther down from a height of about three or four meters. From that height, he would have landed over there right on another bush that could have sprung him straight into the river. These bushes are from the same family as those that grow out of the rock: rigid and thick. They saved your boy, acting like a safety net. This is just my theory, and now, let's go closer and see if I am right."

They approached the bush growing under the imaginary line of fall. The bush was strong, but there were many broken branches and torn leaves.

"See? I was right. Look at the ground around it. There are no footsteps, other than those that we made. The riverbank here is narrow, and I guarantee you the bushes threw him right into the water. He could have hit the land near the shore, but that's not a big deal, only a few bruises. The soil in this place is soft, without rocks or other hard objects, and the river is deep, right at the bank, which means that your son is most likely alive. He could be a little hurt when he got caught on the ledge up there. I can even assume minor injuries, but, in general, you have nothing to worry about. He's alive!"

"If that's the case, then where is he now?"

"I think I know where to find him. The river here is rough, with strong currents. But a few kilometers downstream, it makes a bend. The stream crashes onto the rocks and slows down, making a sharp turn, forming shallow, quiet backwater, which is sort of like an oxbow lake. Do you know what it is? Well, it doesn't matter. I hope he came out of the river over there. It would be difficult for him to do so in any other place, as there are steep banks on both sides."

"Where is this place?" Margaret asked impatiently, as hope still shining in her eyes.

"It is about a mile away from here, if we cut straight through the jungle, or it could be a little longer if we follow the bank."

"So what are we waiting for?" Margaret ran down the bank, easily jumping over boulders and tree trunks scattered along the way, and the others followed her. The soil was quite dense with many small pebbles, which made it easy to run on it as their feet didn't sink down into the muddy soil. Very soon the river made a sharp turn, going in almost the opposite direction, forming a meander, a horseshoe-like bend. A powerful current pounding on the rocks split the stream into two distributary channels: one followed further downstream, repeating the bend, and the second, the slower one, went to the right, creating a quiet backwater.

The rescue team reached the bend about half an hour later. For part of the way they had to go through the jungle, as the bank was blocked with huge boulders and was inaccessible. By the time they arrived, it was almost dark. The sun had already set beyond the horizon, and the day was rapidly coming to an end. Margaret reached the place first, followed by Rupert, and then the rest of the team. Hubert examined the terrain, looking at the muddy soil near the water, and immediately noticed traces of bare feet.

"You see, I was right; Ben was here!" exclaimed Hubert, while catching his breath and wiping sweat from his forehead. "He managed to get out of the stream on his own. Ben is alive, and he can even walk. Your son is lucky, madam, as he survived such a high drop! The fall from that height could have been much more tragic for him."

Hubert widened the search area, and soon, he found other evidence. He called Margaret and Rupert and showed them his findings.

"Do you see these broken twigs on the bushes? Someone broke them off with their bare hands. Over here, someone, I am sure that was your son, dragged driftwood along the shore. All these fresh footprints in the wet soil show it was him. Obviously they are not adult size, more like a child's footprints. And yet another step, and another . . . Looks like he collected driftwood to make a raft. Over here, he put the raft into the water and swam farther."

"Why would he do that?"

"Well, here is what I think: Ben fell into the river, far away from the port. He doesn't know where he is or how to get back. He probably wanted to continue going by the river, knowing that all rivers ended up in the sea. Once at the sea, he could easily find the ship."

"So where is he now?" Margaret asked.

"I do not know, madam, but I hope he is somewhere close." Hubert looked concerned. "There are not that many other places where he could easily get out of the water. Most of the river is not accessible from land, and the current is strong. Besides . . ."

"What? Besides, what? Tell me."

"A few kilometers farther down, the river breaks into a fairly high waterfall, and if he does not come out of the water before that, I'm afraid from there he would not be able to get out. Ever."

The last hope to find her son swiftly faded away, and Margaret fell to the ground, exhausted and hopeless. Within a few minutes, pitch-black darkness blanketed the rescue expedition.

Chapter 6. Downstream

The fragile, crudely made raft floated swiftly down the stream. The river current picked it up so suddenly that Ben did not notice if Emma had followed him into the water. But a few seconds later, he saw her swimming nearby, fighting the extreme current and holding the raft with one hand.

The raft flowed at a dangerous speed, avoiding huge boulders polished by centuries of erosion. They were sticking out of the water, obstructing the path and creating frequent rapids along the way. In many places, the stream flowed over them, making the rocks invisible as the rays of the setting sun reflected off the wet surface. Once, they almost bumped into one, but at the last moment, Emma managed to steer the raft to the side.

They quickly maneuvered downstream, penetrating deeper into the heart of the jungle in the twilight gloom. The sun had already set below the horizon, and only the dim glow of the evening sky was left, giving them some visibility. For Ben it was a mystery how the girl could steer between the boulders in almost complete darkness.

"We go a little more!" Emma shouted, dodging the rocks, raising her voice to be heard above the water. "Dark soon, and we no see the rocks. Big waterfall coming. I know place to go out of river. If we miss it, then we fall right into it."

Many people actually pay a lot of money to visit these waterfalls, but you get the chance to see it for free, Second Ben commented, but his joke came out dark and sarcastic, so Ben let it be; it was not the right time for jokes.

The darkness had swallowed them abruptly as if someone had turned a light switch off. He soon found a logical explanation for this strange phenomenon. They were passing through an area of the jungle where the trees came close to the water from both sides, and the dense canopy was hanging low over the river. The trees interlocked on top, forming a kind of tunnel that completely blocked the sky. Even during the day, the sun rays did not pierce through the canopy, creating a constant gloomy atmosphere.

Emma directed the raft to the shore, and after a brutal fight with the strong current, they reached the steep bank. Ben tried to help her as much as he could, knowing how difficult it was to navigate across the stream, but he suspected that his help was insignificant, even a hindrance, so he finally let Emma do all the work, assuming that she knew what she was doing.

Emma grabbed a snag, one of the tree roots sticking out of water, and pulled the raft closer to the shore.

"Crawl forward and hold that stick," she called to Ben.

He pulled himself up, leaving the raft under him and grabbed it with both hands, moving even farther out of the water. Half the work was done. Emma let go of the raft, and it was immediately pulled by the stream and taken down the river. The riverbank had a rather steep slope, which rose almost vertically. It would be too difficult, if not impossible, to climb it, but they were lucky. During the rainy season, the water level rose significantly and eroded the soil from the bank, exposing the tightly interwoven roots of the trees along the bank. They tangled almost to the top of the slope, forming a ladder.

Ben clung to these roots and pulled himself higher and higher, dragging his useless legs along, only occasionally giving himself a short break by resting his left leg on one of the "ladder steps." If he did not bend his knee, the pain was tolerable. Emma was helping him as much as she could. She climbed ahead, grasping the roots with one hand, and stretching out her other hand to Ben, pulling him higher. At first, Ben tried to climb without her help, but soon, he realized it would be impossible to do so. His hands got tired quickly and he could not pull himself up anymore.

But the higher they went, the fewer roots were sticking out from the soil, and now Ben could not reach the next snag. Then Emma did something that would have made a professional gymnast jealous. She turned upside down, locking her feet in the roots, and firmly fixed herself in this position. Then she reached out to Ben with both hands and pulled him up until he found the next snag to hold on to.

Wow, I could never do that, Ben thought enviously, looking at the little girl hanging upside down. To his surprise, Emma was quite strong for her age, and her apparent fragility was deceptive. Ben tried his best to grasp at stones, plunging his fingers deep into the dirt to get the slightest support just to help her a little. But the soil was loose, and his fingers only snatched away clods of clay.

Soon he felt the slope flattening out, making it easier to climb up, and gradually Ben reached a flat area.

"I can do it myself now." His voice croaked as he moved forward, resting his elbows on the ground for additional support.

They climbed to the top, panting from exhaustion, and collapsed. Somehow he managed to sit up against the tree trunk. His knee was burning with pain, despite the long stay in the cold water and the wet clothes. He was getting used to the pain and only cringed when he bent his leg. The situation would be funny if it wasn't sad. He couldn't bend his left knee, but he could stand on that leg, unlike his right foot, which gave him a sharp shooting pain as soon as he leaned on it, though it could bend well at the knee.

They sat under a tree, letting their exhausted bodies rest. The canopy of the foliage thinned out letting moonlight pass through. Over time, Ben's eyes adjusted to the dim light and he could see silhouettes of the objects in the woods. It was possible to move forward now. But they had no energy left to walk and decided to rest for a while.

Emma was mindlessly staring in front of her. Ben had recovered much faster because the main load had been put on Emma during their climb from the river. He furtively looked at the girl. All the exotic paint on her face had been washed off, and she turned out to be an ordinary girl, not beautiful, but definitely cute, petite, very fragile at first glance, but actually quite strong. Her beautifully arranged hair with the colored feathers of exotic birds framing her head was now wet and muddy, with only small tufts of feathers remaining. It looked as if she had spent the night in the henhouse or in a cage with a few dozen fighting parrots. The two beautiful feathers that Ben had mistaken for the devil's horns had disappeared.

"Thank you for the help, by the way," Ben said, breaking the silence, suddenly remembering he hadn't thanked her yet.

She didn't say anything, merely nodded.

"But how did you find me?" Ben continued.

"I was go home and I heard you fall, so I look for you."

"I thought you were from that village near the port."

"No, I live in tribe. I come port yesterday, bring my grandma souvenirs to sell. I make it and Grandma sells it. Sometimes I help sell it as well. It takes long to get our tribe from port. Today, I was on my way home when I heard your scream when you fell, and go look for you."

Ben listened to her, thinking about his good fortune. He had been one step away from sure death. It was pure luck he had survived.

"But you fall very well, too high," Emma continued.

"What?" Ben was preoccupied with his own thoughts, and at first didn't understand what she said. But then he got the meaning of her words and suddenly started to laugh. He laughed so hard that there were tears in his eyes, and pain in his stomach. This laughter was a release from the stress of the last few hours. He laughed and cried, unable to stop, only wincing from the pain when he accidentally bent the knee of his injured leg.

"You laugh how I speak?" Emma was offended and pursed her lips. "But I don't know how say right. If I say wrong, don't laugh at me, just tell me, and I will say it right next time."

Emma's words made Ben stop laughing abruptly. The last thing he wanted right now was to offend the girl who had just saved his life. Her grammar and pronunciation had just triggered his laughter, like how a little spark starts a fire in the forest. Living in New York, among many immigrants from around the world, he had become accustomed to different accents and pronunciations. Some people had lived in the country for decades, and yet had not been able to learn English, except for a few of the most common phrases. Even then, Ben never laughed at them, knowing how difficult it is to learn and speak a foreign language fluently. But this girl, still in her own country, was trying to talk to him in his language. Why would he laugh at her? Of course it was the result of the stress, and her words just triggered laughter that released the pent-up anxiety. But he was still embarrassed at his lack of manners.

"Please forgive me, Emma. I didn't mean to laugh at you," Ben said. "It's just that my nerves are on edge. I didn't want to offend you. I'm sorry. By the way, your English is quite good, and you speak much better than some of my friends do."

"And you no laugh at me again?" Emma did not seem offended anymore.

"I'm telling you, I wasn't laughing at you. I had a rough day today, and I feel anxious, and that made me act stupidly."

"Okay, but please correct me if I say wrong. I want speak better English."

On that note, the language subject was closed. He stopped noticing her accent and grammatical errors, only occasionally correcting her, as she asked. Emma was a very sharp and quick learner, and she had a phenomenal memory. Once he corrected her mistakes, she memorized them instantly and never repeated them again. Sometimes she inserted words from another language into the conversation, as she couldn't find the English equivalent, but it didn't matter, as the essence of the whole sentence was clear.

"Why do you need to speak fluent English?" Ben asked.

"I sell souvenirs to the tourists, and I must communicate with them."

Suddenly, he remembered her. It was from her that he had bought the souvenir for two dollars just this morning. He couldn't see her face in the dim moonlight, only a vague silhouette, but he knew it was her.

"Emma, do you remember me? I bought a souvenir from you today!" Ben reached into his pocket and pulled out a small amulet on rough lace. He had not even bothered to look at his purchase closely, forgetting all about it, and now he examined the amulet with interest.

"Of course I recognized you, but we didn't have a chance to talk about it yet."

"So what does this amulet represent? Is this some kind of god?"

"No, it's just a figure. Our gods—actually, we call them spirits—unlike in other religions, don't have a certain look. They always have different faces."

"If they look different, then perhaps they can appear like this as well, and I will assume that this is a good spirit that saved my life today." Ben concluded and hid the figure back in his pocket. "This is a good spirit and very cheap, as he saved my life for only two bucks. Did you make them yourself?"

"Yes I did. I carve it from wood logs and roots of the fallen trees. Sometimes I make other souvenirs from clay and paint them. I also knit colored yarn bracelets, bags, and more. When we get to our village, I'll show you some of my crafts."

"Then you bring this to your grandma?" Ben was surprised. "You said it is a half-day walk?"

"I usually get to the port a day before, by the evening, and the next day my grandmother and I sell souvenirs. Later, in the afternoon, I walk back home."

"How often do you go there?"

"Once a week, when the ship arrives. But if we have enough left from the previous weeks I come there anyway, just to help my grandma."

"Now I understand why you speak such good English."

"My English is not that great. I wish I could speak better. But I have sufficient vocabulary to communicate with tourists. My grandmother can also speak English. She used to live in the city and even went to school."

"But what if the tourists don't speak English?" asked Ben.

"I can also speak in German, French, and a little Russian. Of late, a lot of Russian tourists come here, so I learned a few words and phrases."

Ben looked at her incredulously.

"How did you learn so many languages? Did you take any special classes?"

"We don't have any classes. We don't even have regular schools. There are only a few, and they are far away. My grandmother taught me how to read, write, and count, and, of course, some English, but the rest I learned myself."

"What is your native language?"

"We have several languages here. I speak mainly Motu. It's easier for me, but sometimes I use Pisin. We also speak Wagi, but I am not fluent in it."

"What is Wagi?" Ben asked.

"It is the language of our tribe, but there are different varieties of it, depending on which tribe you live in. If someone talks in Wagi,

I understand everything, but I find it easier to respond in Motu or Pisin."

"Don't you get confused with different words in all these languages?"

"Not really, it's not that difficult at all. Many of the words are similar in all languages, while others don't exist in another language. Wagi is actually pretty simple, but it is limited and does not have many words. But Pisin is similar to English."

"How old are you?" Ben asked after a long pause.

"I'm eleven."

Ben was terribly ashamed of himself. He was fourteen, attending an elite private school, yet he did not know any language other than his own. This girl, who had no school education, was fluent in probably a dozen different languages and yet assured him it was easy. Ben rushed to change the subject before Emma asked how many languages he knew. Besides, linguistics was the least of his worries at the moment.

"So, how far do we have to go?"

"I don't know." She shrugged. "Probably far."

"What do you mean you don't know?" Ben was shocked.

"I usually take another route. I go up on the hill before reaching the river. This way is much longer, and I do not know this area well."

"But you know where to go, don't you?"

"Yes, somewhere over there." She waved her hand in a vague direction toward the forest. "Do not worry, we will find the way."

"Say, can you make fire?" Ben shivered, as his clothes were still soaking wet, and the air in the forest was cool at night.

"I sure can, if you have any matches."

"If I had matches, I could have done that myself," Ben muttered. "I thought you could make fire by rubbing pieces of wood."

"Actually, I can, but everything is wet in the forest right now. There was heavy rain recently, and we will not find any dry wood around here. But don't worry, when we walk through the jungle you will get warm, even hot."

"Well, then let's go, if you have had enough rest."

"Okay, let's go." She got up and stretched out her hand to help him.

He was going to try to stand up on his own, but immediately realized how absurd the idea was. He grasped her hand and got up on his feet, grimacing in pain. The first few steps he made with great difficulty, but then, step by step, Ben settled into a rhythm, and they walked into the thicket of the night forest.

Chapter 7. At the Roots of Cannibalism

The rescue expedition went back to the port in complete silence and in total darkness. There was nothing left to say, and nobody was in the mood to talk. Margaret, supported by Rupert, walked obediently at the back of the group, turning in the right direction, stepping over fallen tree logs, and wading through the dense bushes silently. Having lost all traces of her son, she was like a deflated balloon, indifferent to everything around her.

Back near the riverbank, she had been distraught that they were going back without her son, and in despair she had lost control, grabbed the flashlight from Hubert, and ran into the woods, calling for Ben. Everybody had to follow her and go a little deeper into the jungle despite the total darkness, hoping for a miracle. But of course, the miracle did not happen.

Hubert was a good tracker, and he knew that the boy was no longer in the woods and most likely had gone down the river. He tried to explain the futility of the search to her, but she didn't listen. He reassured her that it was unlikely that Ben would go too far by the river in complete darkness. He would probably get ashore somewhere along the way, and someone would find him and bring the boy to their tribe to spend the night there, and in the morning, they would help him to get back to the village. At this point, it would be better if they all returned to the port, where he could reach the local tribes through his contacts.

"Then let's go now and ask all the nearest tribes," Margaret had insisted.

"But, ma'am, it is very far. We won't be able to reach even one tribal village before tomorrow morning. We have many tribes in all directions, and the distance from one to another is quite far. Once at the port, I'll contact almost all the tribes. I have my own means."

Rupert also agreed with his arguments and tried to explain to Margaret the uselessness of the blind search. Finally, Hubert found a convincing argument, saying that Ben may have already returned to the port, and they had missed him going by.

"In our dense jungles," he said, "a person could walk a few meters away from us and we might not even see him."

His words made good sense, and Margaret agreed to go back, as she couldn't do anything else anyway. She slowly trailed behind the group, hoping that Ben was already in the port. Thanks to Hubert they had several flashlights and could safely walk through the jungle despite the darkness.

Hubert slowed down and came to Margaret and Rupert leaving the rest of the rescuers to lead the way. He genuinely felt sorry for these people, for whom a long-awaited vacation had turned to hell. He tried to find the right words of comfort and somehow soothe them from these upsetting events.

"Look, ma'am, I think you have nothing to worry about. Your son is alive; he is just lost somewhere in the woods, and I can assure you, we will find him. Nothing will happen to your boy. We don't have any predators here. In the worst case, he will spend the night in the jungle, which is also not a big problem. He will be okay, believe me. It is more like a small inconvenience for him rather than a tragedy."

Margaret suddenly snapped back from her sad thoughts and looked at Hubert as if she had just remembered something. After a moment of hesitation, she said, "Excuse me, Hubert, can I ask you a question? Perhaps it may seem a little . . . strange, but I would like to ask you anyway."

"Of course, ma'am, ask me whatever you want," Hubert replied, glad that Margaret had come out of the stupor she had been in.

"I heard that here, in New Guinea, some tribes still practice cannibalism. Do you think this is true?"

Hubert was taken aback for a moment. The question was, to say the least, unusual.

"No, ma'am, I don't think so. I don't know where you got this information from, but this is not true. The rituals of cannibalism have long been eradicated; it is all in the past. Earlier, such rituals were practiced, but in present day . . ."

"Rituals? I thought that cannibalism occurred because of a lack of food, but you call it a ritual?"

"Yes, of course it was also due to lack of food, but cannibalism is mostly based on religion. You see, our ancestors believed that if a warrior eats the heart of his enemy, then he gains his strength, power, and courage, and becomes invincible. But if one eats certain parts of the bodies of deceased relatives, it will protect the family and their house from the evil spirits, and so on. It's difficult to explain as there are so many beliefs, myths, and religious rituals that nobody really knows them all. Besides, they actually vary from one tribe to another."

"But this is so wrong! Even animals don't eat their own kind. Well, at least mammals don't; there may be some insects that do so, I'm not sure about that. But humans? We are Homo sapiens, which means 'wise man.' How can we allow things like that?"

"I agree with you, but religion in general defies all logical explanation. For many centuries people worshiped different gods and brought animals and even humans on the altar of sacrifice. In the name of God, millions of people have been killed, burned alive, beheaded, drawn, quartered, and exterminated by other means. Most of the world's wars and local conflicts that claimed the lives of thousands, even millions of people, started because of religious differences. Even today, in your civilized world, not to mention other less developed countries, hundreds of thousands of people are killed in the name of God. And you are telling me it is more normal than eating flesh of people who are often already dead?"

"But this is different!" Margaret exclaimed.

"Is it? How so? How is it different? Why is killing someone considered normal whereas killing and eating a dead person's flesh is not? To kill a man is already an abnormal and horrible thing to do, and so it doesn't matter what happens with his remains. Besides, as I was saying, we don't practice these traditions anymore . . . for over thirty years now," he said after a brief hesitation.

Margaret instantly caught the little pause in his words and looked at him suspiciously. "Are you sure?"

"Well, you know, our island is big, and we have over eight hundred different settlements, communities, and tribes, many of which live in remote, impenetrable jungles and mountains. It is impossible to know everything about all them, and we cannot control the situation on the entire island. Unfortunately, from time to time, we hear in the news that someone somewhere out there returned to the old traditions and practiced cannibalism. But nobody can confirm whether it is true or just rumors. But I must assure you, even if such events took place, it happens somewhere high in the mountains, far from civilization. We have this big mountain that occupies the whole island, and the higher up we go, the more uninhabitable that place is. There is impenetrable jungle everywhere, the roads are completely absent, and it is difficult to control that region. In these places, everything is possible. That mountain region, inhabited by some tribes that we call Highlanders, who . . . how should I say this . . . are a bit aggressive to the tribes that live at the lower levels. Those Highlanders still practice some of their customs and traditions that are remnants of the past, and I have heard that some of them are still practicing human sacrifice and cannibalism during their rituals and holidays. But, once again, this is nothing more than rumors and speculation, as we don't have any evidence of that."

"Oh my God!" exclaimed Margaret, ignoring his last words. "We seem to have returned to a prehistoric era."

"You are right; certain areas are still in the Stone Age. Today, in the twenty-first century, such rituals are unacceptable, and the authorities are trying hard to fight that, but honestly, it is not always effective. Let me tell you a little bit about this country and the situation on the island, and then we will come back to your question on cannibalism. I will try to be brief," Hubert continued, noticing that Margaret had become distracted from her sad thoughts. She had regained energy, and her pace had accelerated. Margaret and Rupert strode briskly and were listening intently to Hubert's story. He was a good storyteller, as his occupation had developed a keen capability to deliver information to the listeners in a sapid and easy to understand way.

"So, in a simplified form, the landscape of our country is the following," Hubert began his geography lesson. "Ours is an island in the middle of which is a mountain range called Mount Hagen. At the foot of the mountain, starting almost on the sea level, the region is covered with dense, humid, tropical forest. We are going through that area right now. As you noticed, this part of the jungle is not very attractive. The air is heavy, with humidity over ninety percent. The ground is saturated with moisture and therefore almost never stays dry, forming swamps with myriads of mosquitoes. The jungles here are dense, almost impassable. If it wasn't for the pass through which we are going right now, there would be no easy way to get back to the port. Local tribes and villagers have created this path to be able to go through this forest. From here, the road goes up to the mountainous terrain. If you remember, we were there today during the excursion. At that level, high above the sea, the vegetation changes. The forest is still thick, of course, but not as much as down here. There are a large variety of trees and shrubs, and even entire palm groves. The fauna changes as well. The low ground is mostly inhabited with snakes and various amphibians, but on higher altitudes there are wild boars, deer, and many marsupials. Of course, birds too, as there are a lot of berry plants that provide plenty of food for them. That area is undoubtedly more suitable for living and is inhabited by many tribes.

"If you go higher, the dense forest thins out, and is replaced with the temperate broadleaf and mixed forest with a sparse growth of trees, which in turn changes to just short bushes on even higher elevation. Then at the top of the mountain, all vegetation disappears, except for occasional small lichens, ending with the snowcap.

"The mountain landscape changes all the time. The slopes often end up in wide plateaus, plains, and valleys, and then rise again, sometimes with a gentle slope or steep descent. I think you get the general landscape of our island."

"I already knew that from the geography course in school," Margaret replied, but Hubert continued, ignoring her jibe.

"Now imagine that this mountain is home to over two-thirds of our tribes. Some live on higher elevation, while others on lower. Living conditions at the lower levels are considered the most favorable. The rivers streaming down from the mountain peaks reach the plateaus at the bottom of the hills and spread out in the valleys, forming ponds and lakes. The presence of water enriches the soil and attracts animals, which brings good fishing and hunting for locals.

"But the tribes living in the higher levels are not as lucky. Lakes and other natural reservoirs practically don't exist, as water streams down to the lower levels, therefore the soil is not so fertile and, as a result, there are fewer animals and game. However, there are still plenty of fruit trees and berries, so the tribes can feed themselves. But those who live even higher don't even have that much. The forest there is thin and consists mostly of some shrubs. There is almost no game, the air is cold, and at night, it can even reach the freezing point. This is the overview of the geography of the island.

"The entire island is strictly divided among the tribes, and they all protect their territory from the neighbor's invasion. But nevertheless, those who live in the higher levels, the Highlanders, sometimes come down to the lower woods to hunt, and this causes frustration of the rightful owners of that territory. Such invasion often turns into war between the tribes."

"But why?" Margaret asked. "The forest is big, and there is plenty of game for everybody."

"It is not as big as it might seem at first glance, and I am not talking about the size. But wait, we will come back to that," Hubert replied.

"As I have said, all these tribes defend their territory probably even better than some countries protect their borders. But sooner or later, someone will violate the territorial integrity, so war between tribes is quite common, and usually, the Highlanders attack their weaker neighbors living below."

"Why are they weaker?" Margaret asked again.

"Margaret, it's obvious," Rupert said, joining the conversation. "Those who are poorer are usually much stronger and more aggressive than the ones who are richer."

"Your husband is absolutely right, ma'am. For example, look at the history of boxing. Most of the famous boxers came from poor families, and their first boxing skills were from the street, fighting for survival, not for titles. The gym cannot give you the level of fighting spirit that you can get on the street. Here, we have exactly the same mentality. Highlanders, the tribes who live in the higher elevation, are mean and ruthless to those living at lower levels, in more favorable conditions, and usually attack them first, robbing and stealing their food and people. But, of course, it happens the other way around as well; if the Highlanders come to someone else's territory to hunt, then the legal owners of that land attack the poacher's tribe in revenge."

"But why would they have to fight over it?" exclaimed an indignant Margaret. "Can't they let other tribes hunt on their territory or cultivate land? Better yet, they can do it together, and I bet it would be more beneficial for both tribes."

"I told you that each tribe is very territorial and they want to protect their sovereignty. Let's look at the country Egypt for example. They have, if I remember correctly from school, fertile land around the Nile Delta, right?"

"Well, I am not sure, but let's say this is true, so what?"

"Beyond the southern border of Egypt is a poor country, where many people live in dire poverty in the desert. The people in that country from behind the barbed wire border see that in the neighboring state of Egypt they have everything: deep rivers, palm trees, fertile land, but they have nothing but desert, sand, and camel thorns. Why can't Egypt open the border and share their natural resources with the neighbor? But no, the border is closed and well-guarded. If someone from the poorer country tries to cross it, the border guards will shoot him without warning. How is this situation different from our case? There is no difference, except the fact that we don't have a formal border and barbed wire between the tribes."

"You cannot compare a country to the tribes. There are politics involved, national security, and sovereignty of the state."

"But here we have the same thing: a kind of politics, sovereignty, and national security, but on a smaller, local scale. Hunting on foreign territory, and even just trespassing, is a serious violation of our unwritten rules."

"But how can they tell that someone was hunting on their territory in such a big forest?"

"It is much easier than you think, ma'am. Don't forget that we are professional hunters and trackers. These skills are in our blood. A good hunter can read the forest like an open book."

"But you don't go through the forest reading it like an open book all the time. You don't walk in the woods with your head down, looking for footprints. How do they know that someone was hunting there, let's say, a few miles from the place where the legal hunters were? I don't understand."

"Of course you don't, because you are not a professional hunter. Let me explain it to you in simple words."

"Yes, please do, Hubert," Rupert insisted. Obviously he wasn't a professional hunter either and didn't know much about it.

"Have you ever hunted for wild boar? Well, why am I asking? Of course you haven't. Wild boar hunting, I tell you, is a very difficult and dangerous job, especially when boars go in a herd. A herd of boars is even more dangerous than any predator, and all living things in their way scatter to their hideouts to clear a path for them.

"So, imagine that you are hunting for boars in your own territory, sitting in the ambush area, waiting for the herd to go to the watering place. You know that on this day boars will go to the river on a certain path, because right now this is the shortest and perhaps the most favorable trail to get water. But during the rainy season, the approach from this side of the river could be difficult, so they go around to another riverbank. The information about the best path is in their instinct and has been developed for thousands of years. Our hunters also know it on the instinct level, like wild boars."

"How can you compare the instincts of man and animal?" Margaret exclaimed.

"Humans are also animals, and we have the same instincts." Hubert laughed. "But in addition to that, we also have the knowledge given to us by our ancestors. Our fathers, grandfathers, and great-grandfathers hunted on this land for centuries, and accumulated certain knowledge, which was passed from generation to generation. Thanks to them, we know the habits of animals, their trails, and we know where and when the herd will go by.

"So you are sitting waiting to ambush the herd. At the same time, poachers from the neighboring tribe come to your land to hunt. It seems like it would not be a big problem, right? Let them kill one or two boars. We never hunt more game than we can eat at one time, as we don't have refrigerators to store extra meat from spoiling.

"The poachers are walking around the woods in search of boars. This is not their land, and they don't hunt here often, don't know the animal trails, their habits, and are looking for game blindly. Of course, they are also good trackers, and sooner or later, they will find a herd, but most likely by chance, somewhere in the open area. It is unlikely that they will have enough time to make a proper hideout. So it won't be easy for them to kill a boar in the herd, especially in open area."

"Why not? I thought it is much easier to hunt animals in the herd," Rupert said. "No need to aim, just fire in the middle, and you will hit one for sure."

"Wrong. Actually, it is the other way around. What do you think our men hunt with?"

"I am sure you have guns even here. The bow and arrow today is an anachronism, even in such wild places."

"Of course we have firearms, but not as much as you think. Very few tribes have shotguns, but they won't use them, especially during a hunt on foreign soil. They don't want to make any extra noise. Besides, you cannot kill an adult boar even with large-caliber pellets. In smoothbore shotguns, they scatter far apart. But you have to hit him in the eye or the heart, otherwise you will only wound the animal and it will pounce on the hunter and crush him. An adult boar is a half-ton of weight, multiplied by his speed and anger at the hunter."

"So, what then? Bow and arrow?" Rupert asked surprisingly.

"Yes, mostly, the old bow and arrow, or as it is called here, the *aral* and *aral-ge*. Maybe also *hagda*—heavy spear—to finish off the injured animal. But even with that, it is not as simple as you think. As I was saying, you have to hit it in the heart or the eye. Because the skin of a wild boar is stiff and bristly, you can't penetrate it with an arrow from a distance, unless you come close to the herd, but it is dangerous for the hunter. So you cannot hit him in the heart. You must aim into his eye and stay in front of him, which requires tremendous shooting accuracy and serious professional skills.

"But let's say they were good hunters and shot the animal right in the eye with one or two arrows. What will the rest of the herd do when they see that a few of their group are dead and the hunters are standing in front of them? Boars are not aggressive and will try to avoid any conflicts, unless injured. Animals will quickly abandon the trail and go to the river by another route. The lucky poachers will get the trophy and go feed their tribe.

"Now let's get back to the rightful owners of the woods, who are sitting for several hours, and sometimes even a day, waiting for their chance at an ambush. The herd, having changed their trail because of the poacher, will not come through this place. The hunters will wait a little longer and then get onto the trail to find out why the boar didn't come. Of course, they will find traces of blood, trampled branches, and the footprints of the strangers. They would know exactly where the poachers came from, how many people took part in the hunt, and which tribe they belong to. Hunters will have no choice but to go home empty-handed and tell their tribe-mates that there is no meat today, and they have to eat rats and chew on some roots again. This scenario is a little bit exaggerated, but in general, everything is just as I said. The offended tribe reports this incident to their elders, and they will give the order to attack the tribe of the poachers."

"So why don't they cooperate?" Margaret did not give up. "Why not share information with the neighbors and hunt together?"

"They do that sometimes. Elders of both tribes, tired of war, get together, drink wine as a sign of a truce, shake hands, and leave, ordering their men to cooperate with each other. That brings a period of unstable peace. The hunters will take their neighbors to the forest, allow them to catch a few animals, and with that, their help will end. You don't seriously think that they would willingly share their knowledge with outsiders, do you?"

"Why not?" Margaret was surprised. "They must obey orders from the elders."

"Madam, hunting skills are very difficult. It is not enough to be a good shooter. You need to read and interpret the footprints and the smallest signs in the woods, know the habits of the animals, their trails, burrows, watering places, and on and on. Our men accumulated these skills little by little, over centuries. We inherited this knowledge from our ancestors, from generation to generation. This is our legacy, like how you inherit your grandparents' family business, house, or money in the bank. It is our capital, and believe me, much more valuable than the one that your grandparents leave you. Your legacy will allow you, for example, to buy a more expensive, prestigious car, but our capital lets our hunters and their families survive and not starve to death. Do you think that someone would voluntarily share their knowledge, their legacy, with their neighbor? No way, absolutely not. None of the orders from their chiefs could make them do so. Besides, if they share all their knowledge with another tribe, soon these neighbors will simply go hunt alone, using this knowledge, which can also lead to a new war. Shaky peace doesn't last for long around here. War and peace replace one another all the time, like black-and-white piano keys.

"But besides hunting interests, there is something else that directly impacts the stability in the region. Many tribes that live on the lower levels have access to the ocean. For them, it is not only an additional source of food, but it also a way to make money selling souvenirs to tourists. Have you bought any souvenirs today in the port?"

"Well . . ." Margaret hesitated, "not that much. We bought many gifts from previous ports."

"It does not matter; if not you, then the others will buy them. But our residents and tribal communities have stable revenue from every ship that enters the port. For you, a few dollars you leave on the shore is probably a small amount, but for them, it is an opportunity to buy goods they cannot grow or make themselves. For example, you probably wouldn't believe me, but common salt is a luxury around here."

"Salt?" Rupert was surprised.

"Yes, salt," Margaret confirmed, as she was well-versed in medicine and physiology. "We need to maintain the percentage of salt in our body. Without it, people will die the same as they do without food, but the death would be longer and more painful."

"That's right," Hubert agreed. "We need salt. In fact, many tribes add a little seawater in their food during cooking. This way they can get at least some salt to their body. Sometimes they even collect driftwood in the ocean, dry it out, and burn it, so they can use the ash as a salt. But, unfortunately, not all the tribes are so lucky. Those who live deep inside the island or high in the mountains don't even have this opportunity to extract salt.

"But there are also many other essential goods we have to buy with real money. But the tribes in the lower levels block the access to the ocean so the people who live higher in the mountain can't make any money at all. Often, port access is a good bargaining tool in their peace negotiations. As you can imagine, we don't have many jobs, and it is almost impossible to make money by other means. Very few people have a permanent job."

"But you have a job," Rupert said.

"I am rather an exception to that rule." Hubert smiled. "I simply got lucky.

"My parents are religious people, and educated. A long time ago, they founded the Franciscan Mission nearby, a little farther south, at the mouth of the Sepik River. At that mission we had an elementary school for tribal children, where my mother was a teacher. I received a rudimentary education in that school. Then my father took ill; he contracted malaria. That place was located in a swampy terrain, and living conditions there are much worse than here. He was transported to the hospital in Madang. We thought he would not survive, but he did. After a long battle with this disease, his condition changed from progressive to a chronic relapse, and doctors forbade him to go back in the forest. Since then, we have lived in Madang.

"In town, I graduated high school and then went to the Lay University of Technology, the Faculty of Forestry. Engineering science wasn't for me, as I was born and raised in the jungle, and the forest is my home and my vocation. That is why I chose this profession. After graduating I returned to Madang, and was hired by a travel agency, receiving a job as a driver-guide."

"It actually explains your strong knowledge of the geography, history, and good English skills as well," Rupert noted.

"Yes. It might seem strange to you, but in our country, only two percent of the population speak English," Hubert replied.

"What language do you speak here?" Margaret was surprised. "As far as I know, the country has long been an Australian colony, and English should be your first language."

"Yes, officially, English is considered our national language. But people prefer to speak another language, or rather languages. Have you heard the term 'lingua franca'?"

"Yes, the language of inter-ethnic communication." Rupert nodded.

"That's right. We also have a lingua franca language called Tok Pisin."

"Wait," Margaret said resentfully, "can someone please explain in simple words what lingua franca is?"

"Of course, madam. You see, in all multilingual countries, there is always one common language for communication between groups of people from different areas. In here, we have such a language for inter-tribal communication, called Tok Pisin, and it is the lingua franca of Papua New Guinea."

"So why not use English for that purpose? Why should you create another language?"

"The fact of the matter is that nobody created it. It was formed by itself over many years. Tok Pisin is a mixture of many different languages, including English, by the way, and this mixture has formed into a separate language. Our country now has two official languages: English and Tok Pisin."

"Oh, okay, I get it now. So our companions speak Tok Pisin?" Margaret nodded at the four assistants, walking in front of the group, talking quietly amongst themselves.

"No, they speak a different language." Hubert laughed. "It is called Hiri Motu, and this language is also our lingua franca. However, Hiri Motu is gradually disappearing and is being replaced by Tok Pisin."

"Now you lost me." This time Rupert was confused. "Lingua franca implies a language for communication between multilingual communities, right?"

"That's right."

"Then where did the second language, Hiri Motu, come from?"

"I'll tell you, but I'm afraid that you are not going to like my answer because it will probably confuse you even more." Hubert smiled.

"Why don't you try to explain, but in simple words."

"Okay, I will do my best. You see, Motu is actually a name of the tribe in the southern part of the island, which in terms of their development, has always been one step above the other tribes. They were one of the first who implemented some innovative tools, household items, clay pottery, and much more. People from Motu sailed on large canoes, *legato*, along the coast and sold their goods, particularly pottery, to other tribes, or traded it for food. Such trade in Motu language is called *Hiri*—to trade or exchange. Many tribes of the region understood and could speak the language of Motu, which was actually more sophisticated than others, and eventually, all the nearest tribes switched to this language and called it Hiri Motu, the language of trade. It became popular, and soon, half of the country used Motu.

"After the independence of Papua New Guinea in 1975, it was decided to make Hiri Motu the national language, along with English. Motu became the lingua franca of New Guinea, not Tok Pisin. By the way, this language has several names; it is also called the Police Motu, Pidgin Motu, and even just Hiri. Almost all cities, villages, and many of the tribes understand it, although they continue to speak their own dialect. The police have used the Hiri Motu language ever since the colonization of the island at the end of the nineteenth century. At that time, the Governor, Sir William McGregor, who started the police force on the island, was living here, hence the name: Police Motu. Many government agencies also used this language.

"In the mid-seventies, Papua New Guinea received independence and had to create its own government, parliament, consulates, and a diplomatic presence in other countries. For these purposes, the official language was English, but people continued to communicate with each other in the more familiar Motu as a lingua franca for communication within the country. Is everything clear to you so far? Please interrupt me and ask questions, because it is going to get even more confusing."

"Continue," Margaret replied grimly. Obviously it wasn't that clear to her, but she decided to wait and keep all of her questions silent for now. Rupert also wrinkled his forehead, trying to follow Hubert's story.

"Modern Hiri Motu is no longer a pure, original Motu. It was mingled with several pidgin and creole dialects. I think people from the Motu tribe wouldn't understand much if you tried to speak to them in this modified language."

"Wait, did you say pidgin? Where did the pidgin and creole languages come from?"

"Pidgin, and there are many of them, is the simplest form of lingual communication between different dialectal groups. Over time, the pidgin language improved and became creole, the more sophisticated dialect. How should I explain it in an easy way?

"Imagine that people from two different linguistic groups came to live together on the island. They have to talk to each other and write letters and documents. But they do not know the language of the other party. They read and write words just the way they hear them, with no grammar rules. Over a period of time, they came up with this new language, called pidgin, which is just a combination of the two languages. Eventually this mixture improves with grammar rules, word pronunciation, and so on, and it became the creole language, meaning improved pidgin. But let's finish first with the Hiri Motu, and then we will get back to pidgin and creole a little later.

"As I was saying, Hiri Motu significantly transformed over time, and it is now mixed with other languages. In the modern day, Hiri Motu has two dialects: Central and Papuan, depending on the region and mixture of other languages. Central Motu is less contaminated by other dialects and is closer to the original Motu. But Papuan Motu is closer to pidgin, and eventually, it advanced into the creole language Tok Pisin. So the Papuan dialect Hiri Motu is actually Tok Pisin, which is now, officially, the lingua franca of Papua New Guinea. But Central Hiri Motu is also widely used today and is also our lingua franca. Now, in our country, we officially have two lingua franca: Tok Pisin and Hiri Motu. I am done now. Please ask your questions. I can see on your faces you have many of them."

"I have only one question," Rupert said. "What language do your kids learn in schools and universities? How about your newspapers, magazines, books, and other publication materials? What language are they printed in? Or perhaps television and radio, do they broadcast programs in English? There must be one universal language."

"This is more than one question." Hubert laughed. "But I will answer them all. Our Constitution says that Tok Pisin is our official language, along with English. This is the language used for most of our periodical publications, books, and television broadcasts. However, many TV stations also broadcast in English, and we have many English newspapers. But guess what? We also have all that in Hiri Motu.

"With education, however, the situation is a bit more complicated. Depending on the location of the school, or other educational institution, classes are conducted in a language dominant for that region. Most of the elementary schools on this side of the island are taught in Tok Pisin, while on the west coast Hiri Motu is more prevalent, or even some Tok Ples."

"I'm sorry to interrupt you with my dumb question. What did you just say? Tok Ples? You meant to say Tok Pisin, right?" Margaret asked in confusion.

"Please forgive me, ma'am. I accidentally mentioned that. I didn't want to touch this subject. You see, a Tok Ples is a tribal dialect used by the tribes. But let's not go into this linguistic group."

"Why not? You already mentioned it, so you may as well clarify it."

"I don't want to confuse you even further. Almost all of our tribes speak the dialect of their ancestors. These languages are called Tok Ples. The problem is that the Tok Ples are also constantly transforming into Motu and Pisin. For example, let's take the local tribes located just a few miles away. Most of them speak the Wagi language. But even that has several varieties, which, in turn, are grouped according to some linguistic characteristics. Today, there are several dialects of Wagi, such as Kamba, Silibob, Foran, and others. This is just one language I took as an example. We have over eight hundred of such Tok Ples language groups. That is why I didn't want to get into this subject. Besides, I don't know much about it myself."

Margaret was disappointed again, as she thought that she had already figured out the linguistic subtlety of this region, but it turned out she wasn't even close.

"What language do you think people speak in the port village?"

"I'm afraid to even assume anything," Rupert said, "but I think they speak Hiri Motu, considering that our companions talk to each other in this language. Am I right?"

"Sorry, but you are wrong yet again." Hubert laughed. "At the port, almost everyone speaks Wagi. You see, that village is unique, different from the others scattered throughout the country. It arose as a result of certain events in our country, which I can tell you about some other time, but all its residents came from other cities, and even from some nearby tribes. Therefore, Wagi became the dominant language in this village over time."

"But this is exactly what the lingua franca is for, isn't it?" Rupert intervened again.

"Yes, of course. Only that we forgot to tell our tribal people about it," Hubert joked. "So they continue to speak the language they know. Our other residents speak Motu, and some even understand Pisin. But the dominant language in the village is Wagi. This is exactly how the Pisin is created. I think this time, we are not going to have another lingua franca, as many of the tribes around here can already speak decent Motu. However, Wagi, or rather one of its dialects, Camba, is still the main language here. Although today, nobody knows anymore which dialect is the original Wagi."

At the end, Hubert grinned and said, "Also, I didn't tell you yet about the impact of the linguistic group Bongy on the local dialects. Many words and names were borrowed from this language. Actually, we have barely scratched the surface of this subject. I think we've added a lot of gray hair to the linguists who tried to understand our philological wilderness."

"All of this is very strange," Margaret said.

"Well, considering the number of different nationalities and tribes living on this island, it is not strange at all. This linguistic confusion is understandable."

"I feel really sorry for these kids who go to school here."

"Actually, it is much easier than you think." Hubert laughed again. "In remote areas, we don't have schools, and not that many kids are getting an education. They don't need math and science. They need a different knowledge here, the one that can help them bring food to the table. Tell me, why would a tribal boy need math?

How can the Pythagorean theorem help him kill a wild boar with one arrow or properly set up bird traps?"

"So you don't have any schools at all?"

"Of course, we do. But the children from tribes rarely go there. It is very far for them to walk every day for several miles through the forest. Even some of our children from the village don't go to school, since in most places there are none within walking distance, and we don't have school buses here."

"But you went to school," Margaret countered. "You've got an education and even make a decent living now. So education is not as useless as you were saying."

"But I got lucky, I told you. I didn't have to go far through the jungle every day. If it wasn't for my father's illness, that would have been the end of my education. But because of it, even though it sounds blasphemous, I could continue my education in a different town and even get a degree at the university. Others are less fortunate, and they have no job other than to sell souvenirs in the port. Many residents of this village come from different tribes and make money for them. Some of the tribes make all these souvenirs and bring them to the port, and these people come from mostly lower-level tribes. There are no Highlanders in the port. They have to pass through the lands of other tribes, and it would be classified as trespassing."

"Yeah, life is very unfair," Rupert said. "Some are lucky to be born in the right place, while others have to suffer on non-fertile lands in the mountains."

"This is the rule of life, unfortunately; we don't get to choose where to be born, nor where to die. Everyone has their own faith. Let's take you, for example, Mr. Rupert. According to your accent, you have British roots, don't you?"

"Yes, you are right," Rupert said, surprised at Hubert's insight. "My grandparents came from a small village near Glasgow in Scotland."

"Now imagine for a moment that if, during the journey to America, your ancestors, by miracle, survived a shipwreck, and were carried out to our shores on a piece of driftwood, then instead of New York, you would now have been living in the jungle. You would no longer be driving to work in your Bentley, but running through the woods in search of some rodent for dinner. Believe me, history has known many instances like that."

"Porsche," Rupert muttered under his breath.

"What?"

"I said I do not have a Bentley. I drive a Porsche."

"I'm sorry. I didn't mean to offend you," Hubert said sarcastically.

Margaret shuddered at the possibility of such a scenario. Everything in our world is only a matter of coincidence.

"But we got a little distracted from our topic. Now you are familiar with the situation on this island, our customs and traditions, so let's get back to the issue of cannibalism. As I was saying, the roots of this horrible phenomenon are based on two main factors: religion and starvation."

"Nonsense," Margaret interrupted him. "People live below the poverty line in many other countries as well, but nowhere else in the world does cannibalism thrive as much as here."

"Are you sure? Can you confidently say you know everything about all the tribes in the world? I can assure you that in other countries, cannibalism still exists even today. Take, for example, some Indonesian islands and countries with similar climate and geographical conditions, such as Borneo and Laos, or the many

Chilean villages on the slopes of the Andes, and many others we don't even know about."

"But there are also other tribes, for example, in the jungles of Africa. I don't think any of them practice cannibalism."

"Actually, the conditions in these African tribes are not as bad as people commonly think. Except for a few Moroccan tribes who stay in the desert, they live quite well, compared to ours. African jungles, and even the Savannah, are rich with fertile lands, fruit trees, animals, and game. Besides, you forget about religion. It plays a very important role in this matter. For example, some tribes believe that by eating human flesh, they destroy the evil spirit Kahua, which gets into the body in the guise of humans from a neighboring tribe. They don't perform an act of cannibalism, but simply protect themselves from the troubles and diseases that the spirit Kahua can bring. Each tribe has its own beliefs, spirits, and rituals. Also, they have to appease a good spirit by offering them tidbits of meat. How can they gratify it if they hardly have any meat for themselves? So they sacrifice the bodies of dead enemies and, occasionally, living prisoners, of course. It's not like they eat their own tribe-mates, although perhaps that could have happened as well, who knows? For centuries, people have committed many horrid acts for the sake of religion, and continue to do so. Believe me, cannibalism is not the worst one yet. Add the lack of food to the mix, and we have what we have.

"Actually, today's religion is weakening. People still continue to worship their God and conduct various rituals, bring human flesh to the altar, but they do it more from habit, in accordance to the established traditions. Old people still believe in the power of spirits, but the younger generation is not as fanatic about religion anymore."

"You see," Margaret exclaimed, "religion is weakening, but the old rites do not change."

"You don't believe in Santa Claus, yet every year you set up a Christmas tree, don't you?" Hubert replied. "You have to understand that our ancestors practiced certain traditions for centuries, and suddenly, it turned out that all they did was wrong, unnatural, unworthy of being human. The government is introducing new laws punishing these traditions, reinforcing the fight against cannibalism. But it's not going to work. How would you feel if someone told you that your grandparents did things that are considered improper and even illegal today? What would be your reaction? Would you immediately agree to that? I don't think so. You cannot eliminate cannibalism in one day, and there is only one way to do it."

"How?" Rupert and Margaret asked in unison.

"It is easy. We need to give them a choice. Do you think people would eat their own kind if they had a choice? Offer a plate of juicy fried pork chop, French fries, fresh salad, and a few bottles of cold beer to the most inveterate cannibal. Then give him a bowl of raw human guts and a jug of muddy water, infested with bacteria, like a flask from a biological laboratory. Which do you think he is going to choose? You see, it's not enough to just say that this is wrong. You have to give them an alternative way of living. Bring electricity to every village, give people refrigerators to keep their food fresh, build water treatment plants, and provide them with vaccinations from deadly diseases. In addition, build a few McDonald's, Burger Kings, or whatever else you have in your Western world—put some ice cream in the refrigerators for children. Of course, the elderly people are conservative, and they would never go to McDonald's, but the children, the younger generation—this is our hope. In a few years they will rejuvenate, and I guarantee you that ten or twenty years from now, you will not recognize this country. But for now, this is still only our dream. Our politicians would rather spend money to build themselves another villa, as your politicians would probably do as well. But people on the ground will continue to live as they have lived for centuries."

"Well, perhaps you're right. Obviously we are not going to solve this problem right now." Margaret steered the conversation in the right direction. "But I am actually more interested to know what would happen if my son got lost in the woods and ended up in one of these tribes?"

"Believe me, nothing is going to happen to him, and he is not in any danger at all," Hubert reassured her. "Cannibalism does not exist here, and hasn't for over thirty years. Everything I just told you was nothing more than abstract discussion. Once in a while we might have rare occasions of this horrible act somewhere high in the mountains, but it is an exception rather than the rule."

"You know, I am offering a reward of five thousand dollars to anyone who finds Ben," Rupert said.

"Ten!" Margaret corrected him. "We are offering ten thousand dollars. Just help us find our son. Please tell everybody. And, of course, we are grateful to you for all you have done for us and will pay for all your time and trouble."

"That actually might help." Hubert nodded. "Tomorrow morning I will contact all the local tribes through my own channels. I am sure someone out there will find your son and bring him back. Everything will be okay, don't worry."

Having been immersed in this informative conversation, they had reached the village. Their walk back to the port took twice as long, considering they had to wade through the dense jungle in complete darkness, except for the dim beams of a few flashlights, which turned out to be very helpful. The port, which some time ago was filled with loud, fun holiday spirits was now empty and silent. Hubert's bus was the only vehicle standing at the parking lot waiting for the driver, along with a few silhouettes of late villagers lingering in the nearby shadows.

As expected, Ben was not at the port, but Margaret had calmed down and wasn't surprised. Hubert was probably right about Ben being picked up by someone from the local tribe if he was still alive at all. But they didn't even want to think about the worst-case scenario. The four volunteers who had gone to the jungle with them went home as soon as they reached the village, expressing their regrets to Margaret and Rupert. Hubert got their luggage from the bus and passed it on to Rupert.

"Where are you going to stay?" he asked.

"With me," said one of the silhouettes that had approached them. It was an elderly woman, with deep wrinkles cutting through her tired face. She was holding big duffle bags and a folding chair in her hands. Apparently, she was a souvenir seller who had finished her hard day at the market.

"Let's go," she ordered without asking their opinion. She then turned around and went down the street. Margaret and Rupert, who had neither the strength nor the desire to search for any other place to stay, picked up their belongings, said goodbye to Hubert, thanking him for his help once again, and followed the woman. Hubert reassured them that everything would be okay and drove off into the darkness of the street.

Part Two

Chapter 1. The Awakening

Ben woke up and looked around. He was in a small wooden hut with a bamboo ceiling. It was more like a completely empty barn except for the piles of straw on which he lay. Emma wasn't there, and Ben panicked. What if someone came in and asked him what he was doing here? That was assuming, of course, that he would understand the question. He tried to sit up and immediately cried out in pain as the swollen knee began to throb. The pain did not go away, but only seemed to increase. At the slightest bend of the knee, a sharp pain streaked through his whole body, as if someone had stuck him with a knife. He leaned back on the straw, abandoning all attempts to get up. It was a wonder he had managed to get to this hut yesterday, or today, technically, as they had spent all night walking through the jungle and arrived early in the morning.

Yesterday, after the unplanned swim in the river and the short rest, Ben had gotten up with the help of Emma, grimacing with pain, and they started a long journey through the woods. For support he had used the shoulder of this fragile girl, who was steering him to the right path.

He had walked step by step through the rough terrain of the jungle, illuminated by the faint glimmer of the stars. Over time, his eyes adjusted to the darkness, and he could even discern the contours and silhouettes of the natural hindrances.

During the daylight, the jungle is a paradise, but after sunset, it changes completely. Have you, dear reader, ever walked through the forest at night? For the fans of acute sensations, we encourage you to try it sometime and we guarantee you an unforgettable experience, even for those with a strong and stable psyche. The trick is actually in the game of shadows.

What shadows, you may ask. *At night? Without sunlight?*

But imagine the weak rays of moonlight breaking through the crown of trees, and every branch, every little twig, casting its pitch-black shadow on the dark, gloomy ground. As you walk through the discolored gray forest, the many shadows under your feet move at the slightest breeze. The bird that suddenly flies from its branch in the dark appears like a sudden shadow that sways, jumping right under your feet like mystic underground forces coming to devour and drag you into the netherworld. All this eeriness is accompanied by the horrible cacophony of sounds of nocturnal birds and predators that come out from their burrows for the night hunt.

Why is it that the sound of birds singing is so pleasant during the day, and can satisfy the most captious listener, while their night cry is ominously hoarse, sending a chill down your spine? Ben thought as he strode along with the tenacity of a programmed robot. *If I ever get out of this adventure alive, I should ask Marcus about it.*

They had entered a zone of the woodland that had many scattered openings within the tree crown, and immediately, the shadows jumped on the footpath under their feet, surrounding them, moving menacingly. Emma did not seem to notice them but Ben was shivering with horror, and his skin was covered with cold, clammy sweat. Emma felt the quiver but interpreted it differently.

"Are you cold?" she asked, already knowing the answer. "It gets cool at night in our woods, especially in wet clothes. It is a pity we couldn't make a fire. But it's okay, our clothes will dry out soon and it will be a little warmer."

Ben didn't reply as he had to put a lot of effort into moving through the jungle. At first, he tried not to apply too much pressure on Emma's shoulder, fearing that she could not withstand the weight of his body. But without her support, walking was difficult, almost impossible, as he could not bear the load on his leg. Emma quickly noticed that.

"Don't worry, I can support you. I'm strong."

He knew that, since she pulled him up the steep incline above the river. Besides, he couldn't walk without support anyway, so he had no other choice than to use Emma's shoulder as a crutch.

Though shattered and worn out from the day's unfortunate events, with teeth clenched together to keep him from crying out in pain, he continued to hobble along. Ironically, the right leg with the twisted ankle bothered him a lot more than the left leg, and it burned with severe pain at the slightest contact with the ground. The pain in the left leg was actually tolerable unless he bent the knee, which was swollen beyond recognition.

Yet, the pain was gradually easing, and after some time, Ben could even apply a little pressure on his foot putting lesser load on Emma's shoulder. Fortunately, the forest was not too thick, and it was relatively easy to walk through the woods. He even learned to step over fallen trees without bending his knee. He sat on the tree trunk and lifted his legs to the other side, carefully supporting the knee with his hands to keep it straight.

After a while, the terrain changed, and they seemed to walk on ascending grounds. But with every step the slope became steeper, making the walk virtually impossible. Ben walked up the hill, cursing himself and whoever the divine landscape architect was, the one who had decided to raise the surface here. It was hard enough walking on flat ground, but to go upwards became excruciating. He climbed nonetheless, taking small steps, leaning on Emma's shoulder more and more, wiping tears from his face, overcoming each challenge despite the pain. He walked and prayed to God for mercy and for this damn knoll to end soon and the road to finally go downhill. And soon it did.

"Well, you asked for it," God said gleefully, or whoever was up there in the celestial office responsible for the surface.

Actually, it wasn't too steeply descending, but even the slight angle was enough to make Ben cry. Until now, he thought the hardest thing would be to walk uphill, but he had been mistaken. It became harder now, since it was not possible to go downhill without bending one's knee.

Ben knew he must continue walking, no matter how difficult and painful it was. So he kept going, grimacing in pain, biting his lip to keep from screaming. Now he had to put full pressure on Emma. She was shorter than Ben, and her shoulder comfortably supported him. This part of the road wasn't easy for her either. Emma could no longer bear the weight of his body, and her legs buckled at the knees, making her sink lower and lower until her legs gave way and she collapsed.

"Let's take a short break," she wheezed out.

They lay on the wet grass, completely exhausted and panting.

"How much farther?" Ben asked.

"Not much. We are close."

"Listen, what if I just stay here, and you go home? My leg will get better in the morning, and I can walk back to the port. Or you can come tomorrow and help me."

He immediately regretted his words. What if she did as he said and just got up and walked away leaving him alone in the woods? But Emma just snorted staring at the ground mindlessly, catching her breath.

After a short rest, she got up.

"Come on, let's go."

Ben rose and established a firm balance. They continued on this endless path. One step forward with the left leg held straight, followed by the right leg with support from Emma's shoulder. Left-right, left-right—step by step, slowly but persistently, they were moving through the jungle, coming a little closer to their destination.

They walked in complete silence, trying not to waste any energy on conversations, except for the occasional order to "stop" for a short rest, and then "let's go" after she had caught her breath. Both were exhausted. Ben lost track of time, not knowing how long they had already been in the woods or where they were. During the next stop, Ben once again asked Emma how far they were from her settlement.

"Not far, very close," Emma replied again.

"Wait!" Ben was outraged. "You already said that we were close a few hours ago!"

"We were close, but now we are even closer," she replied calmly.

A rude, sarcastic comment came up within Ben at this obvious mockery, but then he realized that she wasn't teasing him and really thought like that, so he stopped asking her questions.

The pain dulled a bit, or maybe he just got used to it. We get used to everything in life, including pain. That's how the human body functions. Pain is just a reaction notifying us that something is wrong. But if the owner of the body is already aware of the problem, then the pain becomes less sharp. However, it doesn't go away completely, to ensure that we do not forget about it and will take care of the problem at the earliest opportunity.

They reached the tribal village a few hours later, at dawn. Ben noticed that the forest had become silent; the eerie sound of the night birds and animals fell quiet in anticipation of the coming sunrise. The predators had gone to rest as the new day awakened, and the stars in the sky faded along with the night. The morning haze was painting everything around them in gray tones. The outlines of trees and shrubs became fuzzier, causing the ominous shadows that frightened Ben to disappear. The early morning mist streamed down to the ground. The earth was giving up accumulated heat, which cooled in the predawn air, transforming into tiny water particles and forming morning dew on the grass. Soon Ben noticed the blurry silhouettes of some barns and huts.

"We are home," Emma said casually, as if they hadn't been walking through the woods all night, but had just quickly run to pick flowers in the glade nearby.

They came to a long wooden structure in the middle of the village, and Emma stopped.

"You have to go there," she said, pointing to the piece of coarse leather hanging over the entrance in place of a door. "That's the male *buambramra*. I'll sleep over here." She gestured somewhere behind her.

Ben got scared. How was he going to sleep in that place with a bunch of unknown people who probably didn't even speak English? How would he explain to them what he was doing here if they suddenly woke up?

"Please don't leave," he begged her. "What if I wake someone up? What would they think if they saw a stranger on someone's bed? I will not be able to explain to them who I am or why I am in their house."

"Don't worry, you don't have to say anything. Just go in and lie down in an empty spot. When you wake up, come outside, and I will be here, waiting for you. I cannot sleep in the males' house. It is wrong, because . . . I am a *kekeni*[6] . . . *Khane-Ulato*[7] . . . and you a *memero*[8], you understand?" She stammered in embarrassment, forgetting the right English words. "I have already broken so many rules just by being with you. I can't be with a boy; you have not even passed the rite of passage[9] yet."

Ben understood. Everything was perfectly clear, even with the unknown words. He was a *memero*, and she was a *kekeni*, and they shouldn't spend the night in the same room, or in this case, barn. Although he did not know what the rite of passage was, the details weren't that important. Apparently, they had a certain ritual that every boy was supposed to undergo when they reached a certain age.

However, he also knew that he really didn't want to go alone into that barn, or *buambramra*, as she called it. The situation was ridiculous, but Emma understood his concern, and after a moment of hesitation, she took his hand and led him to another smaller structure, located at the far end of the village. She had already broken so many rules and traditions that day, she figured another violation wouldn't make a big difference. Emma followed him inside the hut, and they both fell to the floor lined with straw. But she stayed at the farthest corner away from him, to keep the last shred of decency, probably because of that obscure rite of passage, which Ben had not bothered to go through yet. But he didn't care much about her doubts and moral standards of the local tribe; he had sighed with relief and immediately fell asleep as soon as his head touched the floor.

Now Ben was lying on the ground looking at the bamboo ceiling, unable to get up without help. He was ready to cry for the umpteenth time in the past day, feeling lonely and helpless, abandoned by his parents and everyone else. His sad thoughts didn't last long, though, as Emma burst through the doorway with a jug in her hands.

"I brought you some water. I thought that you might want to wash up."

Ben looked at Emma, stunned. She stood in front of him, fresh, as if she had gone to sleep right after sunset and slept all night in the comfort of her bed rather than walking all night practically dragging him on her shoulders. She had washed up, changed her clothes, and put on her traditional straw skirt on top, painted her face, donned a few necklaces, and inserted some colorful feathers in her hair, replacing the ones she had lost in the river. Well, a woman is a woman at any age and everywhere on the globe!

She had also run to the creek and brought a jug of water for Ben. She helped him get up and poured water into his hands. The water was surprisingly cold. He freshened up a little and suddenly felt famished, remembering he had not eaten anything since the previous morning.

"Listen, can I drink this water?" he asked. He remembered the warnings of the travel agent not to drink tap water under any circumstances during their travel, but right now, thirst and hunger were stronger than his fear of potential stomach disorder.

"Yes, you can. This is good water," Emma assured him. "We have an underground spring nearby, where the water is clean, unlike the river.

Ben clung to the pitcher and drank half of it. The water was cold, delicious, and dulled the feeling of starvation. Never before had he drunk water so tasty. Life was beautiful again, although full of unpleasant and even absurd surprises.

"Well, what do we have planned for today?" Ben asked Emma cheerfully.

"Come on, let's go." She helped him up and led him out of the barn.

"Where are we going?"

"We are heading to our healer, our *docta*[10]. She will fix your legs."

They went out into the yard. Last night, or rather this morning, in the haze and darkness, he had not been able to see much of the village, and now looked around with great interest. It is not every day an urban man who has lived all his years in modern civilization gets an opportunity to enter an aboriginal primal system. Ben was interested in everything: from the run-down bamboo buildings to the tribal people, their way of life, unusual clothing, and often complete lack thereof. But the first thing that caught his eye was the painting covering the entire bodies and faces of almost every man, woman, and child. The colors—mostly red, yellow, and orange hues in many patterns—no doubt had certain meanings. Ben didn't know the real reason behind all that vibrant body art, and he felt as if he had suddenly walked into a circus arena filled with many clowns.

They crossed the courtyard accompanied by the local children under the gaze of male adults. The women of the tribe were occupied with household duties and had no time to scrutinize the strange white boy who had appeared in their village. The men, however, had plenty of time on their hands. The hunting season had yet to start, and there were no wars going on in the region, so most of them spent their free time shaping their hair into intricate styles, or coloring their faces and bodies. They looked curiously at the pale-skinned boy, and one even shouted something after them, though whether it was a question or a command, Ben couldn't tell. Emma did not bother to answer him, so Ben ignored him too, leaving her to determine the right course of action with her tribe-mates.

Ben hobbled after Emma, following her inside another hut that looked just like all the other houses in the village. Inside the hut, there was a creature of unknown gender and age with an extremely wrinkled face. It looked like a very old woman, but it could have just as easily been a middle-aged man.

This is probably a woman, Ben thought, but decided to leave it at that for now, as he didn't want to be rude asking Emma about the gender.

"Hello," Ben greeted in English, walking into the hut.

The old woman did not reply to his greeting; in fact, she did not even turn around. Emma said something in her incomprehensible dialect. This time, the woman turned her head halfway, replied back to her, and continued with her work. Emma pulled Ben inside the room and sat him down on a makeshift couch. Ben collapsed, grimacing in pain.

"This is Dzhamaya, our doctor," Emma introduced the old lady to him.

Because her name sounded feminine, Ben's thoughts about her gender were confirmed.

After a few minutes, she finally walked over to them. Dzhamaya looked at him, paused at the wound on the shoulder, and examined his knee. Then she knelt down and took off his sneaker from the other foot. She wasn't very gentle, and every touch was excruciatingly painful.

Ben gritted his teeth, trying not to cry in pain, and gripped the edge of the couch with both hands. Dzhamaya touched the swelling around his ankle and harshly pulled his foot, turning it slightly to the side. Ben was about to scream, but suddenly, he realized that

the pain was gone! Ben moved his foot about—nothing. It ached a little, but that was rather a residual discomfort. He tried to stand up, but immediately fell back on the couch crying, as a sharp pain pierced through his knee of the other leg. Dzhamaya pushed his pant leg up and felt the kneecap from all the sides, shaking her head doubtfully. She got up from the floor and rustled through some packages, opening jars and bottles, and finally returned with the necessary ingredients for the treatment. Ben was hoping for the same miracle with the second leg and was looking forward to a full recovery. He even began to plan his way back to his parents, who, he had no doubt, were waiting at the port or running through the jungle looking for him. But the miracle did not happen. His knee was still in severe pain after all her manipulations and even became worse. Her tenacious fingers pressed the swelling so hard that tears poured from his eyes. She soaked a piece of cloth in one of the jars with some herbal fragrance and applied the smelly wet bandage around the knee. The pain, which had been bearable so far, now felt as if someone had stuck a searing iron into his leg. Ben, of course, said nothing and sat, trying to hold back tears. But Dzhamaya hadn't finished her execution yet, and began mending the wound on his shoulder. The cut was deep and would bleed at each hand movement that detached the thin crust of gore formed atop the wound.

The ache in the cut was tolerable, and he hadn't paid much attention to it, since the pain in his legs eclipsed the discomfort in the shoulder. That wound could have waited until he got back home. But apparently, Dzhamaya thought otherwise.

He wanted to ask Dzhamaya (through Emma, of course) to leave it alone, as it was not that important right now, but it was too late. She heartlessly ripped off the scab of gore from the cut, and blood gushed down the shoulder. Ben had felt so much pain in the past day that it didn't even bother him anymore, and he only gritted his teeth harder. Another piece of cloth was soaked in the same jar and pressed against the wound. After a few seconds, however, the bleeding stopped and she removed the bandage. Once again, Ben thought that this would be the end of the treatment and was ready to get up, but Dzhamaya did something that put him into a cultural shock, which was even stronger than the physical shock from the pain. She took a pinch of ground wood from another jar, put it in her mouth, and began to slowly chew it. After she was satisfied with the consistency of the ingredients and had soaked it with enough saliva, she spat it out on the same bandage and re-applied it to the shoulder, while muttering some incomprehensible sounds.

"Hold this on your shoulder," Emma translated.

Ben wanted to rebel against the unhygienic treatment, but he didn't dare to argue and humbly held the patch with the "medicine" on his shoulder.

After finishing her saliva witchcraft, Dzhamaya broke into a passionate speech, talking to Emma. Despite her dark skin, Emma's face turned tomato red and she stormed out from the hut, grasping Ben by the sleeve and pulling him to the exit.

"Thank you," Ben said from the door, carried away by Emma.

But Dzhamaya lost interest in them and hurried back to her household duties.

"What did she say?" Ben asked when they got outside. They sat down on a fallen tree trunk, using it as a bench.

"That was nothing," Emma replied immediately, looking away. "She said that your knee will heal soon, and that it is nothing serious. It was just a minor twist, and some lubricant fluid has spilt inside your kneecap. But the swelling will be gone soon. She was more concerned about that deep cut on your shoulder. She worried that it might get infected and suggested to visit the doctor when you get home."

"I didn't ask about that. She said something else before we left. It was bad, wasn't it?"

"I said it was nothing. Don't worry about it." Emma lowered her eyes.

Obviously, she did not want to talk about it and Ben decided not to insist on the answer right now.

"By the way, what did she put in the bandage?"

"This is the tincture of sandalwood," Emma explained, delighted with the change of subject. "This tree is used for all of our medical needs, for almost every disease. The bark of that tree is ground into a powder, soaked, and applied to the wound. We also use the oil and sap from the tree. I don't know all the combinations, but Dzhamaya knows. She treats everything with the extracts of this wood."

"But was it necessary to chew it and spit it out on the bandage?" Ben looked at the compress with disgust, but left it on the shoulder.

"No, of course not. She could have also peed on it, but saliva works better. It is more viscous and holds the particles of wood together. It is also a good disinfectant and—"

"Okay, stop it. I got it now."

Ben frowned. He certainly didn't expect to see a modern medical facility here, with a wide variety of surgical instruments, first-aid kits, and an assortment of antiseptics and anesthetics, but this was too much. On the other hand, Dzhamaya had healed his leg really well and quick, so he had to give her some credit. Her treatment, despite Ben's doubts, had worked. Now, with one working leg, he could somehow limp back to the port. But the shoulder . . . He disgustedly removed the bandage and, seeing no trashcans around, threw it into the nearest bushes.

"So, what is your plan?" Ben asked. "I have to go back. My parents are probably going crazy looking for me."

Emma shook her head doubtfully.

"We are not going to make it back to the port. It is too far for you to walk. I usually take at least half a day when I go by myself, but with your sore foot, we would not be able to get there by daylight. Right now, half the day is already gone, so let's go tomorrow, early in the morning."

Ben was relieved to hear that she said "we." She would not let him go alone, but would accompany him back when he was ready. He had no idea where they were and how to get back. If necessary, of course, he would have found his way back, as he had noted some landmarks yesterday, but naturally, it would be a lot easier to go with Emma.

"I need to let my parents know that I'm okay."

"If you want, I can go to the port by myself. It will be much faster if I go without you."

"Oh, no, I am not going to stay here alone. Also, it is wrong to put my problems on you. You've already spent two days with me, and you probably have other important things to do."

"I have nothing important to do—Wait! I have an idea. We have a sheriff nearby."

"Sheriff? Is he like a policeman?" Ben asked.

"Yeah, a police officer. He has a phone and even this . . . thing. They call it a computer. From there, you can call to the port and tell your parents you're all right, if they are still in the port."

"Of course they are! Where else would they be? They will not leave me here," he said without hesitation. "Come on, show me how to get to this sheriff."

"You think you can walk?" she asked doubtfully. "He lives not very far, but not close enough for you to walk there with a hurt leg. I can go by myself if you want?"

"No, we will go together. I think I can make it. Listen . . ." Ben hesitated for a moment. "Do you have anything to eat? The last time I ate was yesterday morning."

"We probably have something, but I'm not sure if you will eat it. You Westerners are not used to our food. Actually . . . wait a minute."

Emma ran inside the hut nearby. A few minutes later, she returned with a woven shoulder sack.

"Interesting bag," Ben noted, looking at her unusual bulky bag, woven together from colored fibers of unknown origin.

"I wove it myself," boasted Emma. "It is called a *bilum*."

"Whoa, it's beautiful. What's in it . . . in this *bilum*?"

Emma pulled out a few warm tortillas and handed them to Ben. He looked at them suspiciously, twirling them in his hands, and even smelled them. The tortillas were gray and did not seem appealing.

"What is it?"

"This is *baum*. Eat it. Do not be afraid. This is as close to your kind of food as I could find. It is made of sago, a palm tree. Maybe you've heard of it?"

Botany was not his strong subject, but he still nodded his head. Ben remembered his father told them about this palm tree during dinner less than two days ago, but Ben hadn't cared about it then and hadn't really listened. He looked at the warm tortilla once again and confidently took a bite of it. It was soft and fluffy and tasted plain, slightly bitter, but quite edible.

"Sago is a very good, nutritious, and widely known tree," Emma continued. "We eat all parts of the tree: the leaves, the roots, and even the trunk. We take the roots, clean them, and chop into small pieces, then boil it, until it gets soft. It is very starchy. This tortilla that you eat now is made from the dough of the sago tree. You can even bake bread from it, but we usually don't."

"Why not?" Ben mumbled with his mouth full.

"We use breadfruit instead. It's not quite a bread, just the flesh of the fruit. Sometimes we eat it raw, or we bake it. Once baked, it becomes sweet and tastes even better. We even dry it to preserve some for the rainy season, when we don't have any food. But sago is still better. We also eat the larvae of worms that feed on fallen sago tree."

At these words, Ben stopped chewing and looked suspiciously at the rest of the tortilla.

"Do these tortillas also have worms?"

"No." Emma laughed. "We eat worms in whole, most of the time raw, but sometimes we roast them or even make soup with it. We have to eat meat, and these maggots are a very good meat replacement."

"So you don't have meat at all except these larvae or worms?"

"Of course we do, but not often, especially now. The heavy rain that we had recently, it caused all the animals to go into hiding. Some of them have gone to higher elevations. But there are many rats now. Their burrows have flooded with water, so they come out of their holes and it is easy to catch them."

"Why would you want to catch rats?" Ben was astonished.

"To eat them, of course! But we also eat other animals, like snakes and different types of lizards. We have huge lizards here. They have a lot of meat, especially in their tails. Maybe I can show you one when we go to the—"

"Wait a minute. I get the part about the lizards and even the snakes, but the rats? Is it possible to eat them?"

"Of course. Rat meat is no worse than boars, if you know how to prepare it. You see, it has to be cooked well. But rats are small, and if you cook them for too long they shrink, become even smaller, and their meat gets dry and chewy. The meat of a boar is better as it has a lot of fat and is much juicier, and you don't have to cook it for that long. But it tastes the same: a wild boar, rat, or deer."

As she mentioned fried rats, his appetite immediately died out. Ben opened his mouth to say that they should not eat rats, even when they are well-cooked because all rodents are major vectors of infection, but he decided not to. He had no right to give any advice to people if they had been eating such things for centuries. Maybe they had developed immunity to the infection transmitted by rats.

"Why don't you breed animals?" he asked instead. "Pigs, for example, or chickens."

"We breed pigs, chickens, and other animals, but we only eat them during the famine. When the hunting season begins, we do not touch the flock, and even add more into the pens. But in times of food shortage, like now, we have to use the stock of meat and vegetables from the garden."

"You have a garden here?"

"Yes. We grow our own vegetables: potatoes, carrots, and a lot of beans. By the way, I brought some for the road." Emma patted her voluminous bag. "We can have lunch in the woods on the way back."

"What did you bring?"

Emma pulled out a few weird-looking vegetables from the bag.

"What's that?" Ben took one vegetable from her hands and turned it over.

"This is sort of sweet potato. It is delicious, especially when baked. You will like it. Also, when we are in the woods, we can collect some *moga* for a snack. It's a kind of banana. We have plenty of food in the jungle, many fruits and tubers. I have an idea: let's do a bonfire and bake some yams."

"That is a good idea. We will make a picnic in the woods."

"What's a picnic?" Emma asked.

"Oh, I will explain it to you later. But can you start the fire?"

"Of course I can."

"Have you found the right pieces of dry wood?"

"I sure have." Emma smiled and handed Ben a box of matches.

"Well, then let's go!" Ben said, laughing.

Emma got up from the bench and wanted to help Ben get on his feet.

"I can do it myself," Ben told her, grunting, trying not to accidentally bend his injured leg at the knee.

They hadn't gone far beyond the village when they were suddenly confronted by a half-naked man decorated with a variety of bracelets and necklaces. He appeared in their path so suddenly, it was as if he rose from the ground. Most likely he had been hiding behind a tree. Emma screeched out in astonishment and backed away. Ben also tensed in anticipation of the next predicament. Emma's reaction puzzled him. She was all strained, and her face became as pale as her dark skin allowed.

The guy looked no different from the rest of her tribe-mates— similar paintings on his face, hair style, and necklaces. But Ben felt that something about him was different. He was obviously young, probably no more than sixteen years old, but despite his young age, he looked frightening. Maybe it was because he was wearing a huge boar fang through his nose, bent in the form of a crescent and hanging out on his upper lip like a mustache. With this nasal decoration, he looked scary, even ferocious, and when he spoke, the fang bounced up and down on his lip to the beat of his words. Although he had a frightening appearance, the bouncing fang was funny to Ben, but the last thing he wanted right now was to laugh. He was terrified. The guy was very well built: tall, strong, with the bumps of biceps and triceps on his arms, broad shoulders, and a slim waist. He looked like the New Guinean Apollo.

Meanwhile, Emma recovered from her fright caused by the sudden appearance of this scary-looking man on their path and started talking to him. Her voice was confident, with an authoritative tone. She was once again the same independent, self-willed girl Ben had known from the moment they met. Ben also calmed down, assuming he had nothing to worry about and Emma had everything under control. The man was listening to Emma and occasionally, even hesitantly, replied to her in a shy tone. But a couple of times, he glanced sullenly at Ben with an evil look. Obviously, they were talking about him, and the guy was unhappy with Ben's presence here. But Emma continued to talk to him angrily, stomping her foot, and Ben calmed down. He realized that there was no danger to him. They probably weren't even talking about him at all, but rather, about some tribal issues.

At first, he tried to listen to their conversation, but as he did not understand a single word, he started looking at the guy on the sly. Ben still had a very bad feeling about this guy. Something was wrong and bothered him a lot, but he couldn't understand his involuntary fear. Apparently it wasn't because of his muscles and strength, or even the fang sticking out of his nose. There was something else, something evil that chilled his blood and made goosebumps rise on his skin. Then it suddenly dawned on him, what terrified him all this time: it was his face. Specifically, it was the face paint. He was painted in evil-looking black and white, with white circles around the eyes and mouth, which made it look like the mask of death.

He's not from this tribe, Ben realized. For some reason, he did not like this fact at all.

The conversation was coming to an end. The guy expressed his concerns to Emma, and heard everything she had to say in her sarcastic tone. Then he left. Whatever they were talking about remained unclear to Ben, but he did not dare ask Emma about it.

"Come on," she ordered, and went forward, dragging him along.

When they went far ahead, and the guy had disappeared into the distance, Ben decided it was safe to talk to her.

"Who was that guy?" he asked.

"I'll tell you later," she muttered angrily. Ben didn't insist on an answer, as she obviously did not want to talk about it.

Emma seemed to have forgotten about his injured leg and quickly strode forward. Despite Dzhamaya's effort, his leg continued to hurt, and Ben was barely hobbling behind her, unable to keep up. After walking for about an hour in complete silence, Emma suddenly slowed down and let Ben catch up with her.

"That was Amal, my future *adawa-na*[11]," Emma finally broke the silence to explain.

"Who was?" Ben did not understand what she was talking about at first, preoccupied with his own thoughts.

"The guy we met earlier. He is my *adawa-na* and I am his *adawa-na*."

"What is an *adawa-na*? A husband?"

"Yes, *adawa-na* means a husband or wife."

"Are you going to marry him? Isn't it too early for you to get married?"

"That is why I said future *adawa-na*, husband," Emma said nervously.

"But why did he come? Did he miss you and just stopped by to see you? Tell me more, please."

"I don't want to talk about it. Not right now. I will tell you later, as we will be there soon."

Emma went silent again, continuing to march forward. But Ben decided to fill the silence with clarifying questions that had been bothering him all this time.

"Is this guy, Amal, from another tribe?" He started from afar.

"Yes, he is from Abaga. It is a tribe that lives high in the mountains."

"And what is your tribe name?"

"We are the Wagaba," Emma said proudly.

"Oh, okay. I get it. That's why his face paint looks different than yours."

"Why? You do not like my paint?"

"Are you kidding me? I like it very much. I love it! It is beautiful! Very colorful and . . . intriguing."

"Really? You liked it?" Emma's eyes gleamed. "I actually wanted to draw a butterfly, but I didn't have time to finish it. But don't worry, tomorrow I will complete the painting for sure."

Ben looked at her heavily painted face, with red and yellow tones and a touch of brown and orange. He remembered that she had woken up much earlier than him to freshen and decorate herself so she would look beautiful by the time he woke.

"So what does all of this coloring mean? There must be some kind of meaning behind it."

"There are no specific meanings, or rather, everyone's design has its own meaning. Some people paint themselves to imitate animals, so their strength and agility will pass on to them, while others do it to scare the evil spirit Kahua[12]. Some others, however, paint to intimidate enemies. I do it for beauty, because I like it and I think it is beautiful."

"You are right; it is very nice. Unfortunately, in my country, women do not paint their faces like that." He sighed. "So, what about Amal? What is his reason to paint the face? To intimidate or for beauty?"

"I do not know, probably to intimidate. Why do you ask?"

"Well, you know, he has a bit of an unusual coloring scheme: black and white. It's very ominous, unlike yours. You have beautiful, vibrant colors, but his, on the other hand, are kind of evil and scary-looking. I thought that . . . maybe it means something, like . . ." Ben paused for a second, trying to come up with a politically correct way of saying what was on his mind. "I thought maybe it was some kind of symbol of his belonging to the tribe of cannibals."

Ben remembered yesterday's conversation, when his father told the stories about cannibals. At that time, it had seemed like a joke to Ben, nothing more, and today, he regretted that he hadn't asked more questions about this terrible legacy of some members of humanity. He cursed himself for those inappropriate jokes that he had made, and even thought that all his misfortunes may be due to his impudence. Perhaps the evil spirit Kahua had punished him for these remarks. Or was it a mere coincidence? In any case, he had to find out about that for his own sake and peace of mind.

He looked at Emma's expression, afraid that she would be offended by his seditious thoughts, but she did not seem to be.

"What is a cannibal?" she asked.

"Well, cannibals are those who eat human flesh."

"Oh, that . . . no, I don't think so. It is unlikely—"

"You don't think so? But you do not deny such a possibility, right?"

"I do not know. I have never been in their tribe. I know that we have not eaten people for many years now."

"Did you mean your tribe or all the tribes in this country?" Ben insisted on finding an answer.

"In our tribe for sure, but in others . . . I just do not know. But I've heard that somewhere high in the mountains, in some tribes, they perform such rituals. We call these tribes the Highlanders."

"But you said that Amal also lived in the mountains?"

"Yes, well, sort of, but I do not know. Like I said, I have never been in their tribe before."

"And you are not even interested to find out if your fiancé eats people?"

Emma didn't reply. She shut her mouth tightly, like a clam seals its shell when a foreign object gets inside, and walked faster, leaving Ben behind again.

He realized that this conversation was unpleasant for her. Apparently, the subject of cannibalism bothered her less than her forthcoming marriage. To her, cannibalism was a known evil (or wasn't an evil at all). But marriage was much more complicated, confusing, and scary. Or perhaps it wasn't the marriage she was scared of as much as the candidate for marriage. Whatever it was, Ben decided to postpone the conversation until a later time.

His leg hurt from walking fast. Emma kept saying that the sheriff's house was very close. However, it was still quite far according to Ben's standards.

Ben realized by now that her measurement of space and time did not match with the widely known global standards. In his world, when a person says "close," they mean that the target is within a few blocks, and "soon" means a few minutes. But things were different in Emma's world. A close object could be located somewhere within a few miles, and the word soon seemed to mean that you could probably get there before dark. This time was no exception. Her "we will be there soon" dragged on for a few hours. However, this was partly Ben's fault because he couldn't walk fast enough.

150

The sheriff's cabin was suddenly visible after the next turn, in an open glade amongst the thickets. It was a well-built, strong wooden structure that looked like a hunting cabin, raised a few steps above the ground. The government property, of course, had to be protected from flooding and other natural disasters. Also, the sheriff would have weapons that must be secured from falling into the wrong hands. A humming noise was coming from a small shed behind the cabin.

This is probably the diesel that supplies electricity, Ben thought.

He guessed it right. The diesel engine provided the power to the cabin that had all means of communication. He spotted a satellite dish on the roof, with the label "IntelSat" on it. Ben perked up, as the satellite dish promised broadband in the cabin, which also meant the presence of communications with the rest of the world.

Emma helped Ben climb the stairs, and they went inside. He had expected to see something similar to a police station, with a large desk and various office supplies, room for the temporary detention of felons, and, of course, the armory securely fenced and locked behind bars with a heavy padlock. Instead, it was just a simple, though spacious, room with common household items, such as a couch, a dining table, and a couple of chairs—nothing like Ben imagined. There was also an adjacent room, perhaps a bedroom. That was all. No cage for criminals, no weapon room or other police attributes. Most likely they didn't even have felons here and there was no need to detain them; maybe they didn't even need a sheriff in the middle of the jungle.

But in fact, the sheriff was desperately needed here, and there was a good reason for the creation of such sheriff stations. The precedent was set by certain events that happened thirty years ago, and radically changed the way of local tribal life.

Chapter 2. Deeds of Bygone Days

The twentieth century marked an important historical event for Papua New Guinea. After nearly a century of colonization and endless administrative division in the mid-seventies, the western side of the island received long-awaited independence and began its emergence as a sovereign state. The young republic established a national parliament, which became the country's legislature, and their cabinet appointed executive and jurisdictive powers. They also adopted the first Constitution and established economic and diplomatic relations with various countries, which allowed them to become a member of the Commonwealth of Nations. Queen Elizabeth II, the head of the Commonwealth, or simply the Queen of Papua New Guinea, being the formal head of state, presented the proposal for the provision of humanitarian help to the young republic during the next Assembly of the Commonwealth. The assistance was primarily to uplift the indigenous population and ethnic minorities of the country who still lived in primitive settlements at the end of the twentieth century.

The initiative received wide support from almost all members of the Commonwealth, and soon it was accepted and approved. This initiative under the United Nations Development Program was named Foundation and had its own agenda and approved article expenditure budget. Several skeptics, however, opposed these initiatives, expressing concern that most of the budget would be spent on the bureaucratic structures inherent in the distribution of funds of such magnitude. Nonetheless, their voices were drowned out in the loud applause of enthusiastic supporters.

It was not that these skeptics were against providing help to the people in need. They just had doubts about the efficiency of such a program. Instead, they proposed a transfer of funds to the Red

Cross or similar organizations involved in humanitarian assistance. Their small mobile groups would deliver supplies directly to the tribal settlements. But the supporters of the new initiative reasonably argued that the money would be spent not only for the provision of aid, but also to create a strong infrastructure, allowing them to make regular deliveries of food and other essentials to the consumer. How else can goods be delivered, without a network of roads covering the vast span of the country? There are high mountains and impenetrable jungles and marshes, stretching across more than half a million square miles; this is not including adjacent islands scattered in the boundless sea. Also, the region had to be electrified, at least partially, and many schools for children, hospitals, and water treatment plants would have to be built. The Red Cross could not do that, as the scope of the proposed work was way beyond their competence.

"In ten years, you won't recognize this country," continued the supporters of the new initiative, "purified water, electricity, public education, health care, reduction of child mortality . . ."

It sounded impressive, and all skeptics quickly added their voices to the opinion of the majority. The Foundation for Assistance to the Ethnic Minorities, or simply the Foundation as it later became known, was formed.

As the Chinese adage goes: "Even the journey of a thousand miles begins with a first step." Such a step in the long journey of development was the construction of the Foundation's headquarters in the downtown of the nation's capital, the city of Port Moresby. It was a modern high-rise made of concrete and glass, located in the financial district on Paga Hill, with a stunning view of Walter Bay. The architects utilized this location by placing the oval conference room with tinted panoramic windows on the top floor. Such a room would be used by the Foundation's officials and upper management to conduct important business meetings. The management of this new initiative had to be on the top, in the literal and figurative sense of the word, and this beautiful oval office was best suited for this purpose.

Construction of the Foundation headquarters building was completed in record time. Following that, there was the ceremony of the red ribbon cutting, fiery speeches, and a standing ovation from the audience with press and television broadcasts. The Foundation started its official business. In the offices, telephones rang, faxes rustled, copiers, the most recent technological developments of that time, were shining and blinking with their colorful lights. Endless orders, regulations, decrees, and action plans flowed from the upper floors down to the lower. Subsequently, reports and presentations were going in the opposite direction. In general, these were the normal working days of any big corporation.

The first problem arose in the most unexpected area: human resources. The management of the Foundation realized that there was a catastrophic shortage of qualified specialists in practically all business areas: analysts, economists, financiers, and planners. Even though the country had three accredited universities, it was virtually impossible to find good professionals. They barely filled the most critical positions and even invited one business planner from Australia, offering him a decent salary, relocation package, and a significant discount for the construction materials for his new house in an elite neighborhood by the bay.

Young, talented specialists professionally approached the issues to be addressed. They placed a large, detailed map on the wall and divided the entire region into squares and sectors to determine the number of tribes living in each segment. Then they calculated the length of the communication stretch and possible delivery routes for humanitarian help. The overall picture came out unsightly: the majority of settlements in need of assistance lay scattered across the country and were located in remote, impenetrable areas. These facts were well known, but no one had bothered to look at the problem on a large scale, and now it appeared in all its complexity.

"How do you expect us to deliver humanitarian assistance to the people in such harsh conditions? We cannot even land a helicopter in most of these areas. Besides, it is not cost-effective to carry goods from one coast to another." The indignant workers of the Foundation kept complaining.

It was then decided to build regional branches, establishing the presence of the Foundation in close proximity to the potential consumer. It was also important to develop a chain of distributors for short-term storage and ease of delivery of goods directly into the forest villages to reduce extremely stretched communication lines. Construction of the two regional offices was started, one in the southern part of the island, in Arawa, Bougainville province, and the other on the east coast, in Madang. They were modestly smaller than the main headquarters, but still were modern high-rise buildings located in the business district. There also was a plan to build another branch in Lae later on.

Once again, tractors growled, cranes set to spinning their arms, and mixers roared to life, making concrete in barrels. The Madang branch began operations in record time. The Arawa office also rose quickly. At the same time, many warehouses were constructed, strategically placed along the coast for easy goods delivery by sea to the potential consumer. The construction of one such warehouse began in the vicinity of a regional office in Madang, on the wide strip of flat land near the jungles and close to the shore of the picturesque bay. This facility not only served its purpose, but it also created many jobs for people in Madang and nearby towns, reducing the high unemployment rate in the region.

The management of the Foundation also decided to develop a small town next to the warehouse facility for their employees. People should live closer to the place of their job and not have to travel to work from Madang. They formed a village with a few dozen houses. Each employee was given a piece of land big enough to build their own houses subsidized by the Foundation. The village even had plumbing, electricity, and telephone. In the near future, it was planned to add a few large-scale grocery stores and schools for the children of their workers.

Several years passed. The Foundation kept growing, branching out even farther. It spread throughout most of the key regions of the island from coast to coast. But suddenly, they bumped into yet another major roadblock. This time the problem was of a financial nature. One of the experts, the same analyst from Australia, after moving and settling in his new home, began to plan the further development of the Foundation and was surprised to find out that their budget was nearly exhausted. All the funds allocated for humanitarian aid had been spent on infrastructure and organizational needs. The news was as unexpected as it was unpleasant. Construction of the building in Arawa was in full swing and was almost completed. But the Lae branch that was supposed to oversee the operation of the southeastern region and an archipelago of islands had just been started. Warehouse facilities and adjoining village-satellites were in various stages of development, and many other planned activities awaited their implementation as well. It was necessary to take immediate measures to save the remainder of the budget and start sending humanitarian aid to the consumers. The next plenum of the Board of the Commonwealth of Nations would begin soon, and the Foundation officials had to report cost inquiries and show the results of their activities to justify the continued funding for the next reporting period. After long and heated debates, it was decided to freeze construction of warehouses with their adjoining villages and redeploy resources and remaining construction materials to complete the regional office in Arawa.

It was a pity, as the warehouses were much needed. Besides, employees of these facilities had already been moved from different cities and were camped in tents, waiting for their new homes to be built. Now they no longer had jobs, and their promised houses would never be seen. But often we have to sacrifice small to save something bigger, and the highest priority at that time was to start doing what the Foundation was created for: providing aid to the ethnic minorities in need. It just so happened that the small sacrifice for the good cause was that of the people, the laid-off workers of the company, and their hope for a new home and a better life.

Finally, the humanitarian aid went out to the tribal settlements. Containers stocked with food, household goods, and other essentials were sent to the consumers. The tribes who received the aid were located in easily accessible areas on the outskirts of the mountain, where they could be reached by horses and cars. The Foundation did build a few roads, one of which stretched from Madang to Goroka. It was no multi-lane highway, yet the road allowed for the delivery of aid by trucks to some of the remote mountainous areas.

However, even then, not everything went smoothly. It was impossible to provide necessary assistance to everybody at the same time, and delivery of humanitarian aid to one tribe caused envy and bitterness in others who had yet to receive it. Tribal conflicts broke out in that region. Those who did not get any aid attacked and looted the caravans loaded with goods, killing delivery workers. The tribes who lost their goods, in return, attacked the looting settlements. A vicious war broke out between both sides, with many human casualties. The authorities became very concerned with the surge of hostility between the tribes and decided to create a police patrol in the region to ensure order and peace. Thus came the sheriff.

The sheriff's stations, or rather small log cabins, were scattered throughout the vast expanses of the jungle, on the borders of the most violent tribes. These houses were electrified and equipped with the necessary means of communication with the police departments of the nearest city. The sheriff even had an arsenal of weapons to deal with violence, but in extreme cases, he could request military unit assistance. Fortunately, there was no need for such extreme measures, and the sheriff hardly ever used his weapons for anything other than hunting. The presence of the sheriff in the region stabilized the situation and minimized bloodshed. Most of the conflicts, once occurred, were quickly resolved in a peaceful, diplomatic way. His duties also included the preservation of protected areas from poachers, the issuance of hunting permits, and even the prevention of forest fires. The local tribes often came to him for advice in resolving contentious issues or just to kill some time chatting about life over a glass of wine.

The sheriff outposts had been created by the Foundation and were subsidized from their budget. Due to financial limitations, they were set up only in the most vulnerable areas, but in the other regions, conflicts and tribal wars are still going on even today.

There was another obvious merit of the Foundation that's worth mentioning. The management had suggested involving members of the tribes for the work of the Foundation. Who can do a better job than the people who are going to receive the aid? Obviously, the benefit of such collaboration was mutual. The Foundation received cheap labor, who would work in good faith, as they would be doing it for their own benefit, and the tribal residents, in addition to the humanitarian aid, would also receive a stable job and the money they sorely needed.

As a result, people from the various tribes, both men and women, came to the towns and villages where the distributors were located. There was plenty of work for everyone. Workers often had to visit regional offices in the city, and the Foundation introduced a new law on the compulsory wearing of clothes, so the tribal workers wouldn't shock the urban residents with their exotic attire, or rather the lack of it. Men replaced the harima-koteka covering their genitals with shorts. Women covered themselves with dresses and skirts. Gradually, they began to like the convenience of clothing, appreciating the capacity of pockets on their shorts. Women also liked the variety of colors for the fabrics of their dresses. But it took a few years before clothes became a habit. Today, almost all tribes located near major cities have abandoned their traditional style and adopted the wearing of more civilized clothes.

That was one of the Foundation's contributions to the development of the country. But what about the electrification of remote impenetrable regions, the construction of water treatment plants, schools, and hospitals that the local communities needed so badly? Absolutely nothing! None of those plans ever materialized. The tribes continued to drink bacteria-laden water from the rivers, but thanks to their centuries-old lifestyle, their immune systems protected them from deadly diseases, for the most part. Schools were not popular, since they didn't teach the kind of knowledge that was required to survive in the jungle. But the hospitals . . . Well, the situation with hospitals was somewhat different.

During the first years of operation, there was an attempt to create a medical facility for the local tribes. The Foundation rightly considered the provision of health care to the ethnic minorities as the highest priority, and soon, in the middle of the jungle, the first hospital was built. It was not an actual hospital, but rather a small medical clinic with a few beds and equipped with everything necessary to provide help for almost any medical emergency. They could have placed a cast on broken limbs, pulled out aching teeth, vaccinated against infectious diseases, and even delivered a baby—you never know what medical help one may need in the remote jungle.

The staff of the clinic consisted of three people: two medical students and a volunteer who had previously worked as a male nurse in a city hospital. It was conveniently located near several tame tribes who were in friendly relations with each other, therefore, the region was considered peaceful. The clinic was equipped with a radio; they could ask for any help from the main office, refill their medical supplies, or if necessary, even request a helicopter for patients with severe injuries.

A few months later, the medical department of the Foundation noticed that no one from the clinic's staff had ever contacted them for help, advice, or for the replenishment of supplies. The radio was silent and no one responded to calls made. Puzzled by such silence, they decided to conduct an inspection of the newly built clinic. When the inspectors arrived, they found an abandoned, partially demolished, looted house and the medical staff missing. The officials questioned the local tribes, but it was all to no avail. All attempts to find out anything about the employees of the clinic failed. The jungle kept its secrets well, and the inspectors had to go back with no results. Over time, the interest in this incident weakened, and soon it was completely forgotten, drowned in many other daily routines and concerns. The officials reported this incident to the police and wrote off lost assets. The medical department was switched to another line of the function.

This would have been the end of the story, but after a while, some new facts and unconfirmed rumors emerged. They were spread from mouth to mouth, acquiring new details as they went, and eventually reached the authorities. However, one could not use rumors to solve a police case, and there was no other evidence to support them other than the drunken chatter of one of the guys from a neighboring tribe. Of course, he denied everything when the police questioned him, and told them he had amnesia. In short, these rumors were summarized to the following:

The rain was pouring down hard, as always during this season, and the ground was soaking wet, but inside the *buambramra*, it was dry and warm. A few men were sitting around the fire with a pitcher full of homemade wine while sharing interesting stories with one another, boasting about their hunting exploits. They had nothing to do during the rain and were simply killing time with tales of hunting.

When they had run out of stories to tell, they started pestering one of the guys, a young man who was only sixteen years old. He had a strange, shiny object attached to his *sagyu*, which was a source of pride for him and envy of others. His fellow tribe-mates had noticed that object long ago and kept asking the boy about it, but he answered their inquiry vaguely that he traded it some time ago for the leg of a wild boar.

"What are you talking about? What boar?" hunters asked in surprise. "We haven't hunted for several months now."

But the boy was persistent in his answer. After a few cups of wine, they again pestered him with the same questions.

Those who have tried the local homemade wine might know its miraculous ability to loosen one's tongue. This wine is fermented out of passion fruit and sweetish breadfruit, along with kava extract that is also known as "drunken chili." To make the wine, the entire village—men, women, and even the children—chew the fruits and spit it into a clay pit. The resulting leaven mass is thoroughly mixed with water and the extract of kava to enhance the intoxicating effect, and poured into a large crock, which is then sealed with clay and buried deep in the ground for further fermentation under a constant temperature. After some time, they dig it out and filter the fermented mass to get good wine. It is strong, slightly tart, and bitter (due to the addition of kava), but it perfectly quenches the thirst on a hot day. This wine removes all internal barriers and unleashes the tongue of any grown man, but on the young boy not accustomed to the alcohol, it had the effect of a truth serum, and he began telling his story, wiping away the tears running down his cheeks as he spoke.

Strolling through the woods in search of some eatables for dinner, our young man came across a group of neighbors from a nearby tribe. He knew them very well, as the tribe was friendly and they often visited each other in their villages. They even occasionally hunted together, which is a sign of friendship and trust. After greeting each other, one of them told our young man that there was a newly opened medical clinic nearby that they wanted to visit, as it looked very suspicious.

"Can you imagine, they heal people just like our shaman," added another. "But they don't perform any rituals or ceremonies, yet people still get healed. They are probably some kind of *suangi*[13] doing their *sanguma*[14]. We want to go see what is actually going on there."

Our young man also went along, as he had become curious about this obvious witchcraft, and soon the group of men came to the clinic.

Except for curiosity, none of them had any medical conditions that needed to be treated, and the nurse, a young girl, was disappointed to learn that her help would not be needed. These visitors were a few of the first patients in the clinic, and she wanted to do something good for them. Suddenly she had a great idea: since the visitors were already here, at least they could get vaccinated. Eventually, she wanted to vaccinate the entire tribal population of the region to protect them from deadly diseases, but these few gentlemen could be the first in her plan.

The girl explained the need for preventive measures and the possible consequences from the horrible viruses, but, unfortunately, she made very little success due to the language barrier. She was an urban girl and spoke fluent Hiri Motu and decent English, but she didn't know any of the tribal dialects. She gestured to one of the men to lie face down and prepare for injection. He understood her instruction and lay on the couch, even though a bit surprised with such a strange request. The rest of his tribe-mates were waiting for further developments with great interest. The nurse filled the syringe with medicine and stuck it into his soft spot.

The young girl, a medical student at the University of Papua New Guinea in Port Moresby, passionately believed with all her young enthusiasm that her life wouldn't be wasted if she helped at least one person during her career. That's why she had chosen such an honorable and necessary profession for herself. After getting her diploma, she was going to go with the Doctors Without Borders, and, of course, she gladly accepted the invitation to hold an internship at this newly opened clinic in the jungle to help the people of her own country. Unfortunately, her dreams never came true.

Everything happened quickly. The "patient" clearly did not expect such a cunning and painful action from the girl. He jumped from the couch as if he had been stabbed. He growled ferociously while rubbing the pained buttock, grabbed his long *hagda* spear, shouting angrily "Suangi! Suangi!" and pierced the nurse all the way through her chest, forgetting to even ask her name before the killing. The name of a defeated enemy is as much of a trophy as their scalp or a skull. Alas, it is a tradition of these places.

The brave warrior finished the woman off and waved to the others to start the carnage. But they did not need any signal, as the slaughter of the other workers had already begun. The massacre was short and brutal, and after just a few minutes, none of the infirmary staff was left alive.

Then it was time to collect the spoils of war. In addition to the scalp and skull, under the category of trophies, came everything that was found in the clinic. They especially liked shiny stuff, including medical instruments and sharp objects in particular. One of the warriors with bloody hands immediately tried to attach the scalpel to the tip of his *hagda*. However, the testing of his modified spear immediately failed. The delicate medical instrument, not intended for such barbaric use, broke as soon as the spear hit the wall. But the "MacGyver" of that time was not disappointed with the outcome of the experiment, and with his infinite scientific resourcefulness decided that the scalpel would better fit in his lighter *servaru* spear, designed for close combat. The tip of such a spear is supposed to break inside the enemy. All scalpels and other sharp instruments were fairly divided amongst the participants, but the victim of the treacherous medic received a larger share in compensation for his damages. Our boy, who witnessed this tragedy, also had a trophy, even though he was not involved in the massacre. He got a pair of pliers for teeth removal. He did not know the purpose of this shiny thing, but gratefully accepted the gift.

They also found packages of pills and tried to eat some colorful tablets, licked a few creams, but did not like the bitter taste of it and threw away all the capsules, tablets, ampoules, and various ointments. The only thing that caught everyone's attention was a large bottle of Brilliant Green, which in those days, was widely considered an excellent antiseptic. The brave warriors tried to drink it but weren't impressed with the taste. However, they found another good use for it; this Brilliant Green was a perfect paint for the face and body art and harmoniously complemented the red-yellow-brownish color palette. There were no other faces in the entire region with such beautiful bright green tones. The paint that they used was made out of clay, with the additions of juices from different berries, therefore the dominant colors were mostly reddish. It is common to find brown, white, and even black clay, but a green one simply did not exist.

Besides the instruments and green dye, the warriors also snatched everything they saw, hoping to find a use for it later on. The medical clinic was completely looted.

The rest of the story our young man told by barely moving his tongue as the concentration of alcohol in his bloodstream already exceeded the limit. He was blubbering and sobbing while wiping tears, leaving dirty stripes on his face.

It was a bloody feast. His older friends were eating the bodies of the defeated enemy. Their brains were particularly valuable, because it stored the power of *suangi*, and each warrior strove to consume as much of this priceless flesh as possible. Now the spirit of the witch would dwell in them and they would also be given magic powers, knowledge, and strength.

They decided to bring the remains of the bodies to the tribe and share it with the rest of their tribe-mates. Obviously, they would have to sacrifice some meat to the spirits as gratitude for a good battle, and the elders, of course, would get the hearts of the victims, the best part. But every other man would also get a good chunk of meat. Even women and children could chew on some bones with offal and tripe. No doubt, today was a very lucky day.

As mentioned already, our boy was young and had only recently undergone the rite of passage to become a man. But he had not taken part in any wars and had never seen the death of a human before this day. He stood in the doorway watching this bloody tragedy with a pale face, not knowing what to do. But his older friends decided everything for him. They simply sent him back home, as they thought he unfairly wanted to get his share of the delicacies without participating in the battle. That was wrong. He already had a trophy they had given him from the goodness of their hearts, and that should be enough.

These were the last words the boy uttered. He suddenly stopped talking in the middle of a sentence, looked around the campfire with blurry eyes, and fell asleep. The faces of his listeners expressed nothing but regret that they had not been there instead of this young man. They would not have missed this opportunity. But this boy . . . well, he was too young. What can you expect from him?

These events happened in the late seventies. A few years later the sheriff's presence would be established in the region, and the government would officially classify cannibalism as a crime, introducing a new law that punishes such criminal acts. But at that time . . .

The next morning, the boy tormented by a terrible hangover, said that he had made the entire story up and continued to insist that he exchanged the shiny object for a boar's leg. So it remained unclear whether these events actually took place or were a figment of the imagination of an intoxicated young man.

Thus ended the attempt to provide medical assistance to the local tribes by the Foundation. People still heal themselves the way their ancestors did, sometimes very effectively, and a terrible epidemic that takes thousands of lives, or causes infant mortality, was just natural selection. Life is God's gift, and he can take it back at any time he wishes.

The Foundation exists to this day. However, the scope of their activities is not the same anymore, and financial aid from the United Nations Development Program was significantly reduced. Life dictates new goals and objectives, and the problems of the ethnic minorities of the region were pushed to the background as being less significant.

But we got a little distracted, and it is time to get back from the past, to our story.

Chapter 3. In The Meantime

Rays of sunlight broke through the dirty windows and warmed Margaret's face. She woke up and reluctantly opened her eyes. The day was in full swing. Rupert had already put a kitchen apron on, making breakfast along with the hostess. It was time to get up, but Margaret did not have any strength despite the night's rest. After yesterday's walk in the jungle, her body was indignantly resisting the slightest movement, and every muscle, every cell, was giving her a dull pain. But the thought that she would have to walk to the end of the yard to visit the lavatory, a hole in the floor instead of the clean white toilet bowl she was used to, made her groan. She'd already had the pleasure of visiting this masterpiece of local architecture yesterday, and the memories of that were etched in her mind forever.

Last night they came home quite late, but nobody knew the actual time. In fact, they had lost track of it long ago despite the expensive Rolex on Rupert's wrist. He had flatly refused to adjust his watch for a few weeks of vacation.

"How difficult could it be to calculate the local time? It's not rocket science," Rupert had assured his family. But in reality, it turned out to be a lot more complicated than he expected.

The Australian continent spans across three zones. They were sitting at the Sydney airport, located on the east coast, and while waiting for their connecting flight to Perth, the city of his aunt's residence, Rupert decided to calculate the local time. He surprised everyone with a good knowledge of the Coordinated Universal Time offset and tried to explain it to Ben.

"Listen up, Ben. This city is ten hours ahead of the prime meridian, or the Greenwich Mean Time. We flew from New York going west, and, therefore, crossed only ten zones instead of the fourteen it would have been if we were flying to the east."

He looked at his watch and instantly calculated the local time. But, to his astonishment, he noticed that the results of his computation differed with the time shown on the digital clock at the terminal by two hours. At first, Rupert was surprised by this fact, but then he slapped himself on the forehead and laughed at his stupidity.

"Well, of course! You see, Son, how easy it is to make a mistake? I added the number of zones between the two locations to our home time, without considering the actual time zone of New York and Sydney. Hence the error by two hours. Perhaps it is easier to add zones to Universal Time Coordinate that shows the leading or lagging times from Greenwich. Got it?"

Ben looked indifferently at his father and increased the volume on his music player. He had no interest in the Australian time zones. His iPhone instantly displayed the local time as soon as they got out of the plane, and the rest of it did not matter to him. But it mattered to Rupert, and he continued.

"We are now ten hours ahead of the Greenwich Meridian, but New York is five hours behind. Let's add fifteen hours to our home time, and now should be . . ."

He looked again at the billboard and realized that he had made another mistake. However, his calculations showed serious improvement, as he was mistaken by only one hour. After that he didn't include family members in his computation. He sat staring at the floor and moving his lips silently, while trying to figure out the root cause of his error. Unfortunately, he had to stop it soon after, as they had to board the plane to Perth. However, the trouble with the time zones didn't go away, but became even worse.

Having flown from the Australian east coast to the west, where the town of Perth is located, they got two time zones closer to Greenwich, complicating Rupert's calculations even further. Besides, Australia had already set their clock back to the winter Daylight Saving Time, while New York had advanced one hour to the summer time (which caused the two hours difference in his calculation). At this point, Rupert realized that he was completely lost and stopped looking at the watch.

But the situation worsened every day. His caring aunt tried to diversify their vacation and booked a variety of tours around the country for them. One such tour was in the central Australian time zone one hour ahead of Perth, in the beautiful city of Adelaide. They spent a few days in the resort but barely adjusted to the new time, as they had to go back to Perth. A few days later they went on the cruise, departing from Cairns, which is also on the central time but in northern Australia. Unlike Adelaide, Cairns doesn't have Daylight Saving, as, like other cities in the equatorial region, the sun rises throughout the year at the same time.

This was the last drop in Rupert's cup of patience and he finally gave up. However, another drop was added to his already full cup after which he would have gladly broken it if it had physically existed. While they were on the cruise, the captain said that Papua New Guinea and the Solomon Islands archipelago spans across multiple time zones, but to avoid any confusion, they would not change the clock on the ship and all scheduled excursions would be held strictly by Cairns time.

Now try to figure out by looking at your watch, what time it is in Papua New Guinea, in the province of Madang, if the time there is an hour behind the ship's time but Cairns is fifteen hours ahead of New York. Oh, and don't forget to include Daylight Saving offset to your calculations.

It was very late when Rupert and Margaret reached the house of the compassionate woman who had offered them temporary shelter. They didn't know what time it was although they had assumed it was around midnight. They had traveled for what felt like many hours.

The house was simple but surprisingly clean. There were two small rooms with unpretentious furniture and the kitchen, separated from the living room by a curtain. Margaret sat down wearily. The day had been hard, stressful, and felt infinitely long. She was tired, but most of all, she wanted a shower, or at least to wash and change into clean clothes. After the hike in the jungle, her whole body was covered with sticky sweat mixed with dust and webs they had to walk through. She had no energy left to even get up from her chair. Rupert brought their luggage into the room and placed it such that the suitcases didn't block the entrance. This room was too small and not meant for guests with so many belongings. He pushed the suitcases into the free space under the bed and approached Margaret.

"Do you want to freshen up a little?" he asked, as if he was reading her thoughts.

She nodded gratefully, and Rupert went to the hostess to find out about the restroom and amenities. The toilet was in a small outhouse in the yard. A weak light illuminated the narrow gravel path that led to it and barely reached the far corner of the yard. Although the lighting was poor, it was nearly impossible to miss the bathroom—a strong odor of sewage, mixed with some disinfectants, could be identified from afar. Margaret opened the door and boldly stepped forward. The awful smell struck her nose so hard that she immediately jumped out, unable to breathe.

"I can't," she sobbed. "I just can't."

"Well, my dear, it is not as bad as it looks . . . and smells," Rupert reassured her. "If you want, I'll go first."

Rupert stepped inside and indeed stayed there long enough to address nature's call.

"Well, I've seen worse," he said, coming out of the toilet. "It's a little . . . hmmm . . . unusual, but not deadly. Your turn, madam."

He jokingly bowed his head, pointing toward the open door. Margaret realized that she would have to go in there sooner or later, and she submissively stepped inside.

Washing their hands had also become a newly acquired experience for them. The washbasin was a small metal cylinder filled with water and nailed to the wall of the house. To get the water running all you had to do was push up the conical stick at the bottom, and when you're done, let go of it and the water stops. Everything was simple and clear. Margaret had seen one just like that earlier in a movie about a Third World country, but she had naively believed that this device was connected to the plumbing. They didn't show in the movie that this basin had to be manually filled before use and the bucket with sewage underneath had to be emptied in a special pit after it was full.

Despite the simplicity of this device, it got the job done, and soon Margaret and Rupert had freshened up and walked back into the house. They even got a clean towel from their hostess. Margaret made the last steps dragging her feet, completely exhausted. She forgot about the shower, her missing son, and everything else in the world, wishing only to reach the bed.

That evening, however, they had another unexpected difficulty to overcome, which, to Margaret, was an even bigger challenge than the unsanitary toilet and the outlandish washbasin. When they entered the room, two aluminum bowls with steaming hot dinner were already on the table, waiting for them. Rupert knew his wife very well. He was familiar with all of her oddities and quirks, one of which was an obsession for clean, sterile tableware.

"Dishes should squeak," Margaret kept telling Ben and Rupert, meticulously examining the washed plates, on the rare occasions when they did housework. "If you wipe the dishes and the ceramic does not squeak, that means a layer of fat and grime is still on the plate."

Rupert and Ben were aware of her obsession and tried to finish washing the dishes before she got home. But when Margaret served supper, she would carefully examine each piece of tableware, and "suspicious" plates, cups, and glasses went back to the sink. She did the same thing in restaurants, making waiters change the table cutlery several times, and even at their friends' houses. Close friends who had known her for a long time were accustomed to her compulsion, but new people were sometimes offended.

And now she was offered dinner in an aluminum bowl that had been quickly rinsed in a bucket of cold water. Margaret looked at the bowl suspiciously, carefully took a sticky spoon with two fingers, and skeptically examined it. She also looked doubtfully at the contents of the bowl.

"Eat your dinner," their hostess said sternly. "You need to have energy. How are you going to find your son without food?"

Margaret lay the spoon aside.

"Do you happen to have a cup of tea?" she asked. "I am so tired that I can't eat anything. But I would love to drink some tea."

She found a good excuse, Rupert thought. He knew that Margaret wouldn't eat here, and was interested to see how she would get out of this situation without offending this kind old woman.

"Of course I do! I have a great tea." The hostess smiled.

"But I will eat the dinner if you don't mind. Thank you, ma'am. I haven't had any food since breakfast." Rupert cheerfully sat down at the table. He would rather skip dinner as well, but he didn't want to offend the woman. She also had a long, hard day at the port market, selling souvenirs to the tourists and probably hadn't had dinner yet either, preparing food for her guests instead. He was eating whatever was in his bowl, spoon after spoon, without looking at it, until he finished everything. He was afraid that he could not eat it if he looked at it. But actually, it was quite edible. Dinner was beans with chunks of unknown steamed vegetables.

The hostess put two mugs with hot tea on the table. Margaret took hers and inhaled the fragrant steam billowing from the cup, took a sip, and reasonably decided that the hot water would disinfect the cup anyway. The tea was surprisingly good and pungent with the smell of fragrant herbs.

"Your tea is very aromatic and tasty," complimented Margaret. "What kind of tea is it?"

"This is a good tea, brewed with herbs." The hostess smiled. "I picked the wildflower leaves and dried them myself."

Margaret sipped the tea, holding the cup with both hands. Her eyes were closing involuntarily, as she was on her last drop of energy.

"I think you better go to sleep," the old woman said. She led them into the room, pulled out an old sofa bed, and put clean sheets on it. A minute later, Margaret and Rupert were sound asleep.

Now, the next morning, Margaret lay in bed, squinting at the beam of sunlight shining through the window and didn't want to move. But she realized that sooner or later she would have to get up, do her morning routine with the obligatory visit to that awful bathroom, and then go search for Ben. She would probably even have to go back to that horrible jungle again. Thoughts about Ben woke her up completely, and she briskly got up and got dressed. The first steps she made with difficulty and yielded a dull pain over every inch of her body. But after a couple of minutes, she overcame her pain and strode toward the restroom. The second visit to this unsanitary facility didn't frighten her as much, and she bravely stepped inside.

Having finished her morning routine, she returned to the house, and Rupert put a plate with breakfast in front of her. Margret hesitated only for a moment, and then resolutely stuck a spoon in her meal without further doubts, anxious to start looking for her son again. She needed energy right now, and her principles and obsessions would have to be put aside until better times. The breakfast turned out to be yesterday's dinner, but now wasn't the time for gourmet dishes. She instinctively swallowed the contents of her plate and washed it down with an aromatic cup of hot tea. After breakfast they changed into comfortable clothes and shoes in case they would have to go back to the jungle, thanked the old woman for her hospitality, and went outside.

Coming out of the house, they looked around and stopped in shock. They hadn't noticed anything around them the previous day after returning to the village exhausted and stressed. Besides, it was already too dark. The dim light coming from the solitary lamppost in the square had been barely enough to illuminate a small circle around the pole. Beyond that spot, there was total darkness, lit only by a dim glimmer of moonlight.

Today, in broad daylight, the village appeared before them in all its squalor. Margaret and Rupert were astonished by the changes that had occurred. Yesterday's arrival of the ship had brought to the shore excitement, music, and fun, but when the ship with the tourists left, the holiday spirit and festivities went away with it. The array of bright colors seen on yesterday's waterfront had disappeared. Vendors had packed all unsold goods in bags, disassembled their stalls and chutes, and took them home. The only thing left behind was a pile of debris and garbage that lay motionless, held down by the weight of the heavy, humid air. The single store in the village, where Ben had wanted to buy something edible yesterday, was now closed. The restaurant in the street was empty, with only sticky lumps of ash left behind in the barbeque grill. Empty outdoor chairs and tables were chained together and locked. The dirt and grinding poverty of this place revealed all their ugliness. Just beyond the port area was the dusty and dirty street with a few dozen huddled shacks on both sides winding through the village. The houses seemed to be put together with any material that one could find: logs, trim boards, roofing tar, tiles, and even bricks. In fact, it was true. The entire village had been hastily built from everything that the residents could get their hands on. This was also a result of the professional activities of the Foundation. This settlement, like many others scattered over the country, had been established by the Foundation, but also thanks to them, ended up on the verge of poverty.

These villages were created for the workers of the warehouses, in the early seventies, when the Foundation was at the apogee of its development. People, tired from endless unemployment, enthusiastically accepted the jobs offered by the Foundation and moved with their families to remote, uninhabited places. They started building these houses for themselves, buying the building materials from the Foundation at a discounted price. In the developing village, people pitched tents while building new housing, but these temporary difficulties did not bother them. They planned to complete construction before the rainy season started, and a few months of living in a tent wasn't too much of a problem, given the warm tropical climate. The prospects for the future were optimistic. The intention was to build a settlement of fifty houses immediately, and later, the plan was to double the size of the village, and build schools and shops. The young settlement was already connected to the water plumbing, electricity, and telephone lines. Water, however, was not yet brought into the individual houses, but to the hydrant on the street though the management had promised to pipe water to every home after the construction of the entire village was completed.

But suddenly, all hopes for a blissful future disappeared like dust in the wind. One morning, someone noticed that the construction of the large warehouse behind the village had stopped. Workers did not come to work, construction equipment was gone, and the quietness was broken only by the singing of the birds in the jungle. After the second day of silence, the workers were notified that the construction of the village was halted indefinitely, and the staff of this new warehouse facility was laid off due to the freezing of the project.

When, a few weeks later, the Foundation's management sent down transportation to transfer the remaining lumber to another job site, it was all gone. The angry former employees of the Foundation pilfered all the construction materials they could find to complete their homes and finally move under their own roofs. They also dismantled and carried away the partially built warehouse, the remains of which to this day stand on the outskirts of the village, as a monument to the indifference towards human fate.

Fate, however, was different for everybody. Young people returned to the city to start a new life with a clean slate, but others remained in the village, surviving with fishing and hunting. The village became quiet. There were no more sounds of dogs barking or children's laughter— the main indicator of the well-being of any inhabited locality. Half of the houses were abandoned, gaping with broken doors and shattered windows, and remained empty for another quarter century.

However, this village was much more fortunate than a dozen others scattered throughout the country that were destined to languish in poverty forever. Thanks to the recently opened cruise line, it had been given yet another chance. Someone in upper management had decided to make this place a destination for cruise ships. At first glance, it would make more sense to route ships to Madang, which was already equipped with large docks, but the alternative suggestion turned out to be a wise and far-sighted decision.

Madang is a major seaport, an important hub for maritime transportation for all of Southeast Asia. Cargo ships and barges come there from around the world. But it was not suitable at all for cruise ships filled with tourists, who paid a lot of money for their trip. Long piers tightly packed with containers, incessantly moving cranes, big rigs, and trailers scurrying back and forth, is quite the contrary image to the vacationer. They prefer a picturesque destination with sandy beaches and cerulean water instead of industrial scenery. Then someone remembered this village, which was perfect for tourism. It was located on the banks of a breathtaking bay, enclosed on both sides with the cape jutting far into the sea, forming a secluded lagoon. Tourists could participate in any water sports activities on the mirror-like sea surface, without harsh waves, or simply enjoy the white sand beaches and the azure water. Also, the bay was deep enough for large ships to come in. Considering all this, it was decided to direct the flow of tourists to this small waterfront village. But if someone desired to visit the city, the cruise company provided excursion tours to Madang.

It also cost little to bring the needed improvements to the village. There already was electricity, water supply, a telephone line, and even an asphalt road connecting the village to the city. All they had to do was reinforce the docks, pave a small waterfront area, and build a facility for the port officials. It was decided to not spend money on any improvements outside the plaza and instead build a gift shop and a restaurant near the embankment, which would bring additional revenue to the community.

So the cruise company had decided the fate of this village, which now proudly called itself a port. Since the first ship filled with avid tourists entered the quay, the welfare of the villagers significantly improved. They had found a way to make money from these tourists. People from other less fortunate villages around moved toward the boomtown, occupying empty houses. The village became alive again.

Obviously, Rupert and Margaret did not know the history of this place, and they were horrified. Of course, they realized that this was no Manhattan, and did not expect the living conditions here to be like the Western countries, but the poverty around was still striking. They also did not know that this "revived" village was actually an example of prosperity amongst similar small settlements around the country.

They were walking along the street, squinting as the bright equatorial sun shone right in their eyes. The village was empty, except for a few chickens scrambling about the dust on the roadside, in hope of finding some seeds. The villagers were hiding from the midday tropical heat in the comfort of their homes.

Rupert and Margaret had no idea where to go, what to do, or whom to ask for help. As always, Rupert came up with a bright idea first.

"Margaret, do you remember yesterday, when you—" he paused for a second, searching for a neutral word, remembering how she had clung to the driver's shirt like a wild cat, "—persuaded Hubert, our bus driver, to return to the forest? I think there was a policeman standing there. I am sure I saw one in the crowd. I suggest we go back to the harbor and ask the police for help."

The idea was sensible, so they turned around and briskly walked to the main plaza. The two-story building where the police station was located, along with the other port officials, was closed, with a huge padlock on the door. All services were opened just before the arrival of a ship, and the doors closed immediately after the last tourist left the wharf, until the next time.

"Well, so much for that idea." Rupert shrugged.

Suddenly he slapped his forehead.

"The telephone!" he exclaimed. "All we need is a phone!"

"Would you also like an Internet connection, a fax machine, and a dedicated satellite radio frequency?" Margaret sarcastically joked. "Do you think that they have a phone here?"

"Of course they do!" he replied with confidence. "At the post office. There must be one around here, not necessarily at the port, but somewhere in the village, or even in the town nearby. They have to have some sort of communication. But I do not know where to go exactly. Come on, let's ask our hostess."

Even the most absurd idea would have been better than nothing at this point, if it gave birth to hope. Besides, this idea was not absurd at all. They turned around and went back to the place of their temporary residence.

"Ma'am!" Rupert called out. "Do you have a post office in the village?"

"Of course we do," the hostess replied without stopping her housework.

"Do you know if they have a phone there?"

"Of course there is a telephone. Why wouldn't there be one?"

"Does it work?"

"Of course it works. Why shouldn't it work?" she said calmly. "Most likely it does."

"So where is it, then?"

"What do you mean, where?" she was surprised. "It is right down the street."

Rupert and Margaret looked at each other. They had almost reached the end of the village and hadn't seen anything that resembled a post office. But they decided to walk around once again.

They walked along the street once again, and this time, they keenly looked at all the houses on both sides, and almost missed it again. At the last moment, Rupert saw something that caught his attention as they walked past the post office. Unlike the other houses in the village, this one was built slightly higher off the ground, with a few short steps leading to the front door. It was the same rickety shack, hastily built out of different lumber and other materials, but two concrete steps differentiated this structure from the others.

"This is government property, and they have to take good care of it," Rupert said sarcastically. He ran up the stairs and opened the entrance door.

"Wait, what if no one speaks English here? How would we explain to them what we need?" Margaret suddenly hesitated. "Maybe we should have asked our hostess to come along."

But it was too late for doubts, as Rupert had already stepped inside. An old woman came out of the back.

"Did you want to make a phone call?" she asked them.

Rupert had already prepared a speech, but now he was shocked. He was unaware that the entire village knew about the previous day's events. Tourists, especially children, don't go missing often in here, and the appearance of a white couple in the post office was an obvious connection to these events.

Contrary to Margaret's fears, the woman spoke decent English, slightly influenced by the local dialect.

"Yes, if we may," Rupert replied, happy that there was no problem communicating with the postal worker. "We really need to use the phone. I am sorry, I didn't catch your name."

"You never caught it because you never asked me for it." The old lady smiled. "My name is Beida."

"Thank you, Beida. May we use your phone, please? I will pay you for the call, of course."

He pulled a bill from his wallet without even looking at the value, although he knew it was a large denomination. He thought it wasn't the right time or circumstance to be cheap. Beida took the bill.

"What number should I dial?" she asked.

Margaret and Rupert looked at each other. They had no idea whom to contact. As always, Rupert came up with a solution.

"We need to call the cruise ship company. The captain promised to assist us in the search for our son."

The postwoman nodded.

"Okay, just give me the phone number."

"Ah, you see, we do not know the number. I thought maybe you could somehow find out by calling the directory, or by looking in the telephone book?" He told her the name of the company.

"Okay, sit down and wait." Beida pointed to a couple of chairs in the corner and went out to the next room.

The search for the phone number took about half an hour, but eventually, she handed Rupert a piece of paper with the number on it.

"I've already placed a call for you. Expect a call back from them within an hour."

"What do you mean 'call back'?" Margaret exclaimed impatiently.

"We do not have direct access to the international line. Normally, we call through Port Moresby, and they will call us back, usually within an hour, once the other party responds."

"Within an hour? Can they call sooner?"

"An hour should be fine, Beida. It's okay," Rupert said. "We are no longer in a rush, Margaret. There is nothing we can do to speed it up, so we will wait."

Rupert made himself comfortable on the chair and began waiting.

They called sooner. Within less than half an hour, Rupert was talking to a customer service representative. A soft, feminine voice with an Australian accent (it would be strange to hear any other accent here, like a Texan one) thanked him for choosing this company for their vacation and warned that the conversation would be recorded for training purposes.

"What is your first and last name?" the girl asked.

"Rupert Pearson, but I am actually calling about my son, Benjamin Pearson."

"How can I help you, Mr. Pearson?" she finally came to the point after she recorded their personal information.

"You see," Rupert started, "we lost our son."

"During the cruise?"

"Yes, during the stop in Madang."

"Did the incident occur due to the fault of our company?" Rupert heard the audible noises of her typing through the phone.

"No, it wasn't the company's fault. We booked an excursion into the jungle and—"

"Did you book a tour through our excursion desk or through a private party on the shore?"

"On the ship, but—"

"So, the incident occurred due to the fault of the services provider," she summarized. Her fingers typed on the keyboard even faster.

"I already told you it was no one's fault. Our son accidentally walked to the edge of the cliff and fell down. There is no one to blame for his negligence but himself."

"Don't say that," the girl on the other end of the line replied. "All excursion providers with whom we do our business must comply with the basic safety rules during the tours and take good care of the tourists under our mutual contract. All dangerous areas should be properly fenced and equipped with warning signs and posters. Failure to follow these basic safety rules leads to this kind of incident. Isn't this true, Mr. Pearson?"

"Well, perhaps you're right." Rupert had to agree with her logic.

"I want to assure you, we will conduct a thorough investigation and take all measures to prevent further incidents—"

"Wait!" Rupert interrupted her. "I agree with what you just said about safety and precaution measures, but I lost my son on this island. He fell into the abyss, and we must—"

"Yes, of course, Mr. Pearson. I'm sorry. Let me see what we can do for you."

The girl put him on hold and music began to play. Rupert nervously drummed his fingers on the table. After a few minutes, the music was switched back to the girl's voice.

"All right, Mr. Pearson," she said, her voice filled with glee. "Your case is a good example of the importance of protecting yourself before the trip and the need to always buy insurance. I checked your policy, and your insurance fully covers all the costs associated with the medical expenses, including, if necessary, transportation by helicopter from remote areas. And in the case of death of the insured, we cover all the expenses pertaining to the delivery of the body to your preferred location for the burial and the ritual services. The funeral will also—"

"What!" exploded Rupert. "What the hell are you talking about? What ritual services? What burial?"

Margaret overheard Rupert's last words and got up from her chair. Her face turned pale. Rupert realized that she would misinterpret his words, and he gestured reassuringly that everything was fine, and continued in a normal tone.

"Listen, I didn't ask for any compensation. I simply want to find my son. He is lost in the jungle and we desperately need your help to find him."

"But how can I possibly help you with that from over here?"

"Can you contact the captain? He promised to send a rescue team. We're stuck here and cannot leave until we find our son."

"I'm sorry, but we do not have a direct connection with our fleet."

"Is there anyone who can contact them? Better yet, connect me with your supervisor; maybe he knows how to call the captain."

"There is no one at our help desk who can call the ship. We are here to help our customers to solve their problems, but we don't get involved in operations."

"But I have a problem! Help me solve it!" Rupert raised his voice again, losing his temper.

"You can try to contact our cruise representative at the port and they will coordinate the search for your son with the local authorities."

"We tried that already," muttered Rupert. "Who else can I contact for help?"

"I don't know, but I can connect you to our central operator. Maybe he will redirect you to the right party."

"Okay, please transfer me."

"You got it. I am transferring you to the operator," her voice quivered. "Thank you once again for choosing our company for your vacation."

He heard another click on the phone, and the music played again.

A mechanical voice was telling him that due to a large number of callers the waiting time was approximately twenty minutes. However, it was only a minute later that something clicked again, and the music was replaced by a continuous beep. The call had dropped. Rupert slammed the phone down so hard that the old woman heard it from the other room. Beida wanted to say something reproachful to him but didn't out of respect for their grief.

"Can you please call the same number again?" Rupert asked, handing the woman another bill. "The call was abruptly disconnected."

Beida nodded and dialed the number once again. But this time she did not take the money. Suddenly Margret, who was staring blankly out the window, got up and pulled Rupert out of the post office.

"Thank you, Beida, but we do not need to call anyone. It's just a waste of time," Margaret said to the woman over her shoulder while walking out the door.

"Thank you," Rupert also said as Margaret pulled him out.

They came out on the street. The sun already hid behind the treetops as the day was coming to an end, but they still had no idea what to do or how to find Ben.

Chapter 4. Computer Genius

"Emma!" the sheriff exclaimed, surprised. "I'm so glad to see you."

"I'm glad to see you too, Uncle Sai," Emma replied.

"Unfortunately, you don't spoil me with your visits often. What brought you here? Just don't tell me you missed me." He smiled broadly.

"Of course I missed you!" Emma didn't get the humor, as she seemed to take everything seriously. "But right now, we came to ask you for help. I want you to meet Ben."

Emma pushed Ben forward.

"Well, hello, Ben." The sheriff stretched out his hand to Ben for a handshake.

"Hello," Ben said shyly, stealthily eyeing the sheriff while shaking hands. The sheriff was a strong, muscular man with a firm handshake. He was not too old, but his face was weathered by the tropical heat.

"So, Ben, what brought you to our woods?"

Ben opened his mouth to narrate his misadventures, but Emma stepped forward and started telling Ben's story, assuming the role of an interpreter. There was no need for translation as the sheriff spoke Tok Pisin, a language similar to English, occasionally also inserting English words and phrases. Sometimes Ben had to guess the meaning of the entire sentence, as some words did not make any sense; but it wasn't a problem. Overall, the conversation was going fluently, and both parties understood each other fairly well.

"You know, I heard about this story; rumors that one passenger got lost in the forest and missed the ship. So are you that lost boy?"

"Yes, that's me," Ben confirmed.

"How did you get lost? Did you go to the jungle alone?"

"No, I fell off the cliff chasing some . . . monkey or something. I am not sure what that animal was, as I could not get too close to it."

"Well, at least you survived the fall and are still alive, and that's most important. So, why don't you ask Emma to walk you back? The port is not that far from her."

"Yes, I know." Ben smiled. "We can get there in a half a day or so."

"Ben cannot walk fast." Emma jumped into the conversation again. "He has hurt both legs and walks slowly. It will take him a whole day to get there, and his parents are worrying. We need to let them know that he is okay and will be back tomorrow. I thought you could help him by calling the port."

The sheriff frowned.

"I'd love to help, but I don't have a phone."

"You don't? But Emma told me you have a phone and even a computer," Ben said.

"I have a computer, but not a phone, sorry. I also have a radio, and I could have contacted your ship, but it does not work. The batteries died about a month ago. I will go to Madang to get the new set of batteries next week, but right now, it is completely dead."

"That's just great! Now what?" Ben sighed. "How about the computer? Don't tell me it doesn't work either."

"You are right! It's also broken." The sheriff laughed. "You see, Ben, we are not very comfortable with all this equipment, especially with the computers."

"What happened to your computer?"

"What happened . . . hmm. I don't even know, to be honest. I'm not good at it, as I said. I tried to learn it, but I am too old for computers and wasn't too successful. At first it worked, and then stopped, the screen froze. There was a blue screen with random letters, numbers, and—"

"Ah, the blue screen of death. Can I look at it?"

"Are you well-versed with computers?"

"Yes, I know computers a little bit." Ben smiled.

"Well then, of course, please take a look."

"Mr. Sai, I noticed you have a dish on the roof. Is it for the TV?"

"Not only for the TV, but it's also for this thing . . . called the Internet. I even went on it a few times before this thing broke."

The sheriff walked them to the adjacent room, probably his bedroom because there was a bed on one side of the room, but in the opposite corner there was a table with the computer. It was an old PC, with an even older, low-resolution CRT monitor. But it was a computer nonetheless. Here, in the middle of the jungle, even this veteran of nanotechnology looked strange, like an expensive crystal vase kept in a barn.

"Why do you need a computer here?" Ben asked.

"You see, my management decided that in the computer technology era, everybody should have one. So, a few years ago, a guy from the main office came with a bunch of boxes, set this thing up for me, installed a dish on the roof, and left. I asked him to show me how to use it, but he was in a hurry and did not explain too much. He showed how to turn it on, how to open the e-mail, the Internet, and a few other basic functions. Also, he explained how to order ammunition, receive assignments and write reports. Of course, it is convenient, no doubt. If my computer worked right now, I could have ordered new batteries for my radio, instead of having to go all the way to town. Unfortunately, I don't remember much of what he told me. I should have written it down, but he left quickly."

Ben looked at the computer on the table. It was an old Compaq PC, which today could be found only in a museum as a memorial for the victim of the brutal competition in the computer market.

"Well, apparently it's a Pentium-II, with an AMD processor, 160-166 MHz, probably no more than 128 megabytes of memory, or even 256. The hard drive is about 250-300 megabytes. The operating system could be Windows 2000, given its age, and cable modem with broadband from the dish on the roof. Nothing too complex."

The sheriff and Emma looked at each other.

"Were you speaking in English just now?" the sheriff asked.

"Yes, in English," Emma confirmed for Ben. As usual, she did not recognize the irony.

But Ben was silent, as by then, he had entered a world familiar to him. He turned on the cable modem and started the computer, hoping that the hardware was still working, as everything else could be fixed. It was even older than what Ben had guessed with a Windows 98 operating system. Everything else he had guessed correctly: old hardware that, these days, could not be found even in the homes of families with a limited budget.

The computer began the boot sequence. A list of loaded files and drivers flashed on the screen, but a few seconds later, the red eye indicating the hard drive operation blinked a few more times and went off. The computer froze, and the blue screen was filled with a random binary number. Ben sighed and turned the power off.

"I told you!" the sheriff exclaimed, watching the monitor. "That's how it gets stuck, and everything freezes. I used to see a green screen, with lots of little pictures."

"Icons," Ben corrected him.

"What? What icons?"

"Those little pictures are called icons."

"Ah, yeah, so before it showed this little—"

"What were you doing before it froze?" Ben interrupted rudely.

"Well, I did everything as usual. I pressed the start button, then—"

"Did you go on the Internet, by any chance?" Ben was beginning to lose patience. He had neither the time nor the will to listen to all the details and explanations, as everything was obvious.

"Yes, I browsed the Internet and tried to install a few games. Sometimes I get bored in the evenings, and I thought I could play a little. On that evening . . ."

The sheriff wrinkled his forehead, trying to remember details of that day when the computer had first stopped working, confusing himself with names, terms, and the sequence of his actions, like a patient telling the doctor about his illness, how he felt in the morning, and what his temperature and blood pressure were in the afternoon.

Ben nodded sympathetically, sometimes even asking him to repeat certain parts, but he didn't listen. Everything was clear without his explanations. He started the computer once again, pressed the F8 button during the startup, and selected the Test Mode with the network drivers. Once again, lines of text ran across the screen, showing the loaded drivers and files. The old hard drive rumbled loudly while reading the necessary information and entering it into the appropriate memory cells. Ben looked at the monitor and immersed himself in his own thoughts.

Marcus was right. I should have brought my laptop. So much work could have been done during this trip.

Ben remembered Marcus's smiling face when he came to his house late one evening with his invention, as he couldn't wait until the next morning to share his excitement.

Waiting for the computer to complete its booting, Ben thought back to their special project, to which they had devoted almost a year of their time.

Marcus was an obvious leader in their friendship whenever it came to computer technology. Computers came into his life at a very early age, soon after his parents got rid of his unnecessary diaper changing table and replaced it with a computer desk. So, Marcus learned how to use computers way before he could read, write, or even walk. He was lucky to be born in a family of programmers, who had plenty of computers in their home, and Elmo, from the popular children's show *Sesame Street*, sang to him from the screen of his first personal computer when he was not even a year old. Of course, he did not immediately become a programmer. His first experience was limited to smashing the mouse against the keyboard as soon as he learned to stand. But even such a simple action instilled in him some basic skills. His parents had to shift the computer to a higher table to stop him from breaking it, but Marcus also grew. Soon he nimbly climbed onto a chair, reaching for his favorite toy, and clicked on the keys, removing dozens of needed files and directories. James, his father, not expecting him to have such aggressive "computer skills" had not protected the programs from deletion, and had to reinstall half of them, including *Sesame Street*. But, to his surprise, Marcus never again turned on his once favorite show, but continued to browse around the computer screen with the mouse. However, by this time, all the files were well protected.

When he turned four, Marcus had been able to freely run the command line console, amused with all of the files and directories running through the black-and-white window inside the operating system console, ignoring the colorful icons on the desktop. He discovered this function by accident. One day James, while tuning Marcus's computer, got interrupted by a phone call, leaving the operating system console open, and when he came back, Marcus was sitting in front of the screen trying to type unknown commands. He started asking questions about this little window, but as James couldn't explain the intricacies of software and hardware to a four-year-old, who had barely learned how to read, he instead showed him a simple command "DIR," which had inspired more excitement in Marcus than his Elmo program ever could. He spent hours looking at these scrolling lines of text, typing this command over and over again. James had to show him a few other options to diversify Marcus's entertainment, one of which was "HELP," displaying all possible operating system programs and combinations of their arguments.

One after another, he entered the commands at the prompt and became upset when the same error appeared on the screen.

"The com-mand-was-used-incar . . . incur . . . incorrectly," Marcus read the message, breaking words into syllables, "or req . . . required argu-ment is missing."

His parents had long known and encouraged his passion for computers, but they could not explain the purpose of the operating system to a child, despite all their computer knowledge and experience. But soon they couldn't spend much time with him anymore, as there was a new addition to the family, a baby girl named Liah. Marcus was left with more time to himself.

Within a few years, the little boy who had by then learned how to read and write well, looked yearningly at his parents' bookshelves stockpiled with computer literature. One day he climbed on a chair and pulled a big colorful book off the shelf.

James, passing by, grinned looking at Marcus's choice.

"You are not going to like that book, Son. Start with this one first." James offered him another book instead. It was a small black-and-white book in soft cover, without any pictures. Marcus immediately took the book to his room and returned it back a few weeks later. Flipping through the worn, torn, and food-stained pages, James realized to his surprise that Marcus had actually read the book from cover to cover!

"Did you like it?" James asked. "Did you understand everything? Or anything?"

"No, Dad," Marcus replied honestly. "I didn't like it and understood very little."

"Do you know why? Because books treat us in the same way as we treat them."

"What do you mean?" Marcus was amazed. At that time, he was just six years old.

"Well, Son, how about this," with only two fingers, James held out the disgustingly stained book with ripped pages, barely bound together. "If you do not learn to respect books and treat them well, then they will treat you the same way and not teach you anything."

It was the first and most important lesson in computer technology given to Marcus by his father. They fixed the book as much as possible, gluing the pages back and wrapping it in a new, clean cover.

"Now try to read it again," James said, also explaining to him the key points of the book in simple words.

Little Marcus was stunned by the results when he read it a second time. He understood almost everything. It is possible that the simple explanation by James helped to clarify some points, but the boy firmly believed in the truth of the words spoken by his dad about caring for books. Since then, he had treated every book with tremendous respect, as if it were the Bible.

He was only seven when he read and understood his first book about the basics of computers, which elucidated some rudimentary functions and commands. After this first, he asked for a second, then third, and gradually all the literature from his parents' bookshelves moved into his room replacing fairy tales and other childish nonsense.

His parents did not notice when the level of knowledge in the head of the child exceeded the critical threshold and changed from quantity to quality. When Liah grew a little older, James realized that Marcus no longer bothered him with any inquiries. Earlier, when he came home after work, his son used to meet him at the door and drag him to his room with an arsenal of questions, and now he had stopped. Curious about this, James went into Marcus's room and immediately recognized the book on his desk; it was one he had been planning to recommend that he read in a few years: a manual on local and wide area networks and TCP/IP[15] protocols. At that time, Marcus was not even ten years old.

Ben also became addicted to computers at a young age, thanks to Marcus. Often during sleepovers, Marcus taught him everything he had learned thus far. Little Liah constantly bothered them, interrupting their important business, so they mainly stayed at Ben's house. They would sit up long after midnight, until angry parents ordered them to bed, threatening to take away their computers. But Ben always lagged one step behind his friend. Most of the innovative ideas usually belonged to Marcus, and on that day, too, he was the author of this invention. He came into Ben's home late in the evening, screaming, "I did it, Ben! I truly did it!"

Ben knew that for the last few months Marcus had been working on a project, but never asked him any questions. Ben, knowing his friend well, assumed that he would tell him when he was ready.

"I did it, Ben," he repeated. "You cannot even imagine what we have in our hands and what opportunities have just opened up for us."

Marcus excitedly paced around the room, waving his arms, and began to explain the essence of his discovery, which he summarized as follows:

In the modern Internet network, a vast amount of data constantly travels in all directions. It is transmitted through wires and in the air, via satellites or optical fiber cables. Information goes to its various destinations in the form of documents, e-mails, pictures, computer viruses, music, passwords, messages, money transfers, and much more.

But if you look closely under a very strong microscope (if such a microscope existed) at the data flow, you would see nothing but a long string of ones and zeros flowing in a specific sequence. Change two digits in the string and the entire sequence would be completely scrambled. As a result, the server would refuse access to the user, the message would not reach its recipient, or an ATM would decline your transaction.

"So . . . what?" Ben was surprised that Marcus explained such simple facts to him. "These are basics. I already know all that."

"Now imagine that you want to get into someone's computer." Marcus ignored Ben's comment. "Let's also assume, for simplicity's sake, that it has three layers of security. To pass all three layers, you need the correct combination of user names and password for each layer, which, at the end, will create a string of ones and zeros of a certain length and sequence. And I know this sequence. I can easily pick it up."

Marcus proudly concluded his speech and triumphantly looked at Ben.

"What do you mean you can pick up the sequence? It will take you ten lifetimes to find the correct sequence of transmitted data."

"That's right, even ten may not be enough, especially considering the fact that we do not have them. So, instead, we shall do it in a few days, or maybe even sooner."

"How?" Ben was intrigued.

Marcus put down sheets of paper with his calculations on the table.

"Look at this. Here is a sequence of bits required to pass through all three layers of security. Here is the first block of ones and zeroes—the first level, for example, the firewall. Then we'll get confirmation for successful passing. Then the second block—this is for the entrance to the router, and the confirmation again. A third block is the authentication to the server or domain controller. The entire chain together is rather long, and to try all possible combinations to pick up the right sequence will require a dozen lives, you were right about that. But if you break it down and figure out the sequence one block at a time, then it is much easier. Besides, you will write a program that will generate all possible binary number combinations of this length." Marcus outlined a block of zeros and ones. "Of course, there is a lot more additional information in between the blocks: parity check, permissions, etc., all these little things you can read about later."

Ben reluctantly looked at the scribbled notes scattered on the table. Knowing Marcus as a good computer specialist, he had never expected this. What he was offering was so unprofessional and naive that even a child could see the ridiculousness of his idea. This was not because it is impossible to pick up the right sequence of numbers out of billions of possible combinations. For a fast PC, it would not be a problem at all. But since the request would come from the same address, any device would simply block the access for that user after the third incorrect login attempt, realizing that someone was trying to hack the password. After that, the user would be blocked, even with the correct login credentials. Ben looked at Marcus pitifully.

"You know, Marcus," he said carefully, like a psychotherapist soothing his delirious patient, "what you are suggesting is—"

Marcus smiled again and stopped Ben mid-sentence.

"Catch!" he shouted, throwing Ben a thumb drive from across the room.

Ben caught it and looked at it with amazement, as if he had never seen this simple device before. He plugged it in the computer and started to browse through the material on the drive. Marcus eased himself into a chair with a devious grin, pulled out two slices of pizza from the big pizza box on the table, folded it like a sandwich (he claimed it was much tastier that way), and took a big bite.

After some time, when Marcus had finished his second "sandwich," Ben looked up at him.

"Are you serious? You want to—"

"Yes, Ben, I did it," he mumbled with his mouth full. "I created a network card with a virtual variable address."

Marcus was very proud of his invention, and he had every right to be. The essence of his creation was to change the distinctive identifier of the computer.

All modern computers are equipped with a port through which they connect to the Internet. Usually, it is built into the computer's motherboard, but could also be located on a separate adapter, a wireless card, known as Wi-Fi, or even integrated into the microchip in a mobile phone. But they all have the same purpose: connect to the network or the Internet.

Each network adapter is unique. It has a built-in identifier, called the MAC[16] address that distinguishes each adapter from others. All messages, e-mails, chats, and other communication protocols that leave the computer find their destinations by this address, and all receiving computers know who this message is coming from. By this address, special agencies find hackers, phishers, terrorists, and other criminal elements who use the computers for their illegal actions. Data coming from any device is always followed by the sender's return address, as the tail follows the dog, and there is no way to change it other than by purchasing a new adapter or even a new computer.[17]

Marcus had found a way to change it. He had created a virtual adapter, which kept constantly changing its address. With such an adapter, computer users could remain completely invisible in the vast expanses of the Internet. The MAC address is similar to the fingerprints of the computer. Using the constantly changing virtual address, you could crack the password to any computer in the world and break into the most secured network or server. No device will ever detect that someone is trying to hack the correct combination of ones and zeroes, the right key to enter the gate guarded by a firewall.

Now Ben jumped from his chair and excitedly walked around the room.

"Do you realize what you've done? Do you even understand the importance of your invention?"

"Oh, yes. I realize," Marcus replied with his devious signature grin.

"Now all the doors are wide open for us; I mean computer doors. We can get into almost any network in the world."

"Not 'almost any.' We can get into *any* network."

"Yes, but there are places you shouldn't enter if you want to sleep well at night."

"We will sleep well no matter what. With a variable address, we are absolutely invisible."

This was indeed the truth. To detect a computer with a constantly changing address would be virtually impossible, as their return address simply did not exist.

When Ben overcame his first shock, they began to discuss what to do next and how to use this unique tool.

"First of all, Ben, you need to write a program that will generate a sequential 32-bit binary number for our testing. Then we will do an experiment and think about the next step, based on the results. I mean, it's not like we are going to break into banks and become ordinary thieves. We need more than that."

A week later, everything was ready for the first test. Marcus got permission from his parents to spend the weekend at Ben's house, as they did not want to be disturbed by the nosy Liah. Friday night, they stocked up on pizza and soda and began the testing. Their target was a small company with a weak security system they had discovered a while ago and had noted, just in case. They had researched this company and prepared in advance. By that time, they already knew the IP address of the victim, its open ports, the brand and model of its firewall and its operating system, and now they could better utilize the time for the actual testing.

They ran the application that Ben put together in a hurry, and the counter began sending combinations of binary numbers. The generated messages consisted of a chain of incrementing numbers from zero to the maximum available combination, followed by a constantly changing MAC address.

The results exceeded their expectations: to break the "hole" in the firewall took a little over an hour; they hadn't even finished their pizza "sandwich" before they were through. Half an hour later, the server confirmed their login, meaning that the second level of security was successfully breached. It was a victory! They did not want to go any deeper than that, as this was just a test.

Now they were really dazed. Was it this easy to sneak into any network, regardless of whether it was a bank, ATM, the Pentagon, or a candy store? They had to seriously think about how to use this new tool. It was decided to postpone the decision on such an important matter until the next day, as it required a clear head. Besides, they had run out of pizza, which was a necessary component for productive brain work.

But that night, they did not get to rest much. Soon after Marcus fell asleep, Ben grasped him by the pajamas and shook him violently.

"I got it, Marcus! I got it."

"It works!" exclaimed the sheriff, snapping Ben back to reality. Windows had finally loaded the desktop, and icons appeared on the screen. Ben's recollections of the past had made him forget the day's events, but a few seconds later, he was plunged into reality and began to work.

He went into the command prompt and pinged[18] a known host, verifying the broadband connection. The host successfully returned all four echoes[19], as expected.

Yeah, obviously they aren't spoiled with high-speed Internet here, Ben thought, looking at the return time of the echo packages. But the important thing was that there was a connection; the low speed was just a minor inconvenience.

This was his world, his jungle, where he felt as comfortable as Emma did in her forest. He was quickly immersed in the task and momentarily forgot all his misfortunes, and minutes later, he opened the Telnet[20] session with his provider. Marcus and Ben loved Linux. They respected it for the speed, ease of use, and outstanding reliability, and in such a remote place, where the speed of the Internet remained in the level of the mid-nineties, Linux was simply irreplaceable.

Ben typed a command: Pine[21], and almost immediately, the green text of the simple but reliable mail editor appeared on the black screen, despite the slow network. It would probably take forever to open Outlook or Internet Explorer on this computer. Ben quickly typed an e-mail to Marcus and clicked the 'Send' button, waiting a few more seconds, but the mailer-daemon[22] that monitors the e-mail delivery to the recipient was silent, meaning that Marcus would get this message.

Ben exited Telnet and leaned back in his chair.

What more could have been done under such circumstances?

If I had my laptop with me, I could have broken into the cruise ship's network and let the captain know about my whereabouts, but on this old computer, it is simply impossible. Hmmm . . . Cracking the security of the ship's network—now that seems like a good idea. Not easy, but challenging and definitely doable! I am sure no one has ever done that before! I have to tell Marcus about this idea when I get back home. He will like it.

"Wow, you are pretty versed at it. What did you do?" Ben had completely forgotten that the sheriff and Emma were standing behind him, watching over his shoulder, and he was startled when the sheriff spoke.

"I wrote a letter to my friend in New York and asked him to let my parents know that I'm okay, and will be in the port tomorrow."

"But how can he contact them from New York?" the sheriff asked, surprised.

"He will manage." Ben did not want to go into details. He turned off the computer and got up. "He is very resourceful and will find a way."

"Listen . . ." The sheriff hesitated. "It looks like you are good at this thing. Could you fix it for me so I could . . . well, it's . . . there is one card game I used to play sometimes in the evenings before it broke down."

"Of course, no problem." Ben nodded.

He turned the computer on again, entered the command line, and in the Windows directory, brought the system files up on the screen. The display showed two current files and two older ones—backup that were created when the sheriff had installed a software on his computer. As expected, he had downloaded a program that was infected with a virus. It may not have even been a virus, but just as likely that program was simply incompatible with the version of the operating system, given the age of his computer. But it did not matter. Ben was not going to investigate the causes and consequences of the sheriff's actions. He quickly restored the previous working configuration simply by renaming the backup files into the REG, current configuration, and rebooted the computer. Ben got up without waiting for it to load all the programs, confident that everything would work.

"All set. Everything should work. We can go now."

"Wait, it's yet to be confirmed." The sheriff looked at the computer anxiously.

"Just wait a few minutes, let it reboot." Ben pulled Emma to the exit. "Thank you for all your help," he said, stepping out on the porch.

"I'm glad to do it." The sheriff scratched his head, puzzled. "But I don't know how I've helped. Why are you in such a hurry? Why don't you stay and have tea with me?"

"Thank you." Emma decided to intervene. "Ben walks slowly and we want to get back before dark."

She tactfully did not mention their plans for a picnic in the woods.

"Oh, okay then. Emma, visit me sometimes. Do not forget an old man."

"Of course, Uncle Sai. I will."

A few minutes later, as they were walking through the glade, the sheriff called to them.

"Ben, the computer is working! Thank you!" he shouted.

Ben waved to him, and they stepped into the thicket.

Chapter 5. Picnic In The Forest

"Tell me!" Emma demanded.

"About what?"

"What you were doing there."

"But you don't even know what a computer is, how can I tell you what I was doing?"

"So first tell me what a computer is, and then what you were doing. I want to be able to work on computers as well. I will go to the sheriff and . . . do whatever I can do on that thing. So, will you teach me?"

"Sure, I can teach you," Ben said. "If you want, we can even chat or write e-mails to each other."

Emma beamed.

"Of course I want, just tell me first what 'chat' and 'e-mail' are."

"We cannot start with that until you learn some computer basics, but it will take a lot of time. How far are we from that place where you wanted to have the picnic?"

"Not far, very close."

Ben immediately realized that he had asked a silly question. Of course it was not far. From Emma's perspective, the port is way too far from her settlement as it would take about half a day to get there. Assuming for simplicity's sake that the daylight in the tropical latitude lasts for about twelve hours, it would take half of that time, or approximately six hours, to get to the port. The sheriff, however, is much closer, let's say no more than a half of the distance to the port, or three hours of walking. Emma planned that picnic somewhere in the middle between the village and the sheriff, in a place within a distance of one to two hours of walking. Emma's outlook on time and distance was becoming clearer to Ben. But the estimated time should have been adjusted a little because his injured leg had slowed them considerably. However, his leg was getting better, and Dzhamaya's treatment seemed to have helped. Her healing technique with saliva, like snake's venom, was indeed very good medicine! Back at the sheriff's house, while the computer was booting, he had noticed that the swelling in his knee had practically disappeared.

Ben was in a good mood. He had been able to notify his parents that everything was okay—it was as good as done, as he had no doubts that Marcus would find a way to contact them. They were now going to have a relaxing stroll in the woods, make a fire somewhere in a picturesque forest glade, and have lunch. Tomorrow morning, Emma would take him back to the port, leaving behind all his troubles and worries. He walked through the jungle admiring all of its natural splendor. People usually pay a lot of money for such an excursion, a private, leisurely tour with a local, but he got it for free. Life had taken a sharp meander in his life, but now the road was gradually becoming straight and pleasant again. Emma said something as they walked along, but he did not listen to her, lost in his thoughts, breathing in the fresh air. In the daylight, the forest no longer seemed creepy. The lush green flora was breathtaking in all its beauty, and the trill of exotic birds soothed Ben. Over the past two days, he had gotten used to these woods and now felt comfortable here, because the previous day had perhaps been the scariest one of his life. He felt like a child who had been thrown off a boat into the raging ocean, swimming to the shore, and the next day coming to a shallow pool with a lifeguard on duty, equipped with all kinds of swimming gear and life jackets.

"Are you listening to me?" Emma asked yet again.

"I'm sorry, I was thinking about something else," Ben replied honestly.

"I said, when are you going to teach me to use computers?"

"How about we start right now?"

"I'm ready!" Emma said enthusiastically.

"Okay, let's begin, but please interrupt me if you don't understand something."

Ben cleared his throat and began a lecture on high technology to a Papuan girl living in the Stone Age.

"So the computer," he began, "is a device that performs substantial mathematical computation in a binary system within its processor registry. It consists of—"

"Wait a minute. I don't get that."

"What didn't you understand?"

"Everything. What is a binary system? What are these computations in registers?"

"Well, you know, the binary system . . . it's . . . well—okay, forget the binary system for now. I will explain it in a simple way. A computer is a device on which you can type text, read books and newspapers, play music, view photos and movies, send messages . . ."

At this point, Ben trailed off. He had no idea what else to tell her. Every word that he was going to say would confuse Emma even further, but he couldn't explain the basics of computer technology without the use of these words. All of a sudden, Ben realized that all his computer knowledge was not sufficient to explain what a computer was and how to use it in simple words.

"You know what, Emma, I'm sorry, but I cannot teach you computers. I'd rather show it to you when we have another chance. I don't know when, but I am sure we will have that chance. I'll put you behind the keyboard and explain everything I know myself."

"Put me behind what?"

"Exactly. This is what I am talking about." Ben sighed.

"Well, okay." It seemed that she herself had grown bored with this lecture. "Then tell me something about yourself."

"That I can do," Ben agreed. "What do you want to know?"

"Everything. Perhaps start from your childhood."

"I was born in New York, went to kindergarten, then to school, and finished eighth grade. In September I will start high school, but now I am on my summer break and we came here for vacation. In short, that's all I can tell about myself. I am not sure what else to say. You better ask me questions if you want to know something."

Emma opened her mouth to start asking questions but stopped in hesitation. She was interested to know everything. This was the first time in her life she had met a boy who lived in another country, far away across the ocean, in America. It was probably even farther away than Port Moresby. Of course, she had met people from different countries before, tourists who showed up once a week in the port. They were all dressed in bizarre apparel with these shiny things hanging on their necks or shoulders. Grandma said these things were called photo cameras. But these people all seemed like inanimate objects like dolls, similar to the ones that she once saw in Madang.

A few years ago, when she was a child, she had gone to Madang to do grocery shopping with her grandmother. Walking past the toy store, she saw a big, beautiful doll in the window with golden hair, in an elegant white dress. It was a mechanical doll that moved its hands and spoke some words and even a few short phrases. Emma had liked it very much, but Grandma said it was too expensive and she couldn't buy it for her.

All these tourists in the port were just like that talking doll in the store. They always used the same words and phrases, although in different languages. A sample list of phrases included the following:

"How much is it?"

"Can it be cheaper?"

"Will there be a discount if I take two (or three, four, or more...)?"

"Do you have change for (followed by the denomination of the bill)?"

"Yes, thank you. (Although the more frequently used option was: 'No, thank you.')"

"What a beautiful (variant: smart) girl!"

However, she had not heard this phrase in quite a while. She probably had grown out of being beautiful (smart).

This was the limit of her communication with all of these colorful tourists. However, her responses to them did not vary widely either.

Now, by some weird happenstance or fate, she was in the close company of a boy from another world. He was almost her age, just a little older, and could have told her lots of interesting things about himself and the world he lived in. She wanted to know everything about him, about his life, friends, school, what they eat, how they dress, how they get rid of head lice, how they protect themselves from mosquito bites, escape from the rain—everything.

Emma opened her mouth to ask him something, but suddenly realized that she didn't know what to ask. There was so little time, as he would be gone tomorrow, and she would be left alone again in the forest with her problems and concerns.

"Do you have any friends?" Emma finally asked, after thinking for a few moments.

"I sure do. I have many friends in my school and in the gym. But they are more like my pals. I only have one true friend, Marcus, whom I've known since our childhood. We live close to each other, went to the same kindergarten, and now we go to the same school and even the same class. He also has a younger sister, Liana, but we all call her Liah. When she was little, Liah thought that we were one family and was surprised to find out that only Marcus was her true brother. But she still considers me as her brother, and I also think of her as my little sister."

"How old is she?"

"She is soon to be eleven years old, about your age."

"I'd like to meet her one day." Emma sighed. "Oh, and Marcus too, of course. Tell me something else about them."

"I do not know what else to tell you. Liah can be annoying sometimes, but we still love her anyway."

"What about your friend Marcus? Is he a good person?"

"He's my friend," Ben replied. "Friends cannot be good nor bad, they are what they are. There are a lot of good things about him, and perhaps some bad, just like anyone else. He is also very smart. He knows everything."

"Is he as smart as you are?"

"Actually, he is much smarter than me." Ben laughed.

"But you know computers."

"He also knows computers. In fact, he knows much more than I do, and he taught me everything I know about them. He started to use them when he was just a baby and forced me to learn computers with him. At first I did not like it. It was boring to me. I love sports, aikido, I love to play football. But then I got sucked into computers, too."

"I still think that you are smart," Emma said stubbornly.

"Well, I am just regular smart, but he is a genius. Just recently he invented. . ." Ben hesitated for a moment, unsure whether he should tell her about it; not because she wouldn't understand it, but since all the participants involved in it had taken an oath not to tell anybody about this new invention.

"Tell me, please," Emma asked, catching his indecision.

"Well, you see, I do not know if you will understand, as it is all about computers."

"But you can try to explain it to me in simpler words."

"Okay, I'll tell you, but you shall never tell anyone about it. We vowed to keep it a secret. You will be the first one outside of our group to know about it."

"I can also vow," Emma said. "Just tell me what I need to say."

"That's okay, you do not have anyone to tell it to who would understand it."

Ben began to tell her about their project. At first, he spoke slowly, choosing the right simple words. But he soon got carried away and forgot that he was talking to a tribal girl who knew nothing about nanotechnology. Emma listened to him intensively, trying to understand the meaning of the new words, sometimes interrupting, asking him to repeat unknown terms. But then she was simply skipping past all the technical terms, just catching the conceptual essence.

"You see, Emma," Ben started telling her, "all computers have a lot of information written on them."

"Where does this information come from?"

"The computer owners put it there."

"Why?"

"So they wouldn't forget it, and to process this information further and use it later on. Imagine for a moment that you have a computer. What kind of information would you like to put there?"

"I do not know. I do not have any information."

"That's not true. We all have all kinds of information. You, for example, have information about the souvenirs that you sell at the port. Let's say you have a lot of different souvenirs. Some of them you are making yourself, while your grandmother buys other ones from someone else, right?"

"Yes, that's how we do it."

"Okay then, this is one bit of information that you could have put on your computer if you had one. Every time you sell some souvenirs, you would also record what was sold and how much you sold it for. A computer then will calculate the number of souvenirs that you have sold, how many you have left, and how many you have to make or buy for the next week. Also, it will calculate your profit and losses. Then, a few years later, you would have all this information summarized, and you will see which souvenirs sell better and which ones are more profitable. This data will help you to increase sales, profit margin, and reduce production cost." Ben took a breath.

"Wow, that's really cool! I wish we could do that."

"Here's another good example: The hunters in your village, after each successful hunt, enter into the computer the place where they hunt down the animal and the time of year. After some years pass, they will have information on where the best hunting places are to track down boar or deer. So they won't need to search in the woods blindly anymore, hoping to get lucky, because now they can go to a specific location, depending on the season. The probability of a successful hunt would become quite high."

"This is a good idea, but if we had such computer our men would become lazy. All they would have to do is to go to the certain place at the certain time, kill the animal, and go home, back to doing nothing." Emma started to laugh.

"Computers are supposed to make people's life easier, and it is up to them how to use extra time they get from it."

"So, what did Marcus invent?" Emma decided to shorten the preamble and get to the point.

"If you understand everything this far, let's go back to Marcus's invention. All computers are well protected with passwords and it is hard to break into them. However, it is even harder to stay invisible, once you get in. Imagine that the neighboring tribe breaks into your barn and steals a boar, but the next day your men track their footprints and catch them. But what if the burglars flew into the barn, snatched the boar, and flew away? They would leave no footsteps or any other traces, right? Now let's apply that scenario to computers. It is fairly easy to get into one if you know how to do it, but it is virtually impossible to stay invisible and not get caught. But Marcus came up with the way to break into any computer and stay there completely invisible."

"Oh, I got it. You want to get into someone's computer to steal the information about the boars, right? But why would you need this information? It is only valuable for hunters."

"Yes, for example, for your neighbors. I think they would gladly steal it from you, right?"

"Are you going to steal the information from others and sell it to people who need it? So you are just regular thieves?" Emma was disappointed.

"I knew you are a very smart girl." Ben laughed. "But the thing is that we are not going to steal information, and we're obviously not going to sell it to anyone."

"But then I don't understand—"

"That's exactly what I am going to tell you right now."

It is a well-known fact that everything new is just a well-forgotten old. That long-ago night, Ben came up with the idea on how to use Marcus's invention. It was based on a popular treasure hunting game called Geocaching. The game was invented at the end of the twentieth century, when portable GPS came to our everyday life, allowing the coordinates of the place to be described with a high degree of accuracy.

The rules of the game were simple. The player hides an object anywhere in the world. Usually it is a small container with a souvenir, a little toy, a coin, or a bill from the country of his origin. Then he lists the hiding or "cache" on the Internet, leaving its coordinates and a description of the general area, which occasionally could be in the form of a riddle, based on the level of difficulty. Subsequently, other players have to find the container using the information given at the site and exchange the souvenirs in the container with his own or simply leave a note with his name and the date of finding. That's all. The rest of the game depends on the creativity of the players and the level of difficulty, which may vary from simple ones to difficult and even extremely challenging. The simplest caches are left for children in schools, city parks, and other easily accessible places. The more difficult ones are accessible only to adults. But for fans of extreme tourism, there are absolutely insane ones in inaccessible places. Extreme caches exist in the North and South Poles, high in the mountains, on the seabed, in the deserts, and in jungles.

Anywhere in the world, in every city and country, there are thousands of hidden caches waiting to be found, that vary with different levels of complexity. The game became so popular that millions of people, regardless of their age and gender, roamed around the world with the sole purpose of finding a hidden souvenir. Today, the interest for the game is gradually fading, but many people still play it. Ben and Marcus were no exceptions, passionately searching all nearby and remote caches within reach.

"Wait," Emma interrupted him. "Do you think we have these caches here as well?"

"I don't know. I'm sure there are some, as they are everywhere, all over the world."

"How about we go find some?" Emma suggested. She became enthusiastic about this idea and already looked forward to a new adventure. "Let's go back to the sheriff and you check on his computer where the caches are. Tomorrow morning, we can go look for one. That would be great!"

"It is an excellent idea, but I don't think we can do that." Ben sighed. "Without a navigator, it is too difficult to find anything in the forest. You do not have any landmarks here, just a lot of trees. You can't say '. . . Look under the trunk of the palm to the left of a large oak . . .' We're going to need the exact coordinates. Besides, these caches can be anywhere, maybe somewhere close, or far away, but we don't have much time. Tomorrow morning, I have to go back to the port and then go home."

Emma did not know what a navigator was, nor did she know much about coordinates, and she simply ignored Ben's last words.

"Then stay for a few more days," Emma said in a quiet tone, avoiding eye contact with him. "You can live with us for a while. You said you were on summer break now anyway."

"Emma, that's impossible. I would love to stay here longer," Ben lied apologetically. "But I can't. I have to go home. I have a lot of things to do before school starts."

"Oh well. I guess it's fine then," Emma suddenly agreed. "Please, continue your story."

The idea of geocaching had bothered Ben all through that night after Marcus revealed his virtual adapter. Tossing and turning in bed, thinking of this game, Ben had finally come up with the plan. He could not wait until morning, fearing that he would forget everything by then. He shook the sleeping Marcus.

"I got it, Marcus! I got it!" Ben whispered to him. "Geocaching, computer geocaching?"

Marcus looked at Ben incomprehensibly, trying to grasp Ben's idea. Finally, he fully woke up, and his face stretched into a wide smile.

"Hey, Ben, do we have any pizza left?"

They made some tea in the kitchen, trying to be quiet and not wake up Ben's parents, and got down to the discussion of the new project that did not have any analogies in the modern computer world. Within moments, the project with the codename the "Game" was born.

"The rules are simple," said Marcus, blowing on a cup of hot tea. "For example, one player breaks into the network belonging to a certain company and creates a cache somewhere on the server. The cache is a simple text file with a message."

"After that, he generates a record on our master website and lists all necessary information about it: the company name, the server, its IP address, approximate directory of the hidden file, and time necessary to break into this network," Ben continued, developing Marcus's idea further. "Another player should find that server, locate the file, and read the message. Then he posts it on our website to confirm breaking into the network successfully. If that message matched the one that was left on the server, then the player gets a certain amount of points."

"Excellent. This is simply brilliant. Pretentious and tasteful," Marcus concluded. "One small correction: a text file is easy to read. The system administrator can find the file and delete it. I suggest we create a special encrypted format. It will be even more interesting. Better yet, we generate an electronic marker, a token. A finder will have to copy it to his directory to confirm that he was able to breach the server."

"Roger that. Option two: we do not leave any files at all. Instead, our cache will be a question. Let's say I break into the network of a factory that makes teddy bears and find some information on their server. For example, an employee, who stuffs the bears with the . . .

stuffing, did not come to work due to an illness. Then I ask on our site: what is the name of the worker who missed work on a certain date, in such-and-such company?"

"Great. I think it will make it more interesting and difficult. Here's another scenario: In the hospital's network, we find a patient and post a question—what was his blood pressure on the second day after his surgery?"

"Or who flew to South Africa from Ghana International Airlines last week in a certain seat?"

"Or this scenario: What movie did someone in Paris rent last Sunday?"

They kept coming up with new ideas and scenarios all night long. The next morning, Margaret peeked into their room and saw that they had fallen asleep in their clothes, lying on top of notebooks with scribbled notes.

On Monday after school at Marcus's house, they kicked Liah out of the room, and held the first official meeting of the players. Besides Ben and Marcus, there were three other participants, close and reliable friends who were proven computer specialists.

Marcus briefly explained his invention to them and the basic idea of the Game, and all new members immediately agreed to participate in the project without hesitation. Even the label "not quite legal," as Marcus called it, did not discourage them. In fact, it had the opposite effect, inspiring them even more. They liked the novelty and complexity of the idea and little legitimate nuances didn't bother them at all. After expressing their emotions and congratulating Marcus on his innovative idea, they moved on to the organizational part of the project. By tradition, they had ordered a few extra-large pizzas for better brain function and began the discussion.

"We would have to find more people," started one of the participants. "The more players, the more fun."

"I am sure we can easily find enough people to participate. In our school alone, there are at least a dozen boys who are reliable and competent enough," said another participant.

"But we cannot use them all," Marcus replied. "You do realize that there are endless opportunities for criminal acts using this tool, as you can get into any bank in the world and transfer an unlimited amount of money to any account. Not to mention the opportunity to sell trade secrets to competing firms. It would be difficult to resist the temptation to use it for a malevolent purpose; therefore, we must be careful about whom we invite to the game."

"So rule number one: All the players shall be trustworthy and not succumb to any temptation to use the Game for their own benefit." Ben turned to the computer, opened a Word document, and created a new file named 'Rules of the Game.'

By the time the pizza box was empty, the general rules had been drafted, and it included the following terms:

1. Under no circumstances shall the players use the Game for personal gain.
2. All players shall maintain utmost secrecy about the Game and its participants.
3. Under no circumstances shall the players delete any files and data, or run viruses in the computers they enter.
4. Under no circumstances shall the players interfere in the affairs of the company whose computer was hacked, even with the best intentions in mind.
5. Under no circumstances shall the players make cache on the servers of the municipal, federal, and government institutions,

military bases and agencies, including the White House, the Pentagon, the CIA, FBI, and other federal services.

After a brief debate, they also decided against hacking into the network of airlines, airports, and military aircraft.

The section of the document devoted to the acceptance of new members to the Game was more detailed and meticulously descriptive. The new members shall only be accepted to the Game by the recommendation of other players who could vouch for them and assume full responsibility for their protégé. The candidate for the Game had to be tested thoroughly for both technical abilities and, more importantly, for ethical conduct. However, it was specifically stated that Marcus and Ben reserved the right to veto the acceptance of a new member without explanation, regardless of the test results. The implication was that it would be better to make a mistake in not accepting a trustworthy candidate into the Game than to accept a dishonest person who would jeopardize the Game and its members.

The draft of the proposed acceptance exam was also roughly sketched and turned out more complex than the test for admission to Google. They thought hard over the test questions and finally agreed that it was not necessary to thoroughly evaluate the technical skills of the candidate. If his computer knowledge was not strong enough, the candidate would not be able to play anyway and would soon leave the Game. The test was focused mainly on the issues of computer security and ethics.

For example, one question read: How long does it take to restore your personal data on the new hard drive after your faulty drive is replaced?

That was a very important subject due to the dubious legitimacy of the Game. In case of any problem with the authorities (and this possibility could not be completely ruled out) and even the arrest of one of the players, the police would confiscate all computers that belonged to the detainee. So there shouldn't be any data that could lead to the Game and potentially to the other players. Therefore, security measures were considered of paramount importance, and the only correct answer to that trick question was: It shouldn't take any time at all, because there will be no personal data stored on the hard drive. All sensitive information shall be encrypted and kept on a password-protected flash drive, stowed in a safe place.

Questions on ethics were as follows:

During the placing of a cache on the server of a financial institution, you notice a bank account with a large sum of money that is of a criminal nature. What would you do?

1. Report it to the FBI/IRS.
2. Transfer money to your anonymous account.
3. Split the money amongst the other players.
4. Continue the Game, ignoring this information.

Marcus insisted on this question, saying that he did not want players to become regular computer thieves who use their knowledge for personal gain, and any answer to this question except for the last one would automatically exclude the candidate.

Or another question:

During the placing of a cache in a hospital's network, you find that the "artificial heart" device connected to a seriously ill person is beeping an alarm on its low-battery state, but the nurse has fallen asleep (her computer has been in screensaver mode for a long time). What would you do?

1. Continue with the cache, ignoring the signal.

2. Wake the nurse up by playing loud music on her computer.
3. Attempt to get in touch with relatives of the patient.
4. Complain to the doctor about the nurse who sleeps during her shift and get her fired.

According to the fourth rule of the Game, the player shall not interfere in the operations of the hospital.

All other questions followed a similar pattern. At the end of the test, the candidate must be proven as trustworthy and honest, a person who can resist the temptation to benefit from the Game in any other way than pure enjoyment and fun.

The next section was dedicated to the rules and technical description of the game. It was agreed to create a master website and an additional site for the authentication of the players. Also, every player was responsible for creating a personal web page, which would contain each player's achievements, score, and awards, among other information.

Authentication to the master site was rigorously secured through a secondary page with a neutral content. They decided to use some completely random electronic books for entry purposes. By opening the right book on a certain page and clicking on the requisite word, the player entered a blog with some ridiculous topic, like "how I spent my summer break" or some other nonsense. The number of words in the blog that the player had to type would correspond to his unique identification number, and the amount of punctuation marks in the text was the player's password. The content of the text itself did not matter at all. Only after that could the player get into the master site with all the secret information. Obviously, the passwords were changed regularly, as well as the titles of the books and page numbers through which one would gain access into the blog. This was a very hard but effective safety precaution.

The master page listed all caches created by the participants of the game, sorted by the level of difficulty, and contained descriptions of each cache and estimated time required to find it. A player who wants to find a cache would get an electronic token for a certain period. He must break into that company network, find the information as required, and return the token to the master site, spending no more time than allotted for this cache. To avoid multiple players going into the same network, the token for this cache would be unavailable for other players until it returned to the master site.

Upon successful detection of the cache within the allotted time, the player gets a certain number of points according to its complexity. If a player has spent less time than allowed, extra points will be added to the player who sets a new record, and the author of the cache loses points. If the attempt to find the cache failed to reach the specified time, the electronic token is returned to the master page automatically, and the player loses points.

When the player accumulates enough points, he receives a "medal"—an electronic icon that appears on his personal website. After a certain number of medals, they are replaced by the Order of Honor, which, ongoing higher, is exchanged with a Title.

The master site also contained all the necessary software and other helpful tools to breach the network security. Marcus's invention was just one of many utilities that was required to achieve the goal. The player who created a new useful program received a medal or even a Title, depending on the complexity and importance of the new tool.

These were the rules that had been developed for the Game. During that night, the players had assigned everyone their responsibilities and agreed to officially start the Game at the beginning of the next school year. On that note, they closed the first meeting of the project members and went home.

Now everything was ready to begin, and about two dozen reliable, proven, and competent guys had been selected as players. As Marcus had expected, finding participants was not a problem. All they had to do now was finalize some minor details and begin the Game next month. However, Ben's vacation had suspended all work on this project.

"Now you understand why I cannot stay here? I have to go home and finish the job."

"I understand." Emma sighed. "You cannot disappoint your friends."

"I knew you would understand me."

Emma looked away and didn't say anything. For a while they walked quietly, each engrossed in their own thoughts.

Suddenly, Emma broke the awkward silence, "I don't get it, what are these points, medals, and titles?"

"They are awards for the Game. Whoever gets the most points receives a medal, Order of Honor, or even a Title."

"Real medal?"

"No, not real." Ben knew that Emma had been upset earlier, and now he was glad to defuse the tension a little. "They are virtual ones."

"Virtual? What does it mean?"

"These are the pictures that appear on your website. We drew little images that represent all the achievements."

"I still don't get it."

"What don't you understand? Do you have any questions on some technical details?"

"To be honest, I didn't pay attention to that and completely zoned out on it. I do not get why you are doing this. You don't steal money even though you could have, right?"

"Correct."

"You don't use or sell the information that you find, right?"

"Yes, that is true."

"Then what are you doing this for? Just for the sake of pictures of the medals or a fake title?"

"It is a kind of a competition for us to see who can break through the security of a computer faster. You have similar competitions here, don't you? For example—who can shoot the bow and arrow better or throw the spear farthest. We are also having competitions."

"That's right, but our competitions help us to survive and get food for the whole tribe, and to protect our women and children during the war."

"We also have the same goal. We learn new technologies that will enhance our knowledge. Then we can get better grades in college and find good jobs later on, which also means food on our table, housing, and protection as well. We could work in the agency that fights real computer hackers and criminals. So, as you can see, our competitions are similar in nature to yours, just of a different kind. But at the end, we both have the same goals."

Again they walked in silence for a while.

"Let's go this way. I'll show you something," Emma pointed to a barely noticeable path between the trees.

They went along the trail, skirting a huge tree, wading through the undergrowth of ferns, stepping over a few fallen trees, and suddenly ended up on the edge of a cliff. Far below there was a stunning lake, framed by the forest. Turquoise water shimmered, reflecting the golden rays of the midday sun.

"Do you want to go for a swim?" Emma asked.

But Ben's reaction to this scenic view was completely different from what she anticipated.

He closed his eyes and backed away, frightened by the height. The previous day's fall seemed to have created a lifelong aversion in him to any kind of cliff. Emma, albeit belatedly, realized her mistake and tried to calm him down.

"Don't worry, it is not that high. I have jumped off this cliff many times."

But he retreated even farther from the edge, to a safe distance.

"If you don't want to jump it's okay, but I will swim," she said, and she jumped off the cliff into the lake.

A few seconds later, Ben heard a splash in the water below and carefully came to the edge looking down the cliff. Despite Emma's assurances that it was not too high, he could only see a small black dot on the water's surface. Apparently it was Emma, moving toward the shore, enjoying her swim on the hot sunny day.

Silly, stupid girl, Ben thought angrily after he had ascertained that she was all right. He was angry with her, and even angrier with himself for his cowardice. He looked down again. The distance between the black dot on the water and the shore was rapidly diminishing.

"What am I supposed to do now? Should I wait for her or go down? It is hard to get lost here; there is a good landmark, the lake, and I am sure there is a path that goes down to the lake. But how could she leave me here alone?" he wondered aloud.

He sighed and went along the cliff. Soon he found the narrow path going down the hill. The constant wind blew away the top layer of dirt, and bare roots came to the surface, woven together, creating a ladder-like path leading down. They had seen a similar ladder the previous night when they had climbed from the river onto its bank.

It took him at least half an hour to get to the lake. This improvised ladder was steep and close to the edge, and he had to be extra careful not to slip down. Besides, his leg still hurt at every bend of the knee, giving him a dull pain. On top of that, the heavy bag, or *bilum* as Emma called it, with the food for lunch, which he had gallantly carried for her, was hitting his leg. However, he successfully made it down and soon noticed Emma sitting peacefully on the ground.

During the time of his descent, she had completely dried off in the sun, and the only indication of her recent swim in the lake was the loose, wet hair on her shoulders and the almost-clean face with its paint washed off. It was the first time Ben had seen Emma in the daylight without her feathers and "makeup," and her hair left loose. Without all these outlandish embellishments, she looked like an ordinary cute girl.

If she changed her clothes to jeans and a blouse, she would be just like any other girl in our school, Ben thought, looking at her with surprise.

Emma saw Ben coming down the hill and got up.

"Why did it take you so long? I was afraid you would never find the way down here."

"I found it," Ben muttered, still angry with her. "I'm not a child. Why did you jump? You could have been hurt."

He almost said, 'How would I find my way back to the port then?' But he immediately realized that it wouldn't sound right, and he bit his tongue in time. He did not know why such a silly thought came into his head; probably from the resentment that she left him alone at the top of the hill, letting him find his own way down. He glanced at her, afraid that she could read his unworthy thoughts. But shrewd Emma interpreted his grumpy mood correctly.

"Are you mad at me because I left you alone, or just ashamed that you could not jump?"

"Of course not. Where did you get that idea? I was just concerned about you," Ben muttered, blushing and looking away.

"There is nothing to be ashamed of; it is a very high cliff. Not every man from our tribe could have jumped from there. Once, I went hunting with them, and on the way back we came to this lake. Believe me, no one could jump from there other than me, and they were stronger and older than you. If you must know, I started from a much lower height. There are many lakes in these areas, and cliffs of different heights, so I jumped from the lower cliffs first, and only then went to this height. You do not have to worry about that."

Emma immediately changed the subject, not giving Ben time to object. She got up and grabbed Ben's arm.

"Let me show you something," she said, pulling him into the forest, and Ben obediently followed her. He could not stay angry for too long.

They came to a spacious meadow surrounded by greenery. Rare trees spread their branches above it in the shape of an umbrella, creating a pleasant shade on a hot day, not obscuring the sunlight at the same time.

"We are going to make a bonfire here and have lunch. Isn't it a beautiful place?"

As she mentioned food, Ben again felt a rumbling in his stomach.

"How about we go for a swim before we start making fire?"

"Good idea. I wouldn't mind freshening up after the long walk through the woods. Then we will make a fire and eat our lunch, or rather, dinner." He looked up at the setting sun.

They went back to the lake. Ben suddenly remembered, worriedly, that he didn't have swimming trunks and was wearing ordinary underwear, but then he thought that Emma, who was accustomed to the sight of men wearing *koteka* on their genitals, wouldn't give a damn about his bathing suit. A second later, he had pulled off his clothes and jumped into the water, leaving all his doubts behind.

The lake was probably fed by some underground springs because the water was cold and refreshing on a hot day. Ben heard a loud splash behind as Emma also jumped into the lake, and within a few moments, she caught up with him. She was swimming extremely fast using some indescribable style of invisibly wriggling like a conger eel, without even flapping her hands. For a while, Emma swam next to Ben but quickly got bored and went far ahead. At first Ben tried to keep up but soon left all attempts to catch her, turned over, closed his eyes, and just floated on his back, enjoying the slanting late-afternoon rays of sun on his face. Even though the day was coming to an end, the sun remained strong, and cool water seemed even more pleasant and refreshing. Ben was rocking with the little ripples and enjoyed the peace, coolness, and the complete silence, disturbed only by the singing of wild birds from the woods and the occasional splashes of water.

Nature, in its wisdom, protects us by not letting to look into the future. Fate gave Ben a little breather, before the next chain of events and surprises that could make even a grown man's blood run cold with fear; a set of events prepared for him by some divine writer of human lives with a perverted imagination. The calm before the storm, as they say.

Emma suddenly emerged close to Ben and splashed him with a fountain of water. Caught by surprise, Ben opened his mouth and immediately plunged under, choking on swallowed water. But soon he surfaced again, snorting and spitting loudly. He wanted to yell at Emma for her prank, but said nothing when he heard her shrill laughter.

"Are you hungry yet?" she asked. "I think it is time to go eat."

"Yes, about time. I'm so hungry that I could probably eat a whole crocodile," Ben joked, swimming toward the shore.

"We don't have crocodiles here, as they mainly inhabit the south part of the island, near the Sepik River, where there are lots of swamps and marshes." Emma did not understand the joke and, as always, took everything he said literally. She was swimming next to Ben, deliberately slowing down, adjusting to his pace. "Did you really want to catch and eat a crocodile?"

"I think it is not worth the hassle," Ben replied with feigned indifference. "It is too much trouble to chase one, then kill it and cut off all the meat. We don't have much time for that. Besides, I am hungry now, so let's eat the vegetables that we already have, and leave the crocodiles for the next time."

Emma shrugged.

"Well, if you say so. But you know what, we can quickly eat our lunch and go search for the crocodile. Sometimes they do come here as well. I even know where to find them. You need meat. You're a man, and cannot live only on vegetables."

Ben almost choked on the water again after her words. He stopped, anxiously looking around, but didn't notice any suspicious objects on the mirrored surface of the lake and started to swim faster, trying to quickly reach the shore. Even Emma had to put out some effort to keep up with him. Before he got out of the lake, Ben once again scanned the shoreline, but there were no crocodiles in sight, and he began to quickly pull his clothes over his wet body. He didn't like Emma's last words. Ben knew that she was not joking, as she always took everything seriously.

"Didn't you say that crocodiles inhabit the southern part of the island?" Ben asked, trying to sound indifferent, but he felt that his voice trembled treacherously.

"Yes, usually they live in swamps, but in the rainy season when the rivers overflow and spread out over long distances, crocodiles swim even this far. After the water recedes they return to the lowland. But occasionally they remain trapped in the lake until the next flooding, if the water goes down too fast. It is too far for them to go by land to the place of their permanent habitation."

"So when was the last time there was very high water?"

"The rainy season finished just recently, and in some places the water is still too high. I think we can find a few crocodiles there. I know at least one place, a little farther on the opposite side of the lake, where the soil is silt and there are lots of fallen trees along the shore. They are usually hiding there."

"I think we shouldn't look for them. We cannot eat that much meat anyway, and it is too heavy for us to bring the rest of it to your village. But to kill the crocodile for just one dinner is wrong. Let's eat vegetables for now, okay?" Ben thought he had found a quite clever way to get out of this delicate situation with dignity.

"By the way, what kind of vegetables do you have in your bag? Isn't it time to kindle the fire yet?" On that note, the crocodile subject was closed.

Emma, however, was saddened by that. She had been looking forward to a new adventure and was disappointed as she took out the stockpiled lunch from the bag. She had prudently brought a few dried breadfruit cakes wrapped in leaves of the sago tree, vegetables taro, *kaukay*, yams, and a few tortillas made from the flour of *baum*, as Emma called it; the same one that she treated Ben to this morning before they left the village. She even had dessert—several outlandish fruits including one with a funny name—*cherimoya*.

They collected some brushwood and started making fire. Soon yams and taro were baking on the hot coals. Emma skeptically examined the *kaukay* and set it aside.

"You are not going to like that," she concluded. "Too bad we had to carry it this far."

Breadfruit cakes were quite tasty, slightly sweet, piquant, and hearty, and they quickly satisfied their hunger, not even finishing half of their provisions, as there were still vegetables left in the fire and some sweet and juicy cherimoya fruits.

After lunch, they leaned against the tree trunk, enjoying the coolness of the late afternoon.

"Now it's your turn to tell me your story," Ben said.

Emma sighed. She remembered her promise to tell Ben about Amal, but she really didn't want to talk about him, and Ben immediately noticed that.

"You know, tell me about yourself instead. We will talk about Amal some other time. I still don't know anything about you."

"What do you want to know?"

"Everything from the moment you were born. Tell me about your parents, your grandmother, and all that you know and remember."

"Well, that is a long story. I cannot tell it to you in a few words."

"But we are not in a hurry and still have time until morning. Besides, there are some more yams left in the fire, and also . . . other vegetables, whatever it is. So begin your story."

"Okay then, listen," Emma said and made herself comfortable.

Chapter 6. Dynasty of Broken Hearts

Ben was mistaken. Emma's story didn't start from her birth. It did not even begin with the birth of her parents. It started much earlier, three generations ago, to be more precise.

Her great-grandmother was born during the post war era following the New Guinea liberation from Japanese occupation in 1945. The newly formed 18th Imperial Army, led by Commander-in-chief Lieutenant General Adachi, captured the island at the beginning of World War II and maintained control for over four years. After a fierce battle at the end of 1945, the British Royal Army finally liberated the country from Japanese occupation with support from Australian forces and a civil uprising. The Japanese Army was completely defeated, and a girl was born. That started the dynasty which Emma belonged to. Of course, the birth of a child had nothing to do with the occupation or the liberation of the island. Everything was much more prosaic.

A young lieutenant, a junior officer of the valorous allied army of liberation, had been wounded during the combat near the province of Jarra De Cerveza. The small town of Jarra was the last line of defense for the occupants based nearby, in Rabaul. The enemies were fighting fiercely, realizing that this was their last battle, last chance to regain control over the island. But they could not withstand the onslaught of the victorious army of Her Majesty and soon were defeated and capitulated. Our lieutenant could have easily died on the battlefield from severe loss of blood, if it wasn't for one of the Papuans, who carried him away from the battlefront to a safe place.

The insurgents of the civil uprising formed by the Papuans largely contributed to the liberation of their country. Of course, they did not take part in the military operations because Papuans couldn't handle any weapons, except for spears and bows. However, they were courageous workers, performing any hard and dirty labor, fearlessly creeping into the center of the hostilities without fear for their lives. They worked the supporting services, doing laundry, carrying armory and ammunition to the front line, and even helping to carry bodies of the dead and wounded soldiers from the battlefield. They also contributed to the victory by compensating for the lack of food through use of corpses of the enemies and occasionally the slightly wounded soldiers. The blood-curdling screams of terror of the invaders were often heard on the battlefield, which completely demoralized the enemy. Senior officers were ignoring the gastronomic cravings of Papuans, with the only condition being that they would not outrage the bodies of Allied soldiers and instead, move them behind the front line for burial with full military honor. As for the corpses of enemies . . . well, nobody invited them to this land anyway.

So, our lieutenant was saved by one of these young Papuans, who carried the wounded officer on his shoulders to the field hospital. Even though he was only slightly injured, the wound didn't heal for a long time, festering because of the high humidity of the tropical air. Even antiseptics or antibiotics helped very little, and he stayed in the hospital for over a year. However, the young man won the battle with the illness, and eventually, he was dismissed from the hospital at the end of 1946 and returned to duty. The commander of their division recognized his courage and heroism during the last battle near Jarra and awarded our lieutenant with the Pacific Star, a medal for the Asiatic-Pacific campaign. It certainly wasn't the Victoria Cross, the highest military award, but the Medal of Honor was indeed from Her Majesty.

Besides the medal, the commander also rewarded him a week-long vacation, which was very useful after the illness. Our officer rejoiced about the vacation even more than about his new medal and went boar hunting and fishing in the nearby woods. There, in the woods, he met his savior, the Papuan, who had rescued him from the front line. By that time the Papuan too had been discharged and returned to his home village. They both were delighted to meet each other, and the former insurgent of the civil uprising persuaded him to spend some time in his village.

The rest of the story of our officer was pretty common. Within the few days spent with the tribe, he fell in love with a girl, and at the end of his stay in the village, he brought her to the city where his division was based. Everything was done legitimately, even though he could have picked and chosen any girl to accompany his stay. He did not seduce her, did not abuse his guest-of-honor privilege, and certainly did not compel her by force. He honestly traded her for a few bottles of alcohol from the elders of that tribe.

Perhaps we should explain ourselves a little, before we incur the wrath of the reader.

The tradition of the bride price, or, as it is called in some cultures, bride token or bride wealth, is not new, and is practiced even today in many parts of the world, including some civilized countries. This is simply a payment to the bride's family in exchange for the right to marry their daughter. In remote places, as those where our story happened, such rites are also strictly followed, because for many tribes, the sale of . . . sorry, the bride price, is the only source of income. Usually the elders of the tribe decide who shall marry whom and define the appropriate price. And, of course, they get an equal share of it along with the bride's parents or primary guardians.

When our lieutenant, in accordance with traditions, asked the elders' permission to marry that beautiful girl, they decided that this young man, an officer who received a Medal of Honor, despite his young age, would be terrific company for the girl. After a brief discussion, they also defined the bride price, giving him a big discount for his military achievements on the battlefield. At the end, he paid just a symbolic redemption of a few bottles of liquor, which the newlywed officer immediately sent to the elders as soon as he returned to town.

The prices at that time were certainly different. Back then it was possible to buy a bride for such a small price. Today, you can't even get the ugliest woman for less than a dozen head of cattle. Unfortunately, inflation has spread in all areas of trade.

Often his envious friends asked him, "Where did you find such a smart and beautiful wife?"

And our officer invariably replied with a grin, "I traded her for a few bottles of vodka from the tribe nearby." In fact, that was true indeed. It was just a matter of terminology.

A few years later, in 1949, a girl was born, Emma's great-grandmother. They named her Jarra, in honor of that town where her brave father heroically fought the war. Unfortunately, the joy and happiness of their family didn't last long. Shortly after the birth of the child, our lieutenant was ordered to go to another station for military duty. For an officer, an order is an order, and it is not subject to discussion. One day, the young father said goodbye and left the comfortable home he had built with his family. He asked his wife to return to her tribe for as long as he was gone, promising her that he would come back for them as soon as he served his military duty. The young mother returned to her tribe with her child, following the husband's order, where she spent the rest of her life waiting for him.

He never came back to his family. Either he was killed in combat, or forgot all about them—history has been silent about that, but they never saw him again.

Little Jarra grew in time to be an exquisite girl, just like her mother had once been when she was her age. Many men from her tribe wanted to marry her. But the elders gave preference to a young fellow, an excellent hunter and a good warrior who was constantly pleasing his tribe-mates with his numerous victories on the battlefield. He brought many skulls of their enemies to the tribe as trophies, despite his young age. The wedding ceremony was festive, with the ritualistic sacrifices, marital and martial dances, singing, and of course, with the main dish, *mumu*—a big wild boar wrapped in sago leaves and baked in an earthen oven. The young fellow was the happiest man in the jungle and entertained his tribe-mates with new feats of arms even more often.

One day he came home to some good news: he was soon to become a father. He was once again in favor of the spirits for his exploits, generous offerings, and regular sacrifices. He had everything that a man could dream of: a young, beautiful wife, outstanding warrior skills, and soon he would have a son, to whom he could pass on his knowledge, gained in endless combats.

But he was a bit too hasty in building plans for the future. He couldn't pass the knowledge to his son for two reasons that were out of his control. The first was that the newborn baby was a girl. The second, he never even got to see his daughter, as he was killed in yet another combat with their neighbors who had encroached on their territory, shortly before the baby was born. The skull of our young man, who never became a father, was hung on the tree near the settlement of the victorious tribe for a long time, to intimidate their neighbors.

The young woman became a widow at an early age, and in mourning for her husband, she bit off her first finger, in accordance with the tradition of these places and time.

At this point, Ben interrupted Emma's story.

"Wait, I don't get it. What do you mean she bit her finger off?"

"Well, maybe she cut it off, I am not sure. But, most likely, she must have bitten it off."

"But how can you bite off your finger?" Ben was outraged.

"We didn't have iron knifes or axes at that time, even today we still don't have that many of them, so usually women simply bit it off. You cannot cut finger with the stone axe. Try it, if you don't believe me; you would break all the bones. Biting is much easier and more precise."

"I'm not going to cut my fingers with the stone axe, or an iron one. I'm not talking about that. Why would she want to cut her finger? Or bite it?"

"We have a tradition that after the death of a loved one, a woman should bite her finger to the phalange base, as a sign of mourning. Even today, these traditions still exist."

"But this is simply savagery! Barbarity! How can you do that?"

"How else would you express sorrow for the dead? How would you numb the pain of your loss?" Emma asked with surprise.

"There are many ways to express your grief without mutilating yourself. You can, for example, cry or pray. Many people find solace in religion, it helps them to relieve their grief."

"You cannot drown the pain of loss with religion or tears. The pain can be only dulled by an even stronger pain. But it must be true pain, real. That's the only way to overcome the loss of our loved one."

She had a point and Ben fell silent. Emma also kept quiet, giving him the opportunity to comprehend her words. She pulled out some roasted yams from the bonfire and put the remaining vegetables on the hot coals. However, Ben refused to eat; he had lost his appetite. But Emma ate with pleasure, blowing on the hot tubers.

It was already dark, but they didn't want to leave. Emma wiggled the burning coals with the stick, and the embers caught flame again, glowing blood-red on their faces.

"What about the men?" Ben finally broke the long silence. "Do they also bite their fingers off?"

"No, only women do. Men need all their fingers. What kind of warrior or hunter would they be if they lost one? How would they shoot the *aral*? But a woman can manage her housekeeping work without a few fingers."

"Okay, please continue," growled Ben.

Then, he suddenly asked, "Listen, the woman who treated my leg this morning, Dzhamaya, she had all her fingers missing on one hand. I noticed it but didn't pay attention to it then."

"Yes, she had." Emma nodded. "Dzhamaya lost her entire family one after another, and now she is all alone. She is actually much younger than you think, but she aged quickly, dealing with the deaths of her loved ones. You should see her gallery of mummies and *corvars*."

"Mummies?" Ben exclaimed in surprise.

"Yes, she mummified all her deceased family members, and kept them in the back room. We believe that the spirits of dead relatives protect our homes from the evil spirits."

"What about *corvars*? What are these?"

"This is just a figure of a deceased relative, carved in wood or made of clay. Mummies cannot convey a person's appearance well, so we also make *corvars* to remember them. It does not always look identical to the original, but at least it gives us some kind of memory of that person, as we don't have family pictures here."

Ben shuddered. It was a good thing he didn't know all this when he went to Dzhamaya for treatment. Although what would it change, even if he knew about it? Probably nothing. He was not in a position to refuse help because of some prejudices.

"Okay, I got it, please continue."

Emma's story suddenly fascinated him, and now Ben wanted to hear the rest of it.

"So, that baby girl never got to see her father. That was my *tubuna*[23]."

"Who? What is *Tubuna*?"

"*Tubuna* is a grandmother. She is my grandmother Igissy, the one who lives in the port. I already told you a little bit about her. She is the only relative I have in the whole world."

"Is Igissy her name?"

"Yes, right now, it is her name."

"Right now? Did she have another name before?"

"She didn't have a name before and still doesn't." Emma laughed.

"Explain, please, I don't understand—"

"We have another tradition here, to name a baby after an enemy that father kills in combat. Until then, the child remains without one, or Igissy, which means 'Unnamed' in our language. Therefore, Igissy is the most common name here for boys or girls. Many kids still remain without a real name all their life and are simply called Igissy, like my grandmother. Her father died before she was even born, and there was no one else to get her an actual name."

Ben opened his mouth to once again protest against such a barbaric tradition but said nothing. After all, who was he to tell these people what was right or wrong? He could not change customs and traditions created by their ancestors and followed for centuries.

"Continue, please," was all he said.

The young widow Jarra buried her husband, conducted all the necessary rituals appropriate for such a sad occasion, eventually overcame her grief, and plunged into her daily routine and household chores. Unnamed girl Igissy played with other children and grew up. Life was slowly coming back to normal.

Several years passed by. As Igissy grew older, Jarra seriously thought about her future. In recent years, Jarra had changed dramatically, worn out by the hard work, and though in her early twenties, she looked like a fifty-year-old woman. Her swollen hands were red from constant cold water, and shriveled under the scorching sun. Her smooth skin became yellow and her face was covered with a thin cobweb of wrinkles. There was absolutely nothing positive in front of her, only hard labor day after day, year after year. This was not the kind of life she wanted for her daughter. Even though she was just a child when they returned to the settlement with her mother, Jarra still vaguely remembered their small, cozy apartment in the city, with its warm bed, and hot meals cooked on a real stove. She wanted to give little Igissy what she had once lost. Jarra tried to find a way to go back to town and send Igissy to school. However, her mother was still with the tribe, and she would never agree to move to the city, hoping that her husband would come back for her one day. Jarra had long realized that he was not coming back, but her mother still waited for him. She couldn't leave her mother alone, and didn't want her daughter to stay in the tribe either.

Unexpectedly, she found the solution. Around this time, the Foundation had begun its rapid development and built offices and warehouses throughout the country. Jarra was lucky enough to get a job in Madang. She rented a small apartment and moved back to the city with Igissy. Her job also required her to go to the warehouse facility nearby quite often, and she could visit the settlement where her mother lived.

Igissy went to school. Even though she missed a few elementary grades, she was a clever girl and quickly learned how to read and write, and eventually caught up with her peers. Probably the genes of her grandfather helped her along as well. Obviously he had been a smart man, having been promoted to the rank of an officer at an early age. Ancestral genes, however, did not affect only her intellectual abilities; a quarter of European blood significantly changed her appearance as well. Facial contours were subtler, delicate, with straight hair, not curly, and her skin was much lighter than what the other people in that region had.

Years went by quickly. Igissy matured and became a beautiful young woman. She graduated from school and got a job in a small office, working as a clerk. The job wasn't that great, but it gave her a steady income. Soon, the Foundation closed the facility where Jarra worked, and she, along with hundreds of other employees, lost her job. Jarra went back to her mother, who was still living in the tribe, patiently waiting for her husband.

Igissy was left in the town alone. But it didn't matter anymore, as she was doing fine on her own, living in her apartment and working in the office. Everybody in the office liked her. She became a pleasant, well-educated young woman, who was respectful to others, sharp-witted, and agile at work. Her personal life, however, wasn't as good. Urban residents were reluctant to get involved with the people from tribes, as everywhere else in the world where big city residents avoid villagers from remote places.

But, nevertheless, soon Igissy had a wild and swift romance with her office manager. The reason for wildness was pretty obvious: young, beautiful girl meets a handsome guy—the situation is quite ordinary and does not require further explanation. However, their romance fell apart as soon as the young man found out about her pregnancy. He suddenly wilted and gently but firmly broke up with her. One day, when her pregnancy became noticeable, he called her into his office and expressed deep concern about her and the health of their child. He said that she shouldn't spend all day in the stuffy room, suffocating herself. In her condition she needed a lot of fresh air, daily walks, nutritious food, and lots of rest, insisting that she quit her job and take care of herself and the baby. Naive Igissy perceived his words as true care for her and quit, agreeing with his argument. She had some money saved and hoped that it would last until the child was born if she spent it wisely. The father-to-be visited her a few times, bringing food, fresh fruits, and occasionally helped her with money. They even went for a walk on the beach once. However, his visits became less and less frequent, until he completely disappeared. When the child was born, Igissy didn't see him for several months, and she finally realized that he simply didn't want her in the office and in his life. But it didn't matter anymore; by that time she had a baby girl, and nothing else was important.

Despite the traditions of her ancestors, Igissy named the girl immediately after giving birth and called her Ima, which in Wagi, the dialect of her tribe, meant Sunshine. Over time, the girl's name transformed into the more common one, as the residents of that town did not speak tribal languages, and Ima became Emma.

Several years passed. Emma grew up, and it was again time for Igissy to get back to work, as her savings were melting rapidly. Igissy went to the office, hoping to get her job back, but found that her position was already taken, and that there were no other openings available. She asked around about her former boss, the father of little Emma, but many people in the company didn't even remember his name, and the others did not know his whereabouts.

"I am not sure where he is, but I think he was promoted and moved to the head office," someone said, shrugging his shoulders.

"No, he was not promoted. I heard that he was fired," replied a more skeptical employee.

"What are you talking about? Didn't you know that he drank himself to death?" other people confirmed indifferently.

They all expressed very little interest in his fate. For Igissy he was a big boss, the lover and the father of her child, but for everyone else, he was just an insignificant petty clerk whose whereabouts couldn't be the subject of their concern.

However, Igissy needed a job quickly. She went through several other offices, but the town lacked jobs, as the unemployment rate was high throughout the country. Occasionally, she came across some part-time work, allowing her to stay afloat, washing dishes in the restaurant and sweeping streets. Sometimes she could even set aside a little bit of money for the future.

Between work and raising a baby, time was flying fast. An endless line of days passed by, each like the last, adding up to months and years, like an inattentive reader flipping through the pages of a boring book, without delving into the contents. A few dozen pages skipped, and Emma was a school student. A few more chapters and she was no longer a child but a teenager, with the complexities and challenges of adolescence. Another dozen or two pages of the same monotonous, dull book and school would be left behind, but ahead of her were other monotonous chapters, called the routine life of an average adult. But fate had decided otherwise and severely spiced up the rest of her life.

In the late eighties, the country rose in revolt, which later grew into a conflict lasting for over fifteen years. It was notoriously known worldwide as the "Bougainville Conflict" that had taken place in the Bougainville province of the Solomon Islands, which administratively belonged to Papua New Guinea. At the heart of the conflict, as usual, was money, or rather big money. To be more exact, the fight was over the copper mines located on the island.

As we already mentioned, Papua New Guinea received its independence in the mid-seventies. But soon the island of Bougainville demanded autonomy from the newly formed republic and the nationalization of all businesses and their natural resources. The entire island went on strike, and the mine workers sabotaged the orders of the authorities. The operation of the mines was frozen. The government could not reconcile such a major loss of revenue for the state budget, especially at the beginning of the formation of the young republic, and began an economic blockade of the island. The riot and individual clashes had been transformed into an armed uprising and soon escalated into open civil warfare, with thousands of casualties on both sides. In short, without going into a political discussion, the conflict was resolved fifteen years later, by the full recognition of Bougainville's autonomy. However, twenty thousand lives were lost, and more than forty thousand islanders were deprived of their homes.

But at that time, in the mid-nineties, the conflict was in full swing and the armed clash was gaining momentum. Allied forces of Australia and Britain, who owned these copper mines in Bougainville, moved to the island to help the small army of Papua New Guinea fight the uprising. More and more military units were thrown into the fight with rebels. On the main island, unit bases were formed for allied troops to distribute resources and military equipment to the war zone. One of these bases was formed near Madang.

One day Igissy came home from work and found a note on the table, in which Emma briefly said that she had met a man she had fallen deeply in love with, and now she was going with him to the place of his new deployment in Bougainville. She also asked Igissy not to worry for her and promised to write a detailed letter upon arrival in Bougainville.

The next morning Igissy went to her school and asked a few of Emma's close friends about this mysterious guy. They all admitted that Emma had been dating him for a while, escaping from class to visit him during school. They also said that this man received an order to relocate with his division to Bougainville, and Emma decided to quit school and go with him, because she couldn't imagine her life apart from the man she was madly in love with.

Igissy cried for some time but eventually calmed down. After all, Emma was already a grown woman, almost an adult, and she had the right to choose her own destiny at her sole discretion. But, as it turned out later, Emma had not chosen her destiny; instead, destiny determined her fate.

Emma's sudden departure had a marked effect on Igissy. She quickly turned into a tired old woman with a wrinkled face and gray hair. All her free time she spent sitting by the window, waiting for the door to open and for her daughter to walk into the room. And she did. Two years later the door did open, and Emma appeared at the doorway. After some time required for emotions, accusations, and apologies, and for the tears of joy and repentance that streamed down their faces to dry out, both women sat in the kitchen, drinking tea and talking. Igissy listened inattentively to Emma's adventures, as everything was obvious and did not require further clarification.

Emma met the guy, fell in love, and couldn't imagine her life without him. She was afraid that her mother would not let her go with him and she ran away. In Bougainville, she was recruited by the police forces to maintain law and order on the island, near the front line.

After gaining independence, the new country began the improvement and reorganization of the infrastructure and governmental departments, starting with law enforcement. The first step in this direction was taken with the issuance of a special decree introducing women into the Royal Police of Papua New Guinea. Two

years later, the first twelve women joined the police forces of the country on an equal basis with men.

Integration of the female police was challenging, and it took a long time, in the early nineties, female officers were already full members of many police stations. The new set of regulations in the statutes for the female police personnel were drafted and approved. The statutes defined functions, rights, and responsibilities for women police officers, and the requirements for their training programs and disciplinary action. A special paragraph of the statute was even dedicated to the uniform and living conditions for women's quarters.

The paragraph about the housing was tempting to Emma when she signed up for police forces. However, the deciding factor was not the promised housing but the beautiful tropical uniform: a blue blouse, navy blue skirt, high-toed shoes with laces, and a garrison cap with a shiny badge. Due to the mess that's common for any war zone, Emma applied for the job without documents. She submitted an application claiming she had lost her passport and lied a little about her age. She looked older than sixteen years, and no one had any doubts. Emma was given a temporary passport, a police badge, and was accepted for service in the Royal Constabulary of Papua New Guinea.

Soon after, she faced problems with accommodation. Municipal housing was only allowed for married officers with family. So Emma was provided with just a bunk in the barrack. But it didn't discourage her, since she was hoping to get married soon and then get the normal housing. However, it didn't work out that way, because, according to a special paragraph, a woman was discharged from the police forces as soon as the Chief of Constabulary found out about her pregnancy. A few years later the statute would be revised once again to impose the appropriate changes, and female officers would be provided with a paid maternity leave, but at that time, that was not the case.

At this point Igissy looked at Emma, as she really didn't like the end of this story. She wanted to say something, but only sighed. What else was there to say? Maybe the women of their dynasty appeased the wrong spirits, or the offerings at the altar were too meager, but all four generations of women shared a similar fate, like twin sisters.

Emma said that her contract was terminated, and she was discharged from the police force until the birth of her child. That actually worked out well for her. She wanted to deliver the baby at home anyway, as there were no conditions for childbirth in the war zone. But she would go back to Bougainville again if the conflict was not yet resolved before the baby was born, and reunite with the father of her child.

A few months later, Emma gave birth to a girl she didn't even have a chance to see. Emma died during childbirth, and the newborn girl lost her mother in the first moments of her life. Alas, the maternal and neonatal mortality statistics in this region is frightening even today. Igissy didn't have money for a hospital, so Emma had to deliver at home, with the help of her neighbor, who had some experience at this. Apparently, her experience was not enough, and Igissy lost her daughter.

But she got a granddaughter instead, and there was no time to grieve for her loss. She quickly buried Emma and plunged into the care of the baby. The girl was also named Emma, in honor of her mother. She was restless, demanding attention every hour, every minute, but Igissy was grateful to her, as the constant work helped her to dull the pain from the loss of her daughter. Igissy had no one in this world but this little baby girl, and little Emma had only her *tubuna*, Igissy. They needed each other.

Life develops in a spiral. All this had happened before. Just recently, her daughter Emma had taken her first steps, uttered her first words, and now her granddaughter Emma was taking the same steps and pronouncing her first word—*tubuna*.

Life was gradually normalizing again. Bogged down in constant work and care of the child, Igissy didn't notice how the months and years flew by. Again, there were problems with money. Over the past few years, Igissy hardly ever had time to work, completely devoting herself to the care of her granddaughter. She had been careful to save some money during the previous years, but her savings dwindled quickly. Emma needed good food, fresh fruits, vegetables, and new clothes, as she was growing out of them rapidly. Her apartment was also taking a good chunk of her monthly spending. Something had to be done promptly and Igissy made a hard decision.

One day, she sold all of her furniture and belongings, leaving only the bare minimum, which fit into a small canvas bag, and early in the morning, she grabbed Emma and went back to her settlement, as her grandmother once had. Emma whimpered, not understanding why she was pulled from a warm bed so early and forced to go into the woods. But Igissy said sternly, "We have to go, Emma, we have to."

So they went mile after mile on the muddy soil, getting deeper into the jungle. Emma got tired quickly, and Igissy had to carry her most of the way, but by the end of the day they reached the settlement.

Emma immediately joined the group of children playing nearby in a small puddle, and Igissy went to the elder of the tribe named Akelika Yaga, or just Yaga, as everybody called him. Igissy had not been here for over forty years. She had not been much older than Emma when she left the tribe with her mother, and since then, she had never visited this place. But she always knew that this was her home and she would always be welcome here and find food and shelter if necessary. She didn't even forget her native language. There were people who remembered her and her mother, and even grandmother;

however, there were not that many of them remaining. Yaga was one such person who remembered them all.

He told Igissy that her mother Jarra had died from disease several years ago, and her grandmother died of old age, waiting for her husband until the last day. Igissy asked Yaga to shelter Emma for a while, until she settled in a new place, and then would come back for her.

"Of course she can stay. Children are always welcome here, especially girls, as we need to procreate our race. You can leave her with us, temporarily or permanently, as you wish."

So Emma returned to the place of her ancestors.

Early the next day, Igissy went back on the road. She said goodbye to Emma, chastised her to behave, promising to come back for her soon. But, to her surprise, Emma liked it here. She hugged her impatiently and rushed back to the group of other kids. When Igissy looked back after a few steps, Emma was already running to the meadow nearby with the rest of the kids, forgetting all about her grandmother.

Igissy did not want to leave Emma here, but she had no other choice. She had to carry out her plan for the sake of granddaughter. One of her neighbors in Madang had told her that there was a small village by the bay not far from here with dozens of unoccupied houses that Igissy could live in practically for free. She liked that idea and decided to move there for some time and raise enough money to return to the city with Emma again and send her to school. She knew that in the future there would be nothing for her in the tribe. According to the tribal rules, Emma would get married when she reached the age of thirteen or fourteen. By fifteen, she would be the mother of a child, possibly more than one, and there would be no good prospects for her, just hard work and early aging. Unfortunately, that was the fate of all women in the tribe, and her mother was the first who realized that when she took Igissy to the city. Now she must find a way to protect Emma. Igissy didn't know how she was going to raise money, but she knew that it had to be done at all cost.

This village was the one that the Foundation began to build for their employees. It was located near the gorgeous bay with the breathtaking view of the sea lagoon with turquoise water. There was even a small dock where a few locals kept their fishing boats. But the village itself looked dejected. The only street with rickety, hastily built houses induced depression and gloom, despite the scenic overview of the bay.

Igissy spoke with the villagers, mainly older people who had refused to leave their homes, and they pointed at the few houses that could be occupied. She chose one that was in slightly better condition than the others, cleaned it, bought some simple furniture, and even hung a few curtains that she had found in one of the abandoned houses. It turned out simple, but clean, and even had some element of comfort. Igissy bought a few chickens, seedlings for her garden, and also wanted to buy a piggy for breeding, but there was no money left.

It took over six months to get settled, and finally, she decided to bring Emma, who was now four years old, to her new home. She was happy to see her grandmother, but firmly refused to leave the settlement and her friends, crying and begging to continue living in the tribe. Igissy hadn't expected that, as her existence without her granddaughter didn't make sense anymore. But Emma liked to live there. All day long she played in the woods with other children, climbing trees, catching rodents and small animals, coming home only in the evenings, and falling asleep from exhaustion. In the rainy seasons, and especially after it, when the rivers spilled over for many miles around, the whole forest became one big playground. Children ran through the puddles, let little boats made from tree bark float down the river, and did whatever else children's imaginations came up with.

However, Igissy persuaded Emma to stay with her for a while. She promised to go with her to the beach and collect some seashells and colored rocks. Emma spent a few days with her grandmother, and then she brought Emma back to the settlement. From that day onwards, Igissy was often taking her home but always bringing her back, realizing that it was better for her to be among other kids and the expanses of the forest.

But one evening, about a year later, when Igissy bustled around the house, the door suddenly opened, and Emma walked into the room on the verge of exhaustion. The next day, after a long night's rest, Emma explained that she was playing with the kids, but suddenly felt she missed her grandmother. Without telling anyone, Emma had left for the port village. She was a forest child and oriented in the woods only by her inner compass and intuition. Since then, Emma kept coming to her whenever she wanted, and returned to her friends a few days later.

The miracle that Igissy was hoping for happened a few years later, when, in 2004, the first cruise ship dropped anchor in the bay near the village, marking the beginning of regular tourism in the region. Until then, tourists did not indulge these places with their visits. There were occasional lone travelers, tempted by the exotic beauty of the island. But now a regular flow of tourists flooded the shore of this god-forsaken village, which was now proudly called the port. Igissy did not know why it was decided to route cruise ships there, and she didn't care to find out. The more important thing was that she now had a real opportunity to make some money.

Most of the villagers came to the quay once a week to sell local crafts to tourists and, of course, Igissy was among them. The rest of the time she went through the neighboring towns in search of souvenirs, which she then resold with a decent margin. Selling a few trinkets paid for the entire consignment of goods, and the next sold souvenir onwards was pure profit for her. Over a few years, she was able to set aside some money. She bought a sow and planned to get a boar to breed piglets, which could also be a very profitable line of business.

Emma also helped Igissy at the port. Tourists are much more likely to buy a souvenir from a child than from an adult. She quickly learned the bare minimum of words and phrases, even in multiple languages, and communicated quite decently with potential buyers. Compassionate tourists could not ignore the business ability of a little girl and were always buying trinkets from her, even if they didn't need them at all.

The artists of the surrounding tribes noticed that the residents of the same village systematically bought their crafts in large quantities, and soon the souvenir business became widely known. Immediately, the price of crafts soared to an unimaginable level, significantly reducing the sales margin. Now it became almost impossible to buy anything. Igissy had foreseen this situation and had built up an inventory for a few months in advance, but something had to be done for the future, and a new source of cheap handicrafts had to be found. Then Emma offered to make souvenirs herself. By that time, she was seven years old. It turned out she had good taste in art and now all her free time was spent searching for suitable materials for figures, masks, and jewelry. Every week she came to the port, bringing the next batch of goods and then sold it together with Igissy.

"So, yesterday, as usual, I was selling souvenirs, and in the afternoon I went home," Emma finished her story. "Then I found you. The rest of it you already know."

Ben sat quietly, as the story depressed him.

"How do you know all these details about your ancestors?" he asked, finally breaking the awkward silence.

"My grandmother told me. Often, when I came to visit her I could not go back because of the heavy rain, so then we spoke all evening. She told me everything I just told you."

"Interesting story. You have to write a book about it. Can you write?"

"Of course I can. My grandmother taught me to read and write."

"What about Amal? How does he fit into this story?"

"He doesn't. That is a different story."

"But you promised to tell me about him as well."

"And I will. But some other time, because right now, we have to return to our village. It is getting late, and we have to get up early tomorrow to walk you to the port." Emma had persistently avoided this topic.

However, she was right; it was time to go back. It had been dark for a long time, the fire was almost extinguished, and all the vegetables had already been eaten. Ben put out the ashes, and they went back home.

They reached the settlement well past midnight. Emma, without hesitation, proceeded into the barn where they had spent the previous night and collapsed on the straw. Once again the day had been hard and tiring, although pleasant unlike yesterday. Emma fell asleep immediately, as soon as her head touched a sheaf pillow of straw, but Ben could not sleep. He was turning in "bed," trying to find the most comfortable position, and kept thinking about the day. He had never had so much pleasure from a walk in the jungle and was grateful to Emma for time well spent. Night in the woods, of course, could be a little scary, but it wasn't as horrible as yesterday. He had probably grown used to the blood-chilling cries of nocturnal predators and the dark shadows that were following them through the woods all the way to the barn. He had just stopped paying attention to them and laughed at his cowardice from the night before. Now these awful shades were more like cheerful sunbeams jumping on the ground, only, they were black in color.

The last thought that came to his mind before he fell asleep was sudden and probably important.

Why were there shadows in the village? He was perplexed. Black shadows in the forest are a little unusual but understandable, because they are caused by a moment of swaying tree branches in the bright moonlight. But this village was located in the valley, there were no trees, and yet he had clearly seen some shadows here as well, and they had followed them all the way, almost to the door of the barn.

But he couldn't think this idea over as his eyes finally closed, and he fell asleep.

Ben woke up in the middle of the night, feeling an unusual discomfort in his body. He opened his eyes, but didn't see or feel anything. His whole body was senselessly numb, much like yesterday, when he was lying on the riverbank like a rag doll. The same discomfort was felt right now.

Ben wanted to pull his hands from behind him and suddenly realized that he was tied up. Not fully awake yet, he tried to make sense of this fact, but all of a sudden, a black shadow swung to the side, letting some weak lunar glow pour in from a small window near the ceiling. Ben glanced toward the other corner, where Emma was sleeping, and saw the shadows moving over her.

A treacherous shiver of fear ran through his body. He was about to scream when he felt the touch of hot, sweaty fingers on his neck, and the next moment consciousness left him, and Ben fell into darkness.

Part Three

Chapter 1. Highlanders

Ben had been awake for a while but did not want to get up. He was lying on the ground with his eyes closed, trying to shake off the remnants of his dreams. He was restless and hadn't slept well all night because of nightmares. The dreams were about shadows kidnapping and dragging him and Emma somewhere deep into the woods. Perhaps it resulted from these horrible shadows in the night forest. Also, the previous day's exhaustion from walking through the jungle have added to it. They had walked quite a distance, despite Emma's assurances, saying "It is very close."

Ben opened his eyes. It seemed to be the same barn: the sloped bamboo ceiling, the rough walls built from planks interspersed with bamboo. Though it looked like the same one, he had a feeling it was somewhat different . . .

Ben looked around and immediately saw Emma sitting nearby. She sat beside him, her hands wrapped around her knees, and stared emptily at the wall, like a little faithful dog guarding the master's sleep. The sun shone brightly through the window opening, as it was probably midday already. Something about Emma alarmed Ben. He tried to figure out what he didn't like, but his consciousness remained turbid after the night, and he couldn't think logically.

He abruptly sat up, waking up completely. Contrary to his expectations, he felt fine, fresh and rested. His young, trained body, which was adapted to physical activities, didn't complain about muscle pain, soreness, or any other discomfort from yesterday's long walk. Only his wrists ached slightly, and he felt a residual pain in his knee. But everything else was normal.

Emma noticed that Ben was awake and turned to him.

"Good morning. I didn't expect you to get up so quickly."

"I am awake, but I feel like I overslept through something important. . . I don't understand—"

He said that and immediately realized what he didn't like about her. Emma's face was not painted, nor was her hair combed, or adorned with feathers. She was in the same outfit she had worn the previous day. That didn't feel right. Last morning, by the time Ben woke up, Emma had washed up, brushed her hair, and painted her face, which was the equivalent of the makeup that girls wore back home. She did all that after a long night of walking through the woods, barely able to drag her feet on the ground from exhaustion. She had even decorated her head with those colorful feathers. She probably had a whole collection of them, sorted by color for each set of clothes for different occasions.

Ben smiled, imagining Emma staring at her wardrobe, picking the appropriate feathers that matched her clothes. Emma smiled in return, thinking that Ben was smiling at her.

"Where are we?" Ben asked.

"We were abducted," she said, while smiling.

"Abducted?! So it was for real? It was not a dream? All night long, I had these nightmares that we were kidnapped by some shadows and they dragged us somewhere deep in the woods. And now, I cannot figure out where we are. This barn is similar to the one we spent last night in."

"Yes, it is almost the same. Every tribe has similar barns, as this is the only lockable place. It is strong and cannot be broken into easily. Usually this barn is used for—"

"Okay, I got it. Do you also know who kidnapped us and why?" Ben rudely interrupted her. Now wasn't the time or the place for a lecture on anthropology.

"Amal brought us here. I saw him through the gaps in the wall. Probably someone else from his tribe helped him. He is certainly strong, but not strong enough to carry both of us uphill through the woods."

"Of course it's Amal. I should have known that," Ben groaned. "No wonder I didn't like the guy from the moment I first saw him. Somehow I knew that we would have to deal with him sooner or later. Listen, didn't you say that Amal is from . . . how did you call them? —the Highlander tribe, right?"

"Yeah, I said that, so what?"

"You also said they were cannibals, remember?"

"I never told you that!" Emma was outraged. "I said that in our tribe we no longer eat people, but here . . . I just do not know."

"I really hope they are conscientious citizens like the people in your tribe. I am not sure about you, but I don't want to be eaten."

Ben got up and looked around. It was a small barn, only five or six steps from wall to wall, and the floor was strewn with straw—that was it. In the corner Ben found two pieces of rope and some rags. Apparently, Amal had used it to tie them and had gagged their mouths with these dirty rags, just in case they woke up and screamed.

Ben sat next to Emma and groaned from the new troubles that suddenly pounded on him. He was supposed to be halfway back to the port by now, and this little adventure would have been over in a few hours. Turned out it had just begun.

I wonder why he abducted us, Ben thought, trying to come up with a logical explanation. *Actually, what difference does it make? I have to think of a way to get us out of here.*

"Well, Emma, I think it is time for us to go home," he said casually.

"Of course, let's go." She immediately jumped onto her feet, confident that Ben already knew how to save them, and he would take her hand and get her out of there.

"Wait, let's not rush. First, we need to come up with a plan."

"Ah, okay then." She obediently sat down on the floor again, waiting for further instructions.

Ben wanted to laugh at such humility and the unwavering confidence she had in him, but the whole situation did not leave room for gaiety.

"First, let's look around and think about this situation."

He once again got up and looked around the barn.

"This is interesting." Ben pointed at a narrow window almost under the ceiling. It wasn't even a window, just a small opening, probably for ventilation.

"I thought about it also," Emma replied. "This opening is too small—we cannot crawl through it."

She was right; the window opening was not big enough, even for little Emma. Her head would probably get stuck if they decided to escape through it. Ben looked at all the walls of this flimsy structure, but soon, he had to admit that its fragility was deceptive. Coarse, thick planks were well fitted into one another, with occasional gaps in between the boards, firmly held with entwined rope. Emma explained that the rope was woven from thin, long strips of the *gutur* tree's bark. This tree, once cut, produces a sap that hardens over time, and the rope made from this bark is durable. The hardened sap becomes a resin that cannot be cut even with a sharp knife. Boards and logs entwined with such rope are bound with the sap better than with any glue. In the few places where the boards didn't fit well, the openings were covered with bamboo. Some gaps, of course, were left anyway, sometimes even fairly wide, but the overall walls and the entire barn was pretty solid and built well. But for even better reliability, all the walls were also strapped with several rows of transversal planks. Also, the door was built with the same technology, and it was locked from the outside with a big padlock. Ben looked through the gap in the door and frowned even more: they were secure in captivity.

"Can you climb that wall and peek out of that window?" Ben asked Emma. "We need to know where we are and what is going on around here."

"No, I cannot. It is too high." Emma looked at the small window near the ceiling.

"I'll help you."

He leaned back against the wall under the window and folded his palms. She deftly climbed on his hands with her bare feet and then onto his shoulders.

"Can you see anything?"

"I see some activity, lots of people, mostly women. They are doing. . . ah, yes, I get it. They are bringing a lot of stones and laying them in the pit around the walls. It looks like . . ."

"What? What does it look like? Tell me!" Ben demanded.

"Let me down. I've seen enough."

Ben helped her down.

"So what is it?"

"I think they have a festival and are preparing for a celebration."

"What festival?"

"I do not know. We celebrate for many occasions. If we have food on the table, it's reason for festivity. If the rain starts, yet another reason to celebrate; when the rain finally stops, again we celebrate. This is how we thank the spirits for their help, for their gifts in the form of food or rain or everything else. On the contrary, if they didn't bestow these gifts on us we placate them, appeasing with offerings and donations, asking them to be kinder to us and help whenever possible. In short, festivals are frequent here."

"But how did you know that today is a festival? Did they blow up balloons?"

"Balloons? What is that?"

But Ben just waved it off.

"Never mind that. Tell me what else you saw. How did you know that they are preparing for a celebration?"

"It seemed like they are going to prepare *mumu.*"

Now it was Ben's turn to wonder, but he barely opened his mouth before Emma explained:

"*Mumu* is our famous dish we usually prepare for a big celebration. It is a pig or wild boar baked in an earthen oven. We dig a special pit for cooking and lay red-hot stones at the bottom. Then we cover it with a layer of sago leaves. I already told you about this palm. On the top of the leaves we put pieces of meat, seasoned with the *mola-messi* herb and some other flavored plants and then cover the meat with another layer of sago or banana leaves. The hot stones take a long time to cool, and the meat will stew in its heat. It's a long process, but the meat becomes soft. When I looked out the window, I saw they were preparing a cooking pit for *mumu* and—"

Suddenly she stopped mid-sentence and paused for a while.

"I think I know what they are celebrating," she said, lowering her voice. "Today they had a good hunt, and that's why the festivities."

"So what?" Ben did not understand. "Did they invite us to celebrate their holiday with them?"

"I told you that the rainy season just ended, there is no game at this time of the year. Hunting season will start only in a few weeks. The hunt was on us; don't you get it?"

"So, what does it mean?" He started to vaguely understand, but his mind refused to accept this horrific fact.

"This means they will prepare *mumu* in the earthen oven from us," she said, confirming his worst fears. "One of us will be sacrificed to the spirits, in gratitude for a successful hunt."

"What do you mean sacrificed? I do not want to get sacrificed."

"I do not want to either, but these are traditions. They have to sacrifice part of their spoils. If you don't thank the spirits with the piece of meat, they will not help you next time."

"These are bizarre traditions, you know, to sacrifice people," Ben muttered. "So, how would they sacrifice us?"

"I just told you. They will make a *mumu*, but instead of a wild boar, they would bake one of us and bring the best pieces of meat to the altar. The rest of it they would eat themselves."

"So, they are cannibals after all." Ben sighed.

"Yes, it looks like you were right about that."

"Is it possible they went hunting and came back with a good catch?" Ben asked hopefully. "They could have caught the lone animal that came out of hiding ahead of time. Animals don't always know when hunting season starts, you know."

"No, it's not possible. Besides, I would have known if they did. They have almost no game on this elevation, as most animals are in lower levels, on our territory. But it is forbidden to hunt there by the law. They have to ask our permission, otherwise it will be war again. We have constant wars between tribes because one hunted on the territory of another tribe."

"But what does it have to do with today's hunt? They could have just sneaked into your land, killed a boar, and come home. Your men wouldn't even have known about it."

264

Emma sighed and continued, like a mother explains the basic rules of behavior to her foolish child.

"You see, both tribes agreed to a truce recently, and they are allowed to hunt on lower territory, but only with our hunters. Besides, it is better for them to hunt together, as they don't know our woods well enough and where to find animals. Therefore, if they went hunting, I would have known about it, as some of our men would have gone with them as well. Their hunters wouldn't want to violate the terms of armistice now, when peace has been restored just recently."

"Those are interesting terms of truce: they cannot hunt on your territory but it is okay to abduct people. Wouldn't that also be a violation of the truce?"

"There is nothing in the terms that says about that, as they were only talking about hunting."

"Okay, to conclude, the hunt was us, and apparently it was a successful one. Now they will bake one of us in that earthen oven and sacrifice the best piece of meat to the spirit in appreciation for a good hunt and eat the rest of it themselves."

"Yes, that's right."

"You know what I think? Let's not spoil their festival with our presence and get out of here. For some reason, I don't want to be present on this holiday, especially in the form of their festive dish. I do not like it when someone donates my body parts, even for such a good cause. But, of course, if you insist, we can linger here a little longer and take part in their celebration."

"No, I do not want to. I'd rather go home."

"I am glad we wish for the same thing."

"So, do you have a plan yet?" Emma asked hopefully.

"Hmm, a plan. We still have to come up with one, so let's think logically."

"Okay, let's. But how do we do that?" Emma made herself comfortable, leaning against the wall, all prepared to think logically.

Ben was scared and nervous, and it was difficult for him to maintain this apparent carelessness in his voice. He wanted to destroy walls, break through the doors, and set the roof or even the entire barn on fire. He would do anything to get out of here quickly. But instead, he sat down next to Emma, and began to think logically.

"Let's assume that you are right, and we were kidnapped."

"Okay, then what?"

"Our abduction is a consequence of events that led here. There was a reason that made them do so. It's not like they bumped into us in the woods and thought we would look perfect on their dinner plate. They followed and abducted us when we fell asleep. Something forced them to do it. We must trace the entire chain of events from the cause to the result. And the first question I have is: whom did they abduct?"

"What do you mean—'whom'?" Emma stared at him in surprise. "Both of us, of course."

"No, they meant to take only one of us, and took the other as a precaution. They were afraid that the other would wake up during the kidnapping and start to scream. They didn't need all that noise and wanted to do everything quietly. That's why they took the second person. Isn't that logical?"

"Well, maybe. I don't know. What's the difference? Is this important to us?"

"I am not sure yet, but I feel it could be important. If we know whom they were going to take, we can assume what they plan to do with the other. It is possible we are worrying for nothing, and we were just invited to the celebration as guests. Perhaps they would feed us with real *mumu* and send us back home."

"Yeah, they will feed you with me. I will be your dinner," Emma joked. It looked like Ben's companion had developed a sense of humor in her, although a bit of a dark one.

The girl is holding up well. I wish I had such self-control, Ben thought.

"No, I do not want to eat you. You're too skinny for my taste."

"Why am I skinny?" Emma pursed her lips resentfully. "I am not skinny."

"No, of course you are not." Ben kept forgetting that Emma did not perceive any sarcasm. She was getting better with humor, but still needed to work on her irony skills a little. "Believe me, you would be a great, tasty *mumu*."

"You really think so?" Emma beamed happily.

"I know so. I was just trying to make a joke to cheer you up. But let's not get distracted from our discussion. We have to replay all the events, starting with, let's say, last night, or even earlier, from the morning when we met your friend Amal."

"He's not my friend."

"Okay, whoever he," Ben agreed. "So, your friend-foe Amal comes to your village to meet you. By the way, don't you think it's time to tell me about him?"

"I've already told you, he is my future husband."

"Yes, I remember that, but I want to know more about him. What kind of person is he? Why are you going to marry a guy from another tribe? Who are these Highlanders? What kind of tribe is it in general? I want to understand it all. We need to know all of that because I don't believe that they abducted us just to dine. I am not sure how it would help us, but I must know and understand everything. Besides, we cannot exclude the possibility that we might not be able to get out of here on our own, and would have to negotiate with them."

"Okay, I will tell you all I know about them and Amal, but I don't know that much, because it started a long time ago, before I was born, and even before my grandmother was born. I'll tell you what I've heard in our village." Emma sat back and began her story.

"Once upon a time, it was one big tribe, called Wagaba[24] . . ."

Today, nobody knows all the details of this story, as many facts were irretrievably lost to posterity. Even now there are not that many educated people who can read and write, and in those ancient times, there was no one who chronicled and conducted annals of events. Most of the facts were simply passed from generation to generation by word of mouth, acquiring new details, often untruthful, and to this day, the story has come to us in the way Emma told Ben.

According to the traditions of these places, tribes are usually led by the worthiest elder, or even several elders whose wise leadership could help overcome an endless sequence of life difficulties. This position cannot be appointed. It has to be earned by showing good leadership. Only then would people believe in you and unconditionally fulfill all your directives. But at the same time, rules in the tribe were quite democratic, and anybody could speak up and offer an alternative way of solving their problems, and the tribe-mates would then decide which solution was the wisest and the most effective.

In one particularly difficult and lean year, when all the animals migrated to other places or hid in their burrows due to heavy rain, the one unanimous tribe split apart. A young man who believed he had sufficient life experience to interfere in the leadership of the tribe increasingly showed frustration with the decisions made by the elders and suggested other more radical and effective ways to deal with their problems. As always, controversy retained around the usual topics: where to find food, how to protect themselves from insidious neighbors, and how to sneak into neighboring territories to hunt. The young warrior believed that the elders were way too conservative, and their decisions were not always effective. This could have been true, as people of a certain age tended to conservatism. The warriors rebuked the elders for their abundant caution, which led the once-prosperous tribe to complete impoverishment.

"People have been eating tree roots, and, if lucky, the occasional rodents for many months now," this young man told his tribe-mates. "We need meat. Warriors cannot live on vegetables and rats, and there are many ways to get food for the tribe. We can go, for example, to hunt on higher grounds, to our neighbors, and in the case of an unsuccessful hunt, I am sure we could find some food within their tribe, even if we would have to go in conflict with them."

Many of his tribe-mates, embittered by constant starvation, tired from the endless series of difficulties in life, one after another, added their voices to the young warrior's. The elders, accustomed to foreseeing the consequences of their actions, urged them to wait a little more, when animals would return to the lower woods, and insisted on peaceful coexistence with the neighboring tribes.

"This is a difficult time for everyone, and we all are starving right now. It is not fair to deprive others of their last reserves."

Contrary to the orders and persuasion of the elders, warriors began invasions on neighbors, devastating their barns and stealing cattle. Sometimes the raids were successful, and they returned loaded with food, but most of the time they came home empty-handed. All the tribes in the region were finishing their last reserves of smoked fish and dried breadfruit cakes and were starving as well. Angry neighbors invaded their tribe in retaliation, causing numerous casualties on both sides. On the other hand, the war itself had become a good source of food, in the form of dead and wounded enemies.

The elders tried to bring the young warrior to his senses, urging him to stop the bloodshed, even threatening that the spirits would turn away from them and would not help anymore, but they couldn't persuade him to obey their orders.

"I am not doing it only for myself, but for the entire tribe," the new leader said, perplexed. "And the spirits will get their fair share of sacrifices, if we have a successful raid. Besides, they are not helping us much lately anyway."

They kept invading the neighboring tribes, continuing the bloodshed in internecine wars. But at the end of the day, with the sunset, they scrupulously indulged the spirits with generous offerings, giving them the best pieces of venison, human flesh of vanquished or captured prisoners of war, burned on ritual pyres. They were asking the spirits for their mercy, begging for assistance on the battlefield, and to finally stop that never-ending rain. The spirits gladly accepted the generous gifts (probably the cunning shaman was stealing the donations at the end of the ritual), but didn't rush with their help. Either the offerings were much too modest, or the spirits couldn't stop the rainy season, no matter how many sacrifices they were given. But wars were going on with alternating success, and the rain kept pouring non-stop.

The young leader personally led his men to war, gaining additional respect and fame among his tribesmen. Elders usually gave orders only, letting others do the job. But he, as befitting a real leader, showed the way to a better life by personal example. How can one not respect such a warrior? More and more people in the tribe followed the young man, disobeying orders from elders. Governed by the dual power, at a certain point, the whole tribe was in rebellion.

Dual power is very pernicious in every society, hurting mainly the people led by such a government. This tribe was in the same situation.

Nobody listened to the elders anymore, and willfully attacked the neighbors, resulting in numerous casualties on both sides. Families were losing their fathers, brothers, and children, but they still couldn't defeat hunger. It was impossible to feed over five hundred people with the little that was captured from the others, living from hand to mouth. After yet another senseless slaughter that upset the elders, they made an unpleasant decision, one that was difficult for both parties. Following a long talk with the young warrior, the elders came to the conclusion that the situation was getting out of control and had to be resolved quickly. Therefore, they decided to give everybody an opportunity to leave the tribe, forming their own colony. They were still hoping that the mutineers would come to their senses but, to their surprise, many tribe-mates gladly accepted the offer, and almost half of the people left the settlement forever, following their new leader. A new sovereign tribe named Abaga was born.

The young warrior led his supporters through the jungle in search of a new place to live. However, the perspicacious leader had foreseen this situation and had long been looking for a new place for his tribe. He found this picturesque place in the Wahgi Valley[25], located higher on the mountains, at the foot of Mount Hagen, only a few miles away from their former tribe.

The new location was ideal for the settlers. It had vast, open plateaus in the middle of the jungle with the river flowing nearby, and was reliably protected by the mountain range from the winds. However, there was one small detail that the young man hadn't taken into consideration, which explained the fact that this open terrain remained unoccupied. The river that was flowing down the steep slope through the gorge was inaccessible because of its rocky riverbanks. It was the only source of fresh water for many miles around. Although people could always find a path down to the bank, it was nearly impossible for the animals to access the river, and they chose a more convenient place for water at the lower levels. Therefore, there was almost no game in that area.

But the young Abaga tribe adjusted to the living conditions of this place. They built a few light *buambramra*, corrals and barns for animals, planted a garden, learned to fend and provide for themselves on their territory (but more often, of course, on the territory of their neighbors), and even fished in the fast river. However, the lack of game in the region, as usual, was replaced with the corpses of the fallen enemies and prisoners captured during the wars. What can you do? This is the reality of Terra Incognita, and we cannot judge the customs of this country and the people who struggled to survive in difficult conditions.

The life of the young tribe was gradually improving. Not in one day, of course, not even in one year. It took decades to normalize their life. The young, aggressive leader became more cautious about his decisions, preferring diplomacy in conflict situations instead of war. He felt responsible for the lives of the people who believed and followed him in hope of a better life. There is a difference when you are a part of a large, powerful clan and strike fear in the eyes of your friends and enemies, as compared to if you have just a few hundred people, including women and children. After years, he had become a truly good leader.

Years and generations passed by, and with them the tribe leaders changed. After the wise one, another came to power, intolerant and narrow-minded. The aggressive leader was replaced with a diplomatic one, and instead of a brave one came a coward and a dastardly man. Now, a hundred or more years later, a wise, decent leader came to power, and he successfully combined diplomacy with the language of force. People respected him for his wisdom, neighbors feared his strength and excellent fighting skills. His name was Amal. That was the name that ran in his family for generations. His father was Amal, as well as his grandfather, and probably some other ancestors, whom he didn't know. And, of course, he also named his son Amal.

He was strong, well-built, muscular, and tall—much taller than most of the men in his tribe. The indigenous population of these places were usually short. There were even pygmy tribes due to the lack of nutrients needed for human growth. But suddenly, here was a man taller by far than all his tribe-mates. Amal suspected that he inherited his genes from a foreigner who had been lost in the jungle.

From time to time, tourists vanished somewhere deep in this mysterious island, and it is challenging for one to return to civilization. Try to walk thousands of miles through the vast jungles and not sink in the swamp, not die without food and water, not freeze to death at the snow-capped mountains and, most importantly, not get caught by one of the numerous cannibal tribes. Most likely the poor fellow would have come across a peaceful tribe, remained there forever, got married, and became a full member of that settlement.

Apparently, Amal inherited his large stature and strength from one of these lost foreigners and passed such valuable genes to his son.

Amal Senior led the tribe for over twenty years. During his leadership there were difficult years and not as much; people didn't starve, but there was no prosperity in the tribe either. The woods in that region lacked animals and game, so the men hunted mainly in the lower territories, which often led to clashes with the rightful owners of the land. The Abaga tribe was small but fearless. Led by Amal Junior and under the wise leadership of his father, who also showed strong tactical skills, they kept all their neighbors in the region in fright.

About a year ago, Amal, together with his son, had sat at the negotiating table with an elder, Akelika Yaga, or simply Yaga, from the Wagaba tribe, where Amal's ancestors were from. A vital necessity had brought them to the table. Both tribes, tired of constant wars, had decided to put an end to discord between them and live with each other in good neighborly relations, overcoming life's challenges together. Similar agreements had been concluded in the past as well, but when a new chief came to power, the fragile peace would end once again, replaced with the war. A truce both leaders agreed to many years ago had been canceled along with the death of one of the elders and Amal's coming to power. Now it was the time to renew their peace agreement and friendly relations between them.

During the talks, it was decided to stop all the attacks from both sides and instead jointly hunt on the Wagaba territory, but all the game must be divided equally between the two tribes. Yaga also had to agree with another concession: he had to allow Amal's people to pass through their territory to the port, but in return, he asked Amal to support him in case of war with another neighboring tribe that also occasionally bothered them.

Amal Junior sat at the table silently and looked around, considering it inappropriate to intervene in a conversation between the two leaders. His presence was unnecessary at the talks, but his father brought him along just for the practice of conducting such diplomatic dialogues. In a few years, his son was supposed to take over the leadership of the tribe, provided that the son could prove himself a worthy leader. This position cannot be inherited and must be earned, so the father used every opportunity to bring Amal Junior to the affairs of their community. Some additional experience in diplomacy wouldn't hurt him.

At first Amal listened to the conversation of the elders closely, but soon, he got bored, and looked around. That's where he saw Emma for the first time. It's hard to say what about Emma caught his attention, but he singled her out from her peers for some unknown reason. Perhaps he was attracted by her unusual appearance, as Emma had three-quarters European blood, and she looked markedly different from the others.

Amal leaned over to the father and whispered something in his ear. Amal Senior listened to him in silence and continued the interrupted conversation.

"We agree to all your conditions, Yaga, but we have one more request. You will let that girl marry my son." Amal Senior pointed to the girl playing nearby. "And we'll give you, in exchange, any girl from our tribe to marry any of your men."

Yaga raised his eyebrows in surprise.

"Which one are you talking about? Emma?"

"Well, if her name is Emma, then yes, her," confirmed Amal.

"But she's still a child; she is not even ten years old yet."

"That's okay. Amal will wait a few more years until she reaches the age acceptable for marriage. Is it right, Amal? Can you wait?"

"Of course I will wait."

"Okay then, great." Amal Senior joyfully rubbed his hands together. "So, Yaga, what do you think? Do we have a deal?"

Yaga was hesitating. On one hand, he very much wanted to make a truce with Amal and be his friend, not an enemy. But on the other hand, Emma. No, he wasn't worrying much about her fate. Such a marriage would only benefit her, as Amal was a good party for Emma. Soon he would take his father's place and lead the tribe. They would live in their own home, instead of a general *buambramra* for a half-dozen families. But, there was a different problem . . .

It is considered prestigious for a man to marry a girl from another tribe. Of course, the matter was not as much of prestige as of practicality. In the small tribes, the selection of men and women suitable for marriage is limited. How many young people could there be in a tribe consisting of a few hundred people, more so as many of them are already related by blood? In addition, many families in that region are polygamous, and there was a serious danger that the couple could be siblings without even knowing it. As a consequence, this would seriously affect their future children because they would be born frail, sickly, with an underdeveloped immune system, increasing the already high infant mortality rate. Everyone in the tribes knew subconsciously, without delving into the genetic jungle, that they had to avoid endogamous marriage[26]. To hell with love, first they had to find someone who was not in direct relationship with each other. Therefore, girls from other tribes who had reached the age suitable for marriage were highly valued. Some families paid tens or even hundreds of pigs for the bride from another tribe because she would contribute fresh blood to the dynasty of her future husband.

Yaga, of course, knew all that and was well aware of the high price of such a deal. Letting Amal marry Emma would deprive himself and his tribe the possibility to profitably sell Emma in the future. But Yaga reasonably thought that the peace in the region right now was more important than potential profit later, and he agreed to the deal. Thus, Emma's fate was decided.

"Then they called me over," Emma finished her story, "and introduced me to Amal. Yaga said that he is my future *adawa-na*, husband. That's all."

"And you immediately agreed?" Ben was outraged.

"Nobody asked my opinion. They simply said that in a few years I will marry Amal."

"Does your grandmother know about this?"

"Yes, she does." Emma sighed. "That is why she wants to save enough money as soon as possible, so we can return to the town."

"But they cannot do that to you! How could one decide for you whom and when to marry?"

"We must obey orders from the elders. If Yaga said so, then it must be done. Besides," Emma slyly squinted, "I still have a few more years left until marriage. During this time Amal might change his mind and steal himself a wife from another tribe at the war. Or he may even get killed. Although it is unlikely. Did you see how strong he is? But still, there is no need to worry about it in advance."

"That's true. But let's get back to our problem, otherwise you will be the one to die before the wedding, not Amal," Ben joked grimly. "So, Amal came to visit you, right?" Ben repeated his question. "Does he come there often?"

"No, not often." Emma thought for a while. "He came now because we are in truce with them, otherwise he wouldn't dare to go to our tribe."

"So this should be our starting point. The two tribes are in an unsteady peace, and Amal takes advantage of the situation to visit his future bride. Does it sound right thus far?"

"Yes, everything is correct."

"So, when was the last time he had visited to you?"

"That was a long time ago, during the hunting season, when he was going hunting with our men. And yesterday, he suddenly came again. By the way, he did not even tell me why he came. He was more interested to know about you."

"There," Ben lifted a finger, "that's my point. He didn't expect to see me with you. I already figured that out, but just wanted to confirm that."

"Yes, apparently so. I guess you are right."

"Yesterday, when we walked in the woods, he went back to his tribe and reported about me."

"Reported to whom?"

"I don't know. Probably to those who are supposed to know, the elders. He must have told them that his future wife spends time with the white boy who hadn't even gone through the rite of passage yet. And the elders may have advised him to isolate you from me."

"But they didn't want to touch you, because they were not sure who you are or what you are doing in our settlement. So he decided to hide me for a while until the situation becomes clearer," Emma continued his thought.

"Correct. You are right," Ben praised her. "But apparently, during the abduction, you yelped while they were tying you, and I woke up."

"Yeah, I remember that. I suddenly felt tickled. I thought it was a rat crawling on me and wanted to scare it away, but I couldn't move my hands. Then, I probably yelped, before he shoved the gag in my mouth. So, they abducted me. But because you woke up, they had no other choice but to take you also, to keep it quiet," Emma concluded.

"Yes, sounds right." Ben sighed. "But that means they will eat me."

"Why you?" Emma asked resentfully, as if Ben had taken the largest delicious candy from her.

"Well, this is simple, my dear Watson."

"Who is Watson?" Emma looked at him, puzzled.

"Nobody. I'll tell you later."

"Did you want to offend me?" She did not look appeased.

"No, of course not." Ben was afraid that Emma would get upset at such a crucial moment. "This is from a book. There were two friends, Holmes and Watson. Holmes explains something to Watson and keeps saying: 'this is simple, my dear Watson.' Since then, it has become a popular expression." And then he added, just in case, to calm her down even more, "But if Watson explains it to Holmes, then he says: 'this is elementary, Holmes.' They are friends and get in trouble all the time."

"Like us, huh?"

"Yes, exactly like us."

"Can you give me this book? I want to read it too."

"Of course," Ben promised seriously. "I'll find a way to reach it to you."

"Better yet, bring it to me yourself," Emma said quietly, while looking away.

Ben didn't say anything, not knowing how to reply to this little Papuan girl.

"We will discuss it later; first, let's think of how to escape from this barn." Ben knew that if they ever got out of here alive, he would never come back again, and didn't want to make any promise knowing he wouldn't be able to fulfill it.

"As I was saying, it's simple. They don't need me. I woke up and they had to improvise on the go and bring me here as well. Now what? They cannot take me back now, so they will just eat me. I am a stranger here, a foreigner. I went to the jungle and disappeared with no trace. Lots of things could happen to a tourist who gets lost in the woods. Maybe I got eaten by some kind of hungry kangaroo, who knows? No one would even worry about me. But they will let you go. Yaga would forgive them since you came home, safe and sound. He wouldn't want to quarrel with Amal because of such a trifle. Am I right?"

"No, you are wrong."

"Why am I wrong? I think everything is logical."

"Maybe it is logical, but wrong. They will eat both of us."

"Both? But why? We agreed that they only wanted to isolate you from me."

"Amal doesn't want me to be his wife anymore because he saw us together. We were not supposed to be together at the barn that night. That was wrong. According to our customs, boys can't even talk to girls before they complete the passage rites. Girls are also prohibited from spending time with boys. I already told you that. I broke our rules! Remember when you asked me what Dzhamaya said? The one who treated your legs."

Ben nodded, but he had already guessed what she was going to say.

"She said that I did not behave as a decent girl should. I shamed myself and the whole tribe. Everyone already knows that I spent two nights in the barn with you, not to mention a day we spent together in the woods, and in the lake."

"It looks like I brought you a lot of problems. You shouldn't have saved me over there by the river. But how did Amal find out about me?"

"I do not know, probably someone from our tribe told him, and so he came by to personally verify the rumors, and then he saw us together. Now he does not need me anymore. He is the future leader of the tribe, and his wife must be untainted. You see, if the elders said that I will be his wife, then I should behave like one."

"Caesar's wife must be above suspicion." Ben grinned.

"Who is Caesar?"

"It doesn't matter; I will tell you later." Ben just waved. "So he doesn't want you to be his wife anymore. Fine. Then why did he abduct you? He could have just left and found himself another wife elsewhere."

280

"As a punishment for my wrongdoing. I ruined his reputation also, not only mine. He would never forgive anyone for that, especially a girl."

"I didn't think of that. This is completely changing everything. So, he kidnapped you for punishment, but he had to take me as well because I woke up and became a witness of your abduction. Besides, I inadvertently insulted him as well. You're right, Amal would never forgive both of us for that. This means we cannot persuade him to let us go, and we should only rely on ourselves. We are both going to be part of their celebratory dinner. By the way, this explains why they locked us in the same barn. They don't care anymore if we are together or separate. For them, we are no longer a boy and a girl. You don't put the chicken and the rooster in separate sections in the fridge. Both of them are just meat for the soup. So are we. Why didn't you tell me about it before?"

"I wanted to listen to your logical thinking. What you were saying was so interesting . . ."

Ben opened his mouth to say something rude, but instead, he got up and walked from corner to corner.

Silly girl, Ben thought angrily. *I spent an hour trying to understand their logic, and she didn't tell me that everything is ridiculously simple. So much time lost in vain because she wanted to hear my logical arguments. So stupid!*

However, she was right, and everything she said was logical. All the pieces of the puzzle had their own place in the big picture. Although that picture was a little gloomy.

"When is this celebration going to start? How much time do we have?"

"Usually it starts at or after sunset, when the first stars come out."

"Great! It is late morning right now, so we still have almost half a day, which should be enough for us to come up with a good plan."

"No, we don't have half a day."

"How come?"

"It takes a lot of time to prepare the *mumu* I told you about. It is complicated and a time-consuming process to make it tender. Also, the meat has to be properly prepared, chopped into pieces, seasoned, etc. I think they will prepare *mumu* from only one of us. And the other will be quickly roasted on the fire during the feast and sacrificed to the spirits."

"What? Are they going to give away the entire roasted body? Why would the spirits need so much meat? Can't they be satisfied with just one hand or leg?"

"No, I don't think they would give them the whole body, just a piece of meat, but the best one. Then the shaman will choose a piece for himself and one for the elders, of course. And whatever's left will be given to the rest of the men."

"Wait, how about women and children?"

"The meat is intended only for men. Women, and especially children, don't need meat as they don't do any physical labor. The men will throw them some entrails and offal, or bones with remnants of meat on it, but that's all."

"Didn't you hear about the proclaimed women's movement and equal rights for women?"

"No, we didn't hear that. But what does it mean?"

"Never mind." Ben sighed and continued, "How much time do we have left?"

"As I said before, they will make *mumu* from only one of us, and the second one will be simply roasted. It takes probably half a day to prepare a *mumu*. Whoever they choose for it will be killed much earlier than the other. The meat still has to be chopped into pieces, wrapped in leaves, and put—"

"Okay, okay, I get it now." Ben quickly stopped her, fearing that if he heard a few more words, he would burst into tears, but it was necessary to maintain at least a semblance of endurance, fortitude, and presence of mind. It seemed essential to pull himself together and focus on a plan of salvation.

"Let me peek out the window one more time," Emma suggested. She climbed up on his shoulders again.

"I was right," she concluded, getting down. "The cooking pit is almost ready. There are only a few more stones that need to be heated and laid around the walls. And they have also already prepared the firewood for a bonfire to roast the other one of us."

"We'll see about that." Ben chuckled. "I'm not going to sit around and wait to be cooked. Let's think how we could get out of here. We have roughly two hours to escape, as per my calculations. Do you have any thoughts or ideas?"

Emma shook her head; she didn't have any ideas.

"Neither do I, unfortunately. Let's think further. So, what do we know and what do we have in our possession?" He looked around the barn. "We have two pieces of rope, thanks to our captors who left them for us. Also, we have two dirty pieces of rag and some straw on the floor. That's all. And, of course, we have our clothes and your necklace. I am not sure how we can use all that, but just in case, we have to keep it in mind. Oh, and don't forget the amulet that I bought from you at the port. Although I'm afraid we already exhausted its magic power by now."

Emma sat on the floor, leaning against the wall, and listened to him attentively without interrupting, like an obedient student listens to every word of her teacher. Ben continued on with his discourse, walking around the perimeter of the barn. He got so carried away with it that he forgot about the impending danger.

"So, our goal is to get out of here in less than two hours. We are locked in a small but sturdy barn with a narrow window, which we cannot get through. The barn is locked firmly by a large padlock, and Amal is personally guarding us. However, he is not sitting by the door all the time, just occasionally comes to check on us to make sure we are still here, which is a big plus for us. There are also many people in the yard, minding their own business. Goal number two: after we escape from here, we should run to the forest quietly, unnoticed, attracting no attention. What else? Have I forgotten anything?"

Emma shook her head.

"No, I think that's all right."

"By the way, didn't you say there is a similar barn in your tribe? What is it for? Why do you need to have a lockable barn?"

"To hide valuable things there. If another tribe would attack us, they cannot open it so easily."

"What valuables do you have that it has to be locked?"

"Food, of course. Dried meat and vegetables we saved for rainy season. But also, we hide our weapons, tools—lot of things."

"How about the animals?"

"No, we keep animals in the corral that is equipped with troughs and drinking bowls. Although sometimes we use this barn for the animals that we want to slaughter."

"What?!"

"If you want to slay a boar, it has to be separated from the herd and placed in here. Animals are smart, and they will be disturbed if you slay one in front of the—"

Emma said it and immediately got frightened of her own words. She covered her mouth with both palms and looked at Ben with horror in her eyes. Now it had gotten to her as well. Until now it was nothing but a game, an exciting adventure. She did not seriously believe that they were in any danger, hoping deep down that this little misunderstanding would be resolved somehow. And now, here it was, a confirmation of their brutal intentions. This barn was the butchery, and they both were in it like animals for slaughter. Soon they would be killed and eaten. Both of them! Ben sat down on the floor and buried his face in his hands.

"They are going to eat us."

Emma walked over, sat down beside him, and patted him on the arm. Ben jerked his hand. He didn't need pity right now. One more word and he would burst into tears. But time was running out, and something had to be done quickly. Although nothing appropriate was coming to his mind, and he was sitting in despair, looking away, avoiding Emma's eyes.

Ben got up again, and began to inspect the walls, the floor, and the ceiling in earnest, hoping to find anything that would give them at least a meager chance for freedom. He stuck his fingers into every gap and tried every board for strength. And, of course, he found what he was looking for. As they say "where there's a will, there's a way."

He quickly pulled Emma from the floor and whispered in her ear, "I got it. I have a plan!"

By some incomprehensible conception of the local architect or sloppiness of their builders, the walls were much thinner than originally planned. The door frame, formed by a few downed boards, was designed for thicker walls and, therefore, protruded slightly, creating a small shelf above the entrance, narrow, only a few inches in width. If one climbed to the ledge using a transverse board, it would be possible to stand above the doorway, sticking fingers through one of many gaps between the boards for support.

Ben didn't know how to use this finding yet, but he felt that this was a starting point in the plan of their salvation. And such a plan immediately came up.

Emma beamed.

"Tell me. Please," she said, stamping with impatience. "What's the plan?"

"The plan is the following"—Ben rubbed his hands gleefully, already anticipating a swift freedom— "I climb up on that ledge, and you call Amal or whoever would be nearby at that time. He comes in, and I jump on him, knocking him down. Then we tie him up, take away the key, go out and lock the barn. That's all, then freedom. Of course, we have to discuss all the details—"

"Your plan will not work." Emma wilted again.

"Why not?" Ben had already seen them both at large in his mind's eye and didn't want to hear any criticism against his painstakingly developed plan.

"Have you seen Amal? He is much taller than you and ten times stronger. If you jump on him, he wouldn't even notice it, but will shake you off like a mosquito from his shoulder."

"But what if someone smaller comes in?" Ben did not give up. He knew that she was right and argued just to say something.

"Shorter maybe, but all their men are strong, you won't be able to knock them out. You are not heavy enough."

Ben didn't listen to her anymore. He was going back and forth in desperate thought. *It would be nice to have a large stone to whack him on the head. Then I could do whatever I wanted: twist his arm, tie him up, and plug his mouth with a gag.*

But they didn't have a stone. There was nothing except a pair of ropes. Well, the rope was also a useful tool in their position.

"Okay, another option." Ben cheered again. "We will make a lasso from the rope."

"What is a lasso?"

"This is a loop with a knot that slides along the rope and tightens it. I will show you how it works. I climb up there, and when Amal comes, I throw the loop on his neck and choke him."

Emma quietly walked into the other corner and brought the ropes to Ben.

"Okay, show me."

He enthusiastically began to make a cowboy lasso, and when the loop was ready, climbed up on the ledge, holding the rope with his teeth. Emma stood at the place where Amal would presumably stand when he entered the barn. Ben kept himself on the ledge holding to the board through the widest gap in the wall, while attempting to throw a loop around the neck of a motionless Emma with the other hand. However, it didn't even reach her, falling nearby. He had to repeat the attempt. Ben tried it over and over again but had no success. The loop either fell short or went over, hitting her head. The rope was stiff and tough, thrown from a height of over six feet, it fell on Emma's head with the force of a thrown stone. But she bravely endured, giving him the opportunity to practice. Unfortunately, even the length of two ropes tied together was not enough to make a normal wide loop, and he had to throw it precisely. Besides, he had to do it with only one hand, as he held onto the wall with the other, making the practice even more complicated. However, after many attempts, he managed to throw a loop around her neck.

"Okay, you got it, pull now," she said to Ben with excitement.

He tried to tighten the lasso around her neck with just one hand, but the rope, woven from the fibers of the *nug-sel*[27] tree, as Emma told him, was rough, and the knot didn't slide on it, nor did it tighten the loop. And to do it with only one hand was nearly impossible. When he once again pulled the rope, his fingers, numb from the strain, lost their grip slipping from the gap, and Ben almost fell to the floor. Luckily, he grabbed a protrusion nearby at the last moment and stayed on the ledge.

All attempts were in vain. Ben jumped down and angrily threw the useless rope in the corner of the barn.

I am a very lousy cowboy, he thought in desperation. *If I had a silk cord the knot would glide freely on it, then it would work just fine. But I have nothing except this piece of shoddy, rigid rope. How am I supposed to work with it?*

That's it. Deadlocked again. The plan that seemed so promising had failed ignominiously. Ben looked around the barn once again. There was no escape. A wave of despair washed over him yet again. Hope for freedom disappeared, followed by a complete apathy and indifference to their fate. An hour or two from then, Amal will come through this door, and that would be the end of all their anguish. He would drag them to the tree stump and chop them up into smaller pieces that could be wrapped in leaves and fit in their earthen oven. Or, maybe it wouldn't be him? Maybe they would take Emma first and save him for later to roast on their ritual bonfire. It was a pity that the girl would suffer just because she helped out an arrogant, stupid white boy who appeared in her life. It would be nice to be killed first and not hear Emma cry and scream when they killed her. Although he suspected that she wouldn't give them the pleasure and die quietly. But he would probably scream and screech shrilly like a pig being slaughtered. Literally.

Most likely I would go first and they will make a mumu out of me, Ben thought resignedly. *Emma is much smaller than me and has less meat. But I would be a delicious mumu. They will bake me in the sago leaves, stuffed with some finely chopped vegetables, and insert a sprig of fern in my mouth for decoration. After all, this is a festive dish, and it needs to be decorated in the spirit of the festivities. They would also spice me up a little with some fragrant seasonings to add flavor, like my mom prepares the turkey for Thanksgiving dinner.*

Suddenly a stupid and totally inappropriate thought came to his mind.

When mom prepared the turkey, she usually washed it thoroughly in warm water, skeptically examining the bird, making sure no area was left unwashed.

But they both were dusty and sweaty, and in stale, dirty clothes.

Are they going to eat us just like that, without even washing our bodies? What savages, non-humans. Why would they even need a holiday!?

Holidays. He also loved them, especially Thanksgiving. Usually his mother bought a large turkey, stuffed it with some cranberries mixed with crushed crackers and walnuts, and roasted it in the oven until the bird was dripping fat and the skin became crispy, turning a light brown color. They always had a lot of guests for Thanksgiving dinner, sitting at the ornate table and eating, while watching football.

From all these pleasant thoughts, he felt hungry again. They hadn't even eaten breakfast today, and his heart was filled with even more sadness at that thought. Today, these savages would celebrate their holiday. Perhaps their guests would come from the neighboring tribes and gather around the fire, they would sing songs, dance, and cut the juiciest pieces of meat for themselves.

I wonder what would be the best meat on me and Emma. Probably ribs. Each guest will cut a few from my chest (or Emma's), and eat, dipping it into barbecue sauce, while complimenting whoever cooked the dinner for the perfect mumu.

It would be so cool to run away right before they start serving the meal and spoil their celebration. Then, later, they could catch them and kill, eat, and do whatever they wanted. But their festival would still be spoiled.

I wonder what my mom would have done if her dinner escaped right before guests came? That would be funny if she had opened the oven, but the turkey was not there. All the guests would have come, but there was no dinner. Well, actually, the turkey would not escape from the oven. It should disappear before that, perhaps from the fridge. Mom opens it to get the bird out, prepared for the oven, but the fridge is empty.

No, wrong again. The turkey could not escape from the fridge either; it would already be dead, gutted, and filled with delicious, flavored ingredients. It can only disappear while it is alive . . . alive. It must disappear live; otherwise, it will be too late. How about this . . .

A week before the holiday, Mom went to the market and bought a live turkey, free range, organic, without any preservatives. Fresh turkey tastes better than a frozen one. She bought it in advance, because a day before the holiday you cannot get a fresh bird, even a frozen one is hard to find. So where would Mom keep the live bird till then? She can't just let it walk around the house. We have a little closet, a storage room, where Father keeps all the nails, boxes, and tools on the shelves. But he hardly ever uses it, so the storage room stays pretty empty, except the stuff on the shelves. Yes, this place would be perfect for it.

So she brought the bird home, but who is going to slaughter it? I wonder if my dad can do it. Probably not, as he faints just at the sight of blood on his finger. But this is not a problem. Any butcher shop offers such services. You can bring it to them, or they would even come to your house, slaughter and pluck the feathers off of it—it's only a matter of money. But it had to be done on the eve of the holiday to keep it fresh. Otherwise it would need to be kept in the fridge for a few days. What's the point of buying a live bird if you have to freeze it anyway? You can just buy a frozen turkey and avoid all the hassle.

So Mother invited many guests for the Thanksgiving dinner, and a day before she called the butcher shop to slaughter the turkey.

"So, where is my client?" the butcher said, walking to the kitchen, sharpening his big knife. "Let's do it quickly. I have a lot of calls today."

"Just wait here, I will bring it to you," Mom would have responded and went to get the 'client.'

She opens the closet door, and suddenly, she saw that there was . . . there is . . .

Ben quickly jumped to his feet and looked around, wild-eyed. He picked up a piece of rope again, which he had thrown in the corner after the failed experiments with the lasso, and looked at it again, like he was seeing it for the first time. He got down to the floor and ominously whispered in Emma's ear.

"So you're saying they are going to celebrate a festival today?"

"Yes, they are," Emma replied blankly, staring at the floor.

"Did you say that there are guests coming?"

"What guests? I did not say anything about that." She looked surprised.

But Ben just waved.

"It does not matter." He got up again.

"There will be no celebration!" Ben said solemnly. "I can promise you that! I'm going to cancel it!"

"What? How are you going to do that?" Emma's eyes widened in surprise.

"Very simple. The turkey has escaped! I have a plan!"

Chapter 2. A Day Of Collapsed Hopes

Margaret and Rupert stood in the middle of an empty street and looked around helplessly, not knowing what to do next. The sun was baking them mercilessly, and the smell of dust swam persistently in the heavy, humid air. They were both gloomy from this dreadful situation. Alone in a foreign country, without the slightest idea of what to do or where to go.

"Why is everything here not like in any civilized country?" Margaret mused. "Had something like this happened anywhere else in the world, in France, for example, the police of the entire district or the city would be alerted, and maybe even the whole country along with the rest of the European Union would be in search of the lost tourist. And if they didn't find the boy quickly, they would probably include the UN troops or NATO in the search." She wasn't versed in paramilitary alliances. "But here, you can't even ask for help from an ordinary policeman, because there are none of them around!

"This is just a waste of time. We need to go back to the jungle and search for Ben ourselves."

"We sure can go to the woods," Rupert agreed. "I'm just not sure if it is practical right now. I'm afraid that instead of helping Ben, we would get lost ourselves, and then Ben would have to save us."

"But we cannot just stand here and do nothing."

Rupert knew that Margaret was right, but couldn't think of anything else. Suddenly, he got a practical thought.

"You know, we could ask our hostess to help us find a guide for the jungle."

"Of course! This is a marvelous idea." Margaret perked up. "Why has such a simple thought not occurred to you before? We should have done that early in the morning. So much time is lost in vain; it will be dark in a few hours."

Rupert did not accept her criticism. The most important thing was that they had a plan now, and everything else was just minor difficulties that could be resolved along the way. It was better than sitting in complete helplessness, doing nothing.

"So, let's go back to the house and ask our hostess to find us a guide, and tomorrow, early in the morning, we will go to the jungle. Unless, of course, Ben comes back today. But we can use the rest of the day to prepare for tomorrow's trip. We will get a few flasks of water, some food, and flashlights. I think we might need them."

Without further delay, they went back to the house.

Halfway there, Rupert suddenly stopped and turned at the faint sound of a vehicle at the opposite end of the street. Margaret also squinted, gazing into the distance. The farsighted Rupert showed her a cloud of dust that was quickly approaching.

"The car seems to be coming here, and it looks like Hubert's bus."

Apathy immediately disappeared without a trace from both of them. In a minute, the bus will arrive, and Hubert would get out, followed by Ben, alive and unharmed.

"We must thank Hubert and reward him generously; he helped us so much." Margaret was about to discuss it with Rupert, but she did not have time for that. The bus pulled up, and Hubert stepped out, but there was no Ben with him. The revived hope vanished again as quickly as it appeared.

"Good afternoon, Mr. Rupert, ma'am," Hubert greeted them politely.

Margaret opened her mouth to tell him what she thought about such a "good afternoon," but instead just muttered something unintelligible in response.

"Well, it's all right," continued Hubert, ignoring the hostile expression on Margaret's face. "I've done everything as promised."

"What's all right? What have you done? Tell me."

"I've alerted all the nearby settlements about the missing boy through my channels. Now we just have to wait for results."

"Wait for what? Until someone finds him in this vast jungle and brings him back to us?" Margaret asked, worriedly.

"Well, yes, that's right." Hubert pretended he didn't notice the sarcasm in her voice and continued. "That's exactly what we need to do."

"Wait a minute," Rupert interrupted. "I think we're just wasting time. We should go back to the jungle ourselves. We were about to—"

"No, don't do it. The forest is large; you saw it yesterday. You won't be able to get very far. At best, you could get to one tribe, that's all, and the likelihood that the boy would be there is very slim. Besides, the fact that he went a few miles down the river reduces the chances of locating the right place fast. You have to understand that you physically could not go through all the surrounding tribes in one day. But I have notified all of them in the area, and believe me, they will do everything they can to save your son, and do it much faster than you can. Besides," Hubert said, squinting slyly, "your offer of a reward was helpful, and I'm sure it will speed up the search."

"But we cannot just sit here, doing nothing," Margaret groaned. "I'll go crazy just waiting helplessly."

"Madam, apparently the boy is alive, and that is most important. You have absolutely nothing to worry about, I can assure you. Where would he go from the woods? He might already be on his way here, and it would be ironic if at that time you went into the jungle looking for him! So you would go back and forth, one after another. You better sit here and wait."

"I think Hubert is right, dear." Rupert didn't like this any better than Margaret did, but Hubert had a valid point. "We'd better leave it to professionals."

"That's right. And believe me, our hunters are excellent trackers, and would recognize any barely visible footprints in the woods. I am pretty sure that someone has already found him by now, or at least his traces."

"But how did you notify these settlements in such a short time?"

"We have our own communication system, even more effective than your phone. But I have to be going, I'm sorry. I still have a lot to do today." On that note, Hubert jumped back into the bus. "But I'll be back soon. Meanwhile, use this opportunity and relax, take a stroll through our beautiful place on the waterfront. Or, better yet, go to the beach."

The bus exhaled a cloud of dove-colored smoke and left, once again taking away their hope for a prompt return of Ben.

But, apparently, God was merciful to them. The cloud of smoke, produced by the incomplete combustion of gasoline mixture of the old bus, hadn't even dissipated when a few figures showed up on the horizon, briskly heading toward the village.

They were still too far away. Even Rupert couldn't determine if Ben was in the group. But they knew that the arrival of these strangers was somehow connected with Ben and impatiently went, almost running toward the newcomers. Within a few seconds, it became clear that Ben was not with them.

The strangers were residents of the local tribes, according to their outfits, face paint, and body decorations. It was not clear if they had decorated themselves for the war or for the Sing-Sing festival[28], but it didn't matter. The most important thing was that they probably had information about Ben. The strangers came to Rupert and Margaret, bowed to them, and began their speech, which seemed to have been prepared ahead of time. Only one of them spoke a little English, and the other just came along to keep him company. He was standing a bit farther behind, letting his friend do all the talking and nodding from time to time.

"Dear mister and madam," the English-speaking Papuan began his speech, "we were instructed to bring to your attention—"

"Where is my son? What happened to him?" Margaret rudely interrupted the messenger, not capable of listening to his florid speech at this point.

"We were instructed by our esteemed elder Akelika Yaga"—the messenger calmly continued, not wanting to deviate from the prepared speech—"to bring to your attention that we've found your son."

"So where is he? Tell me!" Margaret couldn't withstand the long, monotonous speech.

"Your son is all right and is currently in our village. He injured his leg, but our medicine woman treated his wound, and tomorrow by noon we will bring him back to you."

"Why tomorrow? Why not now?"

"But . . . you see, madam . . . I just told you that he got injured a little and couldn't walk this far. But we have a good healer, and I am sure by tomorrow he will be able to walk normally."

"If he injured his leg, how did he get to your place?"

But the messenger didn't have a prepared answer to this question and simply ignored it.

"I'm telling you, he's all right. Don't worry," he repeated. "Tomorrow, at noon, you'll see him. And now, madam, mister, we need to go. I'm sorry."

With that, the messengers turned around and went back into the jungle. The nervous tension of the last few days disappeared, and Margaret swayed, feeling weak in her legs. Rupert grabbed her by the arm and looked around, trying to find anything to sit on. He found a fallen tree nearby and seated Margaret on it. He also sat down beside her.

"Well, everything has finally cleared up," Rupert said.

But Margaret did not share his optimism.

"No, nothing will be cleared until I see Ben."

"But, my dear, they said that everything is all right."

"If Ben was all right, he would have come here with them," Margaret said reasonably. "The fact that he didn't come says that something is wrong. And what about his leg? Did he fracture it? If so, then it will not heal by tomorrow. How do they expect him to come back by noon? Are they going to carry him all the way through the jungle? We should have asked them which tribe they are from so we could go to their settlement ourselves."

"You know, I'm thinking that Hubert was right, and his idea wasn't that bad after all."

"What do you mean? What idea?"

"You see, it's not going to do us any good if we sit here and speculate, 'What if he did this?' or 'What if we do that?', 'Maybe we should have done . . .' How about we go to the beach instead? Since we are already here, we might as well use this opportunity to go for a swim and have a nice walk along the coast. Ben will return tomorrow, and a day later, we will be back on the ship forgetting everything, like a bad dream."

They plunged into the warm water of the Bismarck Sea with pleasure, washing away the fatigue, the perspiration, and the street dust. After the swim, they lay in the water near the shore, letting the dashing whitecaps of the waves roll over them, carrying away the stress and exhaustion of the last few days, like the hands of a good massage therapist. The day was coming to an end, and the sun sat just above the horizon, casting sidelong rays on the mirrored surface of the sea. They hastily wrung out their wet bathing suits, walked along the waterfront until the path ran into an impassable cliff, and sat on top of a rock massif, watching the exceptional beauty of the equatorial sunset. Coming to their place of temporary residence, they told the hostess all the day's news, ate dinner, and went to sleep.

The next morning, they woke up early, surprisingly fresh and rested. The time spent at the beach did them good. Also, the news that Ben was all right dissipated their stress enough for them to relax and calmly wait for his arrival. However, after breakfast, they simply couldn't sit and wait quietly. They had to kill the few hours before noon. Margaret nervously paced in the small room, a few steps in one direction and the same distance in the opposite. But the time that passed seemed like infinity.

She offered to help the hostess around the house, but there was not much to do for her. A lot of work had to be done in the garden, but Margaret, being a typical urban woman, could not bring any significant help there. Of course, she knew that all fruits and vegetables most likely don't grow in the fresh produce section of the supermarkets, but that was the limit of her knowledge of this industry.

As always, Rupert saved the situation and came up with yet another good idea. He also wandered around the small house for a while, then went outside, walked along the path to the end of the yard, and came across a small cabin that he immediately recognized as a shower. Suddenly he remembered that they hadn't taken a shower for a few days. Rupert filled the tank on the roof with water (plumbers didn't pipe the house to the central plumbing) and they both had a shower. Cold water refreshed them, and they were in a great mood.

The rest of the morning passed by uneventfully. They changed their clothes and walked slowly toward the woods, hoping to intercept Ben on his way to the village.

But as soon as they came out from the house, they met the postwoman Beida.

"Good morning," she greeted them. "I have good news for you. Your son just called from New York and said that he's all right, and tomorrow, that is already today, he will be here, in the port. So, he asked you not to worry, as everything is just fine."

This message struck them with its absurdity.

How could Ben be in New York, and if he is there, how could he come here today?

"I do not know," Beida replied to Rupert's question. "I was surprised myself. But aren't you the ones who are looking for your son?"

"Well, yes, but he cannot be in New York now. He is here, on this island, and should be on his way to the port right now. We are expecting him to come any minute. It must be some kind of mistake."

"No mistakes." Beida was offended. "I told you word for word what he told me. You're Mr. and Mrs. Pearson, right?"

"Yes, we are."

"So, I am telling you that your son Marcus called and said—"

"Ah, I understand now." Rupert laughed with relief. "Thank you so much, Beida, you did everything right. You see, Marcus is not our son. He is our son's friend, and he is in New York now. It looks like Ben, our son, somehow contacted him, and asked him to let us know that he is alive and well. But I have no idea how he managed to communicate that to Marcus in New York, from the jungle! This is a mystery to us, and I will ask him about it once he is back."

They thanked Beida once again and continued on their way toward the woods to meet Ben. As the sun rose to the zenith, the messengers from the previous day came from the woods, but Ben was not with them. In anticipation of further difficulties, Margaret rushed to them.

"Where is my son?" she shouted angrily from afar.

Panting from the brisk walk they'd had, the English-speaking messenger took time to compose himself. Stumbling and searching for the appropriate English words in his meager vocabulary, he began, "You see, madam, your son is gone."

"What do you mean he is gone? How can he be gone with the injured leg? Where did he go?"

"They went for a walk in the woods. We didn't even notice when—"

"They? Who are 'they'?"

"One girl from our village. I think she was the one who brought him to our settlement."

"That's my boy." Rupert smiled. "Even in the jungle he managed to find himself a girlfriend, just like his father in his youth."

"I don't remember you at his age running through the jungle looking for some girlfriends!" snapped Margaret, who had known her husband since their school years.

"We tried to find them, but they had already gone quite far," the messenger continued, ignoring their short skirmish. "Don't worry, our men are looking for them now, and I am sure they will find them and bring your son back to you soon. We just wanted to notify you that we won't be able to bring him back at the promised time. But I can assure you that he will be here soon. And now we also have to go to search for them."

With these words, they turned around and headed back toward the woods to avoid further questions.

"Wait!" Margaret shouted after them. "We will go with you."

"No, ma'am, you wait here. He is probably on his way to the port, and you don't want to miss him if he is," the messenger shouted from afar as they plunged into the thicket.

Chapter 3. Escape

"I have a plan," Ben repeated.

Emma looked at him, wide-eyed with amazement. She really wanted to believe him, but she was afraid of yet another failure. The stronger the hope, the greater the disappointment.

"What's a turkey? Where does it go?" she whispered, the only thing she could ask.

"Never mind that. I'll tell you later." Ben shrugged.

He grabbed her arm and dragged her to the corner farthest from the door, sat on the floor, and began to explain his plan, whispering right into her ear. She listened in complete silence, and her facial expression kept changing. From despair and sadness, her eyes became interested at first, then narrowed and sparkled with mischief. Her face bloomed with joy, and at the end, she laughed loudly, but quickly covered her mouth, as someone outside could have heard it. Ben kept on talking and talking, gesticulating frantically and pointing to the left, then to the right, and even to the ceiling.

"You know, it actually might work," she said, when Ben finished. "I am sure it will."

Apathy had immediately disappeared, replaced with excitement, and adrenaline in their blood had begun to seethe with renewed vigor.

"How much time do you think we have left?"

"I do not know. Let's look out the window one more time."

Emma climbed onto Ben's shoulder with the agility of a kitten, and clung to the opening.

"Almost all the stones have been laid." Emma reported the situation in the yard after she got down. "I think it will be completely ready in less than an hour."

"What after that? When are they going to lay the meat?"

"Not right away. The hot stones have to be covered with the leaves, preferably fresh cut, and soaked in water. Otherwise, they will be too dry and will catch fire quickly."

"So, we have an hour and a half, no more than that; I guess that should be enough."

"No, we have less time," Emma argued, "as the meat also must be prepared, chopped into smaller pieces and wrapped in leaves. In addition, it takes time to do the killing ceremony. They cannot just slaughter the victim. There is a whole ritual behind that; otherwise, it would be just a murder."

"How do they do this ceremony? What's the procedure?"

"I don't know. I've never seen one myself. I told you that we are not practicing it anymore. Besides, certain formalities may vary, depending on the festival. But from what I heard in our tribe, after the ritual dances, one of the men strikes the victim and makes a hole in here," Emma continued ruthlessly, pointing to the temporal bone. "Or they might remove the top of the head for easy access to the brain. Then they will take out your brain and eat it or maybe suck it out through the hole—"

"How come they are going to take *my* brains . . . or suck it out?" Ben was outraged. "Why not yours?"

"Who would need my brains? I will be just a meat for sacrifice. They will give my arms or legs to the spirits and eat the rest of me. But you are smart, going to school, and knowing a lot about computers. Definitely, they would prefer your brains. So, as I was saying, after that, they would pull out your heart, also a useful and delicious body part, and whatever is left will be chopped into smaller pieces, wrapped—"

"Okay, okay. I got it," Ben hastened to interrupt her. "I don't need more details. By the way, if I was the cannibal, I would definitely eat your brain," Ben complimented her.

"Really? You would do that?" Emma blushed. Obviously, she liked the compliment.

"Of course. Moreover, I would never give away your arms or legs either, and eat it myself. All of it."

"But you have to give some meat to the spirits."

"Then I would have thrown them a bit of your tripe. That would be enough."

Now, when they had a real plan of escaping, they were in a good mood once again and talked about their possible death as something extraneous. All of a sudden, Ben looked at Emma suspiciously.

"You said that your tribe no longer practices cannibalism? For someone who has never seen other people eating human flesh, you are well-versed in all of these rituals."

"There are still plenty of people in our tribe, like Dzhamaya, and many others, who remember the days when it was considered normal. My grandmother told me too, from what she remembered as a child when she left the tribe."

"Did your grandmother ever eat human meat?"

"I do not know. I never asked her about it."

"Why not? Didn't you want to know that?"

"Have you ever asked your mother or grandmother what they ate for dinner thirty years ago?"

"Well, that's different. How can you compare it?"

"How is it different?" Emma said seriously.

"We used to have some traditions and customs. Our ancestors did that for thousands of years, and our parents and grandparents did it. I cannot blame them, cannot say it is right or wrong. It is what it is. It makes no difference what my grandmother or great-grandmother ate. They ate what they had at that time, like we eat baked yams or boar meat now. Today we no longer practice it, but in other tribes, like in this one, they are still doing it. None of us can change our past, and we cannot condemn anybody. Let's drop this subject."

"Yes, you're right. I'm sorry," Ben agreed with her passionate speech. "Let's focus on our escape. We have, let's say, less than an hour left. This means that we have to hurry, but not rush."

"What do you mean? How's that possible?"

"You see, we will have only one attempt to get everything right. If anything goes wrong due to our negligence or some trifles that we didn't foresee, then an hour from now, one of us will end up in the cooking pit, and the second one will be roasted on the fire. This would be the price for our mistake. We have to foresee every little detail and be prepared for any eventuality. Do you agree?"

"I agree." She nodded.

They began to discuss details of the escape, quietly whispering, afraid that someone outside could hear them arguing about every step, making corrections, interrupting each other, and suggesting new options of possible developments of events. At one detail their views differed radically. Emma insisted on her scenario, and Ben tried to prove her wrong, offering his own set of action. They argued, almost quarreled, as both did not want to give in, but they eventually reached a compromise that satisfied both of them.

Half an hour later, the plan was ready and reconciled to the smallest detail, and they began the rehearsal. They repeatedly honed their skills in their respective roles, and calculated the time required for each step to the exact second, which Ben quietly counted due to the absence of a watch. Throughout the preparation, their eyes were also on the door, fearing that Amal would notice their preparations and immediately stop everything as soon as he approached the barn.

Finally, the plan was ready. All the steps were thought out and verified to the smallest details. They still had to figure out the safest escape route, but it was going to be difficult, since Emma had never been in this village before and was not familiar with the surroundings. Obviously Ben had no clue about it either.

To get at least some information about the settlement, Emma and Ben looked through every gap in the wall, not neglecting the one that was high on the ceiling. They moved all the hay to a corner, revealing dry, hard, concrete-like ground. Emma donated one boar tooth from her necklace and, using it like a pencil, scrawled a square on the ground, which represented the place of their imprisonment. Then she looked through each gap, standing on Ben's shoulders, and meticulously drew all the information on the "map" with the precision of a skilled cartographer. For the umpteenth time, Ben was amazed at her natural intelligence and wit.

She needs to go to school. It would be easy for her to catch up on the lost years of schooling, he thought, admiring how accurately she had drawn the layout of the village on the improvised map.

But all that could wait until they got out of here. Right now, they had to focus on their escape. Soon, the general map of the settlement was ready, and they had enough information to put their plan in action. After a short debate, they decided to do a reconnaissance on the go and make necessary adjustments in the escape route.

Everything was ready to execute the plan. They ended up with three scenarios. The main plan was very promising and had a good chance of success. However, in the case of unforeseen complications, they had a second scenario, unpleasant and undesirable. But if that option failed, then it was decided to simply run outside through the open door and flee in different directions, relying only on their legs and hoping for a miracle. In this third case, they had a major disagreement. Ben insisted that he would lead away a group of pursuers, letting Emma run away and hide in the woods. But she firmly declined his plan, saying they either stay together, or both be taken. As a result of the heated debate, it was decided they would just scatter in different directions, and if one got caught, the other would act according to the circumstances. But to avoid confusion during the critical moment and not to run in the same direction, they specified who should go where.

Now they were waiting for the right moment to begin their plan, when there would be the least amount of people outside. They stuck to the gaps in the walls, looking for the shadows of villagers and listening to their voices. Finally, such a moment arrived, and they both agreed: it's time!

"Wait," Ben suddenly stopped her. "One more thing."

"What is it now?" Emma was already embodied in her role, like an actress from the provincial theater personified in the role of Juliet before the premiere; she couldn't wait to start the show.

"You know, from this point on, anything could happen to us. We might get caught and be killed, and I would not see you anymore. I want to thank you for what you've done for me, as I might not have another opportunity to do so." He hugged her tightly.

"If we hurry, then you will have a chance to say it in a more pleasant situation. But if we wait a little longer then I would not need your appreciation anymore. But anyway, I am glad that I met you and could help."

"Then let's get to work!"

"Yes, let's!" Emma replied, laughing, and fell on the floor in front of the entrance door, in accordance with her role.

The plan was simply brilliant, but a little bit childish. Probably none of the adults would dare to do it, doubting in a positive outcome. But that was exactly the idea, a childish solution promised a good chance for success.

Ben picked up the rope and began to tie Emma. The tightness was only visual, because she was holding the ends of it in her hands behind her back, and at the right moment, she could easily get free from it even faster than the notorious Houdini. They had rehearsed her release and after many attempts achieved good results.

They had also prepared the gag, the same piece of cloth that was used during the abduction. Humane Ben did not want to thrust a dirty rag into her mouth and instead offered to donate the remains of his shirt, but Emma said that he should not worry about such trivial matters.

"It is better to suffer a few minutes with a dirty rag in the mouth than forever lose my head. Besides, your shirt is not much cleaner anyway," she noted reasonably.

Without any further doubts, Ben "tightly" sealed her mouth. As in the case with the rope, the gag was also fake, and Emma was biting it with her teeth, to make sure it wouldn't fall out ahead of time, but she could easily push it out with her tongue at the right moment.

They used just one piece of the rag, and Ben folded and frugally put the second piece in his pocket, just in case. You never know what could become handy in the jungle.

So, everything was ready. Emma was lying on the floor, gagged and tied "securely," with her feet facing the entrance door. Ben looked through the gap in the wall, waiting for Amal. As soon as he saw his shadow on the ground, he knocked on the door. That's it, the point of no return. The process had begun.

Ben glanced at Emma one last time to make sure everything was right.

"Remember, just as we planned, no improvisations," he cautioned her.

He had a vague feeling, a concern that something was seriously wrong. Something didn't feel right, which, in their situation, could be vital. He had felt it all day since first awakening and could not figure out what was bothering him. But there was no time for scrutiny anymore as the key grated in the lock and the action began.

Ben quickly climbed on the door, in perfect timing (they also practiced it repeatedly until he achieved an acceptable result), and stood on the makeshift ledge above. Due to the sloping roof, there was enough space to stand relatively comfortably, and Ben leaned back, wanting to embed himself into the wall, becoming invisible. Hearing keys in the lock, Emma moaned loudly through the gag, trying to kick the door. But, of course, she couldn't do it, as her legs were tied (that's why Ben had to knock for her, before taking place above the door).

The door swung open and Amal entered the barn. Strong, over six feet tall, he seemed to be carved out of granite. Looking at his muscular body and wide shoulders, Ben prayed to God that everything went well so they would not have to commence the second option, which was supposed to kick in if Amal did not act according to their scenario. There was one caveat, the unknown factor: it was unclear what plans he had for Emma. If he did not care about her fate anymore and she was nothing more than a part of their holiday dinner, then

Amal wouldn't untie her. Indeed, what difference would it make if she was tied or not, if they are going to kill her soon anyway? But Amal would definitely rush to help her if he still considered Emma his future wife. In this case, Ben had to knock him off his feet. To jump on the standing Amal would be idiotic, but if he bent over trying to untie Emma, then it would be the opportune moment to knock him down. Ben really hoped that Amal would hit his head against the hard ground, losing consciousness. They even removed all the straw from the floor, exposing the concrete-like ground in the place where Amal's head would make contact with the floor. Even if they just stunned him for a few seconds that would be enough time to slip out the door and escape into the woods. The tricky part was to calculate the proper moment of the jump, letting Emma untie herself at least partially. Otherwise, they would lose precious seconds stopping to release her from the rope.

Fortunately, they did not have to execute the backup plan; shrewd Emma did everything correctly. She writhed on the floor, moaning wildly and shaking her head about, trying to free her mouth from the gag. Emma had to "get rid" of it no sooner than Amal noticed her. As soon as the door opened, she immediately raked her mouth against her shoulder and freed herself from the gag. They had made it fit very well. She was writhing and loosening the rope, screaming hysterically. The loudness of the scream was also properly chosen so that her voice was loud enough for Amal, and at the same time, did not attract the attention of the other tribe-mates. To do so, she had to sound a little hoarse, which was quite natural since her mouth was plugged with the gag for a long time. It turned out naturally loud to make Amal act according to their plan, and it could not be heard outside the barn. She rolled her eyes wildly, with real tears, nodding at the window opening near the ceiling and shouting at Amal.

What talent! Ben thought with tender emotion, looking down at the squirming Emma. *The theater world missed getting one great actress!*

Naturally, he didn't understand a single word of what she was saying, but it didn't matter anyway, as her speech was meticulously chosen, agreed upon and rehearsed. She was telling Amal that the ungrateful white boy had beaten her and tied her up and then fled through the window opening. She begged Amal to catch and punish Ben before he had gone too far, while also yelling at him for having left her alone in this barn with the boy. It was important not to give Amal time to think and doubt that Ben could get out through this window. Therefore, Emma was yelling with short, abrupt phrases, distracting him from thinking. Her text would be translated to something like this:

"He is out. He beat me up. Tied me. Escaped through the window. Catch him. Fast. Couldn't be far. Hurry, Amal. He will run away."

But most importantly, he was not supposed to come inside farther than he was allowed. To avoid that, Ben strategically placed Emma on the floor just by the entrance. The barn was small, with no place to hide. They evenly spread all the straw in a thin layer, to make sure there was no protrusion to attract his attention. Amal had to open the door, look at the stage sets, and run in a hurry to catch Ben, forgetting to lock the barn. Why should he spend precious seconds closing the door if the boy had already escaped and Emma was firmly tied up?

The plan worked perfectly, and Amal did everything right! Confused from Emma's cry, he rushed to catch bad boy, who probably hadn't gone far. He sped away so fast that it was obvious that Emma had played her role flawlessly. Standing above the door, Ben regretted not being in a position to observe Amal's face. He would have gladly given up his new laptop in exchange for the opportunity to see the expression on his face, which he would have remembered until old age.

The joy of the success made Ben jump to the ground as soon as Amal left, jeopardizing the entire operation. It was a serious mistake. According to the plan, he had to get down slowly, spending enough seconds to let Amal go far enough from the barn. If Amal had looked back, it would have been the end of their plan, and their lives, because of this small mistake.

But everything was fine, and a few seconds later, Ben and Emma peered out the door. The bamboozled Amal ran after Ben, or perhaps to report to the elders that their dinner had escaped. There were a few women outside making their final preparation for the festival; men were sitting nearby doing their hair. Kids were playing at the forest glade. Everybody was busy, and the path was clear.

Ben and Emma went out to the yard, closing the door behind them, and slowly walked to the planned shelter. Ben took off his shoes and carried them in his hands. Footprints of the soles would be well imprinted on the dusty ground, showing the direction of their escape, but the trail of his bare feet were no different than hundreds of similar ones belonging to the local residents. The shelter that they aimed for were thick, tall bushes that Emma identified after looking through the slits in the barn.

During certain seasons, despite the proximity of the mountain ranges, the strong monsoon winds created a real disaster for the fields and gardens, which are present in every tribal settlement. The wind literally blows away all the crops, after which the entire tribe lives from hand to mouth, since the majority of their food is growing in these fields. To save the crops, the residents planted special shrubs upwind to protect the crop. Such shrubs are usually tall and wide and were a perfect hiding place for fugitives.

They slipped, unnoticed, into the dense foliage and caught their breath. Behind the bushes, there was an open field, and the forest began fifty yards beyond that. The first part of the plan had been successfully completed, but the second part—there was no second part. Their vague knowledge of the surrounding terrain was clearly not enough to develop a strategy, so it was decided to act according to circumstances, improvising on the go.

They looked out from their hideout. The forest nearby beckoned to them like a magnet.

"Let's run into the woods," Ben said impatiently.

"No, just stay down quietly and wait." Emma firmly tugged his arm, forcing him to lie on the ground.

"What are we waiting for?"

"I do not know. But we cannot go just yet. We must wait."

Ben thought that Emma was right, they shouldn't rush away headlong into the forest. First, they should see the reaction of their opponents. He lay down comfortably next to her, choosing a viewpoint between the branches.

"By the way, you promised to tell me what a turkey is," Emma reminded him, "and where did it go? How did you come up with such a great plan, anyway? I thought that they were going to kill us soon."

"The turkey is a bird, like a chicken, only bigger. We cook them for our holiday."

"It is probably delicious." Emma sighed. "I ate chicken a few times when my grandmother cooked it for me, and I liked it."

Ben wanted to tell Emma how his mother prepared turkey for Thanksgiving dinner, stuffing it with crushed walnuts and cranberry sauce, and how it comes out soft, with crisp brown skin. But he said nothing, not wanting to tease a girl who hardly ever gets the chance to eat meat.

"It's not that tasty. Not like your grandma's chicken. So, anyway, I imagined that my mom bought a live turkey for our holiday and locked it in the closet. A few days later, she opened the door to get it, but the bird had flown up on the shelf and sat there quietly. Mom was looking for it on the floor, and didn't even think to look higher. She ran to look for it in the house in such a rush that she left the closet door open. She was nervous, as the guests would be coming soon, and the butcher was waiting to slaughter it . . . From there, I came up with a plan."

"Wow. That was smart. I wouldn't have thought of that. Look, someone is coming, probably Amal." Emma pointed at somebody approaching them.

It turned out that it was indeed the ubiquitous Amal. He sneaked through the gap in the bushes near them and came out to the field. They held their breath, afraid to make a sound, as he was so close to them that they could even smell his sweat. He would have probably noticed them if he wasn't looking down at the loose soil, intently searching for footprints and traces of the fugitives. Amal went along the one side, then the other, and went back, passing through the line of bushes somewhere else, far from them. After yet another minute, the rustle of his footsteps died away, and Amal disappeared behind the *buambramra* in the village.

"We can go now," Emma said.

They quietly got out, trying not to make any noise, and slowly headed toward the woods. Ben wanted to run, but Emma was holding his hand tightly.

"Walk normal, don't run. We shall not attract their attention. And stop looking back all the time. You would know if they noticed us."

"How would I know?" Ben asked.

"You would probably hear the stomping of their feet or screaming. But we would know for sure."

The jungle edge was coming closer unbearably slowly. Trickles of sweat were running down Ben's back, as he had to suppress the urge to run to the forest. But he knew that Emma was right and they should stay calm, not attracting anyone's attention. As soon as they stepped into the protection of the woods, without saying a word, both ran into the thicket. However, they had to stop and spend another minute while Ben put on his shoes. Then, without further delay, they fled down the dale, making their way through the thick bushes and vines hanging from the trees, breaking garlands of moss, and jumping over fallen trees.

After half an hour of erratic running through the rough terrain, both were exhausted and had to stop, panting. Ben was always resilient to physical activities, but the chaotic run had completely stolen his breath. Running through the jungle technique is slightly different from running on a stadium track. Emma also stood nearby, trying hard to catch her breath.

"We cannot run like that," Emma said, calming down a bit. "It is bad. We must save energy, otherwise we will not be able to get far. Also, we are leaving too many traces, and they will quickly find us. We have to be more careful."

"How can we be careful? We cannot fly through the air."

"We don't need to fly, but we shouldn't go through the bushes either, as we break off leaves. It is better to go around the hindrances than to pass through them."

"Then perhaps you should lead the way and I'll follow you. It seems that you know better what to do, this is your field."

Emma nodded.

"Let's go."

They started to move forward again, changing the pace from walking to jogging when the landscape of the jungle allowed. Oddly enough, it turned out even faster than running. Gently, avoiding the branches of shrubs and hanging necklaces of moss, they made their way down the mountain slope. At times, the slope became plains, and in some places, it went steeply downhill and even turned into a cliff. Now they had to go down slowly, but loose stones rolled down the slope too, creating a lot of noise that echoed throughout the forest. Suddenly Emma stopped, listening to the silence of the woods.

"They're coming close."

"How do you know?" Ben was surprised.

"They scared some birds." She pointed to a flock of birds, poised far in the sky somewhere behind them. "Do you see them? That's Amal, or whomever he sent to catch us."

"Maybe the bird just flew away?" Ben asked with despair in his voice. He did not want to believe that they had found them so quickly and were rapidly catching up with them. But he knew that Emma was right. Most likely, they found their trails in the woods and would be here soon. That meant that they had no more than a half-hour head start.

"So what are we waiting for? Let's go."

"No, we cannot rush either. We have to knock them off our scent. I know one place a little bit farther that, if we could reach it, we will be able to break away from them by far."

They ran again, but deliberately saved energy, alternating with jogging and walking. After an hour of running at this pace, Emma stopped again.

"Can you climb trees?" she asked suddenly.

"Of course I can," Ben replied, but he glanced at the surrounding ancient giants and added, "depending on which tree."

"Okay, let's go."

They were moving farther and farther away from the place of their confinement. In some areas it was nearly impossible to move fast enough, and they had to significantly slow down to overcome various obstacles. They had been running for several hours by now and, according to Emma, they had already passed more than half the way. Ben was no longer looking back, as he knew that the pursuers were somewhere close, but Emma didn't seem to worry about it anymore, stubbornly moving ahead and leading Ben.

Soon the jungle visibly changed. The tree crowns covered the sky with a solid green shield, and the woods became gloomier and creepy. The forest here was so thick that often they had to squeeze between closely spaced tree trunks or climb over fallen trees, significantly reducing their speed.

"Why did we come here?" Ben asked. "We should have stayed in the area with the sparse growth of trees, even if it is a longer way home. It would have been much faster."

"Actually, it is the other way around. We made a detour to get here. This forest is our deliverance. Just be patient, we're almost there."

Thus far, Ben thought he had already seen the dense jungles, but he was wrong. The impassable jungles had just begun. It was real forest chaos. This place was located in the lowlands, enclosed on all sides by mountain ranges forming natural barriers to the wind; therefore, the air in here was motionless. The ripened seeds fell to the ground, giving life to a new generation in close proximity to each other. Young growth rose, reaching for the light, vigorously pushing, smashing, and breaking with their strong branches the adjacent century-old giants. Rotten old trees, with the insides eaten by the insects, did not have any chance to survive under the onslaught of the young, powerful ones. Tree trunks huge in girth leaned toward the ground, and eventually fell. Immediately, countless hordes of insects began their work, performing the function of forest cleaners, and after half a century, there would be no trace left of the fallen giant. Many generations of trees replaced one another over thousands of years. Older ones were dying, falling right on the canopies of the younger generation, hampering their growth but not breaking their will to live and their craving for the sun; they skirted around the deadwood with their flexible trunks.

Emma had stopped near one of the trees, heavily banked under the pressure of its powerful neighbor.

"We have to climb up there and go to the adjacent tree, and then to the next one, and the next. This way, we can go quite far over the top and throw our pursuers off the scent."

Indeed, the trees grew so densely that their branches intertwined with each other creating a maze for many miles around. It was practically impossible to determine which branch belonged to which tree.

Ben liked the idea and enthusiastically began to climb the sloping tree trunk, but Emma immediately dampened his ardor.

"No, not from here, you need to go from the other side."

"Why? It is easier to climb on the slope."

"This is elementary, Holmes," quipped Emma. "You will break the bark off and leave marks on the trunk. But the other side is not visible to them. Of course, they will find us anyway, but it will take longer, and we will buy ourselves some more time."

Ben sighed. It was hard to climb from the other side, where the tree is inclined on you. Fortunately, he found a branch located within reach. He jumped up and clutched on it, pulling himself up. A few minutes later he was already moving to the next branch above, getting higher and higher. He was not worried about Emma, as he knew that she climbed trees as good as she walked on the ground. And indeed, she quickly caught up with him and went farther up. Soon she was blithely sitting on the top of the tree, while Ben was clumsily getting up, slowly moving from one branch to another.

When he finally reached the top, Emma gave him a minute to catch his breath and pointed to the thick branch that leaned against a nearby tree, like a bridge. They moved through the "bridge" to the next tree, then the next and the next, and soon they were able to walk a fairly large distance. At first it was easy and fun to travel this way. Ben even tried to compete with Emma, who got to the next tree faster, walking on different branches and levels. They were so excited with this game that at times they even forgot about their enemies. But soon Ben realized that he could not keep up with her. He watched enviously as Emma jumped from one branch to another with the agility of a little monkey, hanging by one arm high above the ground, while reaching the next branch, and hanging upside down, clinging with her bare feet. He couldn't do that. Perhaps not many circus acrobats could have done that either, given that there was no safety net under them, just the hard ground covered with fallen tree trunks, bristling with broken boughs and branches.

Soon the forest thinned out. The distance between trees increased markedly. Even Emma became more cautious and careful in her movements. Ben was moving much slower, gently stepping from one branch to another, balancing with the risk of falling down, and when he reached the next tree, firmly clutched to it. Once the branch that he used as a bridge abruptly ended, not reaching the next tree, and he even had to go back in search of a better route in the endless maze. Soon Emma commanded him to get down to the ground. The forest thinned down so much that further travel this way had become impossible.

"Let's rest a little, but not for too long," Emma ordered.

Ben sat on a fallen tree trunk, giving rest to his trembling arms and legs.

"Wow, it looks like we have come a considerable distance through the trees," Ben said, massaging his numb arm muscles. "How far are we from your settlement?"

"Not far; soon we will be in our territory."

"You know, I actually liked to move around this way, and I also liked this forest, although it is a bit gloomy for my taste."

"Yes, I like it here too. I know this place very well. We call it 'Deadwood'."

"Deadwood? Why is it dead?"

"There are no animals, except the rats and insects. Even birds don't fly here often, though there is a lot of food for them."

"Then why don't they fly here?"

"Did you see how dense the foliage is? The trees almost completely block the sky. If birds get in, it will be hard for them to find the way out. But we sometimes come here to collect the larvae, the worms inside the rotten trees."

"Trespassing?" Ben joked.

"Yep, we are," Emma agreed merrily. "There are a lot of larvae, which I told you about, remember? Many of these fallen trees are hollow, and if you step on it you would fall right through, as these maggots eat away all the insides. They are very hearty and nutritious. We collect and eat them."

"Okay, okay. I get it now." Ben could barely suppress his nausea.

Emma began to look around the deadwood. Once she found the desired trunk, she called Ben.

"Come here. I'll show you something."

Ben reluctantly got up and trudged to her. His whole body ached after the recent exercise, and he did not want to get up. Emma removed the half-rotted bark, and Ben saw the swarming mass of pale gray, almost white, decent-sized worms that Emma affectionately called larvae.

"Here they are," Emma said delightedly, and her eyes flashed with hungry luster. She scooped up a handful of them, each as thick as a man's thumb, and brought them to her mouth. But Ben quickly grabbed her hand.

"Emma, please don't," he pleaded frantically, swallowing saliva and suppressing his gag reflex. "I'm begging you. I believe you that they are tasty, but don't eat it, not right now."

"Why not?" she asked dazedly. "I know that this is not your type of food, so I'm not even offering it to you. But I can eat it." Her hand with the delicacy once again went up to her mouth.

But Ben was on alert and caught it in time again.

"Please, don't. In a few days you can come back here and collect a whole bag of these—" Ben grimaced and continued, "worms . . . well, larvae—whatever you call them, and have a nice meal. But not right now, please."

"All right, if you insist." Emma shrugged and regretfully threw the tasty and nutritious delicacies on the ground, and they immediately crawled back to their mates to continue their meal. Emma followed them with her eyes sadly, and Ben noticed that look.

"I know you're hungry," Ben quickly added before she changed her mind. "We have not eaten since yesterday. I am actually hungry too. If you want, we can find something tasty in the woods. Perhaps some edible roots or other vegetables. We will make a fire, just like yesterday, and I will eat everything. I'll chew on any vegetables, leaves, roots, or even driftwood, anything that you point at. Then we can get some fruit for dessert. Would you like that?"

"Yes, I would love that," Emma said quietly.

"Great, then let's just get to your site and do the picnic there. You said that we are close to your territory."

But such a desired plan was never meant to happen. Emma suddenly turned around and looked back in the thicket.

"Let's move, quickly," she said, looking around.

Ben didn't hear anything suspicious, however, he dutifully got up and went after her. They walked briskly, sometimes breaking into a run when the landscape allowed, and soon Emma stopped.

"We will hide in here and wait for our pursuers to pass by. This will also give us a chance to rest for a while."

At first Ben didn't notice the hideout. They were on open terrain, with some fallen tree trunks like everywhere else. But then he saw the place that Emma was pointing to.

A few big trees fell onto the hillock, forming a small space, a kind of makeshift dugout beneath them, due to an uneven ground. Over time, these fallen trees had overgrown with moss intertwined with vines and completely concealed the space underneath. Emma pointed to the small gap. This was the well-camouflaged entrance to the dugout, which nobody would ever notice, unless one already knew about it.

Unpleasant thoughts about possible snakes flashed through Ben's mind, but he rejected them quickly. Emma knew better what to do, and if she said that they needed to crawl to that hole, then it was safer there than outside, and Ben climbed into the shelter without further hesitation. Emma collected a few twigs and also went inside, masking the entrance with the branches. Now it was impossible to see the hideout from the outside.

"There is also another exit." Emma pointed to the far corner of the "bunker."

"If they find us, we will go through there and run away."

They settled comfortably at the bottom of this small cave and spread the branches at the entrance a bit for a better view. Now they could see everything that was going on outside.

"Are you sure that they are still pursuing us?"

"They're here, and came close. I think they even heard us when we talked."

"I do not understand," Ben said, whispering. "Why is it so important for them to catch us? They are coming after us with enviable persistence. Yes, we ruined their holiday, spoiled the celebration, and took away the holiday dinner. I thought they would search for us for few hours and then let us go. But they have been on the chase for half a day already. It will be dark soon, but instead of preparing for the festival and looking for an alternative meal, they have kept running after us through the forest. This is clearly not convergent."

"First of all, we were the cause of their festival, if you remember. They caught us and made a holiday. We ran away and took a holiday away from them."

"In that case, I think they will not even bother to bring us back home, but instead will kill us somewhere in the jungle."

"Yes, you are probably right. Besides, Amal is furious right now. Not only did he lose his future wife, but a young white boy also outwitted him. He must regain the prestige of the future Chief-of-Tribe, so he will not rest until he catches us. Otherwise, the whole tribe will laugh at him. But you are right, I don't think they will bother with the *mumu* anymore. They will start a bonfire somewhere in the meadow and make a picnic, just like we did yesterday."

"So, they will pursue us all the way to the port." Ben sighed. "But what is our plan? You said that we are on the border with your territory, right?"

"Yes, we need to go a little bit farther and we'll be on our land. Then we have a better chance to escape from them. We could then meet our men, and then we will be saved. Amal is not going to kill us in front of our people. Besides, once we are on our territory, they wouldn't be able to move freely and openly pursue us."

"Listen, maybe we should go straight to the port?"

"No, it is too far. We are not going to make it before dark. But we will leave this option as a backup plan. Shh, keep quiet. They are coming."

They walked openly, laughing and talking, not even bothering to try to conceal their presence. Their voices became louder by every minute, and soon Ben was able to discern even the crunching of the twigs under the pursuers' feet.

Hunters, professionals, Ben thought contemptuously. *They could be heard from a mile away, stomping like a herd of elephants. No wonder they have nothing to eat; scaring away all the game during the hunt.*

They were already close, and Ben could even hear their conversation.

"What are they saying?" he asked in a whisper.

"Nothing interesting, they are just laughing, joking. One of them said that he is hungry. And another replied that soon they will come to a place and have a snack there. And all the others laughed."

"What place? Shouldn't they just be looking for us? Or go by our scent?"

Ben was silent for a while, pondering the situation.

Suddenly, he exclaimed, "I think I got it! I know what they are trying to do. They want to make an ambush somewhere on the border of both territories to cut us off from your settlement."

"So what? It's not a problem. We'll go around it." Emma took the news indifferently. "We've almost reached our territory, and I know where they are going to wait for us and how to get around their ambush."

The three pursuers had walked right above their hideout; Ben could even see them through the gaps in the branches. A minute later their voices faded and soon died down completely.

"Actually, their tactic is clever." Ben continued to develop his theory further. "Why should they chase us through the deadwood, jump on the trees like monkeys, and read footprints? They know where we are going, and will be waiting for us there. If it wasn't for their carelessness, they would have probably succeeded. We should thank them for the warning."

Emma only winced skeptically. There was something in his theory that didn't sound right, but she kept her doubts to herself and began to crawl outside. They got out and looked around. It was all quiet and the pathway was clear, as the pursuers had continued far into the woods. Emma decided to make a slight detour in their route to bypass the alleged ambush.

Ben felt significantly better now. He calmed down as they slowly continued their journey, braking away from the chase. As they were getting farther from the dead forest, the jungle thinned out and brightened as the trees parted from one another, letting more light shine through their crown. The forest was still thick, but with every step it was changing dramatically, and soon they ended up in the woodlands.

The jungle sensibly responded to the changes in the landscape. This part of the woods was located on the hills and the wind blew the seeds away from the trees, scattering them over long distances. Fallen trees had thinned out, and the smell of the rotten wood disappeared. The walk had become more pleasant as the air was filled with freshness, and Ben thanked nature for such a gift. Under different circumstances, this journey could have actually been enjoyable. Even the chase was left far behind, and they could fully enjoy a leisurely stroll.

Their path, once again, went a bit downhill and inexorably descended to lower levels, and the landscape changed once again. The jungle became greener, with more diverse trees and colorful birds. Garlands of moss almost disappeared, replaced with more shrubs and vines.

"Do you recognize this place?" Emma asked suddenly.

"No, I do not." Ben shrugged. "It all looks the same to me: all trees and bushes look alike to me. Have we been here already?"

"Of course we have, just yesterday, when we returned from the sheriff, remember?"

Ben looked around. All the trees were so identical; how could one tell them apart? "No, I don't remember, sorry. Maybe when we walk just a little bit farther I might recognize it."

Amal's warriors appeared so suddenly that Emma cried out in surprise. They were still in the woodlands, descending into a small ravine, passing the invisible border with the thicker side of the forest. Ben was about to part the branches of a long chain of lush, tall thickets of an unknown exotic plant to let Emma get into the opening, when the bushes parted by themselves, and they bumped right into the chest of the warrior. He stood in the opening on the other side of the bushes, holding the branches apart like a passenger holding the door of a bus, allowing the other to complete their boarding.

It is impossible! The thought flashed in Ben's head. *There is no way this can be happening. Is it a specter? I saw them with my own eyes, proceeding in the opposite direction less than half an hour ago.*

But the man standing in front of them was not a ghost. He was alive, in the flesh, and could have even been touched, if Ben wanted to. But he didn't want to do that, of course. Instead, he had another desire: to run as fast as possible, to disappear from here quickly. The warrior was also taken aback by surprise, not expecting to see them here. He was standing with his arms holding the branches, trying to figure out what to do, and that saved them from being caught immediately.

Ben was thinking faster than the slowpoke warrior and took advantage of this situation. He grabbed Emma, who was in stupor from fear, and pushed her right under the man's arm. Emma quickly came to her senses and nimbly slipped through a narrow passage. Ben ducked under the other arm in the opened space in the bushes. They ran on bent legs, slipping past five men stuck in the shrub, jumped out to an open space, and ran into the woods. Each warrior could have easily grabbed them, but no one had time to react. They had not been able to see what was going on behind the bushes through the back of the first soldier. Just that suddenly everybody stopped, and the next moment, unknown creatures ran past them, either human or boar, and seconds later, had disappeared in the woods. It took them a few seconds to realize that the living things that had just passed by their legs were the subjects of their hunt, and they rushed in pursuit, but time was lost.

All five men were covered with ammunition, with bows and arrows in the quiver behind their backs, holding long, heavy spears.

The narrow passage in the bushes did not allow more than one person to go through at a time, and when the warriors turned around, clanging into one another by their ammunition, the fugitives received a half-minute head start and break away. But even this small advantage was now a godsend for them.

Ben ran next to Emma and tried to make sense of the situation. He had already realized that it was a different group of men, not the ones they had seen before. The others were light and unarmed. Not completely unarmed, of course, no self-respecting man would go into the woods empty-handed. They had only small, lightweight bows and arrows behind their backs. But this was a group of thoroughly armed warriors, equipped with heavy javelins, large long-range bows, and axes attached to their waist belt (stone axe, of course, but in a battle it is still a formidable weapon). One of them, Ben noticed, even had a small drum, which seriously puzzled him.

"Emma," he called to her as they ran, "why did they bring a drum with them?"

"That is a ritual drum for dancing," Emma shouted between gasps, barely catching her breath.

A ritual drum, of course. Rituals. Emma had told him that they couldn't just kill and eat someone, and must preserve the ritual with the dances and drumbeats and God knows what else. Otherwise, it would be an ordinary murder. So, they were not going to take them back to the village and would celebrate right here, in the woods, as soon as they caught them, just as Emma thought. They had no doubts that they would catch the fugitives and make a holiday dinner with all the necessary rituals required for this occasion. That is why they had brought the drum along with them. But Ben did not want to participate in the ritual games, especially in the form of a gala dinner, and they ran even faster.

They were indeed good hunters and warriors. How was it possible, in such a vast expanse of dense forest, to predict the route of the fugitives and surround them? Obviously there were other groups in front of them, waiting in the ambush. Amal would not stop until he caught them, to restore his reputation. He would mobilize all the men available, create a dozen such small mobile groups, and scatter them along their path. It didn't matter where they went or how fast they ran; their capture was only a matter of time.

There is no one to blame but myself, Ben cursed to himself in his thoughts. *I relaxed too soon, thinking that we outfoxed the enemies. I doubted the need for precautions, which Emma warned me about. But how gently they came near, silently, no rustle of leaves, no sound of cracking twigs underfoot, and not a single word was said. Sound travels very far in the forest, and we would have heard them if they talked. But no, they crept in complete silence, even for Emma's acute ear.*

Then yet another thought struck him: the purpose of that first group was completely different. They were not going to wait for them in an ambush, they had to drive them away from the village and force them to go this way. They had to walk loudly, laugh and talk, as they wanted to let the fugitives know their plans and make them change the route. Ben had to admit that, despite their primitiveness, they planned a strategic operation better than the NATO generals. He remembered in one of the books he had read, a description of the royal hunt, when group of hunters were chasing animals right into the ambush by the loud noise, barking dogs, and shooting into the air. But the actual hunters sat quietly in the bushes waiting for the prey. But Ben, a naive urban boy, had obviously underestimated the enemy, laughing at their apparent sloppiness.

Emma had told him that they were excellent hunters and warriors; these skills were inculcated in them over centuries, passing down from generation to generation. In the woods, they practically had no chance to get away from these primitive people. But Ben had not believed her, thinking that they could easily disappear in the jungle. And here it was, the consequence of his negligence and contempt for the ability of the enemy. Amal was probably waiting somewhere in the bushes farther down the path with another group, craving their deaths. Most likely he would want to personally unscrew their heads.

Suddenly, as if to confirm Ben's thoughts, another warrior came out on their path, followed by a few other men. Ben didn't see how many of them there were, but he noticed that Amal was not among them. A warrior jumped out from the bushes, but while he was coping with the inertia, Emma and Ben went around him, one to the left, the other to the right, and continued the race, speeding up their pace even more.

Of course, just as expected, Ben thought, jumping over the next fallen tree trunk. *Yet another group, and there will be a lot more of them ahead, waiting for us.*

It was bad. A dozen men were literally breathing down their necks. The pursuit entered its final phase.

Should we stop running and put an end to all this? We cannot escape anyway . . . No, there is no way I will let them eat me so easily! Ben thought angrily. *I'll make them work for their dinner to the very end.*

So they kept running. One time someone even grabbed Ben's shirt, but he miraculously managed to dodge him, and sped up even more. Suddenly, a new thought came to his mind.

"Emma," Ben shouted over his shoulder, panting, "what if they start to shoot us?"

"Not yet, at first . . . stop . . . aim . . ." was all Emma could get out. She was also breathless. "Listen to the noise behind . . . when quiet . . . then shoot."

Oh, God! Now Ben longed to hear the sound of running feet behind him to make sure that they ran and were not aiming at them with an arrow. Emma had told him that they could hit a boar in the eye from a hundred feet away, and to aim at such a large target for them is not a problem at all. Besides, they didn't even have to kill them. It would be enough to just wound them in the leg and drag them to Amal, so he could perform his long awaited ritual killing.

And, of course, as one would expect, the clatter behind them had suddenly stopped. Apparently, God had exhausted the limit of good deeds for today.

They are going to shoot us now, Ben thought. He imagined the sensation of an arrow with the tip of a split bamboo hit him between his shoulder blades. These arrows are dangerous, as it cannot be pulled out easily.

What if they use poisoned arrows? As soon as this horrific idea came to his mind, he immediately dismissed this thought. *No, it is unlikely they would do that because they would have to eat infected meat themselves.* But it didn't give him much relief.

And then Ben did something that he never expected from himself. He slowed down, letting Emma run forward, and stayed behind her, covering her from a possible shot. Maybe at least she could escape. Emma, losing sight of Ben, looked back, but seeing that he was all right, continued to run.

Running had become a little easier; the surrounding flora thinned out with every step, and the path went strikingly downhill. Ben noticed familiar terrain, and he realized that Emma was right. They had been here just yesterday (just one day had passed, but it seemed like an eternity), walking together through the woods. Here was the landmark tree, which was probably more than a thousand years old, huge, all hung with garlands of vines. It was impossible to confuse it with any other tree. They were here for sure. But that meant that— Ben couldn't complete his thought.

"Jump!" Emma shouted on the run, as if she guessed his thoughts.

"No, please don't! Don't jump!" Ben exclaimed in horror, but to his surprise, he couldn't hear his own voice. That was the other Ben screaming, his inner self, while true Ben already made his penultimate step toward the edge of the cliff. For a moment, he stood still over the precipice, and the next instant, he was falling down into the lake, ridiculously waving his arms and legs.

I am so tired of these cliffs. Ben barely had time to think before he breached the glossy surface of the lake. He went into the water hard, not with his head or legs but flopping as if he had sat on a chair. His body was hit hard and burned as if a belt had whacked him on the back, just like in his childhood.

His father was conservative when it came to his son's upbringing and taught him polite manners and behavior in the most effective old-fashioned way, as Rupert's own father, Ben's grandfather, once had with him, and all previous generations as well. Once Ben learned about the strong hand and the flexibility of his father's leather belt, he tried to never again give him a reason to repeat this humiliating and painful procedure. And now these childhood feelings flared up in his memory when he hit the surface of the lake.

He went deep into the water with a huge splash and at a decent depth, thrashing around with his hands and feet, trying to get back to the surface quickly. Just when he thought it was the end and he would drown, the water parted above him and he ascended to the surface, with the last breath of air in his lungs. Ben eagerly took a deep breath, coughing, and immediately went down once again, but this time not for too long. Emma was circling nearby, in case he needed her help, but once she made sure he was all right, she swam to the shore, occasionally looking back at him.

Ben looked up and saw the tiny figures of their pursuers, huddled at the edge of the cliff. They didn't dare to follow them into the water and were now trying to comprehend the situation. Ben wanted to make a rude gesture at them but thought that they were not going to see it anyway and followed Emma to the shore, occasionally turning over on his back, giving himself a short respite.

He tried not to look at the slowly approaching shoreline, swimming with the tenacity of a robot. The water was cold and refreshing, but it could also lead to muscle cramp. However, he did not think about that, or probably did not even know it and simply swam forward, until he felt the muddy soil under his feet. Emma was already on the shore and watched him keenly, ready to jump back into the water at any moment if Ben needed her help.

He had no strength left to stand, crawling out from the water and falling onto the sand, breathing heavily. Now their pursuers could have taken him with their bare hands. He would not even resist, and probably would have thanked them for the deliverance.

It's not a big deal, he thought, helplessly lying on the muddy banks. *They will whack me once with a large stone, cracking my skull open, and that's all, eternal freedom. After that, they can do whatever they want: stuff my brain with maggots, fry it with vegetables, boil it with spices, or just eat it raw—I don't mind.*

"A few minutes of rest," Emma ordered in the tone of an army sergeant, breaking his "pleasant" thoughts. She too was utterly exhausted, drained, and panting, but still found the strength to get up and was ready to continue running at the slightest danger.

"We may have won the battle, but haven't won the war yet," Ben paraphrased the well-known expression, with an ironic smile.

But Emma was not in the mood for a joke and didn't even respond with her usual, "What does that mean?"

"We cannot sit for too long," she continued. "They will be here soon."

Ben knew that. He remembered that yesterday it took him about an hour to go down to the lake through the narrow trail along the mountainside. Today, perhaps, he could get down in thirty minutes. For them it would take even less time, let's say fifteen to twenty minutes. It took about ten minutes to swim to the shore, so, they were left with only . . . nothing! They had to get up and go. Now!

He pulled off his shoes, which were in as bad a condition as his clothes, poured water out, and with great difficulty put the wet shoes back on his swollen feet.

I am not going to get far in these shoes. My feet will blister till they bleed if we have to run again, Ben thought, looking at them in disgust.

He was pretty sure that the chase was not over yet. The deceptive silence of the jungle no longer fooled him, and he knew that their persecutors would be here any minute. They were real professionals. He had no illusions anymore about the abilities of these primitive people. They hastily wrung out their wet clothes, got up, and walked along the lake, listening suspiciously to all the sounds in the jungle.

"Maybe we should swim across the lake to the other side?" Ben asked.

"You are not going to make it there," Emma replied. "Besides, the mountains on that side are impassable. We should go to the port. That is the only option we have left," Emma concluded, and they plunged into the jungle again.

They couldn't run anymore and just briskly walked, slowing down occasionally while overcoming obstacles, or accelerating their pace in the open areas. They heard the noise of the chase within just a few minutes. It was coming from everywhere: behind them and on the left and right, and it was no longer a tactical maneuver. The hunters realized that the fugitives had unraveled their plans, and there was no need to hide their presence anymore. They were simply cutting them off from Emma's settlement and from the lake, just in case.

For the past two days that Ben had spent in the jungle, he had figured out the basic geography of this area. If someone had asked him the way to the port right now, he would reply without hesitation, while gesturing vaguely, "probably this way," as Emma replied to that question on the first day of their acquaintance. Now he confidently led Emma to the port.

They still had a chance to get out from the siege; just a little bit farther, and then, freedom. The pursuers would not attack them after that. This was not their territory. There could be tourists or police authorities, and perhaps his parents with a rescue team searching for their missing son.

Footsteps could still be heard quite far, a few minutes away, and so there was still an opportunity to break through.

"Emma, we have to run, to break farther away from them."

She nodded, and they ran again. The forest was not as dense in here, and they could run freely. If it wasn't for his wet shoes painfully rubbing his feet with every step, it would be possible to run even faster, and for the first time, he envied Emma for not wearing shoes at all, freely stepping with her bare feet on the prickly branches and stones. A few minutes later they made their way through the thick bushes and reached a large, open meadow.

If there was a paradise on Earth, it was surely here. A large, secluded, spacious glade almost rectangular in shape, entirely covered with a carpet of lush green grass, surrounded by the solid wall of shrubs on the perimeter, entwined with vines. Several young, slender trees protected the glade from the direct rays of the sun, creating a pleasant shade without forming an oppressive feeling. If it was possible to move this glade to Central Park in New York, put in a few picnic tables and a barbecue grill, there would be plenty of people willing to spend time here with their friends on a hot summer's day. It was a marvelous place; a paradise in the middle of the chaos of the jungle.

Only one element didn't fit into this picturesque corner, disrupting the harmony of this paradise—standing a dozen yards away in the glade was their old friend Amal, from the tribe of Abaga, a good soldier, and a great strategist.

Chapter 4. Deliverance

Amal stood in the middle of the glade, muscular arms crossed over his chest, looking like the statue of Abraham Lincoln on Union Square in New York. He was strong and over six feet tall, but seemed even taller because of his high, fancy hair, decorated with colored feathers. He looked at them and smiled, revealing two rows of strong white teeth.

Emma ran into the glade first, making her way through the bushes, and even kept running for a little while before she noticed him. She stopped abruptly and gasped, horrified. Ben, who had been running instinctively, following her without looking around, almost bumped into her. The surprised Emma squeaked faintly and darted behind his back. Then Ben saw him as well.

Ben was not scared, nor surprised. He was tired and didn't have any strength left to be afraid. As for being surprised . . . there was nothing to be surprised about. They were playing with professionals in their field, not even knowing the rules of the game. Emma did not count, as she was too little and had never participated in a hunt, and even more so in such hostilities. The outcome of this game was a foregone conclusion from the beginning. Although late, Ben realized he had no more chances to win than a beginner chess player who sat down to play against a grandmaster.

"Sir, I'm going to checkmate you on this square," the grandmaster would say, and the novice chess player would get checkmated in the promised square, regardless of which pieces were used and where he moved them. It did not matter that instead of the sixty-four squares of the chessboard the game took place in the vast expanses of the jungle, and the role of chess pieces were carried out by soldiers armed to the teeth, who did not just take the opponent's pieces off the board but ate them too. Literally! This was a game of chess. Extreme chess.

This meadow was the square on the chessboard of the jungle, where grandmaster Amal would checkmate them. It even looked like one, almost a proper square glade. They had been manipulated to come to this place, where Amal had been waiting the entire time. The game was over now. Checkmate!

All these thoughts flashed in Ben's head while he was urgently contemplating the situation.

What a beautiful combination they played, he thought, admiring their plan, albeit grudgingly. *What a spectacular ending. They were not going to capture us, or shoot us down with a bow. Why should they drag wounded game through the woods on such a hot day if it could come on its own to the place where they wanted it to come? They were just guiding us right into this secluded glade, where nothing and no one would interrupt their ceremonial dinner. They even brought a drum, knowing without a doubt that they would need it today. Hats off, Gentlemen! What a great game, great hunt! Your ancestors would be proud of you!*

Ben looked around, doomed. There was no escape. This was the end. He even considered for a moment that they should split and run in different directions through the bush, but he immediately dropped this idea. The surrounding shrubs were too dense. They wouldn't get out quickly enough. One of them could probably escape, but Amal would catch the other in a few steps and instantly unscrew that one's head. He had the legs of a deer, long and strong.

All the other men were also close, minutes or even seconds away, and their sounds were coming from everywhere. They didn't even hide their presence anymore, talking, laughing loudly, and knowing that the prey was already in the trap. The noise was coming from behind, from the left, and from right, but not in front of them yet.

So, they had less than a minute left. Within that time, they had to miraculously bypass Amal, run through the meadow, and escape on the opposite site. Behind this glade was freedom. He knew instinctively that they would not pursue them beyond this point.

You are running out of time, Ben rushed himself. *Think, Ben, think faster, you are pressed for time.*

But he instantly interrupted his own thoughts. *Wait, what do you mean 'pressed for time'? You just acknowledged complete defeat, you are already in checkmate. No, dear Grandmaster, it's just a check, a hard check with only one move left, and I have to make this move and find the way out.*

But nothing good came to mind. The only thing he could do was at least try to save Emma, who was still hiding behind his back.

"Emma, we cannot escape together. I'll distract him, and you run forward through the bushes and get out of here. Quickly! We only have seconds left. Run!" He tried to pry her hands away, but she clung onto him tighter, leaning onto his back.

"Emma, please, you can save yourself." He realized that he was wasting precious time. But he also knew that she would rather die than leave him alone at the mercy of Amal.

Forgive me. I put you into all this trouble, he thought. *I guess I will have to fight Amal. He will eat us anyway, but at least I might be able to bite his ear off and have something pleasant to die for.*

Amal started to walk toward them after giving his opponents enough time to soak in this dramatic situation. He approached slowly, smiling from ear to ear, exposing his strong, white teeth. The next thought that came to Ben's mind was stupid and inappropriate.

Smile while you can, he thought gleefully. *In ten years you will only have rotten roots remaining of those white teeth.*

Indeed, that was true. In these god-forsaken places, men and women quickly became old due to the harsh living conditions, hard work, and malnutrition. The first sign of aging was the teeth because of the severe lack of vitamins and dental hygiene; their only dental practice being to simply rinse their mouth in the morning with river water. The teeth quickly turned yellow, then blackened, crumbled, and broke, the gums beginning to bleed. By their thirties, the once-white teeth would fall out, or turn into rotten roots. Ben looked at the white smile of his enemy, and with sincere glee wished him speedy caries.

Of course, these thoughts were not appropriate under such circumstances, but there was nothing else to think about. Fight with this savage? The thought was not even funny. Given the difference in their weight categories, Amal would smear him all over the grass with just one punch. He was coming at him, slowly, so lazily, smiling from ear to ear, arms spread wide, as if in anticipation of meeting up with old friends. Fresh and rested, he had probably taken a long nap in the shade of a tree while his warriors did all the hard work for him.

In a few seconds he would reach Ben, put an arm on his shoulder, and say, "Well, my friend, I am getting tired and hungry waiting for you here, on this hot day. Let's go to the shade and have a snack, as I haven't eaten since this morning, thanks to you . . ."

And then he would grab Ben's neck with his huge paw, lift him from the ground like a chicken, and tear his head off. Then it would be Emma's turn. Or maybe he would not kill her immediately. He needed to think ahead and save food for tomorrow as well. There were no refrigerators here, so the meat must be kept fresh, alive, so it wouldn't get spoiled. But he was big, strong, and probably ate a lot, and all the other men were hungry too, as they had been running through the woods all day long. Perhaps there wouldn't even be enough meat for so many hungry people.

No, you cannot let him approach you so calmly. It is certain death, Ben thought. *You must irritate him, make him angry, force him to make a mistake, and then . . . after that . . .* This 'after that' might never happen, but at least there would be a chance. Actually . . . hmm . . . perhaps there was a chance, though scanty. But it seemed that there was no alternative anyway.

Involuntarily, sweat trickled down his back, just from thinking of what he was about to do.

"Emma," he said in a whisper, "step away from me five, better yet, ten steps back. Quickly. I need space."

Emma immediately obeyed his command.

She is good, Ben thought vaguely, getting ready to execute his plan. She understood everything perfectly and did not waste time bickering and asking too many questions. If it was Liah, she would never obey his orders so implicitly and would do nothing, until she knew exactly why, how, and what for. You say a word, and she would give you ten in return.

Ben looked at the approaching Amal and begun executing his plan before it was too late.

"Emma, tell him something rude and insulting."

Emma paused for a second, surprised by his request, but a moment later she shouted a few words in her language.

Amal stopped, and the smile slowly faded from his face.

"Again," Ben demanded. "But something very offensive."

She shouted another phrase that sounded different from the previous one.

"Did you hear that? That's right!" Ben also yelled, and tried to reproduce the sounds he thought were the most offensive, although it did not matter much if it wasn't.

"Come on, scarecrow!" Ben shouted in English, not worrying if Amal understood the words. He would figure it out by the offensive tone.

It was the best moment for an insult, as some other "chess" players waded through the bushes. Some of the men had already stepped into the clearing, making their way through the dense thickets, while others were still on their way. The insults shouted by Emma's sonorous voice echoed across the glade, and everybody turned their heads toward her, looking horrified. A deathly silence hung over the glade. Even the birds fearfully ceased their singing and profusely fertilized the soil beneath them. In the complete silence, Ben could hear Amal's heavy breathing while he was trying to comprehend the insults. He was no longer smiling but was looking evil and sullen. His nostrils were moving, loudly blowing air like a bull before an attack, making his magnificent tusks above his lip move up and down in rhythm with his breath.

He is soon going to stomp and rake his hoofs, Ben thought. *That's good, and he is in the right condition. The distance is probably ten feet between us. It should be sufficient.*

Ben stood up in a fighting stance, like his aikido coach had taught him. He had almost two years of training and hadn't achieved much yet, just rose one step in rank, reaching the fifth kyu, which corresponds to the yellow belt. It was far from the black belt, for which another ten years of hard work in training was required. But for now, the basics he had learned should be enough.

Ben relaxed and took a slow, deep breath, alternating with a quick exhalation. This exercise calms one down before a fight and restores normal breathing. He did not look at Amal, afraid that he would get scared of his opponent. His coach always told him that you shouldn't be afraid of your opponent, but instead properly estimate him and calmly anticipate his moves.

"Fear paralyzes your thinking and delays reaction," he had said, "and as a result, it guarantees defeat."

Ben watched Amal's feet, trying not to miss the moment of attack. Only a dilettante would look at the hands of his opponent. Legs say a lot more to a knowledgeable fighter than hands. Your opponent can make a deceptive attack, feinting to the left, but actually throwing a right hook. But the legs always tell the truth. The punching power is not in the hand but in the body and legs. The hand is only a tool performing the punch. Try to conduct a powerful knockout punch on fixed legs (fighting in a limited space does not count, as there are different rules). It would be just a slap in the face. During a good punch, the leg corresponding to the attacking hand moves forward, slightly bent, and the weight of the fighter's body is transferred to the supporting leg while maintaining balance. This is just physics and nothing more.

By the movement of the legs, good fighters can predict the direction of attack. Right foot forward, left foot straight, slightly behind—straight punch or uppercut. Body turns to the right on the supporting leg—right hook. Feet together, slightly bent, one foot turned for support—punch to the torso. And so forth.

Professional fighters know these basic techniques of a fight, but, unfortunately, Ben was not a such fighter; he wasn't even a boxer. He had just picked up a few basic moves in the gym and now hurriedly tried to organize his disjointed knowledge. He was relaxed, but focused on the feet of the enemy, not forgetting his hands either. In his head, he even heard the voice of his coach as if they were in the gym.

"How do you stand? Feet slightly apart, spring on your toes, one foot turned a little for support, arms close to the body, bent at the elbows." The coach would have been pleased if he was here right now. He would have probably grumbled for a while, as always, but in general, Ben did everything right.

"Come on you freak, attack me," Ben whispered impatiently. "We are running out of time, just a few seconds left."

But Amal still hesitated, looking askance at his enemy. Ben began to lose patience.

"Emma, tell him one more time something *really* rude."

Another incomprehensible phrase came from behind. Ben attentively followed Amal's feet. It was important not to get distracted and not to miss the moment of attack. Amal broke down and pounced on Ben. He understood everything correctly. Ben was the offender, not Emma, as she simply translated what he told her.

Let's get to work, Ben told himself, and a moment later, looking at Amal's slow, clumsy attack, he already knew: everything would be just fine.

The whole fight took only five, not even seconds—moments.

One: Amal rushes forward, swinging his hand for the punch.

Two: His fist whooshes toward Ben's head.

Three: Ben's left leg goes back and slightly to the right, turning his body in the same direction as the rushing Amal. His fist swings at Ben, missing the target by just a few inches, and continues forward taken by inertia. Amal's heavy body follows his fist, going off balance, in accordance with the law of physics.

Four: Ben rests his left hand on Amal's wrist, making a step toward the movement of the opponent. Slight pressure on the wrist brings the hand of the enemy down and back. His strong, muscular arm is now limp, still trying to cope with the inertia.

Five: Ben's right hand rests on the forearm, creating a fulcrum and the axis of rotation, pushing down easily, while the left arm continues moving backwards, taking the opponent's hand back and upwards. Amal gets off the ground, ridiculously waving his legs, makes a full circle in the air around the point of rotation at the level of the forearm, and falls flat on the ground. Ben is standing next to him, holding his unnaturally inverted hand in an armlock. That's all. The fight is over.

Emma gasped in surprise, and everybody else at the glade stared with open mouths at Amal lying on the ground. Ben was triumphantly standing over the defeated enemy with the expression of a conqueror on his face.

That's right, Grandmaster, don't play chess with an unknown opponent. Better yet, go play tag. This game is just right for your level.

It was the time for applause from the audience and for the opponent to bang on the mat with his free hand, acknowledging the defeat. Ben would then release his hand taken into the armlock, nod to the vanquished opponent, and the referee would award him a point for the takedown and positioning control.

But there was no applause or referee, and instead of a scored point, Ben and Emma would get another chance at survival. They still had to get out of here, and with every second, it was becoming more and more complicated, as new people were coming to the glade.

Amal writhed on the ground in pain. Ben knew how painful it was, as he had often been in this same position during aikido competitions. The slightest movement caused Amal severe pain in the wrist, elbow, and shoulder joints, and there was no escape from this situation. Actually, there was a way out. Aikido provides a technique to escape from virtually any position. All he had to do was lift his legs and spin to "unwind" the hand with a simultaneous sweep of the legs of his opponent. Ben could never do that, as this skill was way beyond his level. But he could also bet his heart for their dinner that Amal couldn't do it either and didn't even know about this technique. He didn't need aikido, or any other martial art, chasing boars in the woods. And now a strong man, an excellent soldier, and a good hunter, Amal was lying on the ground and writhing in pain, pounding with his free hand, leaving a deep dent from his large fist, which could instantly kill a medium-sized running boar. With just two fingers, Ben held him in an armlock, and the more Amal tried to pull it out, the more painful it became. His hand, which looked more like a pork gammon, was as helpless as a teddy bear in the hands of a little boy. Ben could tear off his paw if he wanted to, or let it go.

However, Ben knew that he shouldn't let it go and must continue that technique to the end, breaking his arm. One kick to the arm-locked hand, not even a hard one, and the unnaturally twisted arm would be fractured or seriously dislocated, which would also suffice. But Ben wasn't taught to break an opponent's arm. In fact, for the slightest injury in the gym that was done on purpose, he would have been instantly kicked out of the sports club. Their coach always watched closely to ensure that his students practiced clean fights to avoid injuries.

"Aikido is a sport," he would remind them. "It is an art, martial art, not a street fight."

In combat every technique is concluded with a complete neutralization of the enemy. Now the situation was similar to combat, and Ben knew that he could not leave an offended Amal behind. He would never forgive him for such humiliation in front of his fellow tribesmen, and would chase them all the way, ignoring possible witnesses and even government officials.

Ben raised his foot to kick Amal's arm, but he couldn't do it. He couldn't break a man's arm and hesitated, not daring to finish it off. Emma screamed from behind.

She is also sensitive, Ben thought, angry at his cowardice. Of course, she saw and understood his doubts. But had she already forgotten that these men were going to kill them both?

Second Ben, his imaginary friend, crawled from the depths of his soul where he was hiding out of fear.

"Break his arm, Ben. Come on, break it!" the second Ben screamed. "Don't wait. You have just a few seconds left."

But the first Ben, the real one, still hesitated, not knowing what to do.

"Break it, Ben! Grab Emma and run!" Second Ben kept shouting, and the real Ben raised his foot to strike. Emma screamed again, louder this time. Still holding the enemy's arm, Ben turned back and was stunned. There was another Papuan just a few feet away from him. He looked just like Amal, as tall and strong, but much older, with skin sagging, where there once used to be huge muscles.

He was standing behind Ben, and Emma struggled in his strong arms. He embraced her around the waist with one hand, so that her legs dangled helplessly in the air, while the other hand pressed her hands to the sides. She silently and furiously tried to bite his hand and hit his chin with her head, but it was all in vain.

Now, this is the checkmate, Ben thought in horror.

In the heat of the fight, he had forgotten all about the other men, or rather, did not take them into account, naively believing that if he won this fight, then the sight of their defeated commander would scare them away, and they would not dare to attack. But if he lost the fight, then the number of other warriors wouldn't make much difference. He had estimated the situation wrongly once again.

He regretfully put down his leg that was ready to inflict a decisive strike, and let go of Amal's arm, raising his hands and shouting, "Okay, I give up. You have won. Let her go now." He spoke in English, not caring whether the Papuan got the meaning of his words. He needed time, just a little bit of time, a few seconds, and then he would think of something.

"Let go of her. It's all my fault. I persuaded her to run away with me, did you understand me? It's not her fault, I made her run."

His brain was working at the speed of the fastest computer, stuffed with megabytes and gigahertz, as he was frantically looking for a way out. Unfortunately, his knowledge of aikido techniques was at a basic level, and none of them were applicable in this situation. Indeed, the school of aikido is more suitable for defense, not for attack. If that Papuan would strike him, then there could be a good chance to come up with the proper defense technique. But to attack him and free Emma . . .

Ben considered kicking him in the groin, but quickly realized that would not work. He was covering himself with Emma. Ben had heard somewhere that slapping an opponent on both ears with flat palms is quite effective, but the man was too tall for Ben to reach his head. He faced the same for poking him sharply in the eye.

His arsenal of attacking techniques was quickly fading out. Ben kept approaching the Papuan, shouting some nonsense while looking for a way out, but nothing suitable for the situation was coming to his mind. This was the end. It was over now.

Meanwhile, the glade quickly filled with people. More than twenty men had gathered, while others continued to wade through the bushes on all sides. They were coming out from everywhere, all armed to the teeth, painted in all possible colors, as if they were gathered on a Sim-Sim holiday.

But they are actually gathered for the holiday celebration, Ben thought, approaching the Papuan and continuing to search for a way to save Emma.

The last chance for escape had been lost because of his cowardice, because he couldn't break Amal's arm. But he continued moving toward the Papuan, hoping to at least save Emma. Only ten more steps left—nine . . . eight . . . seven . . .

"Let her go! I'm telling you, it's not her fault. Take me instead! Eat me! But let her go!"

He was almost there, a few more steps: five . . . four . . . three . . . *I will go up to him and snatch her from his hands,* he thought now. *He is strong. I don't think I can—*

Suddenly, something changed. The horrible grimace that distorted the face of the Papuan changed into a smile, revealing rotten teeth pitted with caries.

"Aha, you've already got the caries." Second Ben was jubilant.

But the smile quickly faded from the Papuan's face, replaced by a surprised look. He cocked his head as though thinking of something, almost like a parrot that scrutinizes offered food with one eye. His hands loosened, and Emma, who was still squirming in his grasp, dropped to the ground. She immediately jumped up like a rubber doll and rushed to Ben, hiding behind him, tightly clasping her hands around him. And then the elderly Papuan started to laugh. He laughed so hard and loud that Ben stopped in surprise. He fell to his knees, thrashing his fists on the ground, while his eyes filled with tears of laughter.

"Eat . . . you? You! . . . Eat?" He was rolling on the ground, unable to hold back the tears. "So you thought . . ." He was no longer laughing, but cried in a fit of unbridled, wild guffaws.

More and more Papuans were coming to the glade, and they saw the oddest situation: Amal Junior rolling on the ground and roaring in pain, holding his dislocated arm (Ben somehow managed to twist his arm, although not that hard). Nearby, only ten yards away from Amal, his father was rolling on the grass laughing his guts out. The situation was absolutely surreal, and all the men looked at them with their mouths open, not knowing how to react in this situation. But suddenly, one of them snorted and started laughing, then another, and soon the entire glade rang with laughter. Imperturbable Emma, who always stayed calm in the face of mortal danger, and never lost her presence of mind, burst into tears, looking at everybody laughing around her. She cried loudly, sobbing into Ben's dirty shirt. Fatigue and the nervous tension of the day, all the anxiety and excitement spilled out through her tears, and unflappable Emma cried like the child that she actually was. Ben was ready to cry as well, but he held back, as both of them crying would be too much! He stood, silently stroking Emma's head, hugging her, choking back tears and blinking to shake them from his eyelashes. The next moment two other Papuans stepped into the glade, accompanied by Margaret and Rupert.

"Mom? Dad? How did you—What are you . . ."

But as soon as they tried to reply, they were interrupted.

"Please forgive me, madam, mister." Amal Senior came up to them, still sobbing with laughter. "They ran very . . . gee-gee-gee . . . fast . . . gee-gee-gee. They thought we wanted to . . . gee-gee-gee . . . we wanted them . . . gee-gee-gee . . ."

Suddenly, Ben realized yet another mistake he had made, perhaps the biggest one of all. They had not intended to kill them or make the *mumu* out of them! They had not been prisoners of Amal; they were his guests.

Ben's thoughts flashed back like a movie in rewind. Here was Amal, about to strike him, angrily rolling his eyes, and a moment later, he goes backward, smiling. Ben and Emma, still playing backward, sprint from the glade back to the lake, into the water, swim to the middle, and from there, they soar high up to the edge of a cliff. Then they run in reverse through the woods, jumping on the branches of deadwood trees, and then run again, finally reaching the barn.

Now, from here, go slowly. Ben stopped himself.

He jumps up on the shelf above the door and came down again. Stop. He's going to climb up and look at Emma, to make sure that all the requisites were set at the stage. No, perhaps a little bit earlier. Rewinding some more, skipping the discussion of their escape plan and a few unpleasant hours of suspense. Stop. Here it is.

He woke up and had felt great, well-rested and fresh. But their abductors carried them through the woods at night for many miles uphill, with Ben's and Emma's hands tied. After such a march, their bodies should be sore, with pain in every cell. But he hadn't felt anything like that. Apparently, the sleeping captives had instead been gently carried through the woods, held comfortably on the hands so that no branch accidentally grazed them in the dark. In the barn, the captors untied them, took out the gags, and carefully put them down on a heap of straw. No one would do that for someone who is going to be killed in a few hours. Most likely they would just throw them on the floor, leaving their hands tightly bound. Nobody would care how their future dinner felt before the slaughter. Much later, when he was about to climb on the door and looked back at the tied Emma, something clicked in his head, some awkwardness of this whole situation had caught his attention. He would certainly figure it out if he had a little more time to think. But it was too late for that, as the next moment the door swung open, and the play began. So, it seems that they ruined the feast not just for Amal, but also for themselves. They were invited to join the celebration as dear guests, even though in a somewhat extravagant way.

Yesterday they came home late and the whole village was asleep. Amal was probably afraid that Ben and Emma wouldn't want to go with him and would argue, make noise, and wake up everyone in the village. So he decided to abduct them and explain everything in the morning. Surely, if they had knocked on the door, they would have released and fed them, and began preparations for the holiday to which, apparently, Ben's parents were also invited. That is why Amal was waiting by the door, to explain everything to them when they woke up, and he probably wondered why they were sleeping for so long. The lock on the door was to ensure they didn't run away in fear before he had a chance to explain the situation to them.

Amal did everything right, except for one thing: he underestimated Ben.

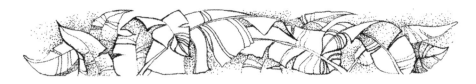

That was Ben's last blunder, the last error, the most critical one. Everything became clear now. The last piece of the puzzle jumped into place, completing the entire picture, and now he stood in shame, blushing to the tips of his ears. Emma did not understand what was going on, clutching Ben with her strong hands as if she was afraid that he might get away from her. She finally calmed down, but continued to sob.

Parents rushed to Ben, trying to hug him, but Emma clung to him tighter, not giving them space, as good manners were not one of her virtues. Margaret came to Ben from the side, not put off by Emma, and Rupert joined awkwardly, reaching his son above Emma's head, and the four of them stood in an embrace.

Laughter in the glade had not abated, but rather grew louder and louder as the new participants of the chase were coming in. Some men came from another tribe, painted in bright red and yellow colors, which, mixed with their neighbors' hues, turned it into a multi-colored crowd. Nobody knew what was going on, not everyone had seen the fight, but the general merriment was infectious, and the new men immediately began to laugh as soon as they stepped into the glade. Only the defeated Amal Junior didn't laugh, slowly rising from the ground, groaning and rubbing his dislocated arm. He had gotten off pretty easy, without any serious injuries, but because of the shame of defeat, he was afraid to raise his head and stare in the eyes of his fellow tribesmen and neighbors.

"How are you doing, Son?" Margaret asked, clinging to him. "Are you okay? We were so worried about you. Is this the girl who helped you?"

Ben freed himself from the three pairs of hugging hands.

"Yes, Mom. This is Emma. She helped me in the jungle."

"When we were told that you went into the forest with a girl, I imagined her to be a little older." Rupert smiled. "But I'm glad that someone could help you. Thank you, Emma."

She said nothing, only clung to Ben even harder. Emma clearly didn't feel comfortable among strangers, and would have gladly went back in the woods again, facing danger and menace, if she had a choice. Back there in the jungle the situation was pretty clear: there was an enemy (even though it turned out to be imaginary) and they had to run from them, hide, jump, cover up their footsteps, do those things that she knew and liked. But here, among all these people, it was unclear how to behave. Definitely she felt more comfortable in the woods.

"Emma, can you speak English?" Margaret asked.

Emma only nodded in response.

"Mom, leave her alone, she had to endure a lot today," Ben told Margaret. "You can talk to her later. Tell me rather how you got here."

"Honestly, I am a bit confused myself. At first two men came—I do not know what they are called—the ones with the yellow-and-red faces." She pointed at the group of laughing Papuans nearby. "They told us they had found you and would bring you back to the port the next day. That was yesterday. But today, at noon, they came back and said that you and Emma went for a walk in the jungle and they were looking for you. Then, an hour later, the other ones came, the ones with the black-and-white faces."

The messengers disappeared in the woods, and Margaret and Rupert stood in silence for a long time as they watched them go. They no longer had any anger or pity, just tiredness and apathy.

"This whole situation is strange," Rupert said, breaking the silence.

354

Margaret shrugged. She did not know what to think anymore.

"If I understood correctly, Ben hurt his leg, right?"

"Yes, that's what they said."

"Now imagine: a boy with an injured leg accidentally ends up in a tribal settlement. Supposedly they treated his wound and promised to bring him back to the port in the morning. But then he wakes up and decides to take a stroll through the woods."

"With a girl," Margaret reminded him.

"Yes, with a girl. Perhaps he met her in the tribal village, or she found him in the jungle and brought him there, it does not matter. So they went for a walk in the woods, knowing that he needs to go back to the port, and given his injured leg, they had to leave early in the morning, probably at sunrise."

"Yes, you are right, go on." Margaret nodded. She had emerged from her stupor and now listened to the logical arguments of her husband.

"They went out into the woods, but went so far that all these excellent hunters couldn't find them all morning. I do not like this at all; it does not add up here."

Margaret was about to comment on his thought when another set of messengers came from the woods. They also had painted faces and bodies, although in a different color scheme, dominated with black and white tones. Their outlandish hairstyles were dotted with colorful feathers, and their necks, arms, and legs were decorated with dangling rows of necklaces and bracelets.

"Who are these clowns?" Margaret asked in surprise, looking at the visitors.

"The clowns" went straight toward them, knowing without hesitation that these were the people they were looking for. Rupert and Margaret did not fit into the local context, as these Papuans wouldn't fit in on the streets of New York. (Although, sometimes in New York, one can meet even more strange individuals!) Coming up closer, "the clowns" addressed them with a speech.

"Mister, madam, we were sent to inform you that your son is in our settlement. He got lost in the woods and hurt his leg. But don't worry, there is nothing serious. We treated his wound, but he walks slowly, and our elder decided to bring him back to the port by the bus."

"Wait a minute," Rupert stopped him, "let's go back a little. Yesterday, two other . . . hmm . . . gentlemen came here and also told us that our son was with them. Are you from the same tribe?"

"No, we are from another tribe," one of the messengers replied.

"But you do not even know which tribe the other men were from."

"Yes, we know. They are our neighbors. But allow me to finish what I had to tell you. Our elder wanted to bring your son to you by the bus. But, you see, we have a festival today. The hunting season will open soon, and we usually ask the spirits for their blessing. So, our elders want to invite you to our holiday. After the celebration, we will deliver you all back to port. Believe me, you will like our festivities with rituals, dancing, singing, and great food. We even bought a pig to prepare our traditional dish."

"Well, thank you. Tell your . . . boss we accept your invitation and will gladly visit your place," Margaret responded politely. "But how do we get there? Shall we go there right now?"

"No, madam, you cannot walk there. It is too far. But don't worry, our elder already thought of everything. He made all the necessary arrangements, and the bus will come to pick you up. We have a road that passes close to our village."

"How close?" Rupert asked suspiciously.

"Very close." The messenger paused for a second. "I think that we can get there before the sunset."

"Ah, then, of course it is close."

"Close, close, don't worry," he assured him, nodding his head, not catching the sarcasm in Rupert's words.

"Okay, then. We will wait for your bus."

The messengers bowed respectfully, and a minute later disappeared into the woods.

"At least now I understand why those reddish-yellow faced ones could not find Ben and the girl. Apparently, he went out for a walk, got lost in the jungle again, and came upon a neighboring tribe."

"Yeah, that's most likely what happened. Do you think I need to change? It's not polite to come in jeans to celebrate a festival."

"I wouldn't worry much about that. I think that even in jeans you will look like Cinderella at the ball. More important is to wear comfortable shoes. I have a bad feeling we will have a long walk in the woods again."

Soon came the transportation, which was the same tour bus with the irreplaceable Hubert. He has already been informed about the upcoming festival and the invitation Margaret and Rupert had received. It was still unclear how they communicated with each other and passed on the information, though.

Just as they were getting onto the bus, two "black-and-white" messengers jumped out from the woods again and shouted, panting fast from running.

"Mister, mister, wait!"

Rupert, who had already stepped on the first rung of the bus, turned to them.

"Wait, let me guess: my son went for a walk in the woods, got lost, and you cannot find him. Am I right?"

"How did you know?" The messenger was surprised. "Who told you?"

"What is going on?" Margaret exclaimed indignantly. "Two tribes, skilled hunters, and pathfinders cannot find a boy in the jungle?"

"We will find your son very soon; you have absolutely nothing to worry about. We have already sent three groups of our men to search for him."

"I am glad that you did, and we are going to help you." With these words Margaret and Rupert went towards the jungle.

The messengers stood, confused and in a dilemma. They were supposed to inform the boy's parents about his escape and to reassure them he would be found soon, and then they were to rejoin the search group. They had an important mission: to intercept the escapees on their way to the port, if they managed to break through all the ambushes on the way. They were strictly prohibited from using weapons or brute force, having been instructed to just stop them and explain that they were not prisoners but welcome guests. On the other hand, they also had to be respectful to the boy's parents, and if they decided to participate in the search then that had to be granted. But if the parents came along, how could they follow the instructions to cut the fugitives off from the port? This conflict of instructions put them in a delicate situation.

But Margaret and Rupert were not the least concerned about their doubts and conflict of instructions. They were briskly going into the jungle, and the messengers had no choice but to follow them.

"And now we've found you," Margaret finished her story. "It's a pity we spoiled the celebration. They were probably preparing for it, cooking dinner . . ."

"Celebration," Ben echoed Margaret's words. "Just as I thought, we were not captives for sacrifice at the feast. We were the guests. I just don't understand why they had to abduct us?"

"I think I know why," Rupert said. He remained silent, though, pondering the situation further.

"You were not abducted but rather invited to celebrate our festival as dear guests."

They all turned around. Amal Senior had been standing behind them, waiting for Margaret to finish her story. He had calmed down and was not laughing anymore, but instead was full of cordiality, friendliness, and smiles. Nobody had noticed when he had come next to them or how long he stood there. It turned out he spoke decent English and understood everything.

"Allow me to clarify the whole situation," he continued. "Mister, madam, we didn't want to kidnap your son, and weren't going to harm him in any way. In fact, we wanted to bring him to you. When we found out that the boy hurt his leg, I hired a bus, as we have a road fairly close to our settlement."

Ben grinned, as he had by now learned the difference in the local notions of "close" and "far." Amal Senior continued as if he read Ben's thoughts.

"It is only a few kilometers away, at the most. We thought that maybe you would agree to come to our village for celebration. And then, at the end, our men could have carried the boy to the bus and sent you all back to the port."

"But why did you—I'm sorry, I do not know your name."

"Amal, my name is Amal. I am Chief of the Abaga tribe. And this is Akelika Yaga, but you can just call him Yaga." He pointed to another old man standing next to him, painted in yellow-red tones. "He is the Chief of the Wagaba tribe. His men also tried to find your son."

The man who Amal called Yaga stood by silently and only occasionally nodded his head. Apparently, he didn't speak English at all.

"Amal, please explain to us why you abducted the children instead of simply inviting them."

"We were going to do just that, and I even sent my son, Amal to tell them that, but they were not in the settlement all day and came back late at night."

"Yes, that is true," Ben confirmed. "We went to the sheriff, as we thought he might have a phone there, so I could call the port. But on the way back we went for a swim in the lake."

"There, you see, Amal was waiting for them in the village all day, but they came back only late at night. My son took the initiative and brought the sleeping children to our settlement. He was afraid that he wouldn't have enough time to come back for them in the morning, as they were going to leave for the port early. Everything was ready for the celebration, and we even sent two of our men to invite you. But in the morning, we found out that the children fled. I honestly still do not understand how they managed to escape from a locked—" He stopped and immediately corrected himself. "A closed space, unnoticed, right under our noses. At first, we were not worried, thinking the kids just wanted to take a stroll in the woods. But after a while, we become concerned about their long absence and went to look for them. But we didn't expect them to run so fast. We could only catch them in here, on this glade."

"I can understand their fear," Margaret said in defense of children. "They woke up and found out they were locked in a . . . barn, got frightened, and ran away. By the way, why did you lock them in?"

"We were afraid that they would wake up and run away without giving us the chance to explain everything. I couldn't even imagine they would think that—" Amal was about to laugh again, and his face twisted into a smile, but he controlled himself and continued, "that we wanted to eat them. You've been reading lot of crappy literature about us at home, in Europe, or America. I can understand Ben thinking that, as he is not from around here, but you, Emma! You know our customs and traditions. How could you think all that nonsense?"

Now everybody looked at Emma, and it was her turn to blush. But she quickly hid behind Ben's back again.

For a long time Amal apologized profusely and lamented the unfavorable circumstances. Ben thought that all his explanations sounded reasonable, except for a few details. For example, why had Amal not intercepted them before they returned to the village? He could have explained everything to them while they were in the woods without fear of waking someone up. He must have followed them through the woods on their way back. Otherwise, how did he know that he and Emma were sleeping in the barn? They could have gone to sleep in a different *buambramras*, as they were supposed to do. But he knew where they were and waited for the right moment to kidnap them. Or, another example, how did he know that Ben had hurt his leg? Did he see him limping? Nonsense. He had never seen Ben before. He could have been crippled from birth. Obviously, Amal's explanation didn't satisfy Ben. But he decided not to express his doubts, as he was sure that Amal would find a reasonable and convincing answer for every question. It was all over now, and the rest of it didn't matter anymore.

In conclusion, Amal offered to visit their village anyway, and even suggested for their men to carry all of them through the woods. Margaret politely but flatly refused, expressing her wish to go back to the port immediately. With that, the noisy crowd of men from both tribes walked along to the port. They were all in a good mood, laughing, talking, and rejoicing at the successful ending of this little misunderstanding.

Emma clutched Ben's hand tightly, not wanting to let go even for a second, as if she was afraid that he would get into another bit of trouble. Seizing the right moment, Ben pulled her aside.

"Listen, we have wronged Amal and ought to apologize to him," he whispered to her.

Emma nodded, and they went to the end of the crowd where the gloomy Amal Junior trailed behind. He was in a bad mood. This boy had seriously offended him for no reason. He had carried Ben and Emma through the forest, carefully covering them from numerous branches. They carried them all night through the dense jungles and then he stood by the door of the barn like a faithful dog, waiting for them to wake up. But instead of thanking him, Ben, a puny white boy, had humiliated Amal in front of all his tribe-mates and neighbors, and almost broke his arm.

Ben, accompanied by Emma, walked over to Amal and offered his hand.

"I'm so sorry, Amal, for what happened. I didn't mean to hurt you. It was just a simple misunderstanding."

Emma translated everything Ben said, but Amal, crimson with shame and resentment, didn't shake his hand but just turned away and stepped aside. Ben opened his mouth to talk again, but when he saw Amal's eyes full of hatred and anger, he cringed and moved away, pulling Emma along.

Of course, he felt sorry for Amal. It wasn't his fault at all. Ben realized now that Amal's ear-to-ear smile in the glade had been a friendly one, not a malevolent one at all. What else was he supposed to do if he didn't speak English? So Amal had been smiling to show his friendliness. Immediately, Second Ben, hitherto pacified with the successful resolution of the conflict, intervened. *Learn foreign languages, Ben. It will come in handy in life.*

Ben and Emma quickened their pace and caught up with parents. They all went together, along with a dozen men from both tribes. They were gallant gentlemen and did everything they could to facilitate the advancement of their dear guests through the jungle, especially Margaret. Each of them strove to run ahead and carefully move apart the branches of trees, while others tore off the cobwebs and garlands of vines in their way and helped her step over the fallen tree trunks. Though Margaret could have easily avoided any impediments in her way, they were seriously offended when she refused their help. She had to pretend that it was terribly difficult for her to wade through and gratefully accepted the help of the gentlemen. At one point, two such gentlemen almost got into a fight over which of them would get to help her. There was a shallow but wide creek along their path. Everybody passed through it without even noticing the water. But Margaret hesitated to step in and was about to take her shoes off when one of the guys immediately offered to carry her to the other side of the creek. At the same time, another guy came and tried to lift her up. The first gentleman, outraged at such impudence, angrily pushed the second man. He, in turn, pushed the first guy back. They would definitely have gotten into a big fight, but Margaret resolved the conflict amicably. She held both of them by the crook of their arms and pulled her feet up, laughing. Both gentlemen were thus able to carry her across the stream. The incident was over.

"It seems, my dear, you have new fans." Rupert grinned.

"Yes, a lot of them. I'm flattered. If they only took occasional showers and used deodorant, it would be great," Margaret replied, laughing and covering her nose.

As the forest thinned out, there was no need to clear the path in front of the guests. Everybody imperceptibly divided into small groups and were walking and chatting with each other. Rupert, making sure that nobody paid attention to them anymore, said to Margaret and Ben (and, of course, Emma, as a direct participant in the events),

"Now I'll tell you what really happened."

Chapter 5. How To Do Business In New Guinea

It was a wise practice to choose the chief of a tribe among its worthy elders. A leader cannot be appointed; he has to be chosen solely by his wisdom and life experience as it cannot be inherited along with a title. It comes with age, with wrinkles on the face, gray hair, and with every fallen tooth. Only a man grown wise by life's twists and turns can be a valuable leader; a man who has lived life through all its complexities and critical situations.

Amal, the chief of the Abaga tribe, without doubt was such a leader: intelligent, prudent, and a visionary. People loved him for his wisdom, profound acumen, and astuteness, respected and even feared his strength, which, alas, had diminished over the years, but even today, he still could compete in endurance and agility with many of his younger men. His natural intelligence and wisdom were well combined with an astute resourcefulness, and his diplomacy skills were equally strong with the language of force, whenever diplomacy failed.

Amal was sitting and thinking in the shade of a large tree, smoking his first morning cigarette made from the local tobacco leaves. Despite being early morning, the heat was already strong and distracting him from his thoughts. But he had a lot to think about.

This morning he heard rumors that were spread all throughout the neighborhood about a lost white tourist boy. The source was reliable, and Amal had no reason to doubt its veracity. He did not know any details, but it didn't matter much anyway. More importantly, he was also told that the grief-stricken parents promised a big reward to those who found their son and brought him back to the port—ten thousand dollars, an amount that, for Amal and his tribe, was surreal and very much needed.

Ten thousand dollars in local kina meant a lot of food, medicine, salt, alcohol, matches, tobacco, a drove of pigs, chickens, etc. It meant iron tools, knives, axes, and even a shotgun for his son—the chief's head was spinning with all the possibilities that opened up with it. There was no dearth of things to procure with the possible reward money. However, it was not as clear where and how to find the lost tourist. Amal knew that he must start looking for the boy immediately, otherwise another tribe would find him and get the reward. All the surrounding tribes were probably roaming through the woods by now, hoping to bring the boy to the grateful parents and earn money for such a trifling matter.

Amal could have deployed all men in his tribe to track the boy's footsteps, but after some thoughts, he dropped this idea. Not that he was concerned much about his men, not at all. It actually would be beneficial for them to run through the woods, to disperse blood through their veins, otherwise they soon will grow fat on their bellies from their sluggishness. Hunting season had not yet begun, and there was no war with the neighbors, thanks to the recent truce, so they were just roaming through the village all day, or doing their hair. The problem was more ordinary. Amal didn't like to do things blindly and preferred to develop a strategy, before sending people to execute his order. But right now, he didn't have a plan yet.

The boy was not familiar with this area and could not navigate through the forest with his urban upbringing. Once gone astray, he would circle around the jungle in panic and get lost even further. His men could follow the trail, but the boy's footsteps would be mixed and confusing; they would go looping around, wasting their time. If they were tracking down a professional like themselves, they could predict his actions in advance and calculate variations of movement. However, professionals find it hard to foresee the movements of a dilettante in the forest, as there would be no logic in his actions. Of course, they would find him eventually, but time was of the essence now. The boy's parents would ask for help from anybody; all local tribes, the police, and even the officials from the town would be involved, and then the Highlanders could kiss the money goodbye. No, he had to sit and think, not run through the woods blindly.

He knew the area of the presumed search well. The boy most likely went on an excursion with his parents. There are three possible places where he could have got lost: the town, the waterfalls, and the jungle. The rest of the tours are all near the beach and do not include trips to the woods at all, so those could be excluded.

It is impossible to get lost in town. But even if he fell behind the bus, he could have taken a taxi to the port, or even gone to the police station. The waterfall area could also be excluded, as there is only one road between the port and the mountaintop, but there are many opportunities to get lost during the trip to the jungle. He could have simply gone to pee behind the tall bushes, turned around, and become disoriented when he could not see the bus, got scared, ran in the opposite direction, and a minute later would have been lost for good.

Considering that the message about his disappearance came early this morning, he must have been gone since yesterday evening, which meant that he never came back to the port and probably spent the night in the jungle. Unless . . . there was one other option that, with some luck, could have a good chance of success.

Yes, I think it's worth trying, Amal thought.

He called his son, Amal, and gave him the necessary instructions.

Amal Junior was a good hunter. He still needed to get some experience and acumen, and then Amal Senior could retire and pass the reins to his son. People would follow him. They respected him now, and even feared a little, but it was too early for him to lead the tribe. He was still young and had to learn the wisdom of life, and therefore, Amal Senior could not retire just yet.

Amal came back a few hours later, even earlier than his father had hoped, smiling as if he had caught a wild boar. Turned out, his wise father was right, as always; the boy got lost in the woods and ended up in a neighboring settlement. There was nothing complicated in this conclusion, as there were not that many places to pass through.

Too bad such a simple thought occurred to my father and not me, he thought sadly, going back to his village.

At the same time, Amal learned details of the story. The boy had accidentally fallen off a cliff, injuring his legs.

"Picture this, Father. Emma, the girl I am going to marry, found that boy and brought him to her village."

Amal's father was listening to his son, while thinking that life was so unfair sometimes. He was sitting here, making plans to rescue the boy, and wanted to send his men out to the woods to search the area, but the money had just fallen into Yaga's hands without even the slightest effort on his part. That was wrong. There was no big deal in healing the boy's leg. Their medicine men could have done that as well, though perhaps not as good as Dzhamaya. Amal knew her very well; she was good at it. In her earlier years, she had been a beautiful woman, and Amal had even tried to date her. He did not succeed, however. Her fate was tough. She lost all her loved ones in a short time while she was still a young girl. One was killed in war, another died from a disease, and others just died of old age. She had bitten off almost all the phalanges on her fingers, one for each loved one she lost. She thought that the spirits were punishing her for her sins and became a healer in an attempt to beg for forgiveness. Whether the spirits forgave her or not, Dzhamaya was the best in her craft, like no other.

Amal snapped back to reality from these sad thoughts. His youth was long past; what was the point in regretting a woman who had never had a part in his life?

"You know, Son," Amal Senior said, puffing his cigarette, "the fact that the boy hurt his leg is certainly bad, but perhaps we could use it to our advantage."

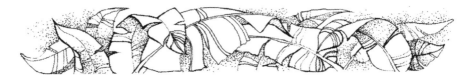

At the same time, no more than ten miles from Amal's settlement, another wise elder, Akelika Yaga, was rubbing his hands in delight.

"Are you sure this is the boy?"

The man who brought the good news to Yaga broke into a smile.

"Of course I'm sure; this is the one. We don't have too many lost tourists running around in our woods."

Yaga closed his eyes contentedly. The money his tribe so desperately needed had fallen into his hands. The main thing right now was to not rush, but to do things the right way and simply avoid any mistakes. Otherwise, the happy parents would unite with their son and refuse to pay the promised reward, saying they found him themselves.

"Tell me everything one more time, with every little detail," Yaga demanded.

"So, as I told you before, I have seen this boy with our Emma. They were going to the woods. I remembered the lost boy about whom I had just overheard this morning. That's all."

"No, this is not all," another man, who was listening to the conversation from a distance, said as he came up from behind. "I saw them coming out of the barn together in the morning."

Yaga's eyebrows shot up in surprise.

"What do you mean? Did they spend the night there? That is wrong. How could she do such a thing? Of course, the boy is not local and doesn't know our customs, but Emma—"

"I think they came to the village well past midnight, and did not want to wake anyone up, so they settled down for the night in a barn."

"Okay, we can talk about it later." Yaga stopped him with a gesture. "I think we will keep a close eye on this little incident. Besides, I already promised her to Amal. Let this be his headache."

"Speaking of Amal," the other man said, "he was here today."

"Why did he come all of a sudden?"

"He came to find out when we are going hunting, as he would like to go with us. Later on, we saw him wandering around the village and talking to Emma. He hadn't seen her for a while and probably wanted to visit her since he was already here."

"This is strange that he decided to come today," Yaga mused. "Did he see the boy?"

"Of course. He was with Emma at that time. She had picked up food, and they were walking toward the woods. I asked her where they were going, but she said—well, you know Emma."

"I don't like this at all. What happened then? Did Amal go back home?"

"I do not know. I did not see where he went."

"Maybe he took them to his settlement? I am sure they have heard about the money too."

"No, it is unlikely. The boy was injured while wandering in the jungle. I think there is something wrong with his leg, so he couldn't go that far."

"What leg?" Yaga did not understand. "You didn't tell me about that."

"I saw him limping in the morning, when they got out from the barn, and Emma took him to Dzhamaya."

"I asked you to tell me all the details!" Yaga exploded. "Why do I have to pull out every word from you? What else have you not told me?"

"That's all I know. There is nothing else. After they visited Dzhamaya, Emma got some food, and they went for a walk to the jungle and accidentally bumped into Amal, who had come to visit Emma."

"I don't like this word 'accidentally.' Life has taught me not to believe in coincidences," Yaga grumbled, though calming down. "Let's do this: Take one of our men who can speak at least a little bit of English and go to the port. Find the boy's parents and tell them we found their son and he is in our village. Unfortunately, he injured his leg and cannot walk. We are going to treat his wound, and tomorrow, by noon, we will bring him back. Got it? Then go."

Yaga sat down wearily on the bench, while messengers ran into the woods. Everything was done and now he just had to wait.

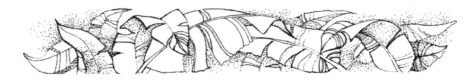

Amal Senior came up with the simple plan.

"We must get the boy to our village at all costs. I don't think we can persuade him to come here, and because of his injured leg, he wouldn't be able to walk that far. So, we have to steal him from Yaga. Then we will also invite his parents and hand the boy over to them. All we need is a good, convincing reason for the invitation so it looks natural . . . Oh! A festival, of course! Tomorrow is the festival! We must invite his parents to celebrate it with us. In this case, they wouldn't have the slightest doubt that we had found the boy and deserve the promised reward. But if they refused to come to our settlement, then our men would simply carry the boy to the port."

Amal called his son again.

"Son, we need to kidnap the boy quietly, without fuss, and bring him to us. Can you do that?"

"Of course I can. But the next morning when they find out that the boy has disappeared, they will get really angry with us."

"They will think that he got up in the morning and went back to the port on his own," father said slyly.

"But he does not know how to get there; Emma promised to walk him back. If we steal him, she would know about it when she wakes up."

"Yes, you're right. Let's bring both of them here. Later on, we will make a deal with the neighbors, give them a few pigs to keep their mouths shut. Take a few strong men with you and bring kids back to us. But you should carry them carefully, making sure they don't have scratches or bruises. They are not our captives, but rather dear guests. Lock them in the barn, and in the morning, when they wake up, explain that they are invited to the feast, and the boy's parents will also be here. Feed them, provide everything they need at their first request; show them our village, make them take part in the preparation for the festival. But make sure they don't run away. Go."

That's all. The process had started. All he had to do now was wait until morning.

Amal had tried to convey all his knowledge and skills to his son, teaching him everything he was once taught by his own father, particularly the skill of lulling people and animals, which would come in very handy today. This technique had been used for ages on wild boars caught in a snare. Try carrying a heavy boar on your back through the woods while it kicks and bites! The task is much easier to do if it's asleep. The boar is still heavy, of course, but at least it calmly rests on the hunter's back. All Amal had to do was press the right spot on the carotid artery and his prey would fall asleep.

The same technique was also used to steal girls from other tribes. Girls suitable for marriage are a valuable commodity. But he had not had many opportunities to practice it on people; mostly he'd done so on animals. The most important thing was to not overdo it, as that could put one to sleep forever. But Amal was a good student and had mastered this skill to perfection.

Amal returned from his thoughts. He knew that his son would do everything right. However, there were plenty of errands yet to be done. He called two other men and assigned them an easier task, which perhaps was just as important. They had to go to the market in town and buy two pigs, one large, and the other one smaller, and deliver them to the settlement no later than the coming morning, as it takes a lot of time to prepare pigs for the *mumu*. To implement this part of the plan, Amal used all the tribe's money that had been saved for an emergency. Right now was such an emergency.

Yaga was waiting for Emma and the boy to return to the settlement. The sun had set beyond the horizon, and in a few more minutes it would be completely dark, and they had yet to return. He was worried. What if he was wrong and Amal had taken this boy to their tribe?

His doubts were soon dispelled by the messengers who had delivered the good news to the boy's parents. On the way home, they stumbled upon Emma with the white boy. The kids were seen by the lake, sitting near a bonfire having dinner. At first, the messengers wanted to bring them back to the settlement, but then they decided against it and continued on to Yaga.

"You did the right thing," Yaga praised them. "The boy is our guest, and we cannot limit his freedom. If he wants to swim in the lake or take a walk in the woods, then so be it."

The next day, Yaga woke up with the sunrise, as he wanted to take the boy to the port himself. While the children were still sleeping, he decided to fix his hair and pick out a suitable outfit. It had been a long time since he had traveled such distances. The years had taken their toll on his body, and even though there was still strength left in him, it became harder and harder to make such long trips. But this important task couldn't be entrusted to the youngsters.

With these thoughts and preparations, he did not notice that the sun had already risen quite high, and he had to hurry to be at the port on time. It was a little strange that the children were not up yet. Emma usually woke up early, regardless of when she went to bed. Yaga called for one of the men idling nearby.

"Wake up the kids. Tell them we need to go back, otherwise we won't be able to make it to the port by noon, as promised."

The man went to the barn, but a few minutes later, he came running back.

"Yaga, they are not there!" he reported.

"What do you mean 'not there'? Where are they? Have they woken up already? I have not seen them in the yard yet."

"I do not know, but the barn is empty."

Yaga, anticipating trouble, pushed the man aside and ran to the barn with unprecedented agility for an elder of the tribe. The barn was empty indeed, except for Emma's *bilum,* which was lying on the floor.

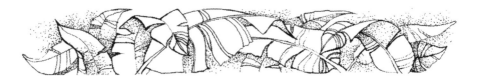

The next morning, Amal reported to his father that the children had been smuggled in and locked in the hut. That's it. The process had started. Amal called for two men who could speak a little English and sent them with a message to the boy's parents that their son was alive and well (thanks to Amal, of course). But since he injured his knee, he was not able to get back to the port on his own. So, Amal invited the dear guests to visit their village and celebrate the feast of a hunt along with them. He even offered to send transportation to bring them as close to the settlement as possible, to minimize their walking through the woods. Then, after the celebration, his men would carry the boy back to the bus and send them all to the port. They could even carry the parents as well, as they were urban people and probably were not used to long walks in the jungle, especially in high heels, which he envisioned the boy's mom wearing.

Two young men received the instructions and ran to the woods.

I should have sent some more people with them, Amal thought belatedly. *The way to the port is long and who knows what could happen to the messengers in the jungle. Their task is very important and cannot be jeopardized.*

But Amal lacked people. There were a lot of things that needed to be done, and not too many young, strong men in their settlement. First, he had to make arrangements to cook the food. He called all the women and gave them a task: to prepare a gala dinner for the celebration. Amal told them to use all their available stock of food. They also had begun preparation for their traditional dish, the *mumu*. The pigs were about to be delivered.

Next, he made arrangements for transportation. He sent two other men to the Franciscan mission nearby to ask for their help. The son of the former missionary was a bus driver and occasionally helped them to deliver goods from the town. Amal, back in his youth, had worked at that mission and knew this young man from when he was a child. Even today, many of his men still worked there, and learn English at the same time. It could come in handy in life, in a situation much like today.

Amal was running around the yard, giving everybody appropriate instructions. The children were sent away to play on the fringe of the woods, as the rest of the adult population began preparations for the festival. Everything should be done in the best possible way. The only thing that bothered him was the money he had to spend, as he had used the entire savings of his tribe for the two pigs. But Amal knew the first rule of capitalism: you have to invest money to make money. If everything went well, then the profit would exceed the cost a hundredfold. Besides, this amount could also be added to the client's tab on top of the promised reward, if he started the conversation right. That required a delicate diplomacy, and that was Amal's specialty.

The main goal was to make the boy's parents come here and to not rush things. First, give them a warm welcome, feed the dear guests, and make a demonstration of the ritual dances with an obligatory sacrifice. That was what the second, smaller pig was for, though it was an additional expense. Only after that would he start the conversation over a cup of wine and snuff. He would tell them all the thoughts weighing on his mind, about children living from hand to mouth, deadly diseases mowing down his people, and so on, and on. These white people were compassionate and rich, and there was a chance to get even more from them than what was promised.

His thoughts were interrupted by Amal Junior, who was running to him, screaming from afar.

"Father! Father! The boy has escaped!"

The meaning of his words did not immediately reach his mind. This simply could not be!

"Wait, Amal, slow down. Did you say that the boy ran away? From a locked hut? How could this happen?"

"He escaped through the window opening."

"You told me that this opening is so small that even an opossum wouldn't pass through it. Then how did he manage?"

"I do not know. Emma said that he beat her up and climbed through the window."

"Let's go. I want to see it myself." Amal got up, and they briskly went toward the hut.

"I hope you still have the girl," Amal said to his son as they approached the wooden structure.

"Yes, I do, she was lying all tied up on the—" Amal stopped in mid-sentence. The hut was empty, except, of course, for a pair of ropes.

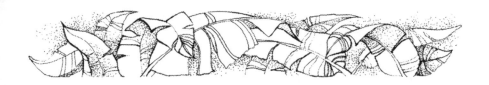

Yaga was shouting and angrily pacing in the small shed, like a kangaroo locked in a cage. All the men in the tribe came to the noise, but after they found out what had happened, they all stood with their eyes downcast.

"Why didn't you make sure they came back? Why did you not put a guard near the barn for the night?" Yaga raged, yelling in fury. However, he had to calm down quickly. He rarely raised his voice to fellow tribesmen, considering it a sign of weakness.

"A truly wise man," he was always saying, "would never yell at a negligent person, like a truly strong man would never hit a weak one. Yelling is a recognition of helplessness, inability to change anything. You can't fix the situation just by screaming. If necessary, you can say things quietly that the culpable person would remember for the rest of his life."

Besides, in this situation, he had no one to blame but himself. He should have foreseen this, knowing his neighbor well (Yaga did not doubt even for a second that Amal had something to do with it). He should have made sure that the kids came home safely. He should have set up a guard for the night. He could only blame himself and nobody else.

Something had to be done immediately but, most importantly, he had to inform the boy's parents that they couldn't bring their son on time, as promised. He'd say instead that the boy went for a walk into the jungle early in the morning.

"That's right, he went for a walk and probably got lost again, so now we are looking for him," he admonished the two envoys, whom he sent back to the port. "Tell them we will find the boy and immediately bring him to them."

Next, he sent a few men to Amal's settlement to conduct a reconnaissance and to clarify the situation.

"But be careful, and don't let them see you. Take as many people as necessary, and send a messenger back to me as soon as you find out what's going on over there. I want to know everything."

This is not the end of it yet, Yaga thought. *I will fight for this boy.*

It took Amal just a few seconds to vaguely understand the entire picture of what had happened, and there was neither the time nor the will to investigate all the details. Obviously, the boy had outwitted his son, and the rest of it was not important at this moment.

"Quick, call every available man." Amal was angry with Junior, but the sermons could wait for a better time, the matter of highest priority right now was to find and return the fugitives, or at least the boy. Messengers were already gone with an invitation for the parents. If they came here, and the boy went to the port, Amal could kiss the remuneration goodbye and would be disgraced for the rest of his life. Not to mention the money spent for the festival preparation.

It was obvious that the boy could not get far, especially with an injured leg, and his capture would only be a matter of time. But because of this incident, he now had to distract people from work. Amal had sent several men in different directions, to determine which way the boy had gone. A few minutes later, they all reported that there were no traces of him to be found in the jungle. How was a white urban boy moving around the woods with the skills of a good hunter? This was absurd. It was more likely that his men hadn't noticed the traces, or that the boy did not run anywhere at all, but just hid somewhere nearby. Amal had decided to personally explore everything and almost immediately noticed two pairs of children's footsteps behind the barn in the field. Seconds later, he also detected traces of their presence in the bushes nearby. Of course, they had hidden here, and then they had run into the woods unnoticed.

"Who checked this side?" Amal growled menacingly at his negligent tribe-mates.

They all stood in silence, afraid to look at the furious elder. But Amal quickly calmed down. They had found traces of the fugitives and knew the direction of their escape. Everything else was not important right now. Amal selected a few men for the chase and sent the first group into the forest.

"Remember, no violence, no weapons. Just persuade them to return to the village, explain to the boy that his parents are going to come for him in the evening. Report to me regularly. The second group will follow you and stay in touch with us."

The situation got out of control and required serious adjustments. Even if they were able to catch the kids soon, there was no time left to properly prepare for the festival.

"What if I do not catch them on time?" Amal muttered aloud, sinking into his worries. "The parents would come and ask, 'Well, where is our son?' And I would have to say, 'He ran away, I'm so sorry.' Now that would be an absurd situation!"

Amal called two of his fastest men, one of whom also spoke a little English.

"Run to the port and tell the boy's parents that their son went for a walk and got lost in the woods again, but we're looking for him.

"Tell them not to worry, we will find him soon and bring him back. But you need to rush and intercept them before they get on the bus."

The two men also disappeared into the jungle.

Why did they run away from us? Amal wondered. Then he immediately answered his own question. "It's simple. They woke up in the morning and found out they were abducted, got frightened, and came up with an escape plan. We should have explained the situation to them and calmed them down. But I, stupid me, relied on my son. It is only my fault, and there is nobody else to blame. I was wondering why they were sleeping for so long; I thought maybe Amal lulled them for longer than needed. But it turned out they had woken up long ago."

Amal was mulling over this whole situation while briskly pacing through the jungle with another group of men. The chase had already been going on for quite some time, and he expected to get news from the pursuers anytime now. And soon he did. However, the news was not what he wanted to hear: they had lost the fugitives.

"Where?" Amal asked, realizing that there would be no quick end to this chase. He had underestimated the boy. Although it was likely that the girl helped him navigate through the forest and hide their traces, otherwise they would have caught him by now. A city dweller simply cannot get far from a professional hunter who knows every path and every tree in the jungle.

"In the dead forest," the pursuers reported dejectedly.

The first news came much faster than Yaga expected. He had just resumed the interrupted morning routine as the breathless messenger came running with a report.

"Yaga, the boy is with them. Amal's got them both!" he shouted from afar.

This time Yaga showed restraint befitting his status. He did not interrupt his business and only said curtly, "Tell me."

"You were right, Yaga, they kidnapped them at night and then locked them in a shed."

"Well, of course," Yaga fumed. "I know Amal very well and didn't expect anything good from him. Please continue."

"But the kids ran away, and now his men are searching for them in the forest."

"What? How can they run away from a locked shed? I'm starting to respect this boy. Where are they now?"

"Amal's men were chasing the children through the jungle, but then lost them in the dead forest."

"Well, looks like we have gotten another chance. We must help them escape from Amal. I am sure they will run toward our village. Amal will probably try to cut them off from us, forcing them to go farther down, though. So what do we have there? There is a lake, and on the right side is the mountain range, almost impassable. On the left side of it is Amal with his men. Therefore, the only option they have is through the lake. Call everybody back. I think I know where he will force them to run, and we will intercept them there."

"In the dead forest," Amal echoed thoughtfully. He knew that area well. "So they went on the top of the trees, and from there, they have only one way out." Shudders went down Amal's back in anticipation as he gathered all the remaining men and explained the situation.

"They are not making their way to the port but to Emma's settlement, which is even worse for us. If they get there, then we can forget about the reward, and yet they will accuse us of kidnapping and breaking the truce conditions. This is bad, very bad. We must cut them off from the settlement and make the kids go further down. If we cannot catch them, then Yaga should not get them either."

He divided all the remaining men into a few groups and pointed out the direction to pursue.

"The first group comes to the left of the dead forest and goes straight along the borders with the neighbor. The second and the third groups flank to the right. The rest of you go straight to the lake. If we are lucky, we can still intercept them before they reach the port."

Amal Junior was about to join one of the groups, but his father stopped him.

"Wait, Son, you're coming with me."

Amal wanted to redeem himself in his father's eyes, by being on the most difficult part of the pursuit, but instead, he had to slowly walk by him and listen to his preaching.

"Father, I better run with my men. It's not too late, and I can still catch them."

Elder only grunted in response. He understood his son's zeal for tracking down the fugitives to restore his reputation. But right now, the most important element was not the speed, strength, or marksmanship, but the strategy and the ability to unravel the plans of the runaways.

"You will, Amal. You will run." His father nodded. "Only to another place. You know the dead forest, right?"

"Yes, I know it well, Father."

"If they had gone by the treetops, the only way out from the deadwood is to the woodlands near the lake."

"Right. There's nowhere else to go from there."

"What do you think our elusive kids would do when surrounded from all sides, forcing them to run toward the lake?"

"They will try to get around it. There is a path going downhill to the shore, and from there is a straight way to the port."

"Or jump into the lake to save time," the father continued.

"But that is a very high cliff!"

"Of course it is. But what other choice do they have if a dozen pursuers surround them? The path down the cliff is steep and dangerous; they would not be able to get down quickly enough. What would you do?"

"I would have jumped, but these are just children."

"Children," Amal mocked him. "Never underestimate your enemy, even though they are not our enemy. Listen, there is a big glade behind the lake, run there and wait for them. They will be there soon."

"How do you know? What if they go to the right bank?"

"You don't have much time, run!" his father shouted at him. "I'll go there too, but I cannot run fast anymore. You have to get there ahead of them. Just remember: this boy is our dear guest, so no violence, only kindness—and smile. Tell him that we want to help him get to the port. Okay, go now; you are running out of time."

Wise Amal had thought of everything and predicted their path correctly. The only way out from the lake was, indeed, on the left bank, unless they decided to swim across it, but that was impossible.

However, he did not consider that the kids would spend some time in the hideout under fallen trees, hoping to ride the chase out. Either Amal did not know about this shelter or may have forgotten about it, but this mistake turned out to his advantage. He had enough time to get to that fateful clearing on time.

Amal saw the children on the way to the glade. They were briskly walking through the thickets, not looking around, confident they had left their pursuers behind. He silently followed them at a distance, trying not to scare them ahead of time. There was no need to rush when he knew that his son was already in place, and the trap was about to snap closed. Once again, he congratulated himself for predicting their route properly. He saw his men approaching the glade from all sides, or rather, felt their presence. They all were good hunters, and could move through the forest so quietly that no leaf on a tree would move and no twigs snapped under their feet. The chase was over. Now he would explain everything to the boy, calm him down, and they would go to the port to meet his parents.

It's even better this way, Amal thought, continuing to follow the kids. "We can eat the pigs ourselves later. Good thing we didn't kill them yet . . ."

However, a second later his happy mood was gone, along with his high hopes. He had noticed Yaga's tribesmen approaching the clearing. The situation was getting out of control, and Amal ran faster, hoping to intercept the fugitives ahead of his neighbors.

Amal saw everything happening at the glade and felt his hair rise in horror. He saw Junior rushing to the boy, trying to crush him with his iron fist.

"No, Amal, don't!" He wanted to shout out, but could not say a word.

A second later, his son, a valiant warrior, a good hunter, and the future chief of their tribe, who terrified the neighbors and their own fellow tribe-mates, who was by far taller, wider in the shoulders, and much stronger than this puny white boy was suddenly soared up in the air. His legs made a full circle, and his big, heavy body fell flat on the ground. But worst of all, the boy was standing near him in such a grotesque way, twisting Amal's arm. He was on the verge of breaking the hand, capable of killing an adult boar with one stroke.

Is this a dream? Amal thought in horror. *Am I sleeping? This is simply impossible.*

But, alas, it was true. One touch, one little kick, and his son would lose an arm forever. Amal could not let that happen. What kind of hunter and warrior would he be with a crippled arm?

Amal made the only right decision. He crept up to the girl, who was watching the fight, and grabbed her, making her squeal to divert the boy's attention. It worked! The boy looked back and let go of Amal's arm. Now he had to calm him down and explain everything, but the stupid boy would not let him say a word. He was coming toward him, shouting all kinds of nonsense, asking to be taken instead of the girl and to let her go. The glade had suddenly filled with men of both tribes, and everybody saw his son humiliated, still writhing in pain on the grass. Seconds later, the boy's parents also stepped into the glade.

That was the end of all his plans and hopes. But then, just when Amal thought nothing could get any worse, he was knocked out with another slap, the last one that brought this story to the logical conclusion. The boy shouted something that cleared everything up. He had thought all along that they were planning to eat him.

Amal wanted to cry, but instead, he laughed. He was rolling in the grass with laughter, choking with tears. Such an elegant plan had collapsed because this stupid white boy was afraid that they would eat him.

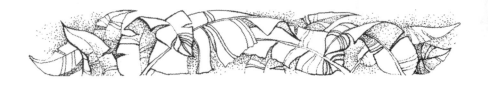

Obviously, Rupert did not know all the details of this story, but he correctly caught the sense of it. The culprit was the promised reward. Obviously, nobody was going to harm his son, but the prize money was much too tempting. Ben became the plaything of two tribes who wanted to earn a big reward by saving the rich tourist. They would have helped Ben anyway and sent him back to his parents, but the temptation of the money was too big and, of course, there was no one to blame for that. People are people at all latitudes.

Chapter 6. Celebration

Despite all the unpleasant events, the celebration was successful, though not quite the way Amal had planned. The road to the port took a long time, and the group entered the village late in the evening, in complete darkness. Everyone was tired, hungry, and could not wait to start the celebration. Residents of this sleepy hamlet usually went to bed early, with the emergence of the first stars in the sky (except for the days when the ship with tourists docked in the harbor). Many of them were already asleep, but dim lights were still visible in some windows, as the owners were completing their evening routine.

But suddenly, the noise of a drumroll, chatter, and the laughter of two dozen people came out of the woods and flowed through the wide-open windows. The villagers jumped out of their beds and peered out on the street through sleepy eyes. A motley, noisy procession marched through the street and turned the quiet village into a circus where, until now, the audience was sitting in the darkness waiting for the show. Suddenly, bright lights flashed, loud music was playing, and two dozen clowns ran into the arena. And indeed, it became lighter as the wind dispersed the clouds and the sky was lit up by the moonlight. The warriors of both tribes, embellished from head to toe with whimsical patterns of many colors, resembled members of the glorious circus métier. Residents of the uneventful village dressed up hastily, and came out of their houses, shaking off the remnants of slumber, and joined the rest of the men getting ready for the festival. Nobody would want to miss such an event.

Preparations began under the leadership of Amal Senior, with the acquiescence of Yaga, and the people of both tribes unquestioningly followed his orders and instructions. One group of men went to collect some wood for a bonfire, the second was instructed to drag a few fallen tree trunks and lay them in a circle, adapting them for the benches around the fire. The rest of the participants went to search for something edible for dinner, led by Rupert, who was the main bursar of the holiday and paid for all the food they could find.

"Mom, where is our luggage?" Ben asked Margaret when they entered the village. "I need to wash off and change."

"At a house nearby. One old woman let us stay with her. C'mon, I'll show you."

"Very well." Emma was delighted. "I will go visit my grandma while you are changing. She lives not far from here."

So they agreed to meet each other again in the glade by the fire, and each went their own ways. But they met much sooner, right at the door of the house where Igissy lived, and where Margaret and Rupert had stayed. Emma raised her eyebrows in surprise.

"Are you staying with my *tubuna*?"

"Are you staying with Igissy?" Ben echoed her question.

"Wait, who is 'tubuna,' and who is 'Igissy'?" Margaret wondered.

"*Tubuna* Igissy, Emma's grandmother."

Margaret nodded sheepishly. She realized that they had been so busy looking for their son that they hadn't even bothered to find out the name of the woman who gave them shelter. Rupert asked her name on the first day of their acquaintance, and she had muttered something in response, but they had no strength or desire to ask her to repeat it.

They all entered the house. The perennially gloomy face of the old woman broke into a smile at the sight of her granddaughter.

"*Tubuna*, please meet the lost boy. I found him!" Emma proudly introduced Ben.

"So, you are Igissy, Emma's grandmother? She told me so much about you."

"And you kept running in the jungle?" the grumpy old woman said peevishly, instead of greeting him. "Your parents worried about you, but for you, it is nothing but a game."

"Not purposely, it just turned out that way. But if it wasn't for Emma, I would probably still be running in the jungles, even now."

"Go wash off a little. Emma will show you where the washbasin is." Igissy handed him a clean towel.

When Ben washed in the strangely designed sink and returned clean and refreshed, Margaret was ready with medical supplies from her bottomless bag containing Band-Aids, iodine, ointments, and antiseptics. Up until now, she had not had the chance to look at him thoroughly, as she was simply happy that he was alive, and the rest did not matter. Besides, a thick layer of dust and dirt covered numerous cuts and bruises. Now, looking at him, she just groaned in horror and opened a box of bandages.

Ben looked at himself in a mirror by the door and saw a haggard, exhausted face, with big dark circles under his eyes. His disheveled, messy hair was more like a bird's nest. Besides the laceration on his right shoulder, his whole body was smothered with bruises and wounds and covered in a mesh of scratches from the branches of bushes they'd had to wade through. Some of them were small, practically healed, while others were deep and continued to bleed.

Margaret was ready to examine his injuries, readying iodine and a box of the Band-Aids.

"Mom, I'll do it myself," Ben said, and took the box of bandages from her, "but later."

Emma was already at the door, impatiently waiting for Ben to finish with all the hygienic and medical procedures. He hastily attached a bandage over the bleeding wound on his shoulder, put the box with the remaining Band-Aids in his pocket, and, accompanied by Emma, jumped out to the street, forgetting to change his clothes.

In the glade behind the village, preparations for the celebration were in full swing, and Ben joined in. He collected wood along with the other men and cut down some thicker branches to make the fire spit, and had a chance to get convinced of the sharpness and reliability of the stone axe, which he had been skeptical about, like all other people living in the comforts of civilization. In skilled hands, it was an effective and rigorous tool, and if necessary, a formidable weapon.

Meanwhile, Emma was helping other women to prepare the holiday supper. Everything edible they found in the village was brought to the glade after receiving money from Rupert. There was a lot of food, but also many people intended to participate in the celebration.

Margaret went to her husband and whispered, "You know, they charged you the price of a good-sized piglet for a bucket of m-m-m— potatoes . . . or whatever it is they are baking."

"I am aware of that," Rupert replied in a whisper. "If you remember, I'm an economist, and the only thing I know how to do well is to count money. I thought that for once in a lifetime, people here have gotten a winning ticket, and they have the opportunity to raise some cash. I'd say let them. I do not mind. For us it's only money, and for them, this is the chance to slightly improve their living conditions, and for some, maybe even the chance of survival. We can earn more money later on."

However, Rupert quickly ran out of cash, and for an obvious reason, this was not the place for ATMs. But the villagers still continued to bring products for free, deciding that they had earned enough from these rich but stupid Americans who couldn't count money.

Soon, all the preparations were completed. The bonfires blazed merrily, and various foods were neatly piled on the broad leaves of an unknown local plant resting on the ground. There was dried breadfruit, vegetables, and sago cakes. Someone brought smoked and fresh fish wrapped in leaves and baked on the coals. Hot beans and rice were steaming in deep bowls. A wide variety of fruits were stacked in one big pile, from ordinary bananas and mangoes to the outlandish cherimoya and passion fruit.

But the main dish was, of course, the pig that Rupert had bought from the villagers for the price of a small herd. He did not even try to negotiate and paid the asking price in full. It was impossible to make traditional *mumu* since the preparation of the earthen oven was a time-consuming and lengthy process, so they simply put it on the spit and roasted it over the fire. Soon, the skin became a crispy light brown hue, and the smell of cooked meat, spiced with seasoning of the local *mola-messi* herb, spread across the glade, causing copious salivation in all participants of the festival. Everybody had completed their work and now longingly looked at the fat-dripping, slow-roasted chef-d'oeuvre.

Then the long-awaited moment arrived, and Amal invited all the participants "to the table." Men of both tribes sat on the logs around the fire. Margaret was sitting with her husband next to the elders. Both of them insisted that the dear guests must sit in the middle. Women and a few children took part in the celebration, but were seated a bit away in the second row. Ben wanted to find Emma, but he was the guest of honor and the hero of the day, and Amal Senior gestured that he should sit next to him. Ben was exhausted from the day's events and gladly sat down and stretched his sore legs. He didn't even want to eat, despite the spicy smell of roasted meat.

Every holiday begins with an official, solemn speech, regardless of whether the guests were gathered: at the table, in a conference room, or at the glade in the outskirts of a small village. This celebration was no exception. Amal Senior delivered his opening speech. However, there was nothing solemn about it. He got up and spoke fast in his language, vigorously gesticulating, nodding at the guests.

Then he added, in English, "Well, Ben, although you brought us a great deal of trouble today, all has ended well, and we all are pleased that we could find you and help you to reunite with your parents."

Ben was taken aback by such impudence and even opened his mouth to angrily deprecate his words, but said nothing. Amal was right, it was over now, and the rest did not matter. There was no point in arguing and finding out the truth.

Amal continued his speech, laughing.

"I actually wanted to thank you for making us run through the woods today. Even Yaga and I had to flex our old bones and disperse blood through the veins."

Yaga, hearing his name, nodded happily. Amal took his *dongan*[29] made of the sharpened bone of an unknown animal and gave it to Ben.

"The first slice of meat to our dear guest of honor."

Ben did not argue. He walked over to the spit and cut off a decent chunk from the pig's thighs. The meat was hot, well-done, and dripping fat. Someone offered him a wide leaf he could use as a plate.

"Thank you, Amal." Ben also decided to give a speech in response. "Please forgive me for all the trouble I brought you and Yaga. That was a simple misunderstanding. However, I shouldn't have this holiday treat. I didn't deserve it. Amal, I know I unwittingly violated probably a dozen of your customs and traditions, but nevertheless, I'm about to do it one more time."

Ben noticed Emma sitting in the second row with the group of women and children. He walked over and handed her a leaf with the meat, but, to his surprise, she recoiled and hid her hands behind her back.

"What are you doing? I cannot, I'm not supposed to . . ." she faltered, frightened.

Ben leaned over and whispered snidely, directly into her ear, "How come you can sleep in the same barn with a boy who did not undergo the rite of passage yet, but you cannot eat meat before other men?"

Emma looked at him despairingly, and then suddenly laughed loudly and took the treat. But Ben didn't give her a chance to enjoy it. He grabbed her by the arm, pulled her up from the ground, and then did a terrible thing: he dragged her to the center and sat her in his place between Amal and his mother. Then he continued his speech, referring mainly to the elders.

"This girl saved my life, and now Emma has to sit in the place of honor, not me. She has earned that right and deserved the first portion of this wonderful holiday dinner. I hope no one would object to that."

"No one will object," Amal quickly replied, looking at the unhappy expressions on the faces of some men, even though very few understood what he was saying.

Ben went back to the skewer and cut another slice of pork.

"I would like to offer the next portion," he continued, gesturing Emma to translate, "to the glorious Amal, the fearless leader, the brave warrior, a strong and smart man, and . . . and . . ."

Ben could not find other adjectives to bestow on his recent sparring opponent.

"A good hunter," prompted Emma in English.

"Yes, a good hunter," Ben finished his speech.

All this time the gloomy Amal Junior had sat apart from everybody, his head lowered and sullenly staring at the ground, reliving his shame. Hearing Ben's words, or rather the shrill voice of Emma, who translated his speech, Amal was roused from his despair. The last thing he wanted right now was to be in the spotlight. His face turned red under the dozens of pairs of eyes, and he glared at his enemy with an evil look. Ben came next to Amal, ignoring his unfriendly expression. Emma regretfully handed Margaret her leaf with the meat, got up, and followed him as an interpreter.

"You're a good warrior, Amal," Ben continued, deciding to make peace with him at any cost, "and if you had not slipped on the wet grass back there, I would not have had a chance to defeat you."

Shrewd Emma translated loudly, making sure that everybody in the glade understood correctly. Amal looked at him incredulously.

Of course I slipped! That elucidates everything. He immediately grabbed this convenient explanation. *It could happen to anybody. Obviously, this puny white boy could not beat me. He just got lucky that the grass was wet, otherwise—*

"Why are you sitting here all alone, Amal? Your place is next to your father." Ben pulled him to the middle, as he had pulled Emma to the place of honor minutes ago.

Amal hesitated for a moment, but then he got up and went to the center of the circle, after Emma translated Ben's words, trying to convey even Ben's intonation properly.

"Here you go, Amal." Ben handed him a leaf with meat. "You deserve this treat, not me. You sought and saved us in a vast jungle, so thank you, from me and Emma." Ben nudged Emma to translate it literally and not to be indignant with this wording.

394

Emma cupped her palms and extended hands to Amal, imitating Ben's gesture, and translated his speech in Wagi. It looked very funny. Someone chuckled quietly, but immediately fell silent, not wanting to disturb the solemnity of the moment.

"And if anyone doubts this," Ben continued, "please step up and tell me right now. I will explain it to the doubters."

Emma, immersed in the role of interpreter, put her hands on her hips, glared around the circle, and translated with a frightful voice.

Nobody dared to doubt Ben's words. Everyone remembered the scene in the glade well, where this inscrutable boy easily knocked their leader to the ground and fearsome Amal roared and writhed in pain. The situation did not fit in their minds. Many had seen it with their own eyes and gladly retold the story to latecomers. Of course, nobody believed the convenient tale about the wet grass, but none of them had the desire to express their doubts. If the boy said that the grass was wet, then it probably was. If he would have said that it was daytime right now, and that the sun shone brightly, everybody would agree with that as well, despite the darkness enshrouding them. There were no warriors brave enough among those present who would want to question Ben's words.

Amal Senior shook his head and leaned toward Rupert.

"He would be a good warrior when he grows up," he praised Ben. "What a pity he does not live with us."

"Yes, he participates in a lot of sports and some martial arts—" Rupert replied, but Amal interrupted him.

"I'm not talking about his physical strength. Muscles are nonsense; they will grow over time, then deteriorate just as quickly. The most important muscle is in here." He tapped his forehead. "In his head."

Rupert did not reply, but he was pleased with Amal's words.

Meanwhile, Ben continued his speech.

"Your place is here, Amal, next to your father. His wisdom and your strength should always be together." He said that and surprised himself; it had come out as a beautiful phrase.

Emma once again delivered his speech in Wagi to all the participants, raising her hands in the air in accordance with the best dramatic act practices, to emphasize the significance of the moment.

Ben walked up to a young man who was sitting next to the elders, and wanted to ask him to move to the side, but the poor guy suddenly recoiled in horror, fell from the log, and quickly crawled on all fours to the end of the row.

"Take your place, Amal," Ben said, and thought that it was time to finish this farce.

Amal sat down on the log next to his father and triumphantly looked at the warriors gathered around the fire. He was completely rehabilitated before his tribe-mates, and his reputation was restored.

Ben handed Amal Senior his *dongan*.

"I think it's your turn to have this holiday dinner."

The crowd roared briskly, hoping that the official part of the celebration was over, but they rejoiced too soon. Amal Junior got up again. He was overwhelmed with emotions and once again loved the whole world, especially the 'saved' boy. He took Ben's hand and began his part of the ceremonial speech. It turned out that he was a rather sentimental man, despite his formidable appearance.

"Ben, I am so glad that I helped you. If you ever need my help, remember: you have a brother in me." With these words, he did something that made Ben shudder inwardly. He took out the wonderful canine from his nose and handed it to him.

Emma, whose great acting talent had been aroused, immediately stood beside Amal and reproduced his gesture, simulating the removal of the canine, and held her hands to Ben. She even imitated his booming bass with her thin voice. Everyone roared in surprise. Nobody expected such a generous gift from Amal.

"Take it, Ben, this is your trophy now."

Ben was not a squeamish person, but he looked with horror at the valuable gift and hesitated to take it in his hand. It seemed that Amal had worn it for a long time, and this gorgeous canine was covered with the brownish-green dried-up crust of boar fat that was stuck on it after years of wearing, as well as dirt and something else that Ben was afraid to even think about.

"Take it, Ben," Emma whispered, seeing his hesitation. "He will be offended if you don't accept it."

But Ben was still hesitating, and the delay was getting disrespectful. Amal held the eerie fang in his palms standing in front of him, slightly bent, trying to be on the same level as Ben, or in respect for him. Suddenly, Ben remembered that this morning, during the escape, he had taken a piece of cloth, which Amal had used as a gag last night. Now he found a use for it. Gently, with just two fingers, trying not to get his hands dirty, Ben gently grabbed this precious gift by the edges, carefully wrapped it in cloth, and put it in his pocket.

I will throw it away later, he decided. *I am not going to bring it to the ship; Mother would go into shock if she saw this up close. She is probably getting her antibacterial wipes ready now.*

"It was very respectful," Emma whispered slyly in his ear. "Amal was pleased with the reverence you showed as you wrapped his gift."

Of course this little devil understood everything correctly. One couldn't hide anything from her. But Ben ignored her sarcastic tone and responded with the acceptance speech.

"Thank you, Amal. I am much honored to receive such a precious gift from a brave and courageous warrior like yourself."

"Brother!" Amal exclaimed through Emma's mouth, and tears of emotion glistened in his eyes. The next moment he embraced Ben, painfully pressing on the bandage-covered wound on the shoulder.

The crowd fell silent under the gravity of the moment. Ben was wheezing in Amal's iron grip and choking from the smell of his sweaty body. He wanted to shout to ask him through Emma to let go or at least to weaken the embrace, but he could not say a word. His voice was muffled by Amal's chest. However, Emma probably wouldn't hear it anyway. After she had finished translating, she stood hugging herself by the shoulders, simulating Amal.

But he soon opened his arms and stood looking at his new brother with affection.

Just wait, Amal, I'll pay you back, Ben thought, rubbing the aching wound.

When Ben was a child, he loved the Band-Aids for children with the motley pictures on them. He stuck the strips on his arms and legs without any necessity, just to look at the colorful images. Since then Ben had grown, but Margaret probably had not noticed it and continued to buy those same packages meant for children.

It was one of these boxes that Ben had shoved in his pocket before he got out on the street. Ben pulled out one strip, removed the protective paper, and quickly stuck it on Amal's arm above his sinister-looking *sagyu* with canines. Teddy bears, dolls, and horses sparkled on the glossy surface of the patch, reflecting the glare of the fire. These funny, colorful pictures looked comical on Amal's strong, muscular arm, especially in combination with the necklace. But Amal did not think so. He gently touched the patch with astonishment, and his mouth stretched into a smile.

"Brother," Ben said, and showed him his shoulder with the similar-colored sticker.

"*Digam-Apa*[30]!" Amal repeated loudly, pointing at his sticker. "*Digam-Apa!*" he repeated again and again, just in case someone in the crowd could not hear and see a sign of his brotherhood with Ben.

Emma did not translate anymore. She stared in fascination at Amal's arm. She pulled Ben's sleeve and asked quietly, "Do you still have another sticker like that? I want one too."

Ben smiled and slipped the whole box into her hands.

"Just don't show it to Amal," he whispered in her ear. "Let him think that he is the only one who has this sticker."

Emma gratefully took the precious gift, and it immediately disappeared into the layers of her clothes.

Amal Senior shook his head again and told Rupert, "Not only would he have been a good warrior, but also a wise leader. If Ben led the tribe with my son, I could finally retire."

He sighed and got up. It was time to close the formal part of the celebration. He said something in Wagi, but Emma had disappeared and did not translate. Apparently, she had grown bored with this melodrama and went back to her place. However, everything was clear even without her services. The official part was over and the actual festival had begun.

Yaga, who was sitting silently until now, presented Margaret with a decent chunk of pork. Besides Emma, she was the only woman honored with a festive meal equal with men. Apparently, the elders decided that they had already broken so many rules and traditions, that another violation would not matter.

Ben looked at his mother, expecting that she would refuse to eat in such unsanitary conditions, but to his surprise, she gratefully accepted the food and boldly plunged her teeth into the meat, forgetting even to wipe her hands with antibacterial wipes. All the other men also gathered around the fire spit as soon as Rupert and both elders first cut themselves a slice of pork thigh. Hungry warriors forgot all about the spirits and sacrifices. The pig, although large, was not big enough for so many starving men to share it with celestial residents.

The essence of the actual holiday Ben didn't understand; however, he didn't even try to. He was sitting on a log next to Emma, forcing himself to stay awake. They were so tired that they couldn't even eat much. One slice of meat that they shared was enough for both to satisfy their hunger.

Ben was watching dancing warriors, shaking their *hagda* under the loud *okam*[31] drumbeat, accompanied by the *ai-cabral*[32]. It was not entirely clear why they called this a dance, as it looked more like a pantomime, although a certain rhythm was noticed in the movements of the dancers.

The first performance was a pantomime-dance imitating hunting, apparently successful (after all it was a hunting holiday), and comprised the capturing of an imaginary wild boar and the alleged killing of it. The dance was short: the pretense animal was caught, slaughtered, and cut in pieces within a few minutes. After that there was a longer, more complex multi-leveled dance that simulated a fight on a battlefield.

The dance was performed by the warriors of both tribes with the intimidation of imaginary enemies, attack, advance, and retreat in turns by each group of dancers—in general, with some imagination, it could have been recognized as military actions. The men lined up by the fire in two rows, facing each other.

At first, one rank of soldiers advanced upon the other, shouting loudly and shaking their *hagda*. Then the opposite group advanced, forcing their opponents to retreat. They conducted an imaginary attack on the imaginary enemy, and some men fell quite artfully from the imitation strike of their opponent's *ure*[33]. Wounded warriors were

400

picked up by their associates and carried away from the battlefield, or rather, from the "dancefloor." It was a whole histrionics in several acts under the dreary *mun*[34] of spectators, mostly women, singing along between the scenes.

At first, Ben tried to follow the dance, but soon his eyelids were involuntarily closing with sleep. He looked at Emma, but she had long been asleep, sitting with her head down. Ben touched her hand, and she immediately jumped up, ready to run again. He gestured for her to follow him. They barely had any strength left; crawling on all fours a dozen yards away from the fire and collapsed in the tall, fragrant grass. While falling asleep, Ben suddenly thought that there could be snakes around there, but he firmly believed in the magical power of a small wooden idol he had bought on the quay for just two dollars that protected him from all adversity.

For them, this infinitely long and difficult day full of surprises, both pleasant and terrifying, had ended. They slept soundly and didn't wake up from the drumming clatter or monotonous voices of women singing along with the dancing warriors, or even from the loud roar of two helicopters of the Royal Air Force of Australia, hovering above the clearing.

Speaking of helicopters: the ship captain had kept his word and called a search and rescue team. They arrived, albeit after some delay. The commander of the rescue party landed near the blazing fire and had a long, heated conversation with Rupert for the false call. But in the end, the crew took off their headsets, unbuttoned their flight uniforms, and joined the celebration and the holiday dinner. In their years of serving in the military, it was perhaps the easiest and the most pleasant rescue operation they'd ever had.

But Ben and Emma did not know any of this and continued to sleep soundly. They did not even wake up when Amal Junior carried them to the house. He stumbled upon the sleeping kids when he took a break from the dance to pee and almost stepped on them. Amal personally brought them to the house and put them in bed, covering and tucking in their blankets. He was about to leave when, suddenly, something caught his attention.

He came back in the room and sat down beside the sleeping Emma. On her arm, just above the elbow, she had the exact same strip of plaster as he had, a sign of his brotherhood with Ben. Emma, of course, could not resist, and had put on a beautiful sticker despite Ben's warning.

A new thought came to Amal's mind.

If Ben is now my brother, and Emma is his dubbed sister, then is she my sister too?

Amal looked at the sleeping Emma. He'd never had siblings before.

Well, with Ben it is more or less clear, Amal continued his thinking. *He's the guy; it would certainly be great if he stayed here with us. I would have taught him everything I know, so we could go hunt together. But what am I supposed to do with Emma?* Life truly makes unpredictable zigzags and twists sometimes. *Not only can I not marry her, but as an older brother, I will have to keep an eye on her, protect her, and choose the right husband for her.* His head spun from the sudden responsibilities, making him dizzy. *But on the other hand, I can get a bride price for her marriage. At least there is something positive in this situation. As for a new wife, I will steal one from another tribe, not a big deal,* he concluded his thoughts.

Igissy walked into the room, surprised by his long absence, and was dazed by what she saw. The formidable Amal was sitting on the bed tenderly looking at the sleeping girl, holding her hand, which looked like a fragile twig in his huge hands.

"Amal, are you okay?"

"S-h-h, keep it quiet; don't wake up my little sister," Amal said in a loud whisper, which exceeded the noise level of the quiet voice of Igissy.

"What sister?" Igissy was amazed even more.

"I'm talking about Emma. She is my sister!" Amal replied with pride, and his face broke into a smile.

"Wait, Amal, are you sure you didn't overdo the dance out there, around the fire?"

But Amal did not listen to her, as he suddenly had a new idea.

"So, you are Emma's grandma, right?"

"Yeah, so what?"

"Emma is my sister now, so you will be my grandmother too."

"Wait, Amal, I'm confused. Let's start from the beginning."

"How can you not understand?" Amal whispered excitedly. "It's simple. Look at this." He pointed at Emma's bandage.

Then he dragged the surprised woman into the other room where Ben slept. Carefully, trying not to wake up his little brother, Amal took his hand and pointed also to the strip on his arm.

"Do you see that? I have the same one too." He put his strong arm closer to her eyes—voila! "Ben and I are brothers, and Emma is our sister. And now you're our grandmother. Do you get it?"

"Yes, I understand now, Grandson." Igissy grinned.

Everything was clear, it was just their children's games! Amal, in essence, was a big child, despite his frightening appearance.

But Amal continued to develop this idea. He took this new responsibility as the older brother and grandson that had unexpectedly fallen on him quite seriously.

"I will look after her." Amal smiled happily. "And for you, I'll bring the live adult boar. The hunting season begins soon, and the first animal that I catch will be yours."

Suddenly he stopped, hesitated a bit, and asked plaintively, "Listen, do you have anything to eat?"

"Eat? Didn't you just have a festive dinner out there in the glade?" Igissy was surprised.

"There were so many people and not enough food—well, I'm still hungry."

Igissy nodded and went to warm up the remains of the supper she had cooked for her guests. It was not going to be easy to feed her newly acquired grandson. According to his size, he could probably eat half a boar for dinner. But, on the other hand, if someone like Amal could protect Emma in the woods, and she could call him for help if she needed it, it was worth more than a bowl or two of pea soup.

But Ben and Emma continued to sleep soundly and had no idea about their newfound ties of kinship. For them, this day had long been over. But it wasn't over yet for the other participants of this story. It was time for Rupert to pay the promised reward. As always in this life, parents pay for the mistakes of their children, and if they are lucky, the payment can be only made with money alone.

Rupert remembered his promise of remuneration, and now waited for Amal to start this conversation, not doubting for a second that they knew about the promised reward. And such a dialog did take place. It was started by Amal, as Yaga didn't speak English at all and he just sat quietly on the other side of Rupert.

Earlier, on the way to the port, the elders had an unpleasant chat. They walked dejectedly, behind the whole group, and both were sullen and angry at each other.

"Why did you do that, Amal?" Yaga broke the silence to say. "Good neighbors don't do that to each other."

"I thought it would be the best for the boy if I sent him back to the port by bus, because of his leg injury."

"Yeah, right, the best for the boy," Yaga mocked him grumpily. "Just say you wanted to make some money. You should have come to me instead of kidnapping the children. Together, we could have done that nice and easy. But you spoiled everything."

"Well, yes, and for the money too." Amal did not deny. "You too did not offer to share the reward with your neighbor. There is a lot of money, and it could have been enough for both of us. You know we desperately needed it."

"We are not in any better conditions. But anyway, it doesn't matter now. We both have made mistakes, as this reward stirred up our minds. But the boy is great. The way he defeated your son, I didn't expect that from him."

Taunts from Yaga were unpleasant, but there was nothing to reply to that. Indeed, the defeat of his son was the event of the day, and everybody was talking about it, so Amal swallowed the hurtful words. The rest of the way both elders walked in complete silence. Only just before they entered the village, Amal said, "Don't worry, Yaga, we still have a chance."

Yaga only nodded in response.

And now, as the official part of the celebration was over, it was time to talk about the promised reward. Amal began the conversation properly, like people discuss important business everywhere in the world: he pulled out a pitcher with a home-brewed wine, and a few aluminum mugs. As mentioned before, people are the same at all latitudes.

Amal poured the chilled wine in the cups and handed the first one to Margaret.

But she looked with horror at the outstretched mug and politely but firmly lied. "Thank you, but I do not drink."

She never refused a glass (clean one, of course) of good wine at dinner, but now, this was too much. She had already forced herself to sacrifice her principles in matters of sanitation, but everything has its limit. Amal did not insist, and handed the cups to Yaga and Rupert, then raised a toast.

"Well, let's drink to the happy ending of this little adventure."

Amal had also translated his words to Yaga, and he shook his head agreeably, and both elders drank the wine. Rupert, like a good wine taster, swirled the alcohol in the mug, sniffed the contents, and took a small sip. Young wine, a little sweet, obviously made from fermented fruits, tasted normal, nothing unusual, and Rupert bravely drank the whole cup to the dregs. Amal immediately filled his mug again.

"And now let's drink to the friendship between our nations," he said solemnly.

"Friendship," repeated Yaga, after hearing the translation. "You, I—friendship."

They drank for acquaintance, then for the friendship between the tribes with all nations, and the strong bond with the foreign guests with each tribe separately.

The pitcher was quickly emptied, and Amal regretfully put it aside. Next, from the depths of his clothes, he pulled out a few cigarettes hand-rolled from a scrap of newspaper. Rupert wanted to bring out some of his fine Dominican cigars, a box of which he'd brought with him on vacation, but changed his mind and took Amal's cigarette.

If I have decided to blend with the local people, then I should go to the very end, he thought and lit the cigarette from the hot coal.

"The youngsters are enjoying the festival," Amal started the dialogue from afar, "dancing and singing. That's good, let them have fun and eat normally while they can. They probably have forgotten the last time they ate meat."

"How come?" Rupert feigned surprise, understanding where the cunning Amal was taking the conversation.

"These are difficult times for them right now, and for all of us. The rainy season just ended recently, but all the game is still in hiding. All we have for dinner now are some vegetables, the roots of trees, and on some occasions, rats. We even slaughtered our breeder boar and sow out of desperation. We had been hoping for offspring for the next season but the barn is completely empty now."

Yaga also sadly shook his head. He intuitively understood what Amal was complaining about. Rupert kept silent, enthusiastically puffing his cigarette while waiting for the rest of his speech. It was like a children's game of "I know that you know that I know. . .", but both sides abided by the rules of the game, playing their roles. Rupert could have just given them the promised reward, as he planned on all along, but he wanted to retaliate for their actions. Besides, there was plenty of time to bring the game to its logical end.

"Even our vegetables are already on the wane," Amal continued sadly. "We have long been eating boiled tree roots. But men need meat, they cannot be grass-fed all the time."

"So why don't you, dear Amal, buy some more pigs to breed?" Rupert asked.

"We don't have any money." Amal sighed. "There is no way to make cash in the woods. A few guys work part-time at the mission, helping them to clean up, while others sell souvenirs at the port. We, of course, have a little savings, but it is not enough."

"You know, I just came up with a great idea." Rupert sustained a long pause, puffing the disintegrating cigarette. "I am not sure if you are aware, but my wife and I had promised a reward of ten thousand dollars to anyone who would help us to find our son. I believe it is about twenty-five thousand local kinas, I am not sure of exact conversion rate. I think that you, dear Amal, along with Yaga, should split this reward."

"Are you serious, Mr. Rupert?" Amal threw his hands up. "We could not have dreamed of that much. I do not know if I dare to accept it, because rescuing the child is the sacred duty of every person. I'm a father myself and understand—"

"Dear Amal, I downright insist that you take the money for your effort and trouble, and share it with Yaga. I am sure it will be useful to both of you."

"Of course, it would be of tremendous help to us!" exclaimed Amal, and translated Rupert's offer to the neighbor.

Yaga smiled hearing the good news. Actually, he did not doubt the diplomatic skills of Amal. He could have conducted the conversation as diplomatically, but unfortunately, because of the language barrier, he was forced to settle for a silent role. But it did not matter now: the goal had been achieved.

"However, I have one small problem," Rupert continued. "I have run out of cash, and I don't know where to get money here. But if you accept checks, I will immediately write you the full amount."

Amal did not expect that. He thought that Rupert would open his plump wallet and pull out a thick wad of bills, counting out a hundred brand-new banknotes and hand them to him, saying, "Take the money, Amal, you deserve it." But a check . . . The bank would never cash it out without identification documents.

"The bank!" He had suddenly come up with a bright idea. "Of course! We need a bank."

"Mr. Rupert, would you be able to get money in the bank, let's say, in Madang?" Amal asked after a brief hesitation.

"Well, I probably could. But it is unlikely that you have a branch of my bank here. Perhaps I could call my bank and ask them to transfer funds to your local branch. I think they should be able to do it."

"Great!" Amal exclaimed happily. "If I am not mistaken, today is a workday at your home, and you can call them right now."

Rupert looked at his watch and thought with relief he would not have to calculate the time again, as it was still showing the home time. Yaga turned his head from Amal to Rupert, not knowing what was going on, but with his gut, he felt the next complexity of life. But Amal didn't want to translate the essence of the conversation to the neighbor, now was not the time for it, as he had to act quickly.

He immediately spotted the postwoman Beida among the crowd, and half an hour later, Rupert was already talking with a representative of the bank in New York. Hearing Rupert's request for a large amount of cash transfer to one of the branches in Papua New Guinea, the clerk paused for a second.

"Excuse me, sir, perhaps this is none of my business and my fears are groundless, but is everything all right? We must protect the interests of our customers, and if you're being robbed or blackmailed, just give me a hint. I will immediately contact the local authorities and the police. Our bank—"

"Thank you for your concern, but there is no need for that," Rupert replied hastily. He smiled, remembering their search for a policeman in this remote village the previous day. "I just need some cash."

Half an hour later the financial situation was resolved. The clerk promised to transfer the required amount to the ANZ Bank— Australia and New Zealand Banking in the Goroka town, through the Australian branch of the Bank of America.

Another fifteen minutes was spent trying to persuade Hubert, who was also present here, to take them to Goroka the next day, for an additional fee, of course.

"Well, everything is done," Amal said with a sigh of relief. "Now we can enjoy our celebration. To do that, I propose to re-fill our pitcher with some more wine."

The word "wine" is conformable in almost any language in the world, and Yaga, hearing a familiar word, nodded happily.

"Agreed," Rupert replied. "Let's get three sheets to the wind[35]. But this time, I'm going to treat you with tobacco. I have a small reserve of good cigars with me."

The glorious warriors of both tribes continued their ritual dances and worship of the spirits in the light of the dying fire, while singing monotonous *munes* that were dreary, like their lives. Let's hope that the spirits would be pleased with the celebration, despite the lack of tributes, and help them in their difficult lives.

Chapter 7. To Everyone According To His Deeds

The hull of the cruise ship approached slowly but steadily. The fragile tender delivering tourists to the ship was rocking mercilessly on the waves, spraying passengers with seawater, which actually felt quite pleasant. The temperature of the air, which didn't cool down much during the night, was quickly rising again, getting way above the average temperatures of the Tropic of Capricorn. It was already possible to discern the vacationers crowding at the lowered ramp. They were excited about the velvety sand on the beaches, interesting excursions, gorgeous rainforest scenery, and rare animals. Not so long ago, Ben had stood at the same open gangway observing the mysterious shores of Terra Incognita.

"A hot shower and a good shampoo," Margaret said, looking longingly at the ship that they were reaching unbearably slowly.

"A bar and a few shots of good Scotch," Rupert quipped, mocking and imitating her tone. He was his usual jovial self and, as always, concealed his true feelings with a joke. However, right now, he wasn't joking entirely.

Ben said nothing. He looked back at the receding shore and the figure of Emma, standing on the dock. Treacherous tears were streaming down his cheeks for the umpteenth time in the last three days.

The farewell was short. The owner of the boat was looking at them impatiently, gesturing at his watch. He got paid by the number of trips to the boat and didn't want to waste time, and consequently, money, on all these sentiments. Ben's parents were already sitting in the boat, but Ben was standing silently on the dock with Emma. She also kept her silence, avoiding eye contact with him. Everything that had to be said had already been said. They had exchanged addresses, and there was nothing left to say. Suddenly, she hugged him with her strong hands, and he, in confusion, gently stroked her head and her hair that flowed down her shoulders, without the usual fancy-colored bird feathers. It was as if he was parting from his younger sister.

"I'll write you letters," she said, pulling away from him. "You can be sure, I will write."

Ben had spent the previous day with Emma, at the deserted beach near the pier. The ship was due to arrive the next day, and they had plenty of time to rest. That was so welcome after all the unpleasant events they had been through. His parents had gone to town to get money from the bank, and Ben and Emma swam all day long. They also took time for sunbathing and eating fruits and sandwiches Igissy made for them. One has to go through all the circles of hell before reaching heaven, evidently.

They lay on the water, rocking on the small ripples, letting the hot sun shine on their faces. There was nothing to talk about. They didn't want to recollect the previous day's events, and even less they wanted to discuss Ben's departure and the approaching moment of farewell. They had a worry-free day of enjoyment at their disposal, and there was no need to overshadow it with thoughts of the upcoming, inevitable parting. That will be tomorrow, but for now . . .

Ben heard a loud splash nearby. Emma had gotten bored floating, and she dove deeper. He did not worry for her, as he knew that nothing could happen to her in the water. She couldn't drown even if she wanted to. She swam so well that even a fish could learn from her. But soon, he started to worry, as it was time for her to surface. And she did emerge, after a while, snorting and spitting salt water, holding an outlandish seashell in her hand.

"This is a souvenir for you." She was breathing steadily, as if she had been floating and rocking on the waves all this time.

The decent-sized shell was pretty, with its surface covered in nacre. Ben had to return to the shore because it was uncomfortable to swim with it in his hands. On the beach, he grabbed his backpack and dumped out the contents. Unfortunately, there was nothing worthy enough for a gift, just some dribs and drabs needed in every travel and his fully discharged iPhone, which his parents had picked up by the cliff where all his troubles began. Why would she need an iPhone? It was a useless thing for her, especially since his remarkable headphones remained hanging on a fork of the tree that saved his life. Maybe someone, in a hundred years, would find them and wonder what they were and how they ended up there, so high above the ground.

He found a baseball cap in his bag, with the embroidered emblem for the Yankees—the only thing suitable for a gift—and put it on Emma, with the visor facing backwards. He also found the second apple that Margaret had given him before the tour. The animal, whose name he still didn't know, had eaten one, and the second was still in his backpack.

"Here, eat this." Ben handed it to Emma.

"What's that?" she asked, looking at the alien fruit.

"Try it, you'll like it."

She took a small bite at first, but a few seconds later there was nothing left of the apple.

"That was delicious," she said, wiping her lips. "I've never eaten anything like that before. Listen, I wanted to ask you . . . Do you remember yesterday, when we ran away from . . . them. You had covered my back so they couldn't hit me with the arrows?"

He stood there and did not know what to say. He had no idea why he had done that. Maybe because she reminded him of Liah. They were even almost the same age.

"I was afraid that if they killed you, I wouldn't be able to find my way to the port."

But Emma did not accept his joking tone.

"If they had killed you then you wouldn't need to go back anymore. You just wanted to protect me," she said with confidence. "I know it because I thought of doing the same thing myself, but you beat me to it, and we didn't have time to argue."

"I'm glad we didn't have time," he replied. "But you know what? I think that you and I, together, we make a pretty darn great team."

At the same time as the children were having this conversation, Rupert and Margaret were dozing on the bus, heading to the bank in Goroka. The trip was going to be long, over a hundred miles each way, yet they expected to return to port before dark, and once again plunge into the warm waters.

The old bus with sagging suspension springs was shaking and swinging mercilessly on the bumpy road, but that did not prevent anybody on the bus from sleeping. The previous day had been hard for everyone, and a night without sleep didn't make it any easier.

The celebrations lasted all night long, and only in the morning did the tired villagers go home. Behind them, when the day was barely dawning, the men of both tribes went to their settlements, like sorcerers fleeing Sabbath before the sunrise.

When the first rays of the sun lit up the glade, there was almost nobody left. Only the two elders continued to sit near the dying fire, lamenting to Rupert about their adversities, emptying the next jug of wine. Margaret thought about going to sleep, but her bed was occupied, and she didn't want to wake up either of the children. So, she went back to the clearing and sat around the fire until sunrise.

In the morning, Rupert filled up the tank with water and everybody took a cold shower, freshened up, and had breakfast. This time it wasn't easy for Igissy to feed that many guests. Besides her tenants and Emma with Ben, Amal, his son, and Yaga, accompanied by his trusted fellow tribesman, also joined in. Hubert, who spent the night at one of the villager's, came a little later and sat down at the table. Igissy looked at the new guest and put down another bowl with a sigh.

After the breakfast, they all went to the bank. Hubert said that it would be better if they all went together, given the large amount of cash they would have to handle. Criminal situations in Goroka, unfortunately, left a lot to be desired. After the short discussion, it was decided that Amal Junior would accompany the trip as well. Of course, his father alone could cope with any villains that came by, if such a necessity arose, but the presence of his son was supposed to purge evil thoughts from the minds of criminals. Yaga also brought his fellow tribesman along, fearing a ruse from his crafty neighbor.

But their fears were unfounded. Everything went smoothly, without incident, except for the excessive suspicion of the clerk at the bank. He looked incredulously at the strange group of people that walked in, and then suspiciously flipped through Rupert's passport, comparing his photo with the original. Then his manager once again read the entire document to the last page, having carefully studied even the visa stamps and the dates of entry from different countries. But Rupert didn't mind; he understood their suspicion, as they had to give them a substantial amount of money. But soon all the formalities were settled, and Rupert received a thick wad of cash in local currency. His bank did everything correctly and on time, and the funds had reached the branch right before their arrival.

Payoff for the reward was uneventful; Rupert casually handed the promised amount to each elder. The tension in the air immediately disappeared, and Yaga, along with Amal, sighed with relief. Until the last moment, they did not believe that this story would end well; the amount of money was unimaginably significant for them. But everything worked out just fine, and the joyful company went back to the bus.

Now it was Hubert's turn to receive his promised reward.

"Hubert, my wife and I are grateful for all your help. I don't even know what we would have done without you, and we appreciate your participation and cooperation."

With these words, Rupert took off his golden Rolex and handed it to Hubert. He looked at the beautiful gift.

"What am I supposed to do with it? We don't have a need for watches here."

"This is an expensive watch. You can always sell it to any jewelry store."

"Yes, it looks exclusive. It is probably worth a few hundred bucks, right?"

Rupert chuckled.

"If you decide to sell it one day and the jeweler offers you less than five thousand dollars for it, then go to another store."

"Wow! Five thousand! I think we don't have a jewelry store around here that would pay that much money for it. Besides, watches are not a commonly tradable commodity here, especially such expensive ones, and the store wouldn't be able to sell it to anyone. Instead, they might probably call the police and accuse me of stealing it from tourists."

He had a good point, and Rupert took the gift back and once again opened his wallet.

"I kind of foresaw that you would refuse it, and just in case, withdrew some cash. But there is much less than you would get for this watch." With these words, he handed him a stack of bills.

"Thank you, Mr. Rupert. This is enough for me. It is safer this way." Hubert smiled, reaching out for his reward.

But Rupert quickly pulled his hand back.

"Actually, Hubert, sorry. I changed my mind. I will not give you the money until you answer my question: How the hell did you notify all neighboring tribes about our problem, in such a short time? This puzzle bothers me so much that I will not rest until I get a clear explanation from you. The jungle is not accessible by the bus, and you couldn't have walked to each settlement. Of course, I've heard about the drums that some African tribes use to transmit messages to their neighbors for many miles. But I don't think you've used this method. Especially since, as I understand, you went to the city at an early age, and it is unlikely that you know how to use such an exotic method of communication. Please explain how you did it."

"You're right, I do not know how to use those drums." Hubert laughed. "Besides, we don't use such methods anyway. It's actually simple, and you would have figured it out yourself if you weren't worrying about your son. You see, we have several missions scattered throughout the jungles: Catholic, Christian, Franciscan, and many others. The only way for the tribe to communicate with the outside world and with each other is through radio. And, as you know, I have a radio on the bus for communication with my dispatcher. I got in touch with the missions on their frequency, and they spread this information further. However, I do not know how exactly they did it. Most likely they sent messengers; they do have such couriers."

"I should have guessed it myself," Rupert muttered, handing the money to Hubert.

"You know, Hubert, what I would like so much?" Margaret said. "Tomorrow our ship comes to the port, and you're probably taking the tourists to the excursions."

"Yes, you're right, madam. I have three tours scheduled: two in the jungle and one in the afternoon to the waterfalls."

"I would love to go with you on that same trip into the jungle again. It was so enthralling, and you were telling us so many fascinating things."

"So, what's the problem? Of course, come with me tomorrow for free. I usually have extra seats in every tour."

"I would really-really love to go, but I will not. I just cannot. I don't have the guts to go there again," Margaret finished her thought. "But, please, be careful, and do not leave someone else behind in the woods."

"I will not. Believe me, madam, that trip was a good lesson for me as well." With these words, Hubert closed the door of the bus and started the engine. Payments for all accounts had been made, and it was time to return to port. That was the end of the story.

Well, actually, the story didn't quite end like that. When Hubert was about to go back, Rupert suddenly said, "Hubert, wait another minute; I will be back quickly." And he jumped from the bus.

He walked into a small, nondescript store, which he had noticed on the way to the bank.

On the shelves, there were bottles of all kinds of liquor in various shapes and sizes. Rupert quickly scanned through them, grimaced in disgruntlement, and picked a flat bottle, with more or less acceptable content and shape that comfortably fit his back pocket. He gave the clerk at the counter a few bills, and without further delay, unscrewed the cap and took a decent swig. It helped. Alcohol, even though cheap (but for the price of an expensive aged cognac), did the job. The block of ice that had been stuck in his chest, not allowing him to breathe freely, now had finally melted. Warmth spread throughout his body, relieving the tensions and stress of the past days. This ice had been stuck in him from the moment Rupert looked down into the abyss, where his son had most likely fallen. He was saying something exaggeratedly cheerful, comforting his wife and was even laughing, but the image of his son sprawled at the bottom of the abyss was constantly in front of his eyes. He was well aware of the possible consequences of the fall. Even the news that his son might have survived, and then meeting him safe and sound had not melted the block of ice in his soul.

The clerk at the counter wanted to tell him that drinking alcohol was forbidden in the store, but he looked at the strange visitor and decided to let it go. Who knows what his life's complexities were. He looked like a decent man, obviously not local, probably a tourist and definitely not poor, according to his liquor preference.

Rupert stood still for a moment, letting the alcohol pass through his body, and then shoved the bottle in his pocket and went back to the bus. Margaret, smelling the alcohol on his breath, looked at him suspiciously, but said nothing. Rupert leaned back in his seat, stretching his long legs into the aisle, and closed his eyes. Life goes on.

In the morning everybody got up early, before dawn, but the ship had already entered the harbor, formalizing necessary custom documents for debarkation of the passengers. Soon the tourists would go ashore, and Margaret wanted to get on board with the first tender. She impatiently paced the small room and hurried Rupert and Ben, who were packing their bags in an unendurably slow manner. Igissy got up even earlier and cooked breakfast for all of them. However, nobody wanted to eat. In less than an hour, they would be able to eat in a clean restaurant on the ship with a variety of delicious foods, desserts, and drinks. They ate a few spoonsful without much of an appetite, just for decency's sake, to not upset the hostess, but they drank her wonderful tea with pleasure.

After breakfast, Ben pulled Rupert aside and asked, "Dad, do you have any more money?"

"Yes, I still have some."

Rupert pulled out his wallet and began to count the remaining banknotes. But Ben did not let him. He took the entire amount of cash and went over to Igissy.

"If possible, I'd like to buy some of your souvenirs you sell in the port."

"Of course. There are plenty of crafts, just pick some that you like. You don't need to pay me." Igissy pulled a big bag from under the bed.

"I like them all and will take everything, if you don't mind. I hope there is enough money." Ben handed her all the cash.

"Everything? Why do you need so many?"

"Because I love it." Ben smiled.

"Sure, you can take everything, if you like. Emma will make some more. But this is a lot more money than it is worth."

"That is less than you need to send Emma to school," Ben replied, not listening to any other objections from Igissy, and packed the souvenirs into his backpack.

However, he couldn't fit much of what was in the bag, and the remaining souvenirs he put back under the bed. Rupert was watching him from a distance, and wanted to tell him that he had already generously rewarded the hostess for her hospitality, and that every night in her simple home had cost him the price of the presidential suite in a decent hotel in New York. But he didn't say anything, not wanting to kill a good initiative of his son, and only muttered grumpily, "I hope you realize that I will deduct this money from your allowance."

The skipper of the tender impatiently fingered the mooring lines, glancing pointedly at Ben and Emma saying goodbye on the pier, and then over at the ship in the harbor. But he did not dare to express his grievances aloud. If it was anyone else, he would have left them to wait for the next boat. But this was Ben, a local celebrity whom everyone in the village was talking about. But he really was running out of time. The parents had taken their seats in the boat quite some time ago, waiting only for the boy.

"Stay, Ben, a little longer." Emma looked pleadingly into his eyes. "Stay! I have so much to show you yet. We could swim in the lake every day, or go hunting in the woods. Our hunters would teach you to shoot arrows, throw a spear, and set snares for birds. If you want to, we could go catch crocodiles. I know where to find them. And I will cook meals for you. You will not have to eat rats. I'll get you real meat, don't you doubt that. Or we could live here with my grandmother and go to the beach every day."

Oddly, over the last few days he had been on the verge of despair many times, ready to burst into tears from his own helplessness, but he never thought that parting with Emma would be, perhaps, the most difficult episode in this adventure. He felt that if she said one more word, then he would not abstain from her persuasions, and would drop everything—civilization, good food, a soft bed, his school, and even their project—and would grab Emma's hand and run into the woods with her. Just one more word . . .

But Emma suddenly stopped persuading, having not gotten a word from him in return.

"But would you at least write me a letter?" she asked with hope in her eyes.

"Of course I will." Ben pulled out a notebook with a pen and quickly wrote down his information. He was in a rush to write everything he wanted, afraid to miss anything important. He wrote his address, phone number, and e-mail, along with his login for Facebook, Skype, and Twitter. He even gave her a link to the web page, where he intended to list all his awards earned in the Game. Ben scribbled down an entire page and tore it from the notebook.

"Here is all my information," he said and handed her the notes. "You write me as well, and stay in touch."

"What is this?" she asked, looking at the bunch of unknown words and symbols.

He explained to her how to get on Facebook and Skype, but then stopped in mid-sentence, realizing the absurdity of his explanations.

"It's better if I write you a letter," Emma muttered.

"Of course, a letter. Here is my e-mail address, you see, over here!" he exclaimed, pointing at the line on the page.

"No, you do not understand. I'll write you a letter, a real one, in an envelope with a stamp."

He looked at her uncomprehendingly, and a second later laughed happily. She suddenly clutched him tightly with her strong hands. And he stood in confusion and stroked her head.

"I'll write you a letter," Emma repeated, pulling away from him. "You can be sure, I will write."

The lump stuck in his throat made it impossible for him to squeeze out a sound. He nodded and jumped on the boat, without saying a single word.

The boats moored near the lowered gangway of the ship, and the crowd of tourists, festooned with cameras, backpacks, and beach towels, hastened in not letting them get off the tender. Nobody expected anyone to be going back to the ship so early in the morning, when everybody else was rushing to the shore. They could barely squeeze through the flow of tourists to the ramp, dragging their suitcases along. A few more seconds, and the on-board scanner would register the new passengers, and they would be back in civilization, enjoying all the amenities that it offers. His parents had already passed through the security checkpoint, and Ben turned around for the last time and looked at the shore.

"Goodbye, Emma," he whispered. "I don't think we will ever meet again. Although, who knows? After all, life is so unpredictable . . ."

Epilogue

They were once again comfortably sitting in the ship's restaurant at the same table with the white, starched tablecloth by the window, watching a beautiful sunset while eating their dinner. The large blood-red ball of the setting sun threw crimson rays through the windows, and that, reflecting from the glass goblets on the table, created a riot of ruby glares, painting the water in the glasses a deep, rich scarlet.

A fresh breeze blew in through the open window and brought with it the smell of the sea. It was like they never happened, these four days filled with adventures in such an amount that it would have been enough for anyone's lifetime. Rupert was sipping his favorite Scotch. Margaret was studying a dessert menu, and from time to time slicing off small pieces from her rare steak dripping with meat juice. Ben, as usual, had withdrawn himself from everything, putting on his headphones. It was not his wonderful Beats, those were irretrievably lost in the jungle, but another set he had bought at the ship's souvenir shop for a few bucks. He quietly ate his shrimp salad looking out the window, admiring the beautiful scenery. Madang and the small village at the port, which had suddenly diversified his leisure vacation, were left far behind. Even though there were a few stops ahead, they were not planning to get off the ship, as they had visited all of them before. They all wanted only one thing: to get quickly to the city of Cairns, the final destination of the cruise, and fly back home.

Dinner was carried out in complete silence, as there was nothing else to say. From the moment they were aboard the ship and had completed all the formalities, there had been plenty of opportunities to discuss everything. Ben received a well-deserved portion of blames, reproaches, and moralizing from his parents, agreed with all of them, and promised to think about his behavior and be more careful and cautious next time. Then he put on his earphones, and leaned back on the sun lounger by the pool, sipping cool drinks. Now they were eating dinner quietly, each absorbed in their own thoughts, not wanting to resume this painful discussion of the recent events.

The same waiter bustled around the table, pouring water in their glasses and bringing yet another shot of Rupert's favorite Scotch, as he had learned his preferences by now. He looked anxiously at Margaret, trying to determine by the expression on her face whether she liked her meal, and not being able to gauge her mood, he dared to approach her directly.

"Madam, did you like your steak?" he asked cautiously, remembering this quarrelsome lady well. "Is it juicy enough for you? If it is overcooked, please let me know, and we will immediately make you another one."

"It's all right, darling, everything is just fine," Margaret beamed at the waiter. "Please tell your chef that the dish he made was delicious. You can be sure I will certainly report to the management about your professionalism. I hope it will help you in career growth. Also, we will no doubt leave you a large tip."

The waiter sighed with relief and quietly went away, not wanting to be too intrusive.

"You have changed, Margaret," Rupert told her. "Did you see how this boy curls around you? He was afraid that you would make another scene. It seems that our little adventure has benefited you well. I think it is good for you to blend with people from time to time and get a taste of real life."

Margaret looked at him with flashing eyes and was about to reply with something offensive, but at that time Rupert's cell phone rang softly. His phone, which had been discharged for the past few days of adventure, had a full battery now and notified him about new messages he had missed. Rupert looked at the screen in surprise. Who could that be? He had specifically instructed everyone at work not to disturb him while on vacation, and to only call in case of any emergency. His employees followed the given instructions and didn't bother their boss without necessity. But Rupert kept his cell phone switched on anyway, just in case.

He read the new message, then read it again, and handed the cell phone to Ben.

"Go on, read it aloud."

Ben picked up the phone and read the short message from his friend Marcus.

"Mr. Rupert, I got this strange e-mail from Ben. I hope you understand what it means. I also tried to reach you through the post office of your last stop, but I am not sure if they delivered this message to you. So I am forwarding you Ben's e-mail, as I think it could be important to you. I quote: Marcus, I am in a bit of trouble. Lost in the jungles. Please try to contact my father and tell him that everything is fine and I will be back at the port by tomorrow."

Ben frowned, trying to recollect how this information had reached Marcus, but the next moment he smiled, and they all burst into laughter.

THE END

San Francisco, 2016

427

Glossary

Many of the items in the book have no analogues in other cultures and their languages, therefore certain names described here are written in the language of their origin. After each word, in brackets, is listed the language from which the word was taken.

[1] **Buambramra** (Bongy) – a public house, separated for men and women.

[2] **Sagyu** (Bongy) – necklaces and bracelets on arms (sagyu) and legs (samba sagyu), beaded with boar and dog canines, seashells, and small, colored rocks.

[3] **Melissa** – fast-spreading computer virus that gets into a computer via e-mail, with an attached Word or Excel file or another format that contains a macro function. The virus is self-propagating by sending infested e-mail messages to all recipients in the Outlook address book.

[4] **Trojan** – a computer virus classified as malicious software (malware). The virus is distributed through e-mail, or can be directly downloaded from the Internet. There are many kinds of Trojans, from simple ones that erase information from the infected computer, to more complex ones that open a port of access to the remote host and disable antivirus software.

[5] **Kina, Toea** – currency (banknotes and coins) of Papua New Guinea. 100 Toea equals one Kina.

[6] **Kekeni** (Hiri Motu) – a girl.

[7] **Khane Ulato** (Hiri Motu) – a girl, a young, unmarried woman.

[8] **Memero** (Hiri Motu) – a boy.

[9] **Rite of Passage** – coming of age, rite of transition for boys, from adolescence into manhood. At puberty the young man is housed for several years in seclusion, away from women, where he is prepared for adult life. Throughout the training period, the boy is not allowed to be around women or communicate with them before the completion of the rite. The final stage of training is the actual ritual of initiation. The ritual is conducted differently in every tribe, but there is a general similarity: this rite is meant to bring the boy as much physical pain as possible. It is believed that the boy cannot become a real man before he breaks a certain threshold of pain. So, as a rule, the father of the boy is prohibited from being present at the ceremony. The rite is conducted by the tribal elders with the help of a distant relative, if there is one, or any other man of the tribe. During the ceremony the young man is subjected to various painful procedures. In some tribes the skin on the boy's body is cut in many places and the wounds are filled with sand to create body scars, for decoration or to prove completion of the ritual. Other tribes practice circumcision, nose and nasal membrane piercing, and tongue incision. After the ceremony the boy, already a man, returns to the tribe, where he is met by the family members and women from his tribe. The return of the young man to the tribe is accompanied by ritual dancing and a festive meal.

[10] **Dokta** (Tok Pisin) – doctor.

[11] **Adawa-na** (Hiri Motu) – husband or wife. Literally translated as "a married person." Hiri Motu does not differentiate by gender.

[12] **Kahua, Kahua-Kumu** – in accordance with the beliefs of certain tribes, Kahua is an evil spirit, encased in the skin of people from other tribes. A man's flesh is eaten by the spirit of Kahua, and it settles into his shell. Cannibalism, in these tribes, is not considered as such, since they don't eat human flesh but the shell of an already dead person to exorcise the evil spirit that is inside him. Kahua-Kumu—the

devil that devours the soul of the victim—must be killed and eaten, to free that victim's soul.

[13] **Suangi** (Tok Pisin) – sorcerer. Also an evil spirit, but, unlike Kahua, he drinks the blood and eats the internal organs of the victim and refills the shell with grass. The victim returns to his tribe, gets sick, and dies. The relatives of the diseased eat his flesh, thereby freeing the soul of the victim.

[14] **Sanguma** (Tok Pisin) – witchcraft.

[15] **TCP/IP** – Transmission Control Protocol/Internet Protocol, used by every computer device for data transmission and routing, in most local and wide area networks. TCP/IP is the main protocol used on the Internet.

[16] **MAC** – Media Access Control. A unique 48-bit identifier (address) to control access to the network. All network adapters are supplied with a MAC address that is assigned to them by the manufacturer and contains programmed code for the manufacturer identifier and the serial number of the adapter.

[17] Dear readers, do not try to reproduce Marcus's invention. In the technical description, we intentionally introduced significant errors and omissions to prevent the use of his creation by some readers for personal gain.

[18] **Ping** – network software utility that tests broadband Internet connection, signal quality, and host availability on the local area network or on the Internet by measuring the time it takes to reach the remote host.

[19] **Echo** – return packets of data that were sent by the Ping command to the remote host. The Ping program sends four (by default) or more packets to a remote computer, and if the host is reachable, it returns the packets back to the requesting computer, indicating the travel time for each echo packet.

^{20} **Telnet** – TCP/IP network protocol is used to connect to a remote host computer through a terminal program.

^{21} **Pine** – one of the first open platform e-mail programs designed for UNIX and Linux. Pine does not have a graphical user interface and uses Pico editor in simple text mode to manipulate e-mails; therefore, it is a fast and reliable program.

^{22} **Mailer Daemon** – a program on a mail server which delivers e-mail to the recipient. In the case an e-mail cannot be delivered, Mailer-Daemon notifies the sender, indicating the possible cause of error.

^{23} **Tubuna** (Hiri Motu) – grandparents (either grandfather or grandmother). The word also has a second meaning, grandson or granddaughter.

^{24} The names of the tribes in this book are fictional. After a long debate, we decided not to use the real names so as to not offend these glorious peoples with inadvertent words. Each tribe portrayed in the book is a collective image taken from several ethnic groups in the region. However, some historical facts and events described in this book correspond to reality.

^{25} **Wahgi Valley** – one of the longest valleys in New Guinea, located on the Western Highlands of Mount Hagen. The name of the Wahgi Valley also gave the name to the language group Wagi, consisting of several similar languages used by local tribes.

^{26} **Endogamy/Endogamous marriages** – the custom of marrying within the local community, cultural group, clan, or tribe. Marital ties between family members or people related by blood.

^{27} **Nug-sel** (Bongy) – a tree.

^{28} **Sing–Sing Festival** – is the main festival of the country dedicated to the Independence Day of Papua New Guinea. It is held annually in Goroka, on the weekend closest to the Independence Day,

September 16th. The festival is attended by many tribes of the region to share their distinct culture and traditions. During the gathering that could last for days, people from different tribes hold the show of the best songs and dances, the most beautiful traditional outfits, hairstyles, body decorations and adornment, and conduct games and sports contests for best marksmanship.

[29] **Dongan** (Bongy) – a sharp knife made of sharpened animal bone (stronger version) or split bamboo. Dongan is not a weapon but rather a household item, and is mainly used for domestic purposes.

[30] **Digam-Apa** (Wagi) – sibling. The Wagi language does not differentiate by gender. It only distinguishes by age: older brother (or sister) – Digam, or younger brother (or sister) - Digam-Apa.

[31] **Okam** (Bongy) – drum.

[32] **Ai-Kabral** (Bongy) – flute made of hollow bamboo. It can vary in length from a few inches to a few feet long.

[33] **Ure** (Bongy) – a short, light spear; a javelin with a few tips.

[34] **Mune** (Bongy) – a song.

[35] **Three sheets to the wind** – the state of being drunk.

Printed in the United States
By Bookmasters